# A Story in Song

# A Story in Song

## Kristen Cornwall

Paintwater Press

*For the forest. You smell good.*

# 1.

Peace, a soft blanket, and the sound of rain settled over Lil as she woke.

The bed cradled her well, and the smell... Crisp sheets with a freshness about them, a little of him, and a little of her. Beyond the linens, wood burned over the scent of apple and cinnamon.

"There you are," a deep voice rumbled from the corner of the room.

She lifted her head from the pillow, her eyes immediately finding him to the right, sitting in a worn leather chair.

He'd dressed in a hunter green sweater that brought out the moss of his eyes, sleeves rolled halfway up his forearms. The weathered jeans had been rolled as well, just below his calves over bare feet... They were not the clothes he'd had on when they arrived.

Steam rose from the mug he held toward his strong face, softening at the sight of her.

In her periphery, to the left, Lil noted a door to the hallway, a fireplace crackling. To her right, a wall of floor to ceiling windows provided a view of the breathtaking landscape coated in falling water. The cool light was filtered by grey clouds, so clear as it fell over him. She imagined he must be seeing her the same way, under varying degrees of white, her gentle curls cascading over some, but not all, of what the sheet revealed.

"I've not yet seen you in the daylight... this time," he whispered. They remained in relative stillness, gazing at each other before he breathed out, "You wear all its shades well, even its absence."

It was true; they hadn't looked openly upon each other in the light of day since she'd awakened. There was relief in being able to see Lu that way, and an unusual dynamic, what with her being undressed and him fully clothed and seated, observing.

Lil wondered briefly why he wasn't in the bed with her. They'd been apart so long, and waking to him was a pleasure such that she did not mind her need for sleep.

"There is *much* self-control in my not climbing in," he confessed, fingers gripping the mug he held tighter, using restraint there as well, as not to shatter it.

"You had an arduous night. To have woken you any earlier than your body required would have been selfish, and now that you've," he inhaled deep, closing his eyes, "*roused...* I think we've kept Magnus long enough. The poor man is down there stress baking."

Magnus did like his muffins and pastries. And it had indeed been a long night.

She remembered barely being able to open her eyes as Lu carried her across the threshold of the old man's house. It had been morning but still dark outside given the time of year. Lu had brushed long, damp tendrils behind her ear, prompting her to look up. She'd raised her attention to Magnus, then allowed her eyes the rest they demanded, her ears not relinquishing their effort quite yet.

"She doesn't look well," the old man had said with alarm, moving quickly to make way for them to enter. "I received word of your departure and an update from Gunnar over an hour ago."

She'd felt the warmth of Lu's tone, as he said, "She is quite content, however extremely exhausted. We detoured to take a swim."

There was a frustrated huff on Magnus's part, but no more talking as she was carried up the stairs.

Lu had spoken softly as he removed her dress, reminding her that, while the sulfurous spring water wouldn't leave an odor when it dried, he was going to use the conditioner he found in the bathroom to brush through her damp hair. It had the faintest scent, like petrichor and basil. She'd been on the cusp of sleep as he massaged her scalp and combed her hair, combatting tangles inflicted by wind and water.

Sitting across from him in the clear light of morning, she could still feel his fingers roaming from her hair, to her neck, and arms. He had continued along her body until he removed the last bit of fabric covering her, replacing it with his hand.

However exhausted, she'd been unable to resist rocking into him. With eyes closed, she'd not seen the glow they'd cast. A soft, almost blue light had hovered over them like a low hanging mist, then fell like drops of water as she melted into a blissful sleep.

Lil still felt the vibrations from the pleasant memory going through her. No, that was Lu, rumbling the corner.

Pulled back into the moment, she saw his nostrils flair as he growled through his restraint. Her cheeks flushed and heart began to pick up speed, anticipating. His arm moved slowly as he set the drink down on the tablet to his side and, holding it there for a moment, he took a deep breath.

She heard the chair skid across the floor as she fell under Lu's weight, his hand between the back of her neck and the pillow, face burrowing beneath her ear.

The fibers of his sweater brushed against her skin where the sheet had been, soft, but scratchy. How could he let something so offensive come between them?

3

She lifted at his shirts until the warmth of his skin met hers, at least a little. She sighed in partial relief against his rumbling chest.

His smile widened such that the seal of their lips was broken. He braced himself on his arms, his abdomen convulsing against hers as he *laughed.*

Lil looked up at him with an amused smirk, delighted for any opportunity to witness his mirth, though she wasn't sure what prompted it.

He rolled to the side, still half entangled with her, wiping tears from his eyes.

"I sat in the chair, as if watching you from a distance could keep me," he said, catching his breath again. "I tried to explain about Magnus while you sat there under a wilting sheet. If I didn't know better, I'd have sworn the linens were sentient, and taunting me." He rubbed over his eyes and scrubbed his beard. "In that moment you were both prey and challenger. Irresistible. And then there was your silent reminiscing…" he sighed. "You unknowingly occupied the room with your memory. I tried to breathe through it, but the air was filled with you."

She reached up and cupped his cheek, digging her fingers into his beard. Bringing her mouth close to his again she whispered, "You didn't stand a chance."

His pants against her were irritating, and his shirt had slid back down.

"I chose my armor well it seems," Lu chuckled. "Magnus had some clothes I was able to borrow, and no, the jeans were not his. They're from one of his staff. Rather remarkable he was able to find something that came close to fitting, though the length was not ideal," he said, unrolling a sleeve to its end, about halfway down his forearm. "He's asked one of his people to clean my suit. I told him this was completely unnecessary, but he'd made up his mind, so it's being done, of course. He offered to find something for you but I told him you'd packed some things."

4

Lu paused for a moment, his focus changing as he traced her curves with his fingers. He produced a deep sound that told of his frustration before he continued.

"I took the liberty of filling in our friend while you slept. I needed more of a distraction than the cold shower provided, and Magnus, of course, needed to know what was going on. I hadn't seen him since before you were born and, considering the way we arrived at the house with your limp, exhausted body in my arms, he deserved some explanation. He was concerned you'd been injured."

"Exhausted, hmm?"

She could have inquired about what was discussed, how much he'd told their friend. Instead, Lil focused on his description of her disposition.

"Yes, you could barely keep your eyes open for him to see you were still living."

"So exhausted was I, that you still felt I needed *assistance* getting to sleep."

Lu raised his eyebrows, and with a straight face he explained, "It was a *deep* sleep you required."

"I recall being assisted at the hot springs... thoroughly."

"You were waking when we arrived upstairs," he rumbled playfully. "My assessment was that more depth was necessary."

Lu scooped his arms under her, Lil letting out a "yip" as she felt herself lifted up toward him. He moved quickly, setting her on the edge of the bed by her spare clothes, already folded and waiting.

"How was Magnus, when you spoke?" She asked as Lu reached for her shirt.

"I didn't share everything. I thought we should both be there when the whole of it was told. He knows we're not human, not mortal, and came here long ago. I relayed that we were betrayed by our kind, that you were unjustly punished, and explained the nature of your affliction. He knows of those trying to kill you, and of those trying to use you. He knows of your last death, and of how you came to live with Nan. He took it well."

5

Magnus did have an affinity for the esoteric.

"He also had a bit to say about the Drakes," Lu added. "The power and influence both the family and their companies hold…"

Lil nodded, "Something we've known for a while… *That* I remember."

"Magnus likely has knowledge of useful details. There will be room for further questions regarding the Drakes, but last night it was more important for me to listen to a friend who'd just learned I was immortal."

Lu slid the stretchy, dark grey tank top over her head and arms, his warm hands enveloping her torso as they slid over her.

"Hmmmmm," he rumbled, questioning something.

His fingers ran along the seams of the racerback. He glanced over her shoulder toward the rainswept landscape, then slid the garment back over her head.

She brought her brows together, puzzled. It was a clean shirt, not that he would have minded otherwise… He'd removed it for a reason, and seemed to be preoccupied with thought, instead of the heat they'd been feeling.

*The heat is never gone,* he reminded her as he rummaged through the bag they'd brought, until finally producing the black long sleeve shirt with the open back. It fit her arms and chest like a second skin, the fabric coming around to a twist low above her hips, leaving her whole back exposed. It looked nice but the stretchy material also allowed her to move the way she needed to: running, climbing, lounging.

Over her head, her arms threaded through the shirt, shoulders barely covered. She loved the feeling of the air over her back, but his fingers… She sighed, relaxing against his chest as he stroked her skin. The sensation was nothing short of hypnotic, immobilizing her every time.

"We'll spend some time with Magnus," he said, fingers grazing along slowly swirling over her shoulder blades. "Then I'm taking you in the sky."

She felt he meant more than flying.

A twinge spread through her, apprehension about using her wings. On the one hand, she knew who she was... She could cut through air like she did water. But so did she remember her feathered limbs catching the wind haphazardly when they'd first emerged the night before, jostling her about. She wouldn't go so far as to say she was *afraid*, certainly not, but she had hoped to practice with a calm sky the next time she went up.

Knowing Lu was cognizant of her thoughts' direction, Lil was appreciative of his patience, and his hands.

"It's raining," she breathed into his shoulder, her head resting there.

Before her sigh had tapered off, he said, "You're not learning to fly, but remembering... remembering who you are. You can cut through falling mist like you can a hurricane," he whispered. "And start one just as easily."

Once Lil had fully dressed, they made their way to the kitchen where Lil caught the eyes of a very relieved old man. He wore a grey linen apron over a white button up shirt, dark grey trousers and, from what appeared to be flannel slippers.

Lil couldn't help feeling a shred of guilt, knowing how he probably hadn't stopped a moment, never mind slept, since she called to report the hunting incident.

"Forgive me Magnus, I was just so tired."

He came steadily toward her, pulling her in for a warm hug, no doubt reassuring himself that she was indeed ok. It comforted Lil as well, to be wrapped in him for the moment; the familiar smell of bergamot, juniper, in a kitchen no less. It felt a bit like home.

"Yes, well," he said, taking a step back. "You certainly had a full day, what with the hunting, the attempted abduction, the darts, as I understand there was more than one, and then somehow had energy enough to *swim*... You still arrived at my door hours ahead of what would have been, had you taken an aircraft, and for that I am thankful." He held his hand out, referencing a thick wooden table by a large window. "Come and sit down, I've been baking. There's hot water in the kettle and I have some fruit as well."

Lil found herself unusually famished, piling food on her plate.

*You've expended quite a bit of energy. Sleep replenishes only so much.*

Lu reached for a scone, and said, "You'll have to forgive me as well, old friend, for not staying longer to catch up with you last night. I wasn't inclined to leave Lil for too long. The last time I left her while she slept… didn't end well."

Magnus puttered back and forth between the table and the counter with mugs, more fruit, another basket of scones, an apple pie… He'd really been at it.

"It ended worse for the intruders of course," Magnus said.

"True, but not the way she would have preferred to wake."

*How you prefer to wake is not unlike how you prefer to fall asleep,* Lu said, keeping his eyes on Magnus. Out loud he continued, "A tranquilizer dart is a less-than-ideal way to start things off."

*Our tastes are similar,* she replied, thwarting a blush and looking out the window, to the rain speckled landscape. Reaching for the other half of the muffin she'd been eating, she found her plate empty, until Lu's hand entered her vision, depositing, a whole, ripe pear, a small pile of almonds, and a scone in front of her.

She met his eyes and smiled, placing an almond in her mouth.

Magnus sat down to join them, *just* reaching for a scone as a muted buzzing came from his side of the table. He followed through with retrieving the scone before removing a cellphone from his pocket.

"It is unlike me to be so rude, but I don't think you'll mind if I take this," he smirked, his smile softer and bright as he said, "Good morning, dear, though dawn has not arrived where you are, has it? Did you get any sleep at all?" After a pause and another smirk, he said, "Yes, they're both here, safe and sound. Hot beverages and warm pastry, not that I'm competing, but I wanted Lil to feel comforted, and I have been enjoying my time baking as of late."

After another a long pause, and a possible blush on his cheeks, he turned to the window, and away from Lil's eyes.

*They've been close for as long as I've lived with Nan,"* Lil started, *"but in the last few years... they've been spending more time together... They pick apples and bake...* she winked.

"I'll put her on, but you *really* must get some sleep after you've been reassured, let the boy open the shop." He shook his head at whatever she said. "White hair suits you just fine," he smiled, turning, and extended the phone. "Lily, dear?"

"Nan?"

"Oh Lil," Nan sighed. "You're alright then?"

"Oh absolutely. Its remote here, and Magnus has been baking. Lu and I plan on staying here today, do some *flying,"* she said, rolling her eyes at Lu. "We'll go to The Mountain after, Uri can fill you in on that. I won't have cell reception, but Lu can communicate with Uri, and I'm sure Magnus has a sat phone lying around, that he'll insist I take."

Magnus shrugged and nodded.

"And Lu, is he managing alright?"

"Yes..." Lil said, heartwarming. "I'll hand you over, then get some rest. Love you, Nan."

Lu's hand rose to cover Lil's fingers as she held the phone to his ear, eyes closing briefly, absorbing her touch.

"Do you still wake early to make pastries then, Nan?" He asked. "I know, I know, I'm teasing. Yes, and we'll be safer still when we arrive at The Mountain... That's another story," Lu said smirking at Magnus, "though I suspect he'll not stay away for long. I will. Take care Nan."

"She wants you to return as soon as possible," Lil said with a wink, passing the phone to Magnus.

"I am quite fond of that woman," he said, sliding the device back into his pocket.

Lil was fond of her too. They all were. Uri and Gunnar's presence at Nan's eased her mind a little, but the idea that such a sacred place had been breached... It didn't sit well with her.

"Why didn't they just come for me at my house?" Lil asked, chilling the pleasant peace that had fallen.

"Perhaps they assumed something so precious would be well protected in her home," Magnus mused.

"They'd have done their research," she said. "There aren't even security cameras."

"Not that I haven't tried..." Magnus groaned.

"You live footsteps from the ocean," Lu said. "They're cautious to approach you so close to water again."

She nodded her head. The water would have put them at a severe disadvantage.

Magnus tilted his head in thought. "How did you manage the aftermath from last night?"

"Sent the bodies back with the survivor," Lil said. "Cleanup isn't Nan's responsibility. They shouldn't have been there."

Magnus allowed a suppressed laugh to escape him. "Yes, Gunnar shared that bit with me. Well played. As disappointed as he must have been, I'd bet Malcom had a good laugh over your response."

"And what did you do with the *remains* I left in the woods?" Lil asked, bodies at Nan's not the only one's she'd left lifeless that day. "Did you have Malcom swing by and pick them up?"

"Don't forget whose table this is," Magnus replied, raising his brows. "Or the focus of my wife's work. The Orn has a number of exciting biological solutions capable of decomposing a human body swiftly and without negative impact on the environment. What's complicated is communicating with Malcom. Silence is also an option, or I could simply phone, saying a friend of mine had been hunting on the property, and approached by trespassers alleging affiliation to the Drake Company. I could say they tried to take her against her will, have since expired, and been disposed of." He looked into his mug like it held fire, drawing him in. "My property should have been off limits in this. He's aware that I know what's happened, of this I'm sure, but it's a different thing to acknowledge it openly. Initiating a dialogue could be dangerous. With names as big as ours, it is our loved ones who become the pawns."

As her parents had been. Lil had been a child with limited control over something much greater than she understood. Having a grasp of the much larger picture, Lil knew it wasn't her fault, but that of a man, of a people who had no trouble creating casualties, who'd sent soldiers to Nan's in the night. Pawns indeed, and the danger never truly gone.

Picking up a scone, Lil breathed in cardamom and vanilla as Magnus cleared his throat. "I knew, from the moment I met you, Lu, that you were more than a hired hand. How it would play out, that was left to be seen, and still is, I suppose. I'm here for you both, for whatever this is that I've found myself a part of."

"I have a way you can help," Lil offered with as straight a face as she could manage. "The bottom of my cup has become visible..."

Before much time passed, the three pleasantly sipped tea, nibbling on the bounty Magnus had prepared. Lil smiled inwardly as she watched him buttering another scone. She thought about what things must have been like for Lu when he lived with Nan; surrounded by nature outside, the warmth of the oven inside. She pictured Magnus coming to visit, hanging around the kitchen, and taking walks in the garden. Things would have been different then, though, as Magnus's wife, Mira, had been alive.

"I knew the two of you had met," Lil began, looking at Magnus. "What with Lu staying with Nan after, well, after the last time…" she trailed off. "Nan told me a bit about how, about when he first arrived…"

Magnus nodded with understanding. "It didn't take long for me to make Lu's acquaintance. I'd become curious about the young man who my friend had taken on to help around the shop and the grounds. I found great depth and deep stillness about him," he said, glancing at Lu, then back to her. "And an underlying sadness…"

"You were perceptive to sense something was amiss."

"We were walking together one day," Magnus continued, "through the miracle of a young apple orchard. We strolled in relative silence for a while, until my thoughts made their way out through my voice. I spoke of my Mira; she was in good health then. I didn't know at the time… of the battle to come." He sighed, regrouping as he sipped his tea, clearly not done with his story.

"The new development of the orchard was breathtaking, but I didn't ask how it came to be so quickly grown. Things reveal themselves as they will. Lu wore a necklace, then, as he does now, but there were two stones dangling instead of one. *Those are very old*, I said. What I didn't say, was that I'd seen drawings of them in my school's archives."

Lil had suspected Magnus knew about her necklace since she was a girl, but he'd seen her seal years before she came to Nan's, before she'd been born.

"Lu and I tended toward quiet exchanges, much as we do, Lily. That day he explained that he'd made the stone pendants. One for his wife, and one for himself, to tell their story. He told me, in what way he could, the tale behind his sadness. *She's not wearing hers*, he told me, my heart sinking at the realization I came to. Instead of prying into the discrepancy between the age of the drawings I'd seen, and his claim of having carved them, I remained present for a friend in pain."

Lil's heart became heavy as she listened to a part of Lu she was never present for: his sorrow when she'd gone. Looking to her beloved, Lil saw his eyes had been on her, not on their storyteller.

*The loss is deep, but so is my faith in finding you.*

"He told me he took it from her body when she'd passed," Magnus continued. "That he would wear it until they met again. *There's nothing in existence quite like her,* you said, Lu. How right you were," he smiled. "I assumed Nan had known of his loss, of course, and kept this information private, as that's what it was. When I saw the stone again those years ago, Lil, on the neck of a fascinating young girl, I knew I was privy to something wonderful. Not a mystery to be solved, but one to witness as it unfolded around me. And oh my, what has unfolded." He paused a moment, looking at Lu. "When Gunnar called me with your name and described the necklaces, you wearing yours and Lil hers… I was relieved at the prospect of her safety improving, but also excited for what would be revealed."

Lil gasped, hand rising to cover her mouth.

"The school…"

# 2.

Magnus quirked up an eyebrow, waiting.

*They don't know what they are anymore,* Lu said. *The burden of knowing became too great, too much risk as the branches of the tree spread.*

Gunnar and Magnus went to the same school. They went to *the* school. It was coming back to her... Uri was the first, of course, then Remi, and eventually Az, too, had eyes that wandered, finding focus on a human woman he'd become increasingly fond of keeping company with. For Az it was just the once... Gunnar knew now, what with spending time with Uri, but Magnus...

*I was in the school, and the archives. Magnus showed me several texts with imagery that depicted our necklaces... but nothing I remember being specific to us, to our kind. Are they still taught our story?*

She had long been separated from matters related to the school, and the memory of it all was slow to return.

*Yes, though much has been removed, save for some images, poems and stories that might be recognized if a need arises. The students are not blatantly taught a mythology to* follow, *but have an awareness of our story as one of many. It's more a philosophy of being that they are encouraged to follow.*

"Uri, Az and Remi share responsibility with the school," Lil started." Lu and I are not hands-on, as circumstances have made that difficult. We were aware some

14

documents related to our involvement in history would be left behind, but I didn't recall what remained. The depictions of our stone seals appears to have made the cut, as it were... Lu told you some of our story, but there's quite a bit more to tell."

"The others like you, they are connected to *my* school, that I attended as a boy?"

*You didn't mention the school when you spoke earlier?*

*No, and it appears Gunnar hasn't either.*

"They founded it," Lu revealed.

Lu looked at Lil, asking with his eyes.

*Go ahead,* she nodded, *tell him everything.*

"For the line of their progeny, Magnus. You are descended from Uri, as is Gunnar, though he has the unique circumstance of also descending from Az..."

Magnus's eyes went wide as Lu detailed the true story of the garden: the beauty, the betrayal, the aftermath... Magnus took it all in, nodding as he listened. He remained stoic as he could, but was unable to contain occasional muted gasps and glassy eyes as he came to know the depth of his connection to those at his table.

"There was only so much the archives could have shown you, Magnus," Lu continued. "We made the decision to discontinue the teaching of our history long ago, you see, for safety."

"Yes of course..."

"When the five of us lived among the people in the beginning. As the population grew around us, Lil and I encouraged the three others to pair off as well, if they desired to do so. Humans are beautiful. Loving is beautiful. In recognizing this, the three of them did so in their own time.

"You were... compatible?" Magnus asked.

"They were."

"Interesting."

"We literally create life with our hands, Magnus. Doing so inside a capable human is not a challenge."

"You'd think I would have known somehow," Magnus whispered. "I have no, *abilities*, so to speak. I cannot levitate or shoot energy from my hands. I cannot heal, though I've tried. I'm *old* for goodness' sake," he laughed.

"The children, initially, lived extended lives beyond that of a normal expectancy. This dwindled over time and so did the spark of greatness that we pass on. It skips generations, sometimes many, sometimes disappearing from a line altogether. You might not grow wings or call storms from the sky, but you are a great leader and global influence. You *inspire*, Magnus. You may age, but you do it well. You are physically fit with few, if any, ailments. It's the spark that is passed on, and why it is so vital that those who carry it are nurtured and balanced. The school was, still *is*, a necessity."

Another aspect of her childhood, of Lil's life that she'd been completely unaware of: Magnus had been, in some distant way, connected to her the whole time.

Lu picked up his mug and sat back in his chair, letting what he'd shared steep a bit. There was no tension in the room, but Lil felt the need to maintain the silence, to give Magnus time with his thoughts, she herself having gone through something similar the night before.

Lu had been so careful with her in retelling their story, and then there was her remembering... Lil's face heated along with the rest of her from the inside out as both her body and her mind recalled the process.

Lu's eyes shot to hers, sending a jolt through her.

Magnus unknowingly provided a well-timed interruption.

"Am I the reason you came here, after Lil was gone?

Lu took a deep breath, refocusing as he turned to Magnus.

"I'm not sure how I came to be on that particular shore the day I met Nan, but it was naught to do with you. I did sense you were a descendent when we met, but our meeting was not intentional on my part."

Magnus nodded, eyes drifting to a faraway place, then back to the table. Lil sipped her tea watching him make his selection from the baked goods spread out before them. A muffin this time, rye. His hand journeyed next to one of the ceramic butter jars. Removing the lid, he looked up to Lil, and smiled. "This one is maple butter… If that won't tempt you, I don't know what will."

She laughed a little outwardly, but more on the inside as she thought of the precious cargo Uri had brought with him to Nan's.

"Don't let my relationship with churned cream keep you from your thoughts, Magnus. Lu and I can communicate silently if we need to but there's no one present who needs to hear their own voice fill the room. We'll let the food quiet our mouths while you mull things over."

"Oh, I plan to ponder my existence a little, but not with you two at the table. I can do that on my own time. What's more pressing, Lil, is your situation. You've spent lifetimes running from credible threats that have repeatedly ended you. You are extremely powerful, but also vulnerable." He turned to Lu and continued. "The threat to her safety would be nullified if she were no longer mortal. It seems to me, we need to get Lil back to her original state," he said, matter-of-factly.

Lil sighed, but continued to listen to him respectfully. If returning to her original state were an option, she wouldn't have been sitting there, having been hunted and darted after a succession of prematurely ended lives. There would be no need for rescues, because there would be no true threat to her. She silently praised Magnus for his ambition in trying to help them take this on, but if there was an opportunity to reinstate her immortality, they would have done it already.

"I know the archives from the school extensively," Magnus continued. "But you mentioned having removed quite a great deal. Perhaps if I had access to your personal library, I could make some progress. I also have a few contacts who deal in historical artifacts, including text. There's also a monastery..." Magnus trailed off, no doubt having noticed Lu shaking his head.

"There are no scrolls, no ancient texts that will reveal the key to all this. The spoken word came before the written word, and we came long before that. There is nothing to uncover that will be of any aid to us."

"How was the change performed?"

Magnus was nothing if not persistent.

"There must be a harmony such that the majority is needed to sing, to weave the change to a soul's disposition. Unfathomable nuance is required, and the participation of more skilled hands than we have, the pitch of a voice that will not sing."

"You need the others."

Lu nodded, "One at least, more would be better."

"They won't do it," Lil added. "If they didn't break rank then, I don't see why they would now. And I don't see the ruling being overturned."

Lil looked for Lu to confirm what she'd said, but this time it was Lu's eyes looking off, out into the grey. There was just a moment's delay in him turning back to her, enough to know something weighed on him.

*What is it?* She asked.

*Thoughts for another time.*

"The unit, The Ten as you called them, this collective was whole before," Magnus said. "And has been incomplete since your change in status, when you and the other three left?"

Lil nodded.

"Trust me," Magnus, face serious, glowing with undercurrents of hope. "They need you. Time works differently for you, I'm willing to wager; thousands of years could somehow be a drop in the ocean. Time having passed doesn't indicate that things won't change. They have been functioning with a short crew, and need you to be whole. Did they replace you?"

Lu chuckled as Lil answered, "They have not."

"Ah, you see? It is as I suspected. You are irreplaceable. You know better than I, what it is that you do… But they cannot run at full capacity without you. Now, that being said, what is your next move?"

"We have a secure mountain home… The less you know the better, but it's safe. We'll head there soon to rest and do a bit of training."

Magnus raised his eyebrows, a sight that brought a smile to Lil's face. She delighted in wondering what spectacular feats the man envisioned, what he waited for her to reveal.

"I won't be putting on a display of miracles anytime soon," she said.

"Please," he scoffed." "I've been witnessing the miracles you sprinkle about since the moment I met you."

"I've only just begun to access my memories, Magnus, there's a lot to navigate. It takes time. I've gone a quarter century without them. Sure, I can swim at length, paint for your dreams, accidentally conjure storms, and grow things, but I can't yet fly properly. I would have crashed last night if it weren't for Lu. And I thought I was going to blow up Nan's more than once, but that's another story."

*One you will likely refrain from telling, but not remembering.*

"What kind of skills will you be honing in on, exactly? Flying, explosives…"

Lu held back an eye roll and answered, "There's no sense in jotting down a list. If you are able to imagine it, then it is within her capability. We cultivated the earth, Magnus."

"Indeed. And when her training is *satisfactory*, will you consider an attack on the Drakes?"

Lu nodded. "We've been facing them for some time, and watching them as closely as we can, but it's not the corporation so much as the family's pursuits that are of concern. Though where they are so heavily staffed by their own, it's difficult to separate the two. Too much collateral damage would be at risk were we to effectively snuff out the threat. There are limits, not in our ability, but in what is acceptable, as far as intervention. We have, for the most part, not been interfered with by what remains of The Ten. What we do on the ground is largely defensive and related to Lil's condition; it also works toward a greater balance. I think it is for that reason we have thus far gone without further penalty from our former colleagues."

"Yes, you mentioned that you've been pursued by the Drake family for a time spanning generations. Forgive me, but however did that courtship begin?"

There was likely only so much Lu had covered while Lil slept, and only so much Magnus would have been able to absorb given what his emotional state was at the time. Perhaps the stories he did hear soothed, distracting him by stimulating his curiosity.

Magnus carved a thin slice from a chocolate tart that had somehow escaped Lil's attention.

"Just a sliver," he whispered to himself, smiling with the simple joy that good food and company can provide.

*Just a sliver.*

That day in the ocean had been just a sliver of time, just a moment. Her memory from before her current life was still hazy at times, taking effort for Lil to find navigate, but recalling the unplanned rescue seemed to clear. It started in the water, as many things do, and as Lil followed the smoke and debris bobbing along the surface, it all came back to her.

"Several centuries ago, Lu and I were at sea together." Lil's eyes flicked up toward the window, where she knew an ocean waited beyond the grey. "I was as I am now, but Lu was a great scaled beast." She turned toward the heat she felt coming from him, his eyes waiting. "So graceful," she sighed. "We were swimming in open water for a time, and came upon the tall masts and billowing sails of a few ships. We watched from a distance as one was destroyed. After a time, the victorious vessels had gone, and only scraps of wood and bodies remained afloat. Then we saw two men swimming; survivors."

It wasn't like them to interfere with what chance had chosen, but she and Lu had been there by chance.

"I rescued the survivors," Lu said, picking up where Lil left off. "They smelled like charred wood and gunpowder, salt water, body odor, and adrenaline. One of them was a Drake."

She and Lu had commented to each other at the time, on the coincidence… that it should be the Drake's namesake coming to his aid. Unbeknownst to him, the origin of his surname derived from a similar encounter in a more primitive time, long ago, when she and the others had walked more freely as dragons among men.

"I remained in my form, scaled as I was, and carried them to the nearest shore. The young drake had a sense of invincibility and providence, while the other was just thankful. Lil stayed in the water, but was seen; she a beautiful woman who swam with a beast in the open ocean. Like yourself at your first encounter with her, Magnus, an impression was made. She became a holy grail of sorts. Bad enough we already had the bloody fanatics attempting to execute her… with the rescue, we acquired a new brand of enthusiast who wanted instead to woo her, and wield her as a weapon."

"Death is on the table I take it?"

Lu slipped into stillness. "Absolutely. Death and agony of the departed soul the likes of which I'd advise you not to imagine."

Magnus's eyes went wide.

"They need not perish if they'd change their behavior, but it doesn't seem likely their kind will. I've thought of attempting to meet with Malcom. I could bring myself to tolerate his existence during his short life for Lil's sake, if he agreed to behave of course. You know Malcom personally, what are your thoughts?"

"He is much like me in that he is ambitious. He lives up to the legacy of his father's reputation as a *means to an end* sort of man. He presents himself as both civilized and a destructive force. He is powerful but wanting more. His power is not stagnant, but ever-building, continuing to accumulate. He is calm, but preparing."

"He is also human."

"Perhaps he has forgotten."

"I assure you, when he is alone in the dark with naught but the ticking of his timepiece lulling him to sleep; he is more than aware of his mortality." Lu paused, Magnus appearing slightly unsettled. "I met Malcom's father. It was the wrong end he justified with his means, and now there is no end for him. No peace."

Magnus appeared stricken.

"You've nothing to worry about, old man. Your soul will pass cleanly on, with or without a song of transition. And I think…" Lu continued, lip turning into a hint of a smile. "I think I'd like to take Lil outside for a little exercise."

Magnus, though still a little pallid, went with the transition smoothly.

Lu removed his shoes and, with a sideways glance at Lil, unzipped his pants. Magnus silently raised his eyebrows, but offered no protest.

In a matter of moments, Lu's sweater had been folded atop his jeans, exposed muscled hypnotic.

Lil arranged her pants, over his pile of clothes. She kept on her shirt and underwear, thinking along the same lines as Lu that it might be best to leave the house with the essentials covered, for Magnus's sake.

Lil glanced out the window, feeling Lu's hands in her hair as he started to braid it. She did very much like a swim in the rain, half submerged, her lower half cocooned in liquid, the part of her above the surface subjected to the pattering of drops. She remembered flying through rain, the most refreshing shower, the water in the air reaching out, connecting with her.

When Lu finished weaving her hair, he brought one arm around her torso, and raised a hand to her cheek.

*There is beauty and excitement out there for us. And peace.*

Lil remembered learning to fly many times; the falling, tumbling into stone before Lu could scoop her up. The time of learning was brief, and well worth the resulting mastery, but still...

Lil looked out into the grey, then back to the unfathomable depth of Lu's eyes. She pressed her toes into the wooden floor, anticipating the earth taking its place...then the air. She felt *ready*.

"Remarkable," she heard Magnus whisper. He stood, beholding them with an expression suggesting he might shed a tear. "Your bodies have become luminous together.

They both looked to him then, and down at themselves, smiling.

Lil slid away from Lu, holding out her hand to Magnus. She brought her palm to his fuzzy cheek, white and silver with age.

"Thank you, Magnus."

There was so much more than those three words said, but with Magnus, what more was there to be spoken.

He took her hand from his face, held it in his, bringing it to his lips for a kiss.

"The miracle of knowing you is not lost on me," he said, glancing between Lil and Lu.

He wiped under his eye before fully releasing her hand, then led them to a door at the side of the kitchen. The mud room beyond was a modest in size, with boots, jackets, all manner of outdoor gear, and two benches.

"There are robes and towels hanging there, a thermos on the bench for your return. I had Thias get some things together and put them out before he left. The thermos is good. I thought you might like something hot when you get back, while you are waiting on the kettle. I might make stew."

"Thias?" Lil asked.

"You were quite somnolent when you arrived, but Lu met him. He's on staff here. There's another house, much larger than this one, a few kilometers on the other side of the mountain. I needed the option of privacy, and had the staff flown over there while you slept. They're just a signal away, though. No security concerns."

*He's worked for Magnus quite some time, and trustworthy,* Lu said.

Lil nodded, warm with gratitude.

"Go on then, children," he said, shooing them with his hand. "Run along to the sea or the sky. Wherever it is, from the depths to the heavens, you will have your privacy so long as you stay on this side of the hills."

"There are windows if you're curious," Lil said, standing in the doorway, sending him a wink. "And if you don't see us, try looking up."

# 3.

With feet on damp earth, Lil felt the unmistakable nearness of the ocean. She stood motionless a moment, pausing her breath to provide stillness, taking in the arresting sight of Lu's body against the landscape.

Water on their skin, floating and falling around them, pushing toward them and rocking reluctantly away at the shore beyond, strong and waiting.

His dark hair had begun to absorb the rain, half of it tied at the back of his head to keep from falling in his eyes, the rest left clinging to his skin as it trailed over his shoulders and back. The shadow between his pectorals made a perfect resting place for the stone he'd once carved, the swathe of black cotton below unable to hide the curves of his upper thigh. Though his muscular body told of brutal strength, it barely hinted at his true capability. She'd known his form for an eternity, as long as her own, and yet he was no less breathtaking standing before her, coated in a thin layer of water.

A delightful thread of electricity preceded the slow turning of his head, his expression somewhere between serene and hungry. Of course he'd known she was watching. In return he took a moment to do the same, consuming what he could without touching her.

Stalking closer, his eyes didn't leave hers until just before their cheeks met.

"Sky first," he whispered.

Lil nodded against him, raising her and clutching his damp hair.

His hand reached around, dipping below the hanging hem of her shirt. His fingers grazed her waist, sliding up the center of her back until his palm pressed between her shoulder blades, warmth radiating from his touch, calling to her wings.

"Before their emergence, changes will begin. Do you remember how it felt to draw them out?"

Did she ever…

The warmth started: the heated sensation somewhere beneath her flesh, as if a map drawn with light had been etched inside her. Blueprints expanded, her body releasing out into a larger space, as it could no longer be contained. Surrounding muscles swelled and tightened to support the new weight behind her.

Raindrops suddenly touched Lil in new places, her eyes on Lu as he watched her unfold. With a stretch, her wings flapped into the falling water, changing the liquid's trajectory and spraying Lu in the face.

He began backing away with a delightfully mischievous grin. "You work well from experience, through feeling, so it's best we just get in the air. You can take off from a state of stillness, but I think for now it's best to get a little speed going."

"Run?"

He nodded and began to pick up his pace, sculpted arms spread wide.

"Do you think you can catch me?" He teased.

Lil ignited with a short trickle of laughter before determination had her sinking the balls of her feet deeper into the ground.

She took off toward him; wings folded, tucked back, black mud splashing up her legs. He dodged her fingertips, cutting to the left with that wicked grin of his flashing.

*You'll never catch me from down there.*

*Down here?*

His wings flared out as he turned into the wind, launching him skyward.

"Open!"

Like feathered arms, her wings followed his command and spread out, drawing her upward as they cut through the air. Her feet, dark with wet earth, left the ground as her newly enhanced muscles push her upward with powerful strokes.

She climbed higher and higher, then angled her wings for stability; the rush that overtook her invigorating.

Lil closed her eyes with the release of a sigh, but just for a moment. As she opened them again, she saw Lu just a few meters away with that look of reverence and hunger she was so fond of.

"Magnificent," he growled.

She faltered a bit under a forceful gust, but recovered, flustered at first, then playfully triumphant as she caught Lu's blazing eyes again. It felt good; more than good. It felt right, like she was conquering something, coming closer to finding herself.

As if sensing her rise in confidence, Lu dropped back and down, smirking, taunting her.

Lil dove toward him, angling her wings back to gain speed. He cut left and she followed, cut right and she followed, then he fanned his wings out and curved upward, beginning to slow.

His wings beat like a hummingbird's as he hovered before her, his body slick with rain, black eyes but for a thin, luminous ring of green surrounding his pupils. In that darkness was a depth greater than the surrounding universe. She should know. She'd been there.

Momentum as much as his stare that drew her closer. He was mesmerizing.

Lil suddenly became aware that her speed remained unchanged, eyes widening with the knowledge of their impending collision. He could certainly handle whatever impact she provided, but Lil had hoped to maintain her dignity. Hadn't she just conquered a gust? Her budding panic was left unassuaged by the mirth and desire on his face.

She pinched her eyes closed, straining her wings against the wind until a thick arm banded around her waist, tucking her into a cocoon of warmth.

With a sigh, she settled in, bringing her wings back before they had a chance to catch air again. His smile was too wide for just his lips to graze her neck. Instead, teeth and breath trailed across her skin until his mouth took hold of the flesh at the bottom of her ear.

*Shall we return to the water?* He growled.

Looking down, she saw they were indeed over the ocean.

Though Magnus had assured them of their privacy, the possibility of a boat couldn't be ruled out, nor the use of binoculars. The need for secrecy brought on a twinge of longing for another time when they'd lived more openly, a time when she'd had her painted gold. They'd lived among the people as themselves once, when it mattered not if it was the moon or the sun shining on them as they took to the sky. People in that time saw magic in the flowers that returned through snow as spring arrived. A creature of their own likeness in flight was no less of a miracle than all the rest. It wasn't their awe she favored, but their acceptance. Lil had, she supposed, found that acceptance in Nan and Claire in her current life, with Magnus, Gunnar and Todd. Her family.

Lil entered the water and hovered, floating just beneath the waves Down far enough that the chop didn't reach her, but close enough to the surface that her body moved in the echoes of the rhythm above.

She felt him from below.

She felt him as she suspected she always had in the pause between breaths.

Five fingers slid slowly over her abdomen while another set gently raked her scalp, threading through her hair.

And then he was gone…

She twisted, swimming down into the waiting darkness, tracking the ripples of his essence.

Pausing, she hovered a moment, hair spreading out like tentacles as the feeling of his presence intensified. He grew stronger in the distance, but she was still unable to see him.

Lil swam further into the deep; the gravity of him almost overwhelming.

Then, the looming shadows came together, taking shape. Lu.

A black, scaled body of fifteen, maybe twenty meters loin length approached her. His four clawed legs were tucked against him, giving the appearing that he was flying through the water, his body trailing with serpentine movement behind a head the size of compact car. Sea dragons had been drawn in his likeness, hers too she supposed, but that had been long ago.

He floated before her, mouth parted just enough to expose sharp teeth, fangs the length of her arm. Lil looked upon him with awe and a deep sense of connection that both broke and mended her simultaneously.

She stretched her arms out, and he moved in, massive jaws sliding into her embrace. His energy thrummed as she rested her head above his mouth. The tears she shed dissolved into the ocean, though she knew he would taste the difference, savoring the love left on his tongue.

A soft glow spread out through the water as vibrations transferred from his body into her.

*My heart is so full,* she whispered.

*It is my pleasure to fill you.*

His body heated under her.

Lil retreated, smiled playfully into his large eyes and took off swimming. She was fast, but fully aware that there was no contest while he was in that serpentine form.

His face arrived beside hers instantly, mouth widening into a toothy smile before he shot forward, looped down, and paced alongside her again. They swam together for some time; Lu racing ahead and looping down. It was blissful to be free in that way: endless space above and below to frolic in whatever form they pleased, chased by no one but themselves.

Once upon a time it had been only them, seeding the oceans with life. It was the bittersweet of remembering their uninhibited togetherness that brought tears to her eyes again, his relentless pursuit, and their reunion. And it was the undying spark between them that sent her swimming ahead, prompting a very brief chase.

He looped around again and came up under her, nudging her belly with his muzzle. The angled protrusions at the rear of his head gently grazed her, Lu waiting patiently until she straddled his smooth, scaled neck. Lil lay forward and rested there as his massive body rippled beneath her.

It was divine.

She imagined her own form changing to match the size of his, as they once were.

*Your body remembers too, and like the wings, you will respond in time, able to master any form of your choosing,* he said, slowly twisting along.

The whole underside of her body pressed against his, water passing over her back. Her dark hair trailed behind with what looked like phosphorescent plankton, but from what she could see, what she knew, it was the residual glow she and Lu emitted.

*Wings first,* she whispered in acknowledgement, pushing back at the twinge of disappointment that attempted to grow in her. It had been a long time since she'd swam as he did, with serpentine skin, but disappointment had no place to take root, not when there was so much to be thankful for.

*I need to feel that voice passing through your lips as air*, he rumbled. *You'll need to breathe soon as well.*

But then the swim would be over.

*We could just surface for a moment.*

*Your voice on my skin is reason enough to rest on the shore.*

Lil held tight as Lu picked up speed and, just below her legs, he sprouted giant, leathery wings. She clenched as he burst through the surface, shattering the barrier like glass, remains spraying outward around them.

Lil took a deep breath, reintroducing air to her lungs.

Lu's wings spread wide as he hovered low over the water, carrying her with him to where rocks mingled with and descended into the ocean. She felt an ominous growl move through her as it escaped him. Looking over one side of his body, Lil saw one of his clawed feet skim the ground, decimating a delicately balanced tower of stones before he fully touched down. Lu met the earth with such ease and control that she barely felt the impact. He circled a bit, nose to the ground and air, before finally settling, lowering his front legs and neck.

*Off you go.*

Her hair clung to her, flowing down her exposed back and layering over the black shirt that fit her like a second skin. She went up on the balls of her feet, placing her hands on either side of his enormous face once again. His eyes, however large, were the same green and brown ring around a circle of unforgiving darkness. The distance between the two orbs decreased, her hands drawing closer together until his body had been transformed into what she woke to that morning.

Raindrops carried both fresh water and remains from the salted ocean with it onto her lips and his as their mouths came together. She felt the life potential in the liquid as it entered her, joining the kiss… a reminder of what they had brought forth long ago.

Sand and stone met skin, molding to her shape as she pressed back into the earth until Lu's face hovered above hers. Though no longer manifesting himself as a beast of the ocean, he still maintained a size that seemed to dwarf her. What would have been shadow between them had been illuminated, capturing rain on the tendrils of his dark hair, falling like drops of light. It was as though she were traveling through stars toward him, toward his eyes. The ground began to move, though the source of the tremor had yet to lower fully into her.

Lil brought down her lids a moment, the combination of sensations and anticipation overwhelming. When she gained sight again, she marveled at the dense collection of steam cocooning them with threads of light shooting up from the ground.

The ferocity of Lu's growl intensified, calling her eyes back to his. She reached up and gathered his wet hair in her hand as he lowered his lips to her ear. She was only going to guide the tendrils back, away from her face, but she couldn't help tightening her grip as the powerful scent of him blanketed her.

"It was sound that brought us to shore, was it not?" He asked, bringing the pad of his thumb to her lips. "My need to feel your voice as it exits this mouth persists."

"Yes." It was all she could say in that moment, existing on the cusp of something. Any more would have thrown her over the edge.

"That word…" He rumbled with a sigh, "Though there is something to be said… for incoherent sound…"

# A Story in Song

Lil gasped pleasantly as his body moved into hers.

Waves crept up, longing to engulf them, though they crashed against some invisible force acting as a barrier, taking shape under the assault of salt water heaving and spraying over it. A dome of water formed above them, impact on one side, rushing water around and pouring over, falling on the other side.

The building force within her felt greater than that of the ocean

*There's naught for you to destroy here, no walls to bring down,* he said.

Still, she felt a knotting thread of fear that she might damage something at Magnus's. It would be devastating, what with his location being so remote. She allowed herself to uncoil her worry, releasing it as light built around her.

With one arm still clinging to him, Lil brought a hand down beside her, grasping for the earth. It was warm and smooth in her fingers; she'd have to dig deeper to get to earth not yet heated by their bodies. With her gaze wandering over his shoulder, Lil noticed stones rising upwards into the air along with the surrounding mist and threads of light. Beautiful, suspended, reflecting the glow she and Lu cast, awaiting a collective rush.

"Release them," he whispered.

Liquid lightning burst through her, from both the junction of their bodies and her soul, resonating through them and out into the world. She was an explosion being washed away, becoming everything before returning back to herself.

Stones fell around them like black rain, the sound of their impact muted by Lu's thunderous roar.

# A Story in Song

Steam lifted off of them as drops of cool water fell down from the above, finally making contact with their hot skin. Invigorated, exhausted, and satisfied, Lil lied back into the cocoon of Lu's body, tilting her head up to the sky, drinking in the rain. Her eyes drifted to the ocean, the stones, Lu, her underwear in his hand. She remembered wearing the garment when she'd emerged from the ocean, having been acutely aware of what separated their bodies at the time. She distinctly remembered the fabric's absence shortly thereafter.

"When did that even happen," she laughed.

"Shall I check my notes?" He asked with mock seriousness, licking his thumb and turning the pages of an imaginary notepad. "Ah yes..." he began. "It appears to have occurred roughly between coming ashore and *entry*."

She tackled him.

Later, Lil's head rested on Lu's chest, one thigh overlapping his, a large arm curled around her.

"First movie," he whispered.

"Out of Africa," she sighed into him. The question to anyone else may have seemed abrupt and out of place, but to Lil it was a comfort. There was something of a routine to their reunion: the remembering, explosive physical connection, and the exchange of firsts, weaving each other back into the missing moments of their lives. What was lost was greater than what could be threaded through, but Lil and Lu were greater than the loss.

"It was early on at Nan's," she continued, "my second week there. Nan didn't watch much television, still doesn't. *Much rather read a book,* she'd say. But I came down one night after she'd just started the film. She was lying on the couch and, when she saw me, she lifted the blanket so I could climb under with her. I didn't make it halfway through the movie before falling asleep, but I still consider it my first."

The moment was slow, slow and smooth, as his fingers gently trickled over her forearm and down the back of her hand before returning up the inside of her wrist. Whether he was following the blue-green trail of her veins or a path inspired by whim, she didn't leave her thoughts to linger on it.

"The first thing you ate," she breathed.

"Manakeesh with cheese, still warm…"

Oh, that sounded good. The chewy flatbread, the salty akkawi cheese…

"Sliced?"

He shook his head. "I tore off pieces. It was figs after that. Uri had them in a dish on the table," he sighed. "I only had a few before the cinnamon French toast… He kept me well fed. They did what they could."

Lil raised her head to look at Lu's face as he listed what he'd consumed upon returning to the mountain… what he'd first eaten after placing her in Nan's care.

"What else?" she asked.

"Croissants, of course, and then a scone… with jam. I helped her harvest wild grapes once when I was there, before," he sighed deep. "She sent me back with wild grape jam, honey, tea, and a leftover scone, perhaps so my arms wouldn't feel as empty without you. She was like a mother packing up her son; tears in her eyes, knowing I was leaving, both our hearts aching. The first thing I ate was the manakeesh, but what I remember most was the jam on my tongue."

Lil pressed her weight into him a little more then, feeling him squeeze where he wrapped around her, a reminder of what his arms had become filled with once again.

"First time you drove a vehicle."

"Nan's old truck-"

"The green one?"

Lil nodded with a smile. Of course he would know that old pickup. He'd probably driven it as well, loaded it, provided repairs.

"I was thirteen. She had me drive the loop out to the back, from the gravel around the barn and the field, over to the orchard... *I'd rather have you peel out than stall out,* she said... I sent a cloud of dirt and rocks flying so far and so fast- if anyone had been out there..." Lil rolled her eyes and widened her grin. "I learned quickly but, safe to say, Todd may not be the only one who gave Nan her white hair. I definitely contributed that day. You know, it's funny what flusters her. I grew that apple tree from seed and she was calm as ever... But Todd puts a naughty keychain on her set for the shop..." Lil chuckled, and Lu along with her, his laughter overpowering the sound of his heart in her ear. He seemed everywhere, not stifled, but no less consuming. She loved the way his presence expanded in a space without walls. A meter of concrete is as negligible as a sheet of paper when the universe is on either side, still, in the open air or in the depths of the ocean, the part of him that wasn't contained by his physical form could expand, breathe. It was like that for her as well, she supposed.

Lil thought back to when she'd seen him at the bar that night, before she knew him. Claire and her friends hadn't noticed him, like a black hole masquerading as a simple shadow. She smiled, recalling how Remi had laughed at Lu gripping the chair and rumbling with such depth it was mistaken for bass or just too low to be heard. Both men had been there, but it was Lu whose presence overpowered the room.

"First game."

"Remi," he smiled. "I relocated all the writing tools," he began, almost too pleased with himself to get the words out. "The progression…" He paused, suppressing his emerging laughter. "I had performed my task and made my way to the kitchen where Uri was working. I said nothing, of course. As I lingered, leaning on the counter, Uri slowed. He paused to raise an eyebrow, noticed I was waiting for something… and then he did the same. And there we were, both waiting. For Uri the gift my mischief provided was twofold. He was rewarded with the surprise as well as Remi's torment."

The grin Lu wore was as priceless as the story.

"He began to watch with me as Remi looked in places that should have housed some writing implement… There was a point when I didn't know which one of us would crack first; we barely hung on. Remi searched his rooms at length, and when he conceded to look elsewhere… He went to Uri's study and we heard the drawer slam…" Tears were forming in his eyes, cheeks bright, his loss to emotion bliss to witness. "*What did you use to write the blasted note,* Rem shouted, and that's when laughter won its battle with our silence."

Lil took a sharp inhale, her eyes wide with delight. "Note? Scavenger hunt! You *didn't…*"

He nodded.

"I did. Rem was quite sour upon finding the first clue in Uri's desk drawer. Uri transitioned from following to joining him in his search at the third clue, and then at the fifth or sixth it became a competition between the two of them."

It brought both fulfillment and longing to her heart, knowing they'd found such happiness while in her absence. It was longing for having not been there, and fulfillment, in a conquering sense. In what they faced, her family did not become bitter and rusted. They were able to flourish, have beautiful moments.

"So where were they?"

"Where were what?" he teased.

Her feet tangled with his, kicking up and down as she threw her head back. With humor and impatience, she shouted, "The pens and pencils!"

*"Where mountain sits on stone, courted by wind and thought, what you seek awaits in darkness."*

Lil brought her brows together during the pause in Lu's speech. Resting her head once again, she felt the rumble build under her before he laughed again.

"I left them in a sack by Az on one of the peaks. Took Rem and Uri about half an hour of searching and bickering."

Lu's eyes crinkled at their dampened corners. His hand came up and scratched through his beard before returning to her neck, and down her back. A dance of laughter and sigh moved passed his lips, carrying memory and air with them.

Oh, were she to have been there with them at the mountain…

"How have they been?"

Such a general question, as if twenty-five years of their lives could be summarized, but still, she asked. Lu knew what she needed; just a little bit about them... Just a tiny taste more until she saw them again.

"Remi has been active with some team of scientists studying ice. He's been monitoring their findings, trying to convince the water to stay frozen. It's also his turn with the school, so he's been busy. He's been carving stone and wood again when he allows himself the time," he sighed. "And he's... I thought he might have found a partner some time ago, but that was fleeting. There's something blossoming now, though," he smiled. "I'll let you uncover the details on your own. Uri has maintained his solitude as far as companionship while positioning himself politically, behind the scenes of course."

Lil quirked her lips up.

"Please," Lu huffed"

"We know war isn't always fought on the battlefield. He does his part where he's needed. Besides, he cleans up well, though he's successfully stayed in the shadows."

Something becoming increasingly more difficult as technology advanced and everyone's pocket seemed to contain a camera.

"Fire has kept Uri's attention as well. He soothes what he can, but the earth is changing, and stopping the necessary cycle of ash is not the answer. Az is Az, comes and goes."

Head nestled on his arm, back to the ground, Lil's had crept up her torso to leave yet more flesh exposed, providing a resting place for the smooth stone she picked up and placed on her abdomen... Up and down in went with her breath, their voices quieting for a time...

Reaching out, Lil selected another stone, smaller in size, and settled it on top of the first. When a third, smaller stone rested on the two, she began to slowly roll her muscles while the little tower balanced there. She thought about the boy she'd met at the school, stacking stones.

Lu exhaled long; his breath dense with thought.

"Would you go back to them?" he whispered.

Them.

He didn't need to clarify, though he did.

"If given the chance, would you choose for us to be as The Ten once more?"

*Together with The Ten...* A vision of death and water invaded her mind. She'd agreed to join with them once temporarily, but they had needed to be sure of her performance, that the flood waters would wash enough away...

Deep breath, in and out.

"We have collaborated, if memory serves."

Pinpointing the amount of time that had gone by only brought her closer to the memory. It had been four thousand years, maybe five. Michael had come to them on behalf of the others with an issue pertaining to the garden and the creatures they'd created. They could all see the need for intervention, and she agreed to assist with little hesitation because it was the right thing to do. Lil agreed, but had only recently been awakened in that life. She needed time to reconnect with who she was. Impatient and untrusting, Michael had seen it necessary to provide her with an emotional jolt. The resulting rage that she released moved oceans, but it hadn't been necessary. Michael could have waited.

What a cruel mess it had all been.

"He showed just how far he lost his way when he took my family before their time."

"One might say it was when your path strayed that he lost his balance. Perhaps it was your betrayal in the garden that led to his lack of trust."

"He had not disclosed his purpose, and when he came forth later, I did not agree. The betrayal in the garden was his. The flood was necessary. We had an accord, but he broke the trust, *again.*"

Lu already knew this, though. Their past fueled a fire that stayed constantly lit, tucked away inside him. If Lu could get his hands on Michael's soul, he would be relentless in rendering accountability, in resetting the errant compass.

"Could compassion for his choices help you to move toward an agreement to join together again, to move beyond what has happened?"

"Move forward? While in a cycle of mortal life, inflicted upon me after *his* error?"

"Magnus is not wrong for advising that you are too valuable for this to continue on, the whole of us is needed. If an offer was made…"

"He would need to make contact for that."

"And if he did?"

It would be too much for Michael to do such a thing. He would need to recognize his fault, and that they all had the potential for such. He would need to see the strength in challenging one another when the righteousness of their path was in question, that it was their duty to do so. If he was going to reach out again, he should have done it ages ago. The earth had long since needed her gardeners, all of them.

The thought exercise was becoming exhausting, having an odd and distant familiarity to it. They'd discussed this before, but when? Lil narrowed her eyes ever so slightly, trying to get a read on Lu. He seemed... conflicted.

Lu released a heavy sigh. "I mean only to provide a healthy challenge, and to assure myself that your position remains as it has been."

His eyes locked on hers, his body shifting as he slid a hand over her belly, knocking the balancing stones to the ground. Her eyes stayed with his as they fell.

Leaning over her, his face grazed hers, his lips coming close to her ear. One would think the ocean could dampen the scent locked in his beard, the space under his jaw... but neither water nor time could diminish his strength, or the way he called to her.

"Your body could use some food after the exercise you've had," he whispered. "And I do enjoy watching you eat."

It wasn't until they were nearly back at the house that Lil contemplated Lu's nudity. She'd known the clothing was gone, she was *well* aware of that, but was only coming to consider what the complete absence might mean for their host upon reentry.

Her eyes drifted down, prompting Lu to release a broad smile as if reading her thoughts.

"A man like Magnus is too cultured to be abashed by the male form," he said.

"He'll raise an eyebrow over it."

"Oh, an eyebrow will be raised, there's no doubt there."

# 4.

Magnus stood behind a large pane of glass, drinking from a mug while staring out into the grey. Lil caught the subtle changes in his countenance as he noticed their approach: a twinkle in his eye, the upturned curve on one side of his mouth and... There it was... the lifting of his eyebrow.

Lil smirked, but before she could say anything, Lu chuckled. "I saw it."

Lu assisted in peeling off her clothes in the mudroom, then she wrapped herself in the soft robe Magnus had left out, wicking the cool dampness off her skin. She smiled at the domestic moment they shared; donning robes and on the cusp of pouring tea from a thermos on a rainy day.

"I feel like we should rinse our feet," she said, scrunching her nose at the grit left behind on her soles and between her toes.

"As much as I can relate to anything that clings to you, I agree."

He rubbed his hands over her sleeves in thought, then puttered around the room, finding a small copper watering can.

Slipping his robe off, he wagged his eyebrows and waved a finger at her, indicating she do the same. She obliged, following him back outside to the ground level deck.

Focused, Lu glanced upward. As if responding to a song in his head, he moved subtly and with grace as the rain collected into rivulets in the sky, flowing downward into the watering can.

"I suppose I could have skipped the can," he said.

The stream of sky water diverted from the spout to where she stood, trickling over her feet. Lu knelt down, taking one foot at a time into his hands, and rinsing away what bits of earth remained.

He stood slowly before her, stepping into the flow of water. One arm wrapping around her, his large hand pressed against the small of her back, an unnecessary but welcome gesture, drawing her closer to his body. Their mouths came together as she leaned into his chest, her fingers rising to his beard, roaming to the back of his neck, up into his hair, gripping him. Water ran off his feet and onto hers. Looking into his eyes she saw the greens and browns of the forest, the depth of the night sky, and the burning fire beyond, smoldering and powerful. She felt him reaching into her, mesmerized by the infinite she presented through gates of her own.

"The blue and grey rings call me to sink into your darkness," he whispered, words like a soft, warm ribbon weaving through her where his arms could only go around. Bringing his mouth to her cheek and along her jaw, inhaling her through the water, he said, "To resist would be an act far more difficult than redirecting rain."

With robes on and tea in hand, They passed through the comforting smells of the kitchen. They found Magnus in a sitting room with large windows, where Lil had seen him from outside. He'd transitioned to the couch, stationed comfortably by an active fireplace. He looked cozy, but amused with himself, like he had a secret, though he was likely fluffing the nest of a clever remark he'd planned, perhaps to acknowledge Lu's nude return.

"It was quite something, to literally watch you take flight as you set off. Things must have been eventful up there, or out at sea… An experience worthy of what was left behind, I trust."

Lil smiled and blushed slightly, leaning into Lu. She felt in limbo, between her life with Magnus as the father she never had, and the concurrent reality where she existed as an eternal being with the power to create and destroy life.

Lu had no such balance to render. Acknowledging Magnus with a deep purr as his hand traveled over the surface of Lil's robe, dipping beneath the overlapping fabric where it crossed, grazing her skin.

"I returned with all I need."

He moved ahead then, selecting throw pillows from the furniture and placing them on the floor in front of an overstuffed chair across from Magnus. The spot he'd chosen left their backs to a large window, a fire at their side.

"The kitchen smells lovely, Magnus. What have you got cooking in there?" she asked.

"Oh, just some stew; help yourselves, please. There are bowls on the table, and spoons. Just poke around, you'll find what you need."

Lil made her way to the pile of pillows, Lu laying a throw blanket over her lap before setting his cup down on an end table, then he disappeared out of the room.

"I hope you don't mind me asking, Lily dear, but had you really no idea there were wings tucked away, waiting for you?"

Lil further nestled into her pillows and blanket, taking in a bit of warm liquid from her cup before forming an answer.

"I felt very much like I should be able to, but it was more of an echo or intuition than a memory that led me to believe it. The ability was... *restricted*. Obviously, not everything was limited..." That prompted a smirk and a huff from Magnus. He'd seen first-hand over the years just how limitless she seemed to be. "It all unravels eventually though, except my mortality."

Lu came back with hands full and eased into the chair behind her, his legs slide into place, cradling her on either side. Lil sipped the last of her tea, the cup in her hand replaced seamlessly with a bowl.

She felt her braid being unbound as she brought the spoon of fragrant stew to her mouth. The flavors didn't burst so much as they seeped into her like water to dry soil. She released a low moan of approval, both of the morsel and of Lu's fingers as they began to massage her scalp.

"Magnus, the stew is so good," she murmured."

"Heat and vegetables do; I simply make the introduction."

Lil smiled and took another spoonful, pleasure and relaxation spreading through her almost enough to distract from Magnus's expression. It was the same as when they'd entered in their robes... Magnus had made his comment about

Lu's arrival, but still, he had that look about him. One could mistake it for pride in his culinary skill enhanced through watching her eat, but she knew the man. He was holding onto something, savoring before releasing it.

"While you were in the sky, there were *developments* on the ground." He allowed a pause to hang in the air before continuing. "Time spent contemplating how to make contact was rendered unnecessary, as I received a phone call just now."

"Malcom," Lu said, not a question.

"Indeed."

"He received the package you returned to him… the one on wheels, containing the deceased and one survivor to tell the tale."

Lil's spoon scraped the bottom of her bowl and, just as her cup had been whisked away, Lu's hands left her hair to remove the empty vessel, replacing it with a second portion, no doubt heated as it was passed to her.

Magnus eyed the exchange. With humor that carried an undercurrent of truth, he looked behind her and asked, "Too many carrots for you?"

Lu chuckled and responded reassuringly, "You've nothing to fear. I share Lil's sentiments concerning the stew, which I sampled in the kitchen. You must understand, Magnus; I eat for sport, while Lil requires it for sustenance, and she has a few calories that need replenishing…" His thumbs ran down the back of her neck until his other fingers wrapped around, resting below her clavicle.

"What of Malcom?" Lil asked.

"He acknowledged having underestimated my involvement, that it was undignified for him to trespass and endanger the family of someone he considers

48

a colleague, if not his equal. I'm sure, given his new awareness of our relationship, that he assumes I have some understanding of your unique qualities, though we respectfully skirted around discussion of his reasoning for the attempted abduction. He did, however, make clear that his objective remains as it was." Magnus held Lil's eyes, letting the words sink in. "He intends to acquire you."

*Acquire.*

With a sigh, Lil put the unfinished stew down on the little table beside her, spoon clinking against the rim. For a moment, the communication Magnus received had felt like a pardon in her favor, but that would have been out of character for such an ambitious man. A temporary reprieve was all she could expect, unless he knew where she was. Would he come for her at Magnus's Iceland home, given his thinking the previous trespass undignified? Would a man like that even consider a meeting?

A large hand held the bowl of unfinished stew in front of her, Lu's other five fingers radiating heat where they rested beneath the fabric of her robe.

*Not a reason to neglect your needs,* he said.

She took possession of the bowl, bringing the spoon again to her mouth as his fingers drifted back to her hair in a gentle act of detangling that served him as much as it did her.

"He knows you're safe," Magnus continued. "He knows that Lu is in play, and that I am in communication with you, but he doesn't know where you are at present."

The now empty second bowl found its place beside the first on the table. Lil gathered one of the blankets around her and climbed up onto Lu's waiting lap, his arms encircling her as she nestled in.

Magnus still had that little twinkle in his eye.

"You discussed meeting, didn't you…" she said.

Magnus nodded slowly. "He agreed to meet, and to pause all attempts on you in the interim. I expect things to proceed delicately, out of respect given our relationship, and, perhaps more importantly, out of respect for you. It's vital that we don't dismiss his ambition but, guarded as he is, Malcom couldn't hide his pleasure at hearing your interest in meeting with him. Details still need to be settled: time, location, rules of engagement and such. He did *gently* suggest a timeline of days or weeks rather than say, months or years. He ages as well as I do, it seems, but neither one of us is getting any younger," he chuckled.

While Lil knew what it was like to live with one's days being numbered, she had a sense of continuation that others didn't. Lil knew she would be reborn. But what must it be like to have one's own hair tell the time as it faded to white? It must be excruciating for a man like Malcom to think he could die at all, let alone leave this world with unfinished business like Lil left behind. He coped with the inevitable end of his days by conquering. Magnus conquered in his own way, she supposed, with his affinity for old things, the archives and such, antiques… Perhaps it was a way of extending his life in reverse. Collectors like Magnus could dive deep into the lives of others, through artifacts and writing… through *diaries*.

"Magnus," Lil asked, just louder than a whisper. "Who gave you the journal I read on the plane to Boston?"

Magnus Stilled. "Malcom."

Lil nodded, confirming to herself what she'd suspected.

"What is this journal?" Lu asked, on the cusp of reading Lil's mind before Magnus cautiously responded.

"A diary written by a young, fifteenth century French woman named Manon."

Lu's head quickly cut to the side, his eyes meeting hers.

"You kept a diary?"

Magnus took a sharp breath, but like everything else around her, the sound faded to silence as she and Lu became each other's focus.

She nodded slowly.

Lil hadn't intentionally withheld the information from either of them. Of course she hadn't known at the time of the flight that she'd been reading words written by her own hand. And the diary hadn't exactly been center stage in her mind after learning who she was. She'd only just been reunited with her counterpart, then there was the attempted abduction. She'd been darted, traveled to Iceland, done quite a bit of connecting with Lu throughout…

*I didn't know*, he said.

*It wasn't important at the time.*

They'd lived this way long enough for her to appreciate these moments of pleasant surprise. Looking into his eyes as they sat across from Magnus, Lil was glad she'd left the book behind, that it could later resurface.

"We met and were married," Lil whispered, looking across to Magnus. "I'm not always close with my birth family. It was my brother then, who I was most connected to. He was busy with his own life, but came and went, staying with us quite a bit after I departed with Lu." She leaned into the warmth that cradled her. "I believe he was with us when we went on to meet your *Italian friend*..."

Another muffled gasp came from Magnus, his hand over his mouth. He knew who the Italian friend was. When he went to speak, she thought it would be to address the identity of the inventor and artist, perhaps discuss the content they'd browsed in the archives, but that wasn't the case.

"How on earth did you manage?" Magnus breathed in awe with heartfelt concern. "How were you not snuffed out for that which makes you extraordinary? People often fear what they do not understand, and you are so much more than that. Frankly, you've been an unintentional danger to yourself and others at times, we couldn't allow you to sleep on my plane, but with love we provide precautions. However did you survive?"

"I didn't survive, Magnus... many times over."

He almost winced. "What I meant to say was, how did you survive *childhood*? It was unspecified in the briefing you provided, but I assume you do not choose from which womb you are born?"

"Roll of the dice," Lu replied, his eyes drawn to somewhere inside the fire, inside himself. "Her *extraordinary qualities*, as you called them, have a somewhat slow release, providing some protection during infancy, but not against all threats. As a man well versed in history and human nature, it's not a stretch for you to imagine *unfavorable circumstances*..." Lu trailed off to a growling whisper as he brought a steaming cup to his lips.

Magnus drew his brows together in question, but Lil knew all too well where this was going.

"Lil continues to have the same appearance, regardless of her birth parents. A paranoid father suspicious of his child's eye color is manageable, but some differences are too drastic for a community to accept. We were sometimes able to intervene, but there were other times when infanticide couldn't be prevented."

Magnus's face transformed, Lil's heart growing heavy as his eyes met hers, holding no mask over his emotions. He was seeing her in metaphor, wearing eternity as a robe, fabric trailing behind her and floating over the ocean to the horizon, blood and tears seeping from thread and into the water.

"We have to let go of more than our possessions as we move through time, Magnus." She said, holding his eyes. "The weight I have released is not for you to carry."

He nodded slowly, a pained smile creeping up from his mouth and through his beard.

"I'd like to say you have wisdom beyond your years, Lily, but I suppose it won't hold now, will it?"

"It still feels right coming from you," Lil smiled back, shifting slightly in Lu's lap as he adjusted the blanket she'd brought up with her.

"Forgive me for pressing, but now does seem like the time to ask…" Magnus started. "When you did survive infancy, how did you manage *childhood*? You came to live with Nan at a young age but must have had some understanding of what capabilities you possessed. Nan is a wonder, but the woman Manon described as her mother seemed largely indifferent. Certainly *she* wasn't leading your training…"

Lil had heard the question but was very aware of Lu's hand resting on her thigh where the parting of her robe had left an opportunity.

"We move guardians in place," Lu answered. "Graduates from the school you attended. The chosen have integrity, mastery of the skills we've taught, and a rapport with one of us who would have recruited them."

The fire crackled, rain pattering as Magnus puzzled over something quietly.

"But there were no alumni positioned with her at Nan's," he observed.

"No. You and Gunnar were an unintended fortune we allowed to play out."

Another long pause stretched, threaded with sounds of fire and rain, with wandering thoughts, and the warmth of Lu's hand on Lil's thigh.

"The diary, Magnus," Lu said. "Do you have it here with you?"

With anticipation and curiosity barely contained, Magnus popped up with a much younger man's vigor, and returned to place a leather-bound *Manon I* in Lu's waiting hands.

Lu opened the book quickly, the binding holding no sentiment, but when the curls of Lil's script graced the pages, he laid his palm to the paper. Though it was not the original, he sighed all the same. Eyes darting back and forth, Lil basked in his expression, his emotions as he savored her thoughts from centuries ago, from another time when she'd not yet known him.

Pages were turned, the corners of his mouth rose and fell, eyes crinkled and widened, breath hitched and steadied.

"This was when Remi accompanied your brother to extend the invitation to your family. We'd agreed with your parents to initiate your transition that way, for appearances."

There was a spot on the next page where the words had smudged, fingerprints left behind. Lu traced the ink and, with his eyes still on the page, reached for her hand, bringing her fingertips to rest against his lips. She watched as he let his lids fall, taking in the moment he'd missed, while holding her close.

"The strawberry jam," he smirked, many pages later. "I remember your brother telling me of the unusual incident. I was thankful that it was your clever bravery, and not one of your other talents that guided the scoundrel to his demise. The flowers weren't yet known as foxglove at the time, if I recall correctly. Are there more of these?" Lu asked.

"Malcom has the original," Magnus began. "And I suspect he has at least one copy of his own to thumb through, as not to damage the original. He passed this on to me as a gift to a fellow collector, though I now know there was more to his motivation in sharing this particular work. He knew. Or at least he suspected."

"Are there additional volumes?" he asked, glancing from Magnus to Lil.

She thought back to the time she'd written what he held in his hands. She'd finished it and there was another... another one of two before she'd been awakened and left the journals behind, left her life as she'd known it.

"I only have this one," Magus started. "However, Malcom alluded to others, and with this being titled *Manon I,* naturally I assumed there could at least be a second or third to look forward to."

Lil nodded. "There are one or two more. I don't think they'd contain anything that could jeopardize me now, though there are identifying details, if one knew what to look for, which Malcom certainly does. But the diaries are written from my perspective before you awakened me. There's nothing of our history here."

"My interest is entirely selfish," Lu smirked. "I only want to read more of your writing."

"By all means," Magnus pleaded. "This copy is rightfully yours. Please, take it with you, I insist."

With the book still closed, Lu squeezed Lil's hand.

"No, I think we'll keep it until we leave tonight. It will be nice to read through a few times and remember together, but I meant what I said upon entering earlier. I returned with everything I need."

Magnus nodded with understanding. He had the limit of his lifetime to collect, but Lil, Lu, and the others, they had to be selective with what they chose to keep with them.

"We leave tonight then?" Lil asked.

"Indeed. There are those at the mountain who've waited too long to see you as you are now."

Remi and Az. She longed to see them as well. She'd stood before Remi just recently, but not knowing who he was. There'd been no running start, no spinning hugs as she'd had with Uri at Nan's.

"And it's best we get you to the mountain so you can explore what you've been holding back. You need more time in the air, and on the ground as well before meeting with Malcom."

"Speaking of Malcom…" Magnus wedged in. "I won't have you slipping off into the sky just yet. We have details to discuss. As far as timing, he will be here in Iceland for the next week, then hosting an event at his chateau at weeks end. It looks to be a small, private gathering, and one which I planned to attend… It will provide an opportunity for the two of us to discuss any further details in person. I'm sure one, if not both of us, will have something to address. Afterwards, he's clear of unavoidable social engagements for a few weeks. Beyond that I would need to check back in, but I think the limited schedule was given in hope that you would meet sooner rather than later."

"Two weeks," Lil said, turning to Lu. "Is that reasonable?"

Lu nodded. *Two weeks should be fine, and you will have us with you.*

"If you don't feel it's too ambitious, I think that will work nicely," Magnus agreed. "As for location, I'd like to extend the use of my house here. To say you've traveled the world over is an understatement, but I think this property would work nicely. You've a feel for the layout, and Malcom has been here as well. It's private. There's access by air, land and sea, but there's a vast openness to the space. We could delay informing him of the location until the last minute, but what Malcom could plan in a week he could easily put in place with a day's notice. The good faith disclosure up front will go farther, perhaps."

Lu nodded again. "Agreed. This location is adequate, familiar to all of us."

"What are your ideas for security?" Magnus asked.

*Uri should stay with Nan,* Lil offered, not wanting to alarm Magnus should Lu disagree.

He nodded. "I'll need to return a few times with Remi and Az. Uri should stay with Nan for continued safety there. It's probable that Malcom will use satellite surveillance once the location is revealed... I should have one of the others stay on here as well, from a distance of course, and perhaps not continuously. You've got a nice property, Magnus."

"The area is vast, but there could be snipers and, with his access to innovation, anything could be in the ammunition. I don't expect a something military, that would be vulgar after the conversation he and I just had, but again, he is ambitious and knows she will be here..."

"I'm not concerned with snipers here."

"His people would be-"

"I've met his people."

"I merely wish to point out that they would be very skilled, capable of accuracy from a distance."

Would they retain accuracy when aiming through a wall of wind and rain? Don't forget, we don't come empty handed. We are not human, Magnus. We prefer these forms, but it is *you* who resemble *us.*

Magnus released a sigh, leaning his brow into his hand and massaging a bit. "My caution and fear have paved the way for my foolishness, it seems. How many of yours should I expect here for the meeting itself? I'll need to decide what food will be served, though I think I'll keep things casual."

*As casual as he is capable*, Lil smiled warmly.

"We will be sourcing the food for this," Lu said. His hands, having not forgotten her, continued along Lil's skin. "Just let us know what you need."

A flash of question crossed Magnus's face, no words spoken, but it was enough for Lu to answer.

"Delivery of danger is not limited to the barrel of a gun, Magnus. Food can be prepared here, by your hands, but we source it, As well as any liquid. We'll have Remi and Az arrive ahead of time, prior to Malcom. When your guest is settled, they will contact me. I will then arrive with Lil. When the meeting concludes, she and I depart first, followed by either Az or Remi. One of them will stay on until Malcom leaves, and perhaps for a time after to ensure your safety, though you're no stranger to security. You can have some say as to when the last of us leaves, but don't take any chances with your life. I won't have you leveraged. No matter how beneath him you think it might be, you said it yourself, Malcom is ambitious and the time he has left to meet his goal is limited."

"He's ambitious, and he is not alone, if I remember correctly. You mentioned an additional threat, the one that has been after Lily from the beginning, or close to it. Malcom wants her for himself but, these others want to cut her down. What protections do you have against them, and how is Malcom the more immediate threat?"

Thinking about those others, the threads of betrayal and tragedy they spawned from, it struck a sensitive chord within Lil. They called themselves Guards of Eden, a name saturated with an irony they would never understand.

"The others you speak of have a name, but I won't use it," Lil said, her whisper laced with calm ferocity. "When we must refer to them, we call them The

Condemned, but anything foul will do. They remain a threat, though it is Malcom who has moved first in this life, and the last. The Condemned could pop up anywhere, poised to strike."

"Forgive my ignorance, but how?"

"They've been recruiting since they first fell, offering righteous purpose, a lineage, a connection to something ancient and divine. A call to arms against the serpent that poisoned the garden is an easy sell..." she sighed. "And they are more than blathering men in robes, carrying sticks and pitchforks, Magnus. They have had *centuries* to evolve as an organization, and, at some point, some of their members evolved to see bits of the future in dreams. One might see a vision of me standing beside a store, eating ice cream on a clear, warm day. From that moment on The Condemned would position operatives by ice cream shops when the sun shines. They would pick out details until the exact shop was identified. They might have one of theirs apply for a job, find a way to purchase the store and staff it entirely with their people. They would do all this months, even years, before the desire for ice cream floated into my mind. We have, over time, found weakness to their sight. We found their visions of me specifically were prompted by my reunion with the others, with Lu... It can be powerful. We learned to avoid this by maintaining my distance from the others while I'm young, vulnerable. The other thing that seems to trigger their ability is a direct encounter..." She trailed off as a recent memory flooded through, a memory of a boy at the school, talk of a dragon, of being taken.

*A dragon*, she smiled inwardly.

*Hmm?*

"When I was at the school, there was a boy there, a relation of Gunnar's named Hamish. He came out to meet David when we arrived, looking quite shaken. He told David he'd had visions... of me."

Lu's breath melted behind her ear, his fingers trailing over the lines in her palm, and up her wrist. He slowed his movement then, silently asking if he should be concerned.

"He said my aim was flawless, and that I smelled good..." Lil began, keeping things light as she eased into the account.

"Both accurate," Lu commented into the space where Lil's neck met her shoulder.

"He must have seen me with the children at Nan's, hunting, and... Magnus you said he spoke of a dragon waiting for me?"

Lu released something of a cough, though the idea that he would ever need to clear his throat was laughable.

*Your dragon certainly came for you, didn't he?* He said, mouth grinning against her ear.

"Indeed, he did," Magnus said. "The boy's description was a little disjointed, but he is young and still developing his gift. There was a dragon mentioned, an arm-"

"I think we got to the bottom of that vision during our swim, Magnus," Lu smiled.

Magnus raised a brow, but continued, saying, "Dragons aside, he did have some concerning and accurate predictions."

It had shaken Lil at the time, even with David telling Magnus not to worry... She'd survived though, she supposed.

"He had seen me being taken, that many would come for me. He'd seen it happen, and not yet happen; I forget the exact wording he used. Magnus?"

Before Magnus could speak, Lu's voice, clear and low, asked, "He was able to see both the past and the future?"

Magnus nodded. "Apparently so. The boy said he didn't know when she was from, but that they always come for her. Of what he saw, he said some was from before, and some was from *not yet*, and that she was safe for now. And you've heard the piece about the dragon, as well as the colorful descriptions of Lily."

"And what was the nature of the boy's exposure to her prior to his vision?"

"David said Hamish, age about eight or nine years, had been in the kitchen when we arrived, and had accidentally cut himself when the vision came. He'd been indoors without view and perhaps between fifty and two hundred meters distance from her given the time it would have taken for him to manage the wound care. He cleaned, stitched, and dressed the wound all before coming to find David. The boy approached us just after we'd first entered the building. My guess is that we were approaching in the car, in the garage, or just outside at the time Hamish had his experience."

"A strong reaction..." *I need to speak to Remi and David,* Lu said. *And likely the boy himself.*

*I'd like to go with you.*

*Of course.*

"Could you not have alumni of the school gifted with these predictive visions assist you in negating the upper hand held by these *Condemned?*" Magus asked. "And if the alumni have these traits, are they not derived from yourselves? Could you and your companions not provide *yourselves* with what the future holds?"

*This will be a tricky one to explain.*

"Sometimes…" Lil sighed. *Where to start?* "We are different. While your gifts or talents may have derived from one of our kind, you are human, and traits present in you differently than they do for us. For the first few generations offspring live longer, like myself with mortality, heal faster, have greater enhancements, but…" It was a struggle to simplify. Lu gave her a squeeze of encouragement.

"We have a similar ability," she continued. "Though it manifests with greater strength in some… Az, and of course Michael… but where our ability is like a sphere, that of, say Hamish or those of The Condemned, would be a circle. Another difference is that Hamish has no control over what he sees, whereas one of us would have a consensual relationship with vision. Something else to consider is that what is seen is subject to chance, and change. Vision, time, and the future are delicate. As we have the wisdom not to interfere with the garden, with this place, we also avoid use of vision. It can be misinterpreted, and one can get lost to it. The most effective use of this strain of ability is the intuition or early warning; seeing a fist come at you a few moments before it strikes, allowing one to move out of the way. I'm not sure if that answers your question, Magnus, but I gave it a good try," she smiled softly; the gesture honest, but with a sense of heaviness about it.

"It's a wonder you don't just stay put in the middle of the ocean," he said wearily.

Of course she could, but what life would that be for a creator of worlds and one who wields the breath of life.

"In the case of both the Drakes and The Condemned," she started. "We could stay within the walls of our mountain home indefinitely and maintain safety. They would not threaten me there. But it is not our way to be confined. We are not of this earth, Magnus. It is my weakness that keeps us here, but I won't be sequestered to a cave because of it, however sacred that space is."

She leaned into the warmth of Lu's body, tilting her head back. His hand slid behind her neck, his forehead easing forward to touch hers.

*You were not meant to be contained, not by walls, not even by me.*

"And so, we move forward," Lu said. "We will try things differently with Malcom this time, though we will remain vigilant."

"I do look forward to meeting with Uri, Az, and Remi," Magnus said, releasing an almost dreamy breath of air. "What a reunion. I saw Remming- *Remi*, just the other day, it seems. What a wonder it will be to see him under these new circumstances."

*A reunion.*

Plans were discussed and light faded, until midnight had passed, and Lil was standing in the doorway, transferring from Magnus's embrace to Lu's arms. The two walked forward, air before them like liquid, ready to transport them to the mountain.

As she turned one last time to offer a smile, Lil felt there was something almost ceremonial about the departure that she knew would not be lost, certainly not on Magnus.

# A Story in Song

# 5.

The refreshing rush of frigid air hit the portion of Lil's body not flush with Lu's. Wind passed over them, thin as the ocean was deep, but with a lightness to it the sea didn't carry. Water could become firm, but air could spread itself, rendering breath useless. Both had the potential to be unforgiving, but not this wind, not to her. From her face to her feet, it playfully threaded between strands of her hair, receiving her, welcoming her home.

Lil and Lu stood together above the clouds on a broad, flat section of the mountain where a small lake spread like glass, still, reflecting the clear blue sky and surrounding snow-covered peaks.

When Lil looked up to her left, she felt a pang in her heart.

Whether from earth or sky, the mountain's entrances were obstructed by stone and darkness. A more central passage was located not too far off, but the formation Lil had her eyes on went directly to her room.

Remi, Uri, Az, Lil and Lu, they all had other locations they'd been drawn to throughout time, but the mountain was a place the collective called home. A constant, belonging no more to one than the other, thus far impenetrable to outsiders.

Few humans, if any at all, had made it as far as where she stood. The mountain was considered sacred by the surrounding peoples, restricting travel there. And the rare curious who might somehow manage to set foot by the lake would not get a chance to look up because, well, mountain weather was fickle... If they were fortunate enough to make it back out, they'd have a survival story to tell, never knowing what was inside, never knowing who dwelled there.

Lil closed her eyes, brought in breath. A fragrance mingled with the fresh mountain air, deep and warm, a scent she knew. His body came around the side of her until her chest pressed against his. A relaxed smile formed as his lips brushed hers, parting as his tongue met hers, then retreating to whisper at her ear.

"Shall we?"

His fingers trickled down her back, lowering the already deep scoop of her dress. She sighed audibly as he flattened his palm between her shoulder blades and, as if he'd pressed a button inside her, Lil's wings released.

She wanted to stay there with her body against his, but there could be no dancing without movement. Instead, opening her eyes, she caught his hungry stare and, with a devious grin, she backed up, stepping out of her flats.

Lil receded, watching him as he slung her bag off his shoulder and placed it on the ground. He removed his shoes next, never breaking eye contact. His nostrils flared, catching her excitement as he slowly unbuttoned his shirt, savoring the anticipation of the chase.

A white glow hummed over his skin, eyes deep and expression flat until she noticed the slow change of his stance into a subtle crouch, his feet digging in at the toes, heals raised.

Lil's focus adjusted from the ground up to where his eyes waited.

She inhaled sharp, and the corner of Lu's mouth lifted. He emitted a low growl that echoed through her, off the surrounding stone. Then it was his voice in her head...

*Run.*

The tiniest squeal escaped her as she turned and sprinted. She tucked her wings initially to gain speed, and then threw them out, catching the wind. With one tilt she was up, toes raking ripples into the lake, Lu's feet pounding against the earth behind her.

She looked back.

His velocity would have left him a blur to human senses alone, but her eyes locked with his. Teeth bared, his wings sprung loose, catching air instantly.

Lil yipped and tore through the sky. Impressed with her own speed, she ascended fast as the joy soaring in her heart.

She'd had help bringing forth her wings again, but needed no assistance with her takeoff, which had been both exhilarating and flawless. She felt home again, at the mountain and in the air, but also within herself.

Lil came upon one peek that met with another to create a small valley. She tumbled suddenly, the change in air current as she went through the slope throwing her off kilter, tossed her up and back, her head cracking against the rock. Lil faltered as she fell, then her feet shot out, catching the surface and pushing off. She steadied herself, abrasions already healing as she angled back around and down toward the lake.

She sensed Lu watching her, but as she scanned the space from rocky ground to sky, she couldn't see him there among the blue, grey, and white.

Her skin tingled with awareness and, as the shadow fell over her, Lil tilted her head up to the left. Craning to see directly above her, she gasped and laughed, cutting down and to the right as Lu plummeted toward her, his wings tucked back as he charged.

Recognizing the entrance she'd seen before, that she knew by heart, Lil banked right, quickly swooping down toward her sanctuary.

Touching her feet to the ledge, her heart pounded. She stumbled a little upon landing, as she turned her head trying to see if he was behind her, but he wasn't there. In a distracted instant the wind pulled at her wings, drawing her back toward the mouth of the cave and leaving her struggling to escape the draft. Tucking her wings behind her, Lil found relief.

Facing inward, she observed thin shadow, a recess in the rock to her left about ten centimeters wide and running from floor to ceiling, purposefully made. She looked to the other side of the opening; finding it there as well. The same recessed space ran along the ceiling, connecting the two spaces on either side.

Reaching in to the space at her left, she felt a handle. Pulling, she discovered a thick, glass door. Had it been there before? Memories of the inner room came back to her as she investigated. The rock ceiling of the entryway became smooth, mother of pearl tiles peppering here and there as she went further, becoming denser until they reached the inner room, her room. Lil knew the entire ceiling was inlaid beyond, though her view was obstructed by three rows of sheer curtains. Spaced about a meter apart, fabric flowing down from the high ceilings, fluttering in what gentle breeze was able to make it that far in. She reached up, fingertips just grazing the material when it suddenly billowed away, parting to provide a glimpse of the place where she had lived.

Several strands of her hair lifted, blown over her shoulders…

He was there. She could feel him.

Lil turned slowly, her wings brushing against the drapes.

His hair was loose, stone cylinder resting at his chest. He had a wild look about him as he discarded the bag, shoes, and clothing on the ground. Stalking forward, his eyes never broke contact with hers as his wings disappeared.

Lil backed to the wall, feathers against stone. Lu planted his palm against the rock surface above her head, his other arm wrapping firmly around her waist, filling her with his presence.

"Put them away."

His voice was low and textured; all around her. She knew he could easily speak directly to her mind but, there was indeed something to be said for the vibration of sound with breath.

She eased into him, into the heat, his scent engulfing her everywhere his arms didn't reach. He moved his mouth until it hovered over hers, lips making the slightest contact as he whispered, "Do you need help?"

She let just enough air escape her to respond. "Yes."

His tongue slid against hers as he growled into her. Lil relaxed, sinking slightly, releasing a sigh into his mouth as her wings receded.

When the rock began to quake around them, Lil felt Lu slow, felt him pause. She looked into his eyes to find he was assessing her thoughtfully. She'd been so worried about losing control before; of destroying something she loved by letting go. Those thoughts had no place at the mountain.

*I'm ok,* she thought, his mouth soft against hers as she joined him again. *If these walls were going to come down, they would have done it long ago.*

*

Lil woke, partially covered by smooth, soft fabrics that felt glorious on her skin; the blanket over her a billowing, tufted white, similar to the one she'd chosen for her home by the ocean.

She breathed deep as her eyes drifted open, Lu's smoldering smell, like myrrh, moss and cardamom, tangled with her own. She stretched out on her back; arms and legs lengthening, toes pointing as she reached. The air she took in released as a sigh, her fingers grazing warmth, Lu's large hand moving across her abdomen.

"This room has been missing your scent for too long. I'm never washing the sheets," he rumbled, sliding her toward him.

Lil nuzzled his body. They were in their bed. In their room. Real.

"When this languid spell wears off," he continued, leaning his head down to graze his mouth against her ear. "You'll find you are hungry and eager to explore."

"I'm surprised the others haven't broken the door down yet." *It wouldn't be the first time.*

"They wanted to, but I forbade their entry. They settled for an update on events transpired, and promise of ample time in your presence once you're rested."

Lil wondered if she'd find them pacing the hall when she emerged.

Resting her head on Lu's shoulder, lips on his neck, Lil was exactly where she wanted to be. It was in this moment that her treacherous stomach rumbled with need.

She sat up, feeling his eyes on her as she took in the room, their room.

Layers of woven rugs covered large portions of the stone floor, gold tiles interspersed amongst the mother of pearl on the ceiling, increasing in distribution over her the giant bed where she'd slept. Doorways flanked the large fireplace across the room, each leading through respective closets and terminating in the same, moderately sized bathroom. Her eyes fluttered at memories of the bath, more like a bathing pool. Food could wait. She'd wanted a lazy morning or whatever time it was, wanted to wake slowly, then there'd be more time for their hands to explore again. The bath...

Lu breathed in deep and released a rumble from his chest. When his sound stopped, it was her stomach that continued to growl.

"The bath isn't going anywhere, and neither are my hands, nor the rest of me," he chuckled.

"Clothing then, I suppose," she sighed. "When did we even start wearing clothing?"

"When they did, or sometime thereafter."

Lil paused on her way to the closet, a hanging piece of art catching her eye and her memory. A framed sketch on aged paper, similar to one she'd seen in a book at the archives, depicting a pair of hands, a couple seated together, their necklaces visible, and their faces clear. Lil's head was drawn resting on Lu's shoulder; her eyes closed as he leaned in to smell her hair.

*He was so determined to fly with us.*

Lil turned, feeling heat greater than that coming from the fire. Lu was there with her at arm's length, reclined against the stone wall, wearing as little as she was.

She needed to get dressed.

Beautiful clothes in luxurious textures hung from long wooden rods in her closet, drawers containing more. Atop dressers and bureaus rested small boxes carved from alabaster, ebony, agate, and river stone; some by Lu's own hands. They contained little bits of things she'd collected over the lifetimes. She was selective about what she kept; they all were.

Lil smiled, thinking back to when Lu had come to her house on the ocean and taken her to Nan's.

Her fingers ran over the peaked lid of a rather large jar, peppered with gold dust. She lifted the lid and grinned at the generous mound of powder shimmering back at her. Looking to the surrounding objects she noted the brushes, the oil.

*Overwhelmed with options? Shall I choose for you?*

*Later,* she sighed with a knowing smile, putting the lid back down. They'd never leave the room if she came out in gold.

*Later?*

*You'll see… No, I can dress myself. I'm just getting a little distracted.*

She was sliding fabric over her head when she heard him in the doorway.

"Do you need a chaperone?"

His hands came up, helping the dress fall into place. Not because she needed help, but because he needed his hands closer. The garment was a blueish grey in color with gold thread wrapping the bottom hem. It draped comfortably over her, coating her shape.

Dark pants hung low on Lu's hips, his chest still bare. The exception, as ever, was the necklace; the mate to her own. His hair was pulled back casually and, as her eyes slid over him, Lil found she had very little confidence she could maintain motivation to leave their room.

*Perhaps I should chase you out,* he whispered, lips stretching to reveal sharp teeth.

They did enjoy a game of pursuit.

Lil ran through the hall with Lu following close behind, still barefoot and shirtless, a wicked smile on his face, his heart radiant.

She slowed as she came to a large, open room where pillars connected a high ceiling to the stone floor, steps carved out and leading down into a stone pool.

Lil navigated through memories as she passed the pool and paused where another set of stone stairs led down to a garden. Roughly two square kilometers of life spread under the open sky, pathways winding through fruit trees, fragrant flowers and herbs, the occasional statue, and a stream.

Lu stayed close behind as she descended, Lil taking the lead as she explored. Her fingers seemed to reach out toward everything she passed, nerve endings drinking in the variety of sensations her skin received.

The scent of ripened fruit came strong with a distinctly *green* smell, and that of the soil, the stone. She heard the trickling of the water, the sound of insects, and the flutter of a bird. The little garden was remote where the rest of the world was concerned, but it was thoroughly alive.

A gentle curve of stone emerged from the ground before her; a hand about a meter in length, partially covered in moss and thyme. As she surveyed the area, she saw another hand, toes, the tops of two thighs, a face. The face was smooth, with barely discernible features, but the curve of the lips led her to believe the subject was happy, content. The collective of the stones gave the appearance of a woman floating in water.

Remi had indeed been busy.

*He carved this after your visit to the school. He and I were still connected and, as a result, he saw you through my mind when I came upon you in the lake.*

*It fits our garden well.*

The life around her had an awakening energy to it, but it was changing suddenly, a tingling on her skin…

The others.

She turned before hearing their footsteps, covering her mouth as she took in a sharp breath.

Her eyes became glassy at seeing the two standing before her. Somehow the number of times she'd cycled through life couldn't dampen the intensity of emotion that rushed in upon seeing them again.

Remi was more or less as he had been days before at the school: light tweed suit, waistcoat and jacket over a white shirt. His blond hair was tucked behind his ear on one side, a little stubble on his jaw catching the light. Blue eyes, cool like glacial water, warmed at the sight of her, edges crinkling as the corners of his mouth raised just so.

Az stood beside him; not quite as tall but built like a stone wall; his wide base a grounding comfort. He still had short, black hair that lay flat against his head, thick, angular brows, and his eyes… His dark eyes were like Gunnar's, almost indistinguishable circles of darkness, though Az had flecks of the universe there, just beyond the center.

He wore a tight grey t-shirt that was well worn, and black pants that came in close at the ankle but remained loose through the rest of the leg, tying at the waist. He tended toward comfort and movement when he dressed, though he preferred as little clothing as possible.

Her feet brought her forward in a run, arms outstretched with no chance of wrapping around one, let alone both of them. Ever patient, Az allowed Remi to take the force of her impact.

Lil breathed in the scent of melting snow, lichen, and birch.

The times they'd flown together, flown with crows and eagles, singing to bees, to grapes at the vineyard... she'd forgotten about the vineyard. Oh, and how she'd adored when playing with his children, but that hadn't been for quite some time. He wasn't as prolific as Uri, but Remi had planted seeds in more than just the ground.

"I'd expected to see you at the bar," he whispered. "But at the school... I was awestruck. The world fell away and, for a moment, I was home."

Steadying her breath, tiny offerings of water welled at Lil's eyes.

"I took a few days off from the students to work with my hands. Lu's vision of you at the lake inspired the new piece in our garden," he smiled, nodding to the stone rising up through the plant life. "I only saw you for a moment before the connection was severed."

"I'll never apologize for my selfishness," Lu quipped behind her.

*It was an experience I thought best to keep private.*

Lil smiled, raising her head to look into Remi's eyes.

"What a puzzle that all was, knowing but not knowing, seeing you, Remi. I felt home as well, and when I saw Uri in Boston, my *goodness*... But you I haven't seen since before I was born," she trailed off, turning to Az with fresh sparkles in her eyes.

His large arms were around her, pulling her towards him until she'd been secured against his chest. He had almost no smell, but when close enough, it was something like clay. He was warm, solid, and could ground her second to none except Lu, but without the heat.

"When did you start wearing shirts?" Lil sniffled with a smile, pulling back to look up at him.

He raised his brows and shrugged.

"I haven't been around to provide him with the lifestyle to which he has become accustomed," Uri's voice announced with mock seriousness. "And when he eats elsewhere, they make him cover up."

Uri had entered quietly by the pool, and leaned against an archway in the distance, wearing a mischievous expression that told of how pleased he was with himself.

Lil's grin was unstoppable, not just for seeing him, but for the evidence that he'd been spending time with Todd.

Uri wore grey denim pants and a black t-shirt stretched over his muscular form that said *Coffee, Leggings, Lipstick* in swirly script. That he'd been able to find a shirt with those words in his size was astonishing.

"You, too?" Lil laughed, her face wet with tears. "You're not even supposed to be here!"

"Oh, they'll be fine for five minutes," he said, strolling in toward her. "The kid is on high alert, and if anything threatened that cousin of yours, I think Gunnar might muster enough fury to shake the ground himself. Apple doesn't fall far from the tree, or trees with that one."

Separating from Az and Remi, Lil embraced Uri who, of course, picked her up and spun her around. Lil laughed, legs swinging through the air, but Uri's face transformed to a scowl as he looked over her shoulder to Lu. Gently, he placed her back down. It was then that she noticed Lu's emotions had darkened a bit.

"Enough, Uri, she needs food. She's ravenous."

"Of course she is," Uri smiled, brushing off Lu's grumbling. "You've been *reuniting* since I last saw you." Turning his attention back to Lil he asked, "How long has the beast kept you in that room with him? Truthfully, when is the last time you came up for air?"

Lil blushed and burst out laughing as she pushed away from him.

"Uri…" Lu rumbled low.

"Have you stayed hydrated at least?"

She thought his serious expression would crack at any moment.

"I only just woke," Lil said, regaining composure, but with cheeks still high and blooming. She continued backing up until her body was flush with Lu's, his arms coming around her, his chest vibrating through her back. "And, while I don't owe any explanation…" she continued, raising her eyebrows. "If it wasn't for him, I'd still be in bed."

Lil closed her eyes as glowing wisps formed around her, feeling Lu's engulfing warmth, the heat of his breath on her neck as his chin dipped down, beard grazing her skin, lips along the rim of her ear. Through his scent, she detected something like the strong smell of rain in the air, like something was going to happen.

And then Az spoke.

"Your radiance… has been missed."

All present stilled, acknowledging the impact of his speech with reflective silence as his sound settled, the echoes of his breath resonating within them.

His words were a rare gift.

Lil's eyes became coated again with unfallen tears, her lips upturned into a sweet smile.

"And it feels good," she sighed. "It feels good to have returned."

The moment hung heavy with emotion such that one could have rested a stone on the air between them. They all felt it, the relief and the hope, the bittersweet thankfulness.

Uri put his hand to Lil's cheek before clapping Lu on the shoulder.

"Food and conversation," he announced, waving at the trees and bushes. "Grab some fruit. You can eat on your way to the kitchen, and we'll talk while I cook."

Lil sighed again, feeling she was capable of cooking, and more than interested in showing Uri a thing or two…

*It's been a quarter century since he's prepared a meal for you.* Lu said. *Allow him this.*

Uri bounded up the stairs, calling out, "I expect I'll find my apron where I left it."

Lu let out a huff that became a deep, suppressed chuckle, stopping Uri in his tracks.

"Where?" Uri asked, Lil rapidly piecing together that Lu had hid the apron as part of a game.

"Main library," Lu grinned, "adorning Remi's carving of that Lynx."

He was fond of that animal's likeness. The carving was both incredibly detailed and comfortable to lounge against with a pillow. It was enormous.

"Were there clues?" Uri asked with obvious disappointment at the opportunity wasted.

"Forty-seven."

"Forty-se-…" Uri shook his head, raised his hand and was silent, the proverbial gears turning.

"Right, while I'm preparing a short-notice feast, you find a new object and final hiding spot, replace the last clue. After we've eaten, we'll have entertainment."

Lil felt her own laughter bubbling up along with Lu's. Remi began to grin, and even Az had a look of creeping delight about him.

Without waiting for a response, Uri started on his path toward the library instead of the kitchen, calling out, "I *am* on a tight schedule. Safety at the shop and all that, but if I don't make it back before dawn, that woman will start baking without me."

# 6.

Lil leaned her palm against the wall, winded, not from the running, but from abundant laughter. As she paused to catch her breath, Lu scooped her up from behind, carrying her at high speed around the corner into a sitting room, close behind the others.

The circular perimeter of the inner room had been carved into repeating archways, the outer hall a square, hanging lanterns dispensing a warm glow throughout the space. The footprint of the room was relatively small; however, the height of the domed ceiling, they way they'd carved and inlaid it, opened the space. Mother of pearl tiles reflected light down from the ceiling, similar to her own room, but with silver instead of gold woven in. Lil had taken time to assist with chiseling and sanding the stone into shape when the work first started, they all had, but the vision was Remi's. He'd carved both the arches and walls like lace, with fine detail, intricate floral and geometric designs starting at six meters high and continuing until the tiling of the ceiling began.

The center of the room housed a wading pool a little over two meters in diameter, water still and steaming in the cool air. Around the pool, large pillows had been piled atop layered carpets, three chairs, and two couches. As Uri approached one of the couches, he held an arm out to fend off Remi and, tossing aside a throw pillow, revealed the last clue. All but Uri had known where the note would be, but only Lu knew what it said.

Paper crinkled as the message unfolded, not a breath escaping anyone present. Uri held up a hand to ensure maintained silence while he read aloud.

"Between your body and the air, the flour dusted space you wear, in suspended darkness it rested while you tarried; your eyes preoccupied, what you seek you've carried."

Stillness.

Any sound heard was external to the sitting room at that moment, beyond the mountain.

The last clue fluttered to the floor as Uri slowly reached down into his apron pocket. His large fingers emerged, pinching a tiny silver spoon, the prize, with elaborate filigree about its handle. His eyes shot up, looking just over Lil's shoulder to Lu, who still held her in his arms. Uri had a twinkle in his eye as he nodded.

The spoon Uri had followed forty-seven clues to find had been in his pocket the whole time.

There were no words needed.

After a show of respect for a game well played, Lil reclined on a couch with her head in Lu's lap. Remi sat in an overstuffed chair; Az on the floor amongst the pillows.

"Forty-seven…" Uri began shaking his head, hovering in the doorway, ready to return to Nan's. "When did you have the time?"

When *did* he have the time?

Lu had something akin to omnipotence when it came to souls departing their human forms. His awareness was like a great net cast over the living, sensing their passage. From the time of Lil's first death, Lu had vowed not to let the unworthy pass without atonement, and he'd been true to his promise. Many were caught, though some eventually passed through, others not yet able, others still who never would, and some… There were some whose nature was so twisted; they demanded his immediate attention upon separation from their bodies. For those, he preferred to be wholly present, and though he could do many things, he had never, to her knowledge, manifested wholly in more than one form at a time.

So, when had he constructed a trail of clues for Uri?

She and Lu had been together almost constantly since she'd awakened… How many days had it been? They'd been at Nan's, and that's when it was decided that Uri would stay on there, so it couldn't have been before then. They'd gone for a swim, then to Magnus's house, then to the mountain…

*While you slept in our bed, recuperating from exhaustion.*

*Exhaustion…*

*Indeed. I believe you had been thoroughly exhausted when it was sleep that came for you.*

*I was-*

"Lil slept while Remi, Az and I had the discussion you joined remotely," Lu started, thwarting Lil's attempt at a witty remark. "Her slumber provided ample time for both our talk and the construction of a game."

While she was sleeping. Lil *had* been quite exhausted, what with the flight, the swim, the hours they'd spend discussing plans with Magnus, and then flying again...

*You were energetic still when we arrived in our room,* he said, smooth and low as if his lips had been brushing against her ear.

"Are you off to Nan's then?" Lil asked.

Uri nodded. "I want to get there well before dawn. There's baking, but also the movement and exercise they get on with out in the field most mornings. I don't think the women would mind seeing me waltz through thin air, but the questions could become burdensome for Nan." He turned to Lil, advancing a few steps. "The weather has been mild since my arrival there, but what do you do when it's not so obliging?"

"Downstairs in the barn," Lil began as Uri approached her. "We just shuffle things around and run yoga in there."

He reached his hand to her shoulder, leaning in to kiss her forehead before clasping arms with Lu.

"Keep me looped in," he said, tapping his temple before turning to leave.

Lil sank into the feeling of Lu's fingers through her hair, staring off into the details of the ceiling. Several concentric circles of rock rimmed the dome, receding toward the shimmering apex. Remi had indeed worked some miracle of lacework with the stone.

There was such ease in that moment, the scent of Lu entering her with every breath. The stability of the room and surrounding mountain was comforting; the presence of her family, the one she'd had for lifetimes, since before race and species, since the beginning. There was ease, like the gentle sway of calm water, but there was also the chaotic reintegration of Lil's life since her current birth into the timeline of her existence.

She had hovered once in the dome above, revealing details and fitting tiles. She'd sat beyond the ceiling, between the stone and sky, her hair chasing the wind. She'd grown trees from her palm and made juice with their fruit in the little garden just down the hall. The memories were all there, but it would take time to settle, for the hum of activity to soothe and quiet. And still, there was the need to plan and train, to play.

"Alright," she sighed, turning on her side, Lu's fingers moving from her hair to gently massage her ear. "Who's up first?"

Remi's face lit with amusement as he shifted, Az motionless save for his eyes meeting hers briefly before Lu spoke.

"Az will accompany me to Magnus's while you get started with Remi."

Lil wasn't put off by Lu's dictation of their schedule, felt no sense of being uninvolved in decisions made. There was a foundation of equality and trust with them unparalleled in any other creatures she'd encountered. That and, aside from having already discussed a preliminary framework for how the days would be laid out while she and Lu were still with Magnus, Lil knew Lu had gone over quite a bit of the details with the others while she slept. They didn't require sleep as she did, and the wheels shouldn't stop turning because her eyes closed.

The plan was for Lil to be with one of them at all times, not arm and arm, but in the same primary location. Lu would take turns traveling with Az and Remi to Iceland, though Lil looked forward to when the three of them would go at once. When that happened, she'd spend some time with Uri and visit family at Nan's. She was rather looking forward to the visit, witnessing for herself how Uri had integrated into life at the shop. She'd already seen the evidence of Todd's influence, and of Nan's in the way Uri left with concern for *that woman* baking without him. Until then… well, she could still pop over there with one of the others maybe.

"Do you have an agenda for our time together, or should we just *wing it*," she asked Remi, wagging her eyebrows to accentuate the obvious pun.

Flight with Remi was something Lil looked forward too. He was graceful and even-tempered, both on land and above.

"I heard you'd flown, but wasn't sure…" he trailed off, looking to Lu for guidance.

Lu's thumb crossed Lil's lips as she turned her face up toward him.

"You've taken to flight with excellence, but need practice calling forth, releasing your wings and tucking them away. But I think more *private* study is needed, before taking off in my absence."

There was an unmistakable heat in his words accompanied by bright, floating sparks of light reflecting off the ceiling and the water.

*I hope you're joking, because there is no way-*

She wasn't about to wait for Lu to advance her flight progress, not that she didn't mind how their lessons ended…

"I say this without challenge," Remi began, pausing to let his introduction take effect. "Perhaps if Lil had additional flight instruction that was less *distracting*, she would wean sooner. Again, not a challenge. If you'll recall, this has been an issue not isolated to the wings…"

Steam thickened above the pool; she thought the water might boil.

*Really*, he growled. *The very idea that I'm incapable of preparing you… Or that I would want you to remain anything less than independent…*

A memory bubbled up. Embracing, but not losing herself to the undertow of it, she said, *when you had me pressed against the wall earlier, you weren't thinking of flight lessons or how best to progress my self-sufficiency.*

The surrounding temperature had risen such that there was no longer steam above the pool, just still water reflecting the shimmering tile and soft glow of the room.

*I wanted to be inside you, as I do now and always.*

She stared at him, brows raised. He'd made her point.

*Indeed…* he conceded.

"You should study what you see fit, but prioritize teleportation. It has been our error in the past not to ensure this skill mastered straight away. Flight is important, and I won't deny how thoroughly satisfying it is to have you in the air. Fast and skilled as you might be, they can still take you from the sky, but they can't take you from the ether. We'll rehearse your escape from Magnus's in the event of an emergency, but in that instance, I want you to return to the mountain directly without turning back. If by chance someone were to latch onto you, they would struggle upon arrival here, what with the sudden change in altitude and weather."

Lil nodded, Remi as well.

*I still intend to continue private lessons…* Lu growled playfully.

*And are you always to be the instructor?*

*You teach me patience, constantly. And I must continue waiting, it seems. Remi is clearly on the edge of his seat.*

Lil caught Remi sigh, raising his eyebrows.

*You have a knack for provoking him,* she smiled.

"Teleporting usually takes some time for you," Remi began, having sensed the personal conversation had ended. "But it's a skill you once practiced flawlessly, and will again. I'm curious about this new approach with the Drakes," he went on. "You said Magnus reported Malcom had been pleased, perhaps honored, to be meeting." He looked into Lil's eyes then. "What are your thoughts?"

"Maybe he thinks to use a gentle hand as not to repeat history. Perhaps his motivation appears to go beyond acquisition of a tool at this point. He's human; he ages. His family will continue on, but the loss of my life in this cycle could result in a total loss of opportunity for him. Malcom would not live to find me again. This feels personal.

"He's covetous," Lu growled. "*Infatuated.*"

Remi raised a brow. Az observant and still.

"I kept journals during my youth in France, and they were left behind," she explained. "It was some five hundred years ago or so. You remember my brother from that time, Estienne?"

*I can think of one he'd recall more fondly than that brother of yours, though he was also a loss we mourned.*

"If not Estienne," Lu teased. "Certainly, you recall a certain fanged creature… soft, grey as ash, loyal, capricious… deadly as any of us…"

*Cendres…* she whispered.

*Indeed.*

"Yes, I recall them both," Remi said, his thoughts appearing to drift a moment. "You kept journals from that time? Did you not take them with you? I don't remember anything of it."

"Neither did I… but Malcom now has the books in his possession, though he didn't make it known directly. He passed a carefully constructed copy of the first journal to Magnus, posing it as a gift from one collector to another. Magnus enjoyed it for what it was initially, but you can imagine how he delighted in the pieces coming together when it was revealed to be *my* writing from another lifetime… Magnus has not acknowledged to Malcom his awareness of the gift's origin, or that he'd shared it with me. Malcom hasn't divulged his suspicion that I am the author."

"A delicate and dangerous game they're playing," Remi breathed.

"Malcom doesn't understand what we truly are," Lu said, voice low and textured. "Or he might have taken more caution to avoid our meeting after his demise."

Lu did take his time when working.

Lil shifted onto her stomach, head still in Lu's lap, his fingers tracing their way from her neck and down her back left bare by the low drape of her dress.

"The Drakes have been ruthless in their attempts to acquire me, but it's more than my usefulness Malcom is after. There's something emotionally significant to it for him, possibly existential."

"Did you ever think it would come to this," Remi sighed. "Engaging thusly with the pieces on the board as if we were players ourselves?

"You've been *engaging* for some time, evidence of your efforts residing in a unique school to the north…" Lu teased.

It was because of her, Lil thought, that they lived as they did for so long. The five of them maintained a careful balance between living on the earth and not interfering too much with it; seeing needs, but only minimally responding to them.

"We could always trigger another ice age," she suggested, quickly adding, "the five of us. We could manage it and be done with Malcom. Whatever has been thawing will be sealed in its frozen tomb again."

She was only half serious, though the idea had been tempting over the last several lifetimes. The earth needed a refresh by water, as ocean or ice. "I certainly never expected…" Lil began again with a whisper, Remi's question still moving through her. "I never expected all this. Who could have? I do wonder, and it cannot be the first time, though it's hard to remember, but I wonder what his endgame is." She wasn't speaking of Malcom anymore.

Lil continued, her words loose, following a floating train of thought. "He sought us out once for the flood, but things weren't nearly as dire then. What could he be waiting for? Or is he not? I've heard… I was having lunch with a colleague of Claire's, well he doesn't work directly with her, rather his company works with Magnus's… but I heard the underground is increasing in volatility… seismic activity. Is it the garden moving forward on its own, or is it us? The other six? If Michael was moving forward with something, certainly he would have reached out as he did before."

Lil's thoughts were interrupted by pulse vibrating through the room. Rings of moving water mirrored the carved details of the ceiling above, the surface of the wading pool undulating with circular symmetry until fading back to stillness. A low vibration burst from Lu, progressing through her. She sought clarity from Remi and Az, but their focus was elsewhere. Their eyes were silently locked on Lu, whose fingers never had ceased in their gentle trickling over her skin.

She didn't have to hear their words to know they spoke silently, intentionally excluding her from their discussion. There was some degree of discord among them, set off, perhaps, by something she'd said… She'd been questioning Michael's plan…

Lil felt the flutter of a breeze through the ends of her hair, ruffling at the hem of her dress where it hung over the edge of the couch.

"What don't I know?" Her voice echoed.

Lil's firm whisper hadn't persuaded Az and Remi to speak, their expressions conflicted. Lu's fingers remained calm along her neck and back.

Lil's brain ran rapidly through information, experiences, moments.

# A Story in Song

The stones… There'd been stones outside her house. *Contact with you would have been unwise,* Lu had said. And there'd been stones waiting for them on the shore in Iceland, stones he'd knocked down.

Fires flared in their lanterns, the surrounding hall flooding with warm, pulsing light. Ripples in the water trembled, crashing against the sides of the pool as a strong wind spiraled up the dome and down, through the hall, tearing at the flames until they were naught but a flicker.

All the while, Lu maintained the gentle action of studying her skin with is hands, grounding both of them. As she evened out, her heart beat with more force but remained steady, her breathing deeper, but controlled. The movement of air in the room quieted altogether, surrounding them in stillness, fires once raging along the perimeter barely holding back the dark.

Lil rolled in Lu's lap again, his fingers tracing lightly along her neck as she turned, resuming their gentle strokes along her chest and shoulders, his hand coming up to frame her jaw as his glistening eyes finally rested on hers. Lil threaded her palm beneath his shirt, her skin against his as she snaked her hand upward, brushing aside stone to rest against his heart. They looked into each other, finding the calm, the connection they both needed, that had always been there.

*What don't I know?*

"I asked you after our swim, if you would choose to work with him again… if contact was made. Your response was as it has been every cycle I ask, though this time…" he sighed. "This time was different. Michael left the stones on the shore at your home, and in Iceland, in an attempted to get my attention. We met after the first incident; the second display a reminder, as business was left very much unfinished."

"So close…" she whispered.

"I'd have made things very uncomfortable for him," Lu rumbled, "if he'd so much as passed you in the street." Lu might not be able to end Michael's existence, but he could, as he'd said, render considerable discomfort if he set himself to it. There had been much restraint on his part over time not to have done so thus far.

"He's been careful not to overstep, not to make direct contact with you," Remi said. "But his intention is to open a dialogue."

"You didn't tell me," she whispered.

Lil found turbulence in the depths of Lu's eyes as she gazed into them. He wanted to comfort, to envelope her, to bring Lil in that she might find respite on the mossy earth surrounding the black pools of his eyes, to slip down into the darkness. Lil felt his relief, desire, and his anger. He was furious, having wanted to protect her where the others thought to burden her with the weight of what she should have known outright.

"I understand," she said, reassurance seeping through her words. "You didn't desire to *keep* me in the dark, only…"

"Only while easing your transition. Timing of disclosure has been a point of contention," he growled, eyes flicking over her to where the other two sat. "You'd only just been attacked… and after the way you reacted when I spoke of him on the shore… I thought to wait at least until you'd been home a few days;

after our meeting with Malcom at most, though I'm not sure I could have made it that long."

"It's possible, that what Michael has to say may impact the meeting with Malcom," Remi offered.

Lil looked at him with furrowed brows. "How so?" Turning back toward Lu's waiting eyes, she asked, "What did you discuss?"

Lu brought his forehead down to rest against hers, his breath warm, the smoldering scent from his skin like embers and cardamom, like new life bursting through the forest floor.

"He's made the same observations we have, and doesn't wish to wait any longer before... thinning things out."

The garden had become overgrown in an unhealthy way, no longer thriving. They'd known for centuries what needed to be done for the survival of the whole, but a careful approach would be imperative for humanity to succeed. The earth already seemed to be gearing up on its own.

"And was a method discussed? Timing? When you-" Lil inhaled abruptly as the realization came to her. "He was in the arctic. Amka saw him when they found the mammoth carcass thawed..." It had been Michael, all of it. The arctic, the man Claire said her friend reported present in the lab, and in the caves... No amount of lichen tea could reign in what he intended. The *cleanse* needed to be large in scale, of epic proportion, but also required a delicate touch. It concerned her greatly that Michael was too reckless.

Lu slid his arm under Lil's back, pressing his palm flat, supporting her as he sat upright again. She adjusted until seated in his lap, her head drifting down on his shoulder.

"He's not limited his efforts to the north," Lu said.

"Pestilence," she whispered.

He and the six had likely set off the volcanic activity as well. Lil hadn't seen the effects of what he'd started in Asia, but Cambridge Bay had been leveled as a result of the illness unleashed there. If Michael was the cause, the pathogen wouldn't stay buried.

Disease was natural, but what Michael had initiated was not, and the process should have been discussed as a whole. Reluctantly, she gave him a fragment of credit for attempting contact, though he had started before she'd even woke, and then again so soon after her transition. Why the urgency?

After thousands of years, Michael could give her the weeks she needed to sort things out with Malcom, and this time he wouldn't use her family as leverage. Uri would be at Nan's, and at least one of the others with Magnus's until the meeting.

Lil couldn't help but let her mind wander to a negative place… to a place where insidious thoughts fester. Once Michael got the idea he was on the right path, putting word to action and fulfilling what was to be done… he hadn't been known for flexibility. What would be the fate of the mortal family from her current life? What would her own fate look like if things went poorly? Lil needed human life to succeed that she could continue having vessels to be born through…

Breath moved in and out of her, but she needed conscious effort to remain steady. She shifted her focus to Lu's body pressing against her, his hands, the slow waves of his scent moving into and around her, the almost undetectable sound of water in the pool.

"If he cannot be reasoned with… if he takes them all… How will I be reborn?"

There was a subtle sense of something impending, a sound, barely audible, but like water being drawn into the formation of a giant wave. Az moved his eyes to hers.

"When this star grows tired, we will have moved on, and you will be with us."

# 7.

"Denim?" Remi asked, not with distaste, but with humor that only suggested it lightheartedly.

Lil sighed and rolled her eyes with a smile. "Apparently Lu made a closet run while I slept earlier. They're quite soft, more like leggings really. I just thought, since I didn't know what we were getting into, the durability might suit."

"Were the sandals put on with similar initiative?"

Her shirt was something between a tunic and a dress: silk, inky like deep, dull indigo bordered by green along the bottom hem and running up the center where the garment was fused and split. The low neckline left her stone visible. Lil's arms were fully exposed, as was most of her back, a braid of silk running down her spine. Her leather sandals had been threaded with decorative beading in gold and bone.

"Why don't we just get started."

Remi nodded, transitioning from fashion to his lesson plan. "You'll remember this from before. If you haven't already, the practice will bring things back."

Gesturing to a cluster of boulders, he said, "I'll just have you sit this time while I demonstrate."

Lil settled down on the rocks and began breathing with purpose, slow and steady. She felt good. The sun was low, light dramatic, the lake was coy, flirting with the darkness that never quite left her. The wind was present, but respectful.

"Close your eyes. Feel the change, then let yourself remain for a bit. Let the sensation sink in. We'll move forward when you're ready."

Like sunshine suddenly breaking through shadow and flooding her skin, Lil felt something akin to warmth; the raising of hairs over her body, but on the inside as well. The initiation of the portal was a blossoming of sorts, the space before her opening with a potential that the fabric of her recognized. The familiar hum was there, distant, calling to her, but she remained. She sat still, allowing the vibrations to wash over her, a reminder.

The trick was in producing that initial burst, like the manifestation of her wings. It was the spark between feeling something below the surface and releasing it out of one's self.

She opened her eyes to find Remi where he'd been, looking at her with a contented smile. The shimmering wall of space beside him faded, and the thrum of energy with it.

"I'll try, then you?" She confirmed, with a bit of asking.

Remi nodded, and Lil began recreating the sensation within herself, but there was a connection missing. "I can feel the change in energy," she sighed, "but it's the pushing it outward…"

"Here, take my hand."

Lil ceased her efforts and placed her palm over his, fingers wrapping around. She closed her eyes.

"Open," he said. "See the change as you feel it this time."

She watched the hum as she felt it, feeling Remi's intention, the response of the fabric before them building as the portal bloomed.

"Shall we?"

Her hand remained in his as they walked through, the roar of ocean waves engulfing them and receding.

Everything was shades of green as she emerged; grass rolling upward into hills that could perhaps be called mountains by some. The air was pleasantly cool, the sun was warm against her at just past midday. The surrounding rocky ruins had been partially overgrown with moss, as was the stone cottage that stood strong before her, well maintained.

"I rebuilt it long ago… though it's much smaller than it once was."

"I know."

"You remember where we are?"

Lil nodded. He'd brought her there many times in the past, and she'd come on her own many times before that. "You lived here with Thyra and the boys… and little Frejya."

"*Little*," he huffed with a smile, catching Lil's eye. "She took after her auntie, that one… beautiful, clever, and formidable." He began to walk toward the house then, not turning back as he said, "Come on, it's still well-stocked."

She remembered that too.

He placed two mugs on the table, filled a kettle with water he collected from the air.

The cup in front of her was simple stoneware, speckled in grey. The body of it had ripples as if a spiral worked its way from base to rim, an impression at the handle that her thumb just slid and settled into. Remi's cup was ceramic as well, appearing as stone with creeping greens at the base like the moss and lichen growth on the rocks of the small home they sat in. She thought about what the vessel would have looked like as it was formed, pictured her hands at work.

She glanced up to the plank that served as a wooden shelf as water pouring from the kettle, the sound pleasant, laced with the aroma of something once rooted in the earth, drifting into the air, into her. She absently pulled her cup so the steam warmed her chin, cheeks, and hands, all while her focus remained on that shelf. A collection of drinking vessels had been lined up there, some ceramic, some wooden, all familiar.

"I made those," she whispered, testing the water, testing her words for truth.

Remi pulled deep from his drink and nodded. "We each hold on to pieces of you in our own way…"

They couldn't forget as she did, but had to endure their awareness of her absence. Guilt seeped in, for what the others had to bear while she was free to live unburdened.

"Your suffering would not have eased mine," he said, not needing to read her thoughts to know the path they took. There was much she had let go of; they all did, in their existence. The emotions she felt were a normal part of transition, and Remi's words a necessary reassurance.

Lil drank and nodded, pressing her memories for the lifetime behind each vessel on his shelf.

"I've been working with clay," she began. "I could create another, if you'd like, so you'll have one from this time." The idea that there would be a time after was an uneasy truth.

"I'd prefer one that you made when we were a longing and a mystery, from before you remembered."

"I have a few at the ocean house, one is sure to be the right fit."

"It already is, whichever one you choose."

Silent understanding passed between them until Lil's cup was almost empty, and Remi spoke once more.

"Are you ready to try again?"

"Yes," she sighed. "But... I felt the change in myself when the portal first manifested, and thought I needed to push out, but then when I watched the second time... Is it more of a reaction in space to what is happening within? I'm struggling not to feel foolish. I've done this so many times..." She thought of her wings, of being tossed around by the wind while struggling like a baby unable to wield their own hands.

"Many times... And we could chat about it at length, but its *feeling* that will get you opening doors. Don't worry about trial and error, I'm not going to let you unravel the universe or transport us into a magma chamber."

Tea, an hourglass of a different kind, didn't tell the time passed in minutes, but in stories. When the pot was empty, Remi returned their cups to the wooden shelf, prompting Lil to follow him outside.

She closed the wooden door behind her as he exited the stone cottage, once again awestruck by the natural beauty of her surroundings. It could have been minutes or moments that she stood by the cottage, witness to the billowing clouds combing sunlight into dramatic strands raking across the emerald landscape.

"It never gets old, does it," he breathed.

"No, nor should it."

Breaths passed; degrees of stillness.

"When you're ready," he began. "Eyes open or closed, focus on taking us home to the mountain."

Both compass and map, Lil focused on her destination until she literally resonated with it. More than just the idea of the place, but the intent to *be* there vibrated throughout her, calling on the fabric of her surroundings to respond. And it did.

The air before her took on a familiar liquid appearance, and Remi's hand slid into hers. Maintaining a hold on the connection to what she created, Lil turned to him and caught his smile, his validation.

"Well done," he said, gesturing with his eyes to the portal, then back to her. "Shall we?"

The act of stepping forward, of passing through, another milestone.

She was transitioning more than just in location, but by recognizing what she had done, what she'd accomplished, conquered; what was behind her, and what she was moving towards.

The sky was dark but for the stars suspended within it, their reflections in the still water below. The night air was crisp and cold, but it always was at the mountain. Lil expected to feel stones beneath her feet, but it was the playful wind that greeted her first, invigorated at her sudden presence through the portal she'd conjured, that Remi had led them through.

She was falling.

Remi looked upward toward her in assessment as he continued down, but her mind was elsewhere, not in a place of fear, but of sweet memories.

*I'm plummeting toward the stars, thinking of you.*

She felt her wings like phantom limbs, tingling under the force of the rushing wind until air passed over feathers, and she was flying.

Both Remi's brows and lips moved upward in surprise and satisfaction. He turned, his own wings shooting out before his body hit the water, sending ripples over the lake as he passed it by. A sound like crashing waves followed as Lil's toes skimmed the surface, though it was not from the contact she made. It was the sound of another arrival.

Lil touched down gracefully at the shore and continued past Remi to where Lu had broken through. Low celestial light refracted through the steam lifting off his body, vapor wisping upward as it condensed, leaving him silhouetted in a glow that was both ethereal and menacing.

"You're wet," she whispered, almost unaware of the steps she'd taken toward him.

He stood still, stalking her with his eyes as she approached until all restraint snapped and he moved like lightning, hands finding their place around her before the sound of his thunder caught up.

*It was raining in Iceland, heavily*, he said in her mind as his mouth met hers with welcome ferocity.

Their contact heightened the excitement she'd developed from the fall, but also relaxed her, wings dissolving. Lil felt her muscles liquefy like warm syrup flowing from her neck down her body, sparking with flecks of energy throughout. Lu's warmth and his scent surrounded her like fire and earth, a rainstorm and the morning after.

His hands rapidly disregarded her clothing's attempt to lie against her skin.

Remi's annoyance betrayed his calm voice only slightly as he said from somewhere behind, "Flight lessons appear to have gone better than advertised. You produced wings without hesitation, though it's difficult to ascertain whether or not their reintegration upon landing was unassisted... what with all the hands."

"He's clearly irritated," Lu said just loud enough to carry.

"You did interrupt our lesson," Remi countered coolly.

"The lesson is over," Lu growled.

"Az is waiting in the lake."

Lil's head whipped toward Remi, her nose scrunched in question, but the answer was not yet to come.

"And your concern is that Az will become impatient?" Lu quipped flatly. "He's content to sit a few moments more."

"Moments…" Remi huffed under his breath as he walked toward a freshly forming portal. "I'll be in Iceland, working out logistics alone, apparently." Magnus would be off for a few more hours attending the climate summit, and Lu was supposed to be at the house with Remi so the two could work together while she and Az did who knows what in the lake.

The tension between Rem and Lu was justifiable, but would soon dissipate. The two understood one another's perspectives too well. Both felt concern, a primal instinct to protect her, longing, and love. Remi knew that she and Lu needed to make contact, Lu knew that she needed to acclimate, to train, and that their togetherness could, at times, become distracting… Lil had watched the dynamic play out over lifetimes. No animosity would be retained.

"The lake?" She asked.

"Yes," Lu said. "Az arrived a little earlier to ready himself. You're to sit with him and find stillness. Unfortunately, I need to return to Iceland before Remi broods too long. I may need to steal his pencils again to convince him of his worth."

Lil smiled against his face, letting a little laughter bubble up as he lowered his lips to her neck.

"I couldn't stay there, not when you sent that image of the stars below. I felt you falling in my heart… so beautiful."

And then it was as it had been in the beginning; darkness and breath.

*At its most poetic, the spoken word has not range enough...* she said. "But I wouldn't give it up entirely."

*Mmm*, he agreed. *I do very much delight in your sounds.*

His arms were around her, as hers were around him; fingers in hair, palms against skin. Lil felt so filled, that tears formed in her eyes, just enough to stretch the light in her vision, to blur the surrounding glow before collecting into a drop, and streaking down her cheek.

"I'd like to watch you walk into the water before I go," he whispered.

Lil filled her lungs with as much of him as she could breathe in before stepping back, his fingers reluctantly releasing her as she took another step. Lil slipped out of her sandals and padded over to a small boulder, leaning against it as she peeled off the denim leggings, slowly. Lu's short growl halted her fingers as they gripped silk. She released the fabric, letting it fall back into place around her hips as she raised an eyebrow at the source of the sound.

His restraint was limited, and so was hers.

She turned, feet molding around uneven stone as she approached the lake and eased in. There was tranquility to her movement, ripples barely sounding as her body vanished beneath the waterline. The silk draped around her torso spread across the surface, exposing back still veiled by her hair.

*Beautiful,* he whispered as her head went under, before thunder sounded and Lil was left to the relative silence of the deep.

She found Az seated in a state of meditation among the shadow shrouded stones of the lake floor, as if he were one of them. He made no move to welcome her, no shift of his body, his hair too short to catch the current she stirred in her descent. She felt him, though, as sure as she felt the water around her, a liquid marble nestled deep within the universe.

Without needing direction, Lil settled across from him, her hair drifting, billowing out. The details in the darkness became sharp with focus, until she allowed them to blend together.

Her eyes closed.

She eased into that pause between breaths that had become a sacred place. Time passed, and she began to hear the distant rumbling of a troubled sky, felt echoes of turbulence in the water. Her eyes opened in question, heart speeding up a bit, but Az kept his eyes closed, his position relaxed. Glancing upward, Lil saw that the moon's light had intensified, the shadow of a large object passing overhead along the surface. She closed her eyes again, and the screams started.

Her eyes flew open and, as if no water came between her and the boat, Lil heard the cries of its passengers. Gunfire. A boat capsized in the distance, bodies slowly raining down, the shadow flickering above, moonlight erased as lightning lit the edges of the vessel passing over her. Lil pushed off from where she sat, frantic as she hovered, searching, then another body began to sink. Dark brown skin, delicate limbs, and tightly coiled hair stretched out. Lil's most recent birth mother, Nora, fell through the water, lifeless beside her. Though she was still in the lake, Lil tasted salt as her lips parted in panic, as her mother slipped through her fingers, her father following close behind.

# A Story in Song

A storm raged above, but it was the strong and sudden pulse from below her that called Lil's attention from the chaos inside her, the replaying of her parents' death. Az sat still where he'd been, eyes closed, heart open, solid, calling her to find the anchor within herself.

Lil descended, heart still pounding. She settled in across from Az once more, unable to use her breath as a means of focus. Instead, she felt the water around her, the pulsing fluid within. She closed her eyes to the bodies falling like stones, no longer just her parents, but other loved ones lost over her lifetimes, too many to count, and deserving of so much more than a number.

The water became an extension of herself, as her wings were when she flew; something that wasn't a part of her until she called upon it, something dormant. She opened her eyes, aware that harrowing memories plummeted in her periphery.

She kept her gaze steady on Az. He nodded, and she closed her eyes again, letting her mind become still and clear, and then her surroundings.

A vague awareness of time and the requirement for oxygen drifted into her consciousness. Lil felt no urgency, only understanding of the forthcoming need, though she was content where she sat.

With an unwavering sense of calm, Lil maintained her pose, legs crossed and hands resting as the water began to move as one, rising upward.

The lake lifted around her, maintaining its shape as it rose out of the rocky basin where Lil continued to sit, mind and body still. When the waterline slipped over her top lip, she tilted her chin down and took a breath. The air was chilled and damp, like cave air but without the brooding. As the barrier crept upward, her hair continued with it until the top of her head was free. She rolled her neck, calling the flowing strands downward until they fell wet against her body.

Lil opened her eyes.

Az looked at her then, his lips forming the softest smile. He was very much the mountain, grounding and solid and strong, but he also helped her to find the mountain within herself, the place that remained when everything else fell away.

*Will you be swimming or walking out,* Lu purred.

The voice sent a sudden plume of heat through her. She paused a moment, drawing out the sensation of knowing what she'd see before finally turning her head, heart racing.

His eyes were ablaze, the low sound vibrating from him surrounding her as it echoed between the water and rocks where she stood.

His clothes were dry this time; black pants and jacket, white shirt unbuttoned at the top. Perhaps it had stopped raining in Iceland, or he had changed before his return. Another possibility was that he'd been watching her long enough for any retained moisture to have steamed away. The idea sent a tingle through her, a ripple through the liquid she held aloft.

Lil brought her attention back to Az, still sitting content under the translucent roof. The water that had been nearly opaque with shadow began undulating with sparkling threads that told of dawn's arrival. Had she really been down there that long?

"Thank you," she whispered, watching as he inhaled her words like food for his soul. He brought a hand to his heart where it rested for a beat, another, then he closed his eyes again.

Lil walked slowly between water and stone, toward eyes that glowed with more than the sunrise. Lu made no movement other than, perhaps, the muscles flexing in his hand, his jaw, his feet digging in a little. He stood there watching as he had when she'd walked away hours before, witnessing as she returned, savoring, anticipating.

She broke eye contact to turn, to see what she'd done.

Slivers of sunlight managed to break between the peaks in the mountain, shimmering through drips and crests along the liquid edges of the lake as it hovered. Az remained in the center, water slowly covering him again as she eased it back down.

Lil imagined she could sink into the manipulation of water as a meditative act of short-term creation. She enjoyed working with clay, not just for the resulting stoneware, but for the transcending calm that came with pressing deep, feeling the shape change.

"You're wet," he said. His words were low, spoken a hair's breadth from her ear, the heat from his body calling her to lean back.

Lil found herself suddenly exploding into the bedroom entryway, a flurry of curtains and Lu's arms around her. The speed of the transition was such that she was left unsure if they'd flown or moved via portal, the momentum that followed rendering her uninterested in pursuing the mystery further.

*

It was the scent that greeted her first as she drifted into consciousness, before the sound of ocean waves and crackling fire had registered. Stronger than flame and salt, were the earth and spice and embers that had merged with whatever Lu loved to inhale from her skin. They came together, creating a scent that lingered in the air, and would certainly walk with them for some time.

Lil's eyes were still closed as his lips pressed against hers, soft, his tongue teasing the seem of her mouth until she smiled, opened.

*I only vaguely remember our arrival here,* she whispered.

*You said you wanted to wake to the ocean.*

So, he'd brought her to the ocean house.

"I never used to sleep this much," she sighed, opening her eyes to the depths of his. "Nan joked that I survived on tea and saltwater."

"You've been exerting yourself extensively," he said, mouth tilting up at the corners before he dipped his head, smoothing his lips over her neck.

"Yes, and you've explained your philosophy on assisting me in achieving a *deep sleep*," she chortled.

"Indeed," he said, inspecting her hands like treasure found. "How was your time with Remi and Az?" While she and Lu had spent some hours together awake before they arrived at her home by the water, they'd not yet discussed her training experience.

"Remi and I had tea in the cottage."

"Mmm. Where he keeps your cups. He'll need another one."

Lil nodded. She wanted to say there was no rush, that they had time, but one never knew when her life would be taken again.

# A Story in Song

Her fingers, having found their way to rest at the curve of his neck, laced through his hair. The small movement doing wonders to soothe both of them. "It took some time but I managed a portal, fell from the sky."

"Yes, that I recall," he said, eyes fluttering as she slowly twisted and released a lock of his hair, rested one of her legs over his. "Stars above and below…"

Relative silence stretched while the fire burned and the ocean sighed, both breathing in and out.

Lu didn't ask again, didn't push, but he wanted to know, and she needed to share, however tempting avoidance may have been. "Things with Az were difficult," she said. He'd have felt her distress during her time in the lake, though with the knowledge that she was safe and her torment was part of a valuable lesson.

"What did he show you?"

"The death of my birth parents from below: the storm, the boats… their bodies."

The stone at the end of her necklace slid to the side, resting on the bed. Lu's palm took its place on her chest, the weight and warmth of him reassuring as she spoke.

"I should have been ready… Their bodies fell from the surface. I scrambled to catch them, and they kept falling." Her vision quivered as unshed tears filled her eyes, though the images that replayed in her mind were clear. She'd told Magnus it was a load she didn't carry through time, but when their bodies fell… "It was more than my parents. It was all of them, everyone who perished for having known me. I've trained my whole life, all my lives, to stay calm, to maintain control…"

"Had it been me beneath the lake, and a thousand of you raining down, the water would have boiled before rising."

Her breath hitched, then a breath released like a burden become weightless and given wings. She was not alone in her vulnerability; there was no weakness or shame in it.

"You're not stone in motion," he said gently. "Though our ability to see beyond the fleeting may cause us to appear thusly. You've lived as both an eternal and a mortal. You've seeded worlds, and served tea. Rem, Uri, Az, and I, we'll never be the same after the depth we've experienced here, with you."

Lil could see the flame flickering beyond the darkness in his eyes as he spoke, as his hand pulsed hot energy.

"Stay calm, maintain control, maintain an awareness of your surroundings and potential collateral damage…" he went on. "We know all these things, but we still feel. Please don't forget, we're not training you to be *emotionless*, Ilati. It's practice in feeling all those things while maintaining the ability to act rationally in the moment, so that those you love, those that *I* love, stay safe. And when the threat is over, that you may unleash the torrent of your tears and grow another ocean," he smiled with tenderness, placing a palm to her damp cheek. "And with all that challenged you, it was not Az that lifted the lake," he whispered with stillness and ferocity. "Your silent triumph sang to me as you walked beneath the water. I savored every step you took."

Lil hadn't strutted out, she'd sauntered. It wasn't with the arrogance of one who's ego is fed by conquering that she'd emerged, it was with serenity.

The light from their skin radiated with soft, brilliant light, blue against the warm tones cast by the fire beside the bed.

"I was at peace," she said, curling her lips into a smile. "Though I'm not now because I haven't eaten since before tea with Rem, and I'm *starved*." Lil leaned fully over him, kissing his mouth as he laughed. She noticed a bit of black fabric peeking out from beneath a pillow and reached for it, finding what had once been Lu's black t-shirt, before she'd torn at the neck and relieved him of it at the mountain.

"It was amongst the blankets in our room, and somehow in your somnolent clutches as we departed," he explained.

She sat up, straddling him as she slid the shirt over her head, the excess of it pooling at her thighs. Tugging at the stretched-out collar, Lil inhaled from the fabric. "Smells like you," she smiled, echoing the sentiment he'd once offered while wearing her apron.

His thumb ran up the insides of her legs until his hands spanned her hips beneath the shirt. Fire flaring in the hearth and in his eyes, light pulsing between them.

"If I don't get up now…" she began.

Lu closed his eyes, eased his grip, and nodded slowly.


Lil put the kettle on, watching Lu as he scooped granola from a glass canister into two bowls. His black sweatpants hung low on his hips, the rest of him a display of uncovered skin over deeply ridged muscle.

"These dried blueberries are delicious," he said, spooning a generous amount into his bowl. "How many scoops for you?"

"At least as much as you put into yours," she said, scootching him out of the way so she could access the drawer he'd been blocking. "And sliced almonds."

Lu nodded, briefly placing a hand on her hip as she dug out two stainless steel tea infusers from the drawer. "I'm going to do lavender and chamomile. Do you want something different? The pantry is extensive…" she smiled, remembering how he'd made tea for her before she'd known who he was.

"I'm aware," he smirked as she continued assembling the dried flowers. "Fennel. Just a pinch."

"Mmm," she hummed, adding the ingredients to the infusers, the sound of her voice joining with the breath of the ocean, the soft glow from her body aiding the moon and fire in lighting the open room. She felt warm contentment in being close, in preparing food together. They created a sense of home, no matter their location, but it was not lost on her that they were inside the walls of a place where she'd dreamed of him, where Mira's apple blossom hung beside the pantry door.

Lil reached up on her toes for their mugs, her focus wandering back to Lu's waistline, then to his face as he turned toward her, his eyes cast down to where the hem of her shirt, his shirt, grazed the top of her thighs.

"Mmm," Lu purred, satisfied with whatever he was imagining, then turned back to open the fridge as Lil took down the mugs.

"You have no fruit," he said, sauntering over to the back door and unlocking it, container of almond milk in his hand. "Best if used within fourteen days," he read from the carton. "When did you open it?"

"Are you concerned I'll get a tummy ache?"

"I'm concerned it will taste foul…" He said, unscrewing the cap, and smelling the contents. "It's fine," he proclaimed pouring it over her granola, then his. "Where did your fruit go?"

"Claire came by with Gunnar and cleaned out most of the produce," she shrugged. "I didn't know when we'd be back. I'm surprised you weren't on top of that."

"I was preoccupied."

"Mmm. Whatever were you doing while I slept this time? During my first sleep at the mountain, you managed to hold a meeting and compose a scavenger hunt while I rested."

"Remi did help with the game."

She raised her brows, still smiling but trying hard for at least a little seriousness.

He came in close, leaning his forehead against hers. "Your room upstairs has a door to the ocean," he began. "I remember a moment when curtains billowed against the breeze from a different balcony. You'd been painted in gold, and I'd wanted nothing more than for luster to coat my tongue, until I heard their heartbeats…"

A touch of frost spread through Lil like snow in her veins, overtaken by warmth in an instant, but with something unsettling left behind.

"I watched your chest rise and fall," he said. "And also, I snooped around your room," he added, running a hand up the back of her thigh and squeezing lightly.

Before she could say a word, there was a knock on the glass door. Without waiting for a response, Uri entered, holding two brown paper bags.

"Midnight snack?" He grinned, holding out one of the bags to Lil as he approached. "Heard you killed it with that portal earlier."

"I have no idea what time it is, or how long I slept," she said, pulling a pastry from the bag and inhaling. "A cinnamon rose," she sighed before sinking her teeth in, closing her eyes.

"There's chocolate and plain croissants in there as well," Uri said, putting his arms around her for a quick spin. "It's about midnight here," he added, both of them walking back to the counter where Uri slid the other bag across to Lu. "That's from Todd."

Lu unfolded the top and peered in. "He works fast."

Lil gave him a look, raising her eyebrows, wanting to know what was in there.

Lu raised his brows back at her, curling the bag back in on itself, then slid her granola toward her, took a bite of his own.

Uri patted his lap for Lil to put her legs up. "Claire is doing yoga in the morning, so hopefully the woman will sleep late and I can get some work done," he said, massaging her feet. "What are you guys getting into tonight? Wanna go for a swim? Cause a raucous?"

Lil took a silent inventory of her body and the rest of her self. She'd recharged some, but...

*How do you feel?* Lu asked, pushing a mug of tea toward her as he sipped from his own.

*Tired.*

*You haven't slept nearly long enough, Ilati. You'll better face tomorrow's challenges if well rested.*

"I need to get a little more sleep, Uri," she sighed, handing him her bowl and drinking from her cup. He took a bite of the granola as she tore off a piece of pastry.

"This is excellent with the blueberries," Uri said, then pointing up to the mugs on the shelf, he asked," Has Remi been over yet?"

Lil shook her head and smiled, "No, just you two."

His eyes widened. Easing her legs off his lap and onto the ground, Uri stood, walking toward the living room with the remains of her granola in hand. He looked over her art supplies, ran a finger over dried paint, then halfway around the edge of a ceramic bowl of saltwater, black sediment deep beneath the surface.

As much as she needed time at the mountain, time to reacquaint herself with who she was, the others needed to find a connection to where she'd been in her absence, the bits of her they'd missed.

"Lu was the only one who came, in that place between dreams and awake," Uri said, carefully placing the empty bowl of granola down on the table, freeing his hands. "He's the only one who'd been here, before you knew." He gazed at the curiosities on her shelf with reverence, seeming almost overwhelmed by all there was to take in.

"Come any time, with or without me, Uri, it's ok," she said gently.

Lu came up behind where she sat at the counter, and Lil eased back into him as one of his arms came around her.

"I'm working with Lil in the morning, but we could delay our start tomorrow and spare a few hours after sunrise," Lu began with a smile. "Perhaps I can distract Nan for you,"

Uri nodded.

"And let's take that swim soon. Remi or Az can camp out over at Nan's, we'll have Claire and Gunnar over, Todd can go surfing. You should see that kid out on the water."

Uri's face lit with promise as he picked up his bowl and walked it to the sink. "That sounds like a good time," he said, rinsing the dish and placing it in the drying rack. "You two head upstairs. I'll get out of your hair."

Lu shook his head. "We're going back to the mountain; I need to drop something off for Remi."

Lil sighed, her hand stroking his arm. "I'd love to sleep in the garden again."

"Sleep," Uri chuckled under his breath as he grabbed a croissant and headed back the way he came. "Just give me a head start, I need to pick some oranges."

# 8.

"And do you know where we are now?" Remi asked.

They'd just been at the school again with Remi and Marissa from the greenhouse after another session with Az. Lil had grown more lichen, tons, not in the greenhouse, but around the grounds. She still needed to connect physically by making contact between her hands and the stones or trees the organism grew on on, but she was able to start it where there'd been none, as she'd done with the cloudberries.

Standing beside Remi in a large, grassy clearing, Lil surveyed the ring of distant evergreen trees as a cool wind whipped through their hair. She observed the landscape, accepting the inevitable forward-movement of memories as the portal faded behind her.

"It's changed," she breathed, recalling the land as it had been during her last visit: felled trees encircling her, a forest knocked down, bodies among the trunks and the boughs. New grass had grown where the trees thought the land no longer suitable, and who could blame them after what she'd done.

"I haven't been here since… since before," she said, her heart picking up pace.

It had been called the Tunguska Event, named for a nearby river. She'd been ambushed by so many, and simply exploded with energy.

"You've not returned since the trees went down, I suspect. I've visited a few times… no match for nostalgia, it seems," Remi said with a sigh, partly to himself as he battled memories of his own. "I didn't bring us here solely to reminisce, though. You've done well managing portals so far, and I want to add an increased level of emotional disturbance, as you will likely encounter some discomfort should you transport in need of escape."

He'd done this type of training before, but not in Siberia… and it had been far worse than what Az had done.

"I was hoping for a gradual increase," he said. "When we rush things, they don't go well and subsequently take more time than if we'd gone slowly to begin with, but you did well under the lake, from what I understand. Go ahead, center yourself and get started."

Lil took another moment, a deep breath in and out. She could travel anywhere, as long as she could get the portal started, of course, which she could. She'd done previously.

"I want you to begin by growing pumpkins, white ones," he said, to her surprise. "And I want your eyes open. You'll continue working until I signal for you to initiate the portal."

"White pumpkins, *specifically*?" She asked, raising her eyebrows.

He raised his brows right back at her, silently.

It could have been any plant, but naming something specific took away the pressure of choosing, though there was the added challenge of having a target. Lil crouched down, pressing her hands to the soil, and closed her eyes.

She opened them again when Remi cleared his throat...

A picture formed in her mind as she developed her intent, then pushed energy into the earth. She thought of curling vines covering the ground around her, until sprouts burst forth, leaves unfurled, and green fruit swelled. As long vines curled and stretched over grass, Lil noticed other changes taking place around her. Fog rose up, taking the shape of trees standing strong, and of figures moving toward her from every direction, morphing into what had been. She knew it wasn't real, or rather, that it was only real in the sense that water vapor was being used to haunt her... She *knew* this, but the effect was sill jarring.

"Go ahead and attempt the portal," Remi said from behind her. "Take us anywhere you'd like, but be mindful of the usual. We don't want an audience..."

His voice sounded somewhat abrasive. Was he being a little more gruff than necessary? Lil pulled her hands from the dirt and started to rise from where she'd been kneeling

"Quickly."

A puff of air pushed at Lil's back as she stood, causing her to take an unanticipated step forward as she tried to maintain balance. She was startled and caught off guard, but before Lil could deliver an annoyed glance, the bodies in the mist changed form.

Todd stood not five yards in front of her beside a tree that had once been. He waved, then a shadow came upon him, and his head twisted, body slumped down.

*"Quickly."*

Another jolt of air hit her back, and though her heart raced, Lil's footing remained steady as she felt for a location to project, some instructions that the air before her might know what to manifest. But the air was mist, and shadow, and memory, and with each breath she felt more stifled by it.

The false trees crowding around her were as they had been during her last visit, just before she'd knocked them all down, and everyone with them. Perhaps if she released another explosion, one of destruction, she'd clear the air that seemed to be keeping her from steadying her breaths. Did she need it, though? In her mortal state, Lil required respiration, but not often. Her lungs had provided no rhythm while she'd been in the lake with Az.

Mountains didn't breathe.

Nan's body hovered above Todd's, the mist beside her shifting into Claire releasing a silent scream. The space between Lil and the horrific scene began to ripple like rain falling on water, shimmering as Lil's heart slowed, and the vibration of her body changed. Lil kept her eyes open, finding the place in herself that remained as lifetimes passed, as civilizations rose and fell, as stars were born. The mist would move around her, as would the memories, as would life, and she would let them hold her back. She had work to do.

The portal began to form, and-

Lil's arms flew out as her feet were swept out from under her, Remi sending another blast of air into her chest, forcing her to the ground. With a firm grip on the soil, Lil sent the earth undulating toward him, and he rode that wave with perfect balance.

Magnus came through the trees then, approving smile on his face as he reached outward and shook hands with Remi. Rem clapped him on the shoulder, then reached for his own belt, pulling it out swiftly like one might draw a sword. Like a whip, the leather wrapped around Magnus's neck.

Lil screamed as the old man's fingers clawed at the strap, then Remi's foot came up, delivering a forceful kick to Magnus's chest. He went down, belt coiled around his neck, Lil clutching the soil at her fingertips, a guttural growl forming somewhere inside her.

Vines thick as her arms shot out from the ground, mercilessly encircling Remi's legs. Lil felt nearly bottomless with potential as she fed her energy into the earth, vines growing longer and thicker as they worked their way up his body.

Body still humming with intention, Lil stood and faced the portal as the vibrations built up within her. She felt, as well as saw, the space before her reacting, answering her, paying no mind to the fog figures advancing through the trees that once were. Lil took a step forward, then turned around.

"Well done," Remi smiled.

\*

A light breeze carried the dunes' surface across the sky, a trail of sand stirred upward as an airborne tribute to the setting sun. Orange and gold blazed like fire, as though the dunes themselves were star born, which, of course, they were.

"It's called the Skeleton Coast now, I believe," Remi whispered. "She's beautiful as ever."

Lil nodded, surveying the dramatic landscape where desert literally met the sea. The ocean showed her strength in the expanse of shoreline, providing a relentless reminder that she was both breathtaking and remorseless.

"The portal will close with distance of intention. The same effort used in construction is not necessary for its departure," he said, returning to his instruction though still marveling at the way the sand sloped down toward the water.

Lil remembered the local people calling it, *The Land God Made in Anger.*

"Do you still come here?" she asked.

"It has been a while. Sometimes there are tourists driving four by fours along the dunes…" He paused a moment, then said, "You did well with keeping a level head, maintaining the portal during the attack. Your reaction was quick, but felt intentional. The vines were effective, but I'd still like you to work on connecting without making contact, as you do with animals, yes?

Lil nodded. She didn't need to be touching an animal to connect with it.

Remi looked distant for a moment. She followed the path of his eyes, but it was only open sky they drifted toward as his focus detached. And then, just as abruptly, his eyes were like glacial water meeting hers.

"Field trip."

Lil gave her brows an exaggerated raise, her expression questioning as she gestured with her hand to their surroundings. Were they not already on a field trip?

*Enjoying the dunes?* The welcome voice vibrated through her body as if Lu had been standing close enough to wrap her arms around...

*The sun is setting brilliantly over the sand, painting my skin gold...*

His rumbling response heated her more than the disappearing star could.

*But the sun's light doesn't reach everywhere,* she added.

*It would if you had less on.*

*Should I remove something?*

*No,* he growled. She saw Remi startle and wondered for a moment if Lu's outburst wasn't contained to her mind...

*I think Remi heard that,* she smiled.

*It was intentional. So, are you interested in running an errand? Magnus has asked for help with a situation similar to that of the artic scenario you assisted with, though there's no need for planes and such now.*

*Is it the same pathogen?*

It had been brutal, killing all those who'd become infected within just a couple days of exposure. The one positive thing Lil could find was that the illness disabled people so rapidly; there wasn't much time for it to spread to others.

125

*Indeed, it looks that way, but your eyes on site could be useful.*

*Another mammoth?*

*Research station. Arctic, but on the Asian side. Not one of Magnus's. There are a lot of details coming out presently. It appears the military may have been called in. There's some urgency about clearing the site.*

Lil's involvement before had been prior to waking, to knowing who she was, but since then… There were ethics about altering the course of things, though there was the *Michael* factor… If this was something he'd intentionally unleashed, she found herself objecting less to the idea of correcting the course, at least until she better understood what he was thinking.

*You're not alone in your concern, but with things moving so quickly, and likely under Michael's influence, I think we should intervene.*

*As do I.*

*Remi has the location. I'll meet you there.*

\*

The rushing sound changed rather than faded at their arrival. What was a receding wave had been overcome with a rhythmic, grinding sound, like the mechanical heart of a hummingbird, but devastatingly loud.

A helicopter, rotors spinning, was perched on the ground in front of a blue and red compound, colors bright against the snow. The chopper stood out as well in red and grey, but there was something else… The windshield was cracked, with blood and presumably brain matter on the inside of the glass. Bodies were slumped in both the pilot and copilot's seats.

As Lil scanned her surroundings, the ferocity of the engulfing sound dampened, the spinning blades slowing to a stop.

Lil's eyes landed next on a woman in the snow, not dressed for the weather. She wore pants, boots, thick sweater and a hat, but no coat. Lil observed the tracks from the nearest facility door, the blood trail from the helicopter to where the woman had apparently collapsed, gun resting loosely in her right hand. The woman released a groan so soft, if Lil had been human, she doubted she would've heard it.

Remi positioned himself slightly in front of Lil upon approaching, as if to absorb any potential threat.

"Selfish cowards," the woman managed with pained breath.

"You stopped them," Remi said in soothing tones, crouching beside her. "And the unknowing world thanks you for your bravery and sacrifice."

Lil assessed the woman's body while Remi spoke, paying close attention to her energy, her life force, to the fluid already lost. Her injuries were not survivable, though illness would have taken her otherwise. The woman's skin had a purple tone over half her neck, eyes sunken, corners of her mouth dark. Her hands looked bruised, skin peeling. It was a wonder she'd been able to grip the gun long enough to have been effective. Persistence was a remarkable quality.

"There were two... helicopters," she rasped.

Lil looked around, as did Remi, confirming what they already knew. Just the one remained.

"The cowards called for evacuation. Two helos came. When no one exited the building, three men entered. Two of them made it out, flew away. The other one, he's inside there," her eyes swiveled to the nearby helicopter. "Two of the infected forced their way on. I joined them... managed to stop this bird, but the other, it flew."

None of the infected had been on the helicopter that left, but its two passengers had been exposed.

The woman's eyes rolled back. She was spent.

Remi pressed a palm to her chest, and hummed a song both distant and familiar. He eased the separation between body and what passed through, then guided what remained back down into the snow.

Lu paced towards them out of a fading ripple in the air, not stopping his stride as he evaluated the surrounding story. Lil had sensed him just prior to hearing the sound of thunder crack, her body and soul aware of his impending nearness.

"I felt the woman's valor, and the ease in her suffering," he whispered, placing a hand on Remi's shoulder. "Let's see if we can honor her effort by cleaning up this mess." He gave Remi a pat on the back before his eyes met Lil's.

"Do you feel any life inside?" She asked.

"No survivors; this woman was the last. Magnus has asked us to get samples to Martine and Saul to see if it's the same strain they're working with, and if the tea is still an adequate prophylactic. Rem," Lu turned, though a hand, perhaps absently, slid up her back, fingers grasping at her hairline. "Where are we with cultivating this lichen at the school?"

"Coming along nicely; gardening is in their blood."

128

# A Story in Song

It was a small fortune. There was only so much they could do, and Lil had no qualms about the students being among those spared.

"How did Magnus know about this incident?" she asked. He'd had known people at Cambridge Bay, then again, he knew people everywhere.

"Malcom."

Her eyes went wide, but Lu shook his head. "The facility isn't one of his, but he was called in for assistance. Malcom was apparently unaware of the details behind what occurred in the arctic on the North American side, but is being looped in presently. Magnus was still on the call when I departed."

Lil and Lu ventured into the facility, making short work of collecting what was needed, though the inside was far less tidy than her experience at Cambridge Bay. Leaking bodies were strewn about, slumped where they had fallen within what had become a tomb.

"Remi will burn it all down, ash to feed the soil," Lu whispered, comforting her with the idea that the remains they'd come upon wouldn't be left to waste in the rubble. The earth would not have to wait long before reclaiming what was left behind. She always took what was hers, eventually.

When they emerged into the white of the arctic snow, Lil saw that Remi had wasted no time in getting started. Steaming black patches of ground remained where the helicopter and body had been.

Lil thought of the garden she'd sprouted from the corpse in the lab those weeks prior, of the animal carcass she'd incinerated after meditating to the sound of Gunnar's breath. That had been before she'd known the story behind the stone around her neck, behind the smell that lingered in the barn.

"I'll get the buildings when you leave to make the drop-off, meet you in Iceland after."

There was a silent moment between them before Lu nodded, then he stood there beside her, as if waiting, a spark of something knowing in his eyes.

"You're waiting for something... What?" She asked, lip curled up with curiosity as she glanced to Remi and back.

Lu's look melted her where she stood, a look of lifetimes, a look of love and mischief.

"I'm waiting for you to open the portal."

\*

Lil continued over moist ground, through the darkness toward Magnus's Iceland house after a brief and uneventful drop off with Saul and Martine. Cool air misted over her, not quite rain, but making its presence known, as did the ocean in the distance.

Lu's arm began to tighten around her waist, his body an anchor. With her back pressed against his chest, his teeth grazed her neck until his lips came to her ear, her eyes relaxing.

"I couldn't possibly let you into the house like this," he whispered, her legs nearly liquid as his knee slid between them.

*What alterations would you make?* She asked, replaying his words in her mind. "Wait… *let* me into the house?" She clarified, as if she needed permission, to be allowed, as if he could stop her… He *could*, and the challenge would be immensely entertaining for both parties involved. They did enjoy a game of chase, though sparring was near impossible. With the close contact, it never lasted long. "This dress is perfectly acceptable, save for the clawing you're presently subjecting it to."

"Shall I stop?"

A pause, and his grip began to loosen, her skin uncomfortable in his absence as he pulled away, though his lips remained at her ear.

"Shall I stop?"

"No."

His body molded to hers once again, his scent coming around to envelop the rest of her.

"Your remarkable form is covered in enough of that pathogen to make for an unpleasant experience for our dear friend Magnus."

Understanding washed over her. *Of course.* She'd donned protective clothing during her last encounter, but this time she and Lu had just waltzed in with no such barrier. It felt wrong being so close to the house...

"We need to shower," she said briskly. "We need soap, hot water, friction…"

"No, Ilati, *you* need to shower," he laughed, deep and breathy. "I require no such thing."

A feral smile came over him as she turned in is arms, and a pleasant warmth ran through her. He took a few steps back and, to both her surprise and delight, burst into flames.

His figure became barely discernable in the blaze, but his eyes, the look he gave her through the inferno, delivered more heat than the fire itself.

As the light quieted and his form took shape, she saw that the flames had taken his clothes, Lu standing before her in steaming glory, not a stitch left.

He stepped forward, verdant eyes taking hold of hers.

"If you touch me, you'll just be contaminated again," she said, both serious and smiling, fighting instinct as she retreated a step.

"I find that unacceptable. Water it is then. I'll assist with the friction."

His gaze held as his hands rested warm against the outside of her thighs, fingers catching the hem of her dress, sliding it upward.

*I'm having Uri call Magnus. He'll leave robes in the mud room, though we could easily pop back home and grab something...*

"I like the robes."


Lil and Lu found a hot tea kettle waiting in the kitchen, Remi beside Magnus near the fireplace, smoldering embers and casual flames bringing back memories of what had burned outside. They'd swam in the ocean for what felt like an hour, until Lu had relented to their time-sensitive responsibilities and acquired soap from somewhere, then there was the hot spring.

It was when her eyes began to stay closed more than open that Lu reluctantly admitted they should return, not wanting to bring her to the house the way he had the first time, exhausted and incoherent.

Lu rummaged for fruit and pastries while Lil leaned against the counter, pleasantly tired, content to drift between what had just been and what was, Lu's fingers drifting up her neck and into her hair.

*You could take a nap after you've eaten. Or we can bring this plate upstairs.*

Lil smiled and shook her head, a yawn escaping. She needed a solid nap, but could put it off a little bit longer. *No, it's no hardship.*

Lu sighed and delivered a kiss soft enough to both wake her up and usher in her dreams. Balancing two scalding mugs and a plate of food in one hand, he placed the other at the small of her back as they entered the sitting room.


"Lily, dear," Magnus beamed, opening his arms and pulling her in. He smelled like Earl Grey and the kitchen. "Your presence lifts a weight I somehow carry in your absence."

Lil pulled back, seeing a brightness in his face that seemed ever present, in the lines branching out on either side of his eyes, framing the light within.

"I missed you too, old man."

She glanced at Remi on the couch as she pulled away. He'd sat back down and was less than discrete in staring at Lu, who was less than interested in whatever silent reprimand was being delivered.

*His nipples are in a twist over our arrival time…*

*We were rather inconsiderate given the circumstances.*

"I spoke with David," Magnus began as Lil settled in. "It's a relief having him fully in the loop."

"I wouldn't say fully," Lil said.

"He's seen him with feathers," Magnus shot back with a nod toward Lu. "David relayed that Hamish continues to dream about you since your last visit. He mentioned you drinking tea, something about a dragon, and being in his arms."

Lil smiled knowingly as she nestled into the cushions on the floor, leaning her head back against the pillow Lu had positioned in his lap. One of his arms came to rest around her.

*Naughty boy enjoys watching us swim together, doesn't he,* Lu smiled, leaning down to nuzzle her neck.

"I think we're clear on the dragon imagery, Magnus…" Lil said. "We explained that to Hamish when we visited."

"I feel for what the child may have been subjected to during those particular visions," Remi added.

"Was there any more talk of Lil being taken…?" Lu asked.

"He mentioned a skirmish in the sky, a battle, but he couldn't say when things occurred, past or future."

"We've taken to the sky in battle more times than I'd care to count," Lu sighed.

*Remi still looks grumpy,* Lil said, peeking over her mug at his brooding.

"Please accept my apology for our tardiness, Magnus," Lu offered. "We didn't want to track anything in after having come in contact with the microorganisms we encountered. Decontamination is rather simple for Remi and I. Lil, however, must suffer through soap and water."

*I hardly suffered…*

"You've earned your time together," Magnus said, eyes sparkling with understanding. "And Lu, you've been here *constantly* over the last few days. The time apart must have been difficult on both of you, though, I understand that you, Lily dear, have been keeping busy."

He arched his brows toward her, fishing for details of her activities.

"I'd rather discuss Malcom and how he acquired a pathogen he shouldn't have known about," Lil said, leaning back and sliding her hand around Lu's leg, giving his calf a squeeze. "Baked goods make better party favors, Magnus."

*Careful, Ilati, or I'll have to take you back outside.*

"How it was acquired is still unknown, but it wasn't from my lab or Cambridge Bay. Malcom has quite a network, particularly plugged into the military, globally. He was contacted when a helivac was requested at the facility you visited earlier. Given the gravity of what was described to him, his awareness of your unique qualities, Lily dear, and those of your associates, Malcom phoned… and the rest is as you encountered it. As for the one that got away, well, we're still working out what happened with those on board the second helicopter. Malcom has put his people on it, discretely."

*He doesn't know about Michael?* Lil asked.

*Not his part in this, no.*

135

"We are fairly confident," Lil began, "that a former colleague is responsible for the spread... We think he's who Amka saw at the mammoth, and I'm sure you're aware of some things popping up in Southeast Asia..."

"Popping up..." he huffed. "There's talk of suspending air travel."

"The inevitable cannot be prevented if Michael is set in his path."

"*Michael?*" Magnus asked, brows rising, seeking to confirm the identity he suspected.

Lil nodded with a sigh. "He reached out, apparently, but I've yet to return the invitation for contact."

"And despite his poor choices," Lu growled, "he has somehow retained the wisdom not to come near her without permission."

"Do you know the nature of his sudden desire to communicate? I'm assuming it's sudden, based on the history recounted..."

"We think it something to do with what's already started, with what, if we're being honest, is needed... He and the others haven't reached out since the flood... *that I know of,*" she added, eyeing Remi, Lu's fingers never stopping on their path as they trickled over her neck, under the robe at her shoulder, over her clavicle and back. He passed Lil a scone with his free hand before the impending rumble in her abdomen had a chance to voice her need.

"I see..." Magnus breathed, and she believed him, believed he saw beyond the hurt and the bitterness, beyond the strength of her righteous indignation. He saw her fear also. "He's come to cleanse the earth again... Yes, I understand your apprehension, my dear. What assurances will he make now that the need is far greater than it was at the time of the flood?"

"He can make what assurances he likes, but *we* will ensure the safety of our mortal loved ones this time regardless," she said. "I have to meet with him, and soon. The boulder he's set in motion cannot be slowed, but we can perhaps alter the *course* of the stone. First, we must come to fully understand what his plan is, and for that we must meet, though my hesitancy is an ache..."

"You've lived long enough that you don't need my advice on continuing in fear..." Magnus said, though he still gave her the eyes of understanding.

*I need to see Claire, Nan, Gunnar, and Todd,* she said, acutely aware of their human lifespan, of the potential for their years to be cut shorter still for having been loved by her.

*Would you be amenable to working with Uri during the visit?*

*Of course,* Lil nodded, receiving a partially filled mug of tea, hot as it had been when she'd first poured it. *He must be chomping at the bit to get some training in.*

*I'd planned to meet with Magnus here in the morning before his flight to France. You'll train with Uri overnight at Nan's. The time will make no difference to him, and you'll be well rested.*

Claire, Todd, and Nan, though, they'd be sleeping. If she rallied and they left sooner, Lil could visit right away and train after... *then* nap. There were so many things she needed to talk with Claire about, and Gunnar. Lu could go with her, spend some time with Nan, get to know Claire a little more... He could surf with them when darkness fell, Todd would love that, Uri too.

*I think I could go a few more hours,* she said, inhaling her tea. It was the blend Nan had been preparing for Magnus over the years to assist with sleep... Lavender, chamomile...

*You might think you can go for hours, and perhaps you could...* he said thoughtfully. *But it would be selfish of me to keep you awake longer than necessary.* He sipped from his own cup behind her before adding, *It won't take much time to get you to sleep...*

Lil paused the cup where it was angled at her lips, too aware of the crackling fire, of the mist outside that had turned to rain. Warmth spread out from her center, from the path the tea took, and from his words. She noticed Remi suddenly sit up straighter before flashing a subtle smirk, a roll of his eyes, then diverting Magnus's attention by engaging him in conversation about the school.

*It's a restorative sleep that you need. Your ocean house might be nice...* Lu continued, *what with the waves.*

*...a deep sleep,* she whispered, her mind flooding with a montage of nearly every time she'd drifted off since waking to who she was.

*Indeed.*

# 9.

"You need to chop it very fine," Uri said, his instructions floating out from the kitchen to the front of Nan's shop, mixing with the low chatter from folks sitting at tables, the sounds of weight shifting in chairs, spoons stirring and set to rest. "Yes, perfect. Ok, throw it in."

Lil turned and smirked at Claire as they steeped their tea behind the counter, thankful Duncan and a couple of the other kids had been coming in to help out. Lu had brought Lil over sometime before sunrise on the island, the plan being to visit with their family of early risers before privately doing some training. Visiting had run long, though, Lil reveling in the slow morning while it lasted.

The two cousins walked through to the kitchen, each holding a mug, though Claire had the addition of a cribbage board in her other hand, eager to see what Uri and Todd were up to while Nan was outside. They found the two men with clever shirts obstructed by well-worn aprons. They stood at the counter with mixing bowls and spoons, measuring tools and ramakins, a chopping board, the flour and sugar bins...

"Rosemary," Claire sighed, then inhaled deep. "I can smell it from here. I *love* rosemary."

Uri turned and winked, his eyes lit and smile wide. "I know you do, Sunshine, and I'm not the only one who's noticed. Do you mind passing the coriander? I should've just taken the jar out, but I wasn't sure..."

Claire eyed the mixture. "Is this for scones? I'd better go ask Nan..."

"No, no, there's no reason to go bothering the woman; she'd make a fuss..."

"Nan doesn't really do savory scones."

"They're not *savory*. And it's hardly ground-breaking to use something other than vanilla in a sweet dough. Look, I'm not starting a revolution, it's just a small batch of six. I'd get the spice myself but I have flour on my hands." And Nan had scolded that habit out of him; she really didn't like a dusty spice rack. "Lil? The coriander?"

Lil's cheeks were practically sore from smiling after only a few minutes of watching the two men work. She set her tea down, retrieved the spice and handed it over.

"Do you mind putting a teaspoon in this ramakin? Thanks."

"What's with the board," Todd asked. "You guys gonna set up in here, play while we bake?"

"Cribbage ladies left their board at their table when they cleared out," Claire said. "They would have come back in eventually, but Duncan was nervous they may have forgotten."

"You know where to find them," Todd smiled, shaking his head.

"We sure do…" Claire practically giggled.

"Those women are shameless," Uri said. "I can feel the heat from their eyes on me while I'm working around the shop," he grinned. "I love it."

"Living their truth is what they're doing," Todd added. "So, the wet ingredients?"

"Yeah, once the dry ones are all whisked together. Just measure out the cream and pour it right on top." Then, back to Lil, Uri said, "So aren't you supposed to be training? You've been hanging around the shop all morning. Whose turn is it?"

"I'm working with Lu…"

Uri raised his eyebrows and Lil smiled, knowing she and Lu were hours late getting started. They'd just been so content to visit, lending a hand here and there. It felt good.

"When these come out of the oven, I'm gonna eat one on my way outside," Uri said. "And I want to find you two working when I get out there. *Working*," he repeated with eyes suggesting he was well aware of their potential for distracting each other. "If you're not making progress, we're sparring. I don't care if it's daylight; we can just go to the orchard. It's on."

Claire snorted, and Todd lit up, saying, "I wanna be there, camped out with popcorn when you guys train."

"You may observe when we get started, but there's no telling where we'll end up. Don't overmix. Just pour it out as it is and shape it into a disc about this big," Uri said, gesturing with his hands.

Lil held the door for Claire, then walked out beside her, a playful breeze gently competing with the autumn sun on her skin. Birdsong welcomed her, soft voices, and a loud *crack* that rang out across the garden every three to five seconds.

"We could spread a blanket right here and bask in the sun," Lil said.

"Mmm," Claire replied, sipping her drink. "You have work to do, though. I'm not complaining or anything, but we haven't talked yet," she smiled, tilting her chin down, both their cheeks getting a little pink. "And I haven't seen your wings!"

They had a *lot* to discuss… About Lu, Gunnar, about so many things. And not in short bursts over the phone, or in the busy kitchen at the shop. They needed some proper time on the couch. She'd had a chance to connect with Nan earlier, and felt the lifting a weight she hadn't known she carried. It meant that much, the little things, the love between them. They'd folded two loads of laundry and talked about nearly everything, though the details Lil spared Nan, she'd probably give to Claire…

"We'll make time," Lil said. "I'm working with Lu now, then Remi. He and I are supposed to go work with that lichen at Magnus and Gunnar's old school. While you're attempting to nail down what's useful about the lichen so it might be isolated, they're just trying to grow more so they can produce their own tea. So, probably not today, but maybe tonight, or tomorrow night."

The cousins came to a natural pause in their steps as three women came into view, sitting together on a shaded bench. Nan and the cribbage ladies sipped from their mugs, engaging in quiet conversation that seemed secondary to what they all had their eyes on.

Lu's t-shirt hung from the back pocket of his jeans, swaying as his body twisted. His muscles worked with effortless rhythm, swinging that axe through the air and sending split logs to the ground as he chopped wood. The sweat sparkling over his skin was a clear indication that he knew he was being ogled. Lu had no physical need to perspire, but it amused him to put on a show.

"And you didn't hear anything?" Audrey whispered.

"Well, there was the storm," Nan said.

"Right. Took some time for power to come back. We were thankful to have the generator," Audrey hushed back.

"It's a full two stories above the other trees," Joan cut in.

Nan drank from her cup. "Stranger things have happened, I'm sure."

Lil saw Claire smirk beside her.

"And those seedlings did mature rather quickly when you planted them," Audrey said, voice drifting as she continued watching Lu chop wood, her focus not likely on the axe. "And he hasn't aged a day."

Lil looking over the rim of her mug, attention drifting to the orchard, to the tree that had grown some twenty feet in height above all the others. Her eyes darted back to Lu, who had stopped chopping to stare at the apple trees as well. Slowly he turned toward her with a knowing, satisfied grin. Nan hadn't said anything to her about the anomaly, but Todd hadn't hesitated to comment at the first opportunity.

Lil approached the bench, Claire beside her, cheeks raised with a smile as Lil held out the cribbage board and passed it to Joan.

"Duncan was worried you'd forget it," she said.

"We might not need it if this keeps up," Audrey said, tilting her head toward Lu as Joan tucked the board into her bag.

Claire looked from the women to Lu, and back. "I didn't think he'd be your type of eye candy."

"Oh, please," Audrey laughed.

Joan took a deep breath, giving Claire her full, serious attention. "I rest my head beside Audrey's at night. She's in my heart, and I'm in hers, but, Sweetie, I am too old to limit where my mind wanders. Love is about supporting each other's dreams, and I'm content to sit beside Audrey, and join her in daydreaming about that man chopping wood over there. Oh, now look. He stopped."

"That's a shame," Audrey sighed.

"He's coming over though," Joan said. "Now Lil, it helps when they're easy on the eyes, but a good partner takes more than good looks. You're a strong woman, and I know you would never settle…"

"She never did before," Audrey cut in. "I've never seen a man come around here at her invitation. Claire, you brought that boy in that time, though, I only saw him the once."

"Mmm, the one who came in with his friend," Joan added. "We were happy for you, of course, but he seemed a little shifty. Much happier now seeing you keep company with the other one. He's attentive."

Both Audrey and Nan nodded in agreement.

"Joan is *very* attentive," Audrey added.

Claire blushed, and then there seemed to be a collective sigh from the bench as Lu put his shirt on, though the fit didn't hide much.

"I preferred it off, but I can't say I mind it on," Joan said under her breath as Lu drew closer. He wore a grey cotton t-shirt with the word *original* written across his chest. He'd been wearing long sleeve's when they'd left the mountain…

*I had it on underneath,* he smiled.

"Claire, Ladies," Lu said, with a tip of his head toward her cousin and the bench as he walked over, then his eyes landed on Lil with such strength, her surroundings nearly slipped away. His hand came around her mug, gliding it out from her hands and passing it to Claire. Then, his arms enveloped her, and his mouth against hers. The kiss was brief, but thorough, before his lips slid along her cheek and neck. The sweat on his skin cool for an instant, rapidly heating.

He pulled back enough for his forehead to rest on hers. "You taste like lavender and mint, and me."

"Have a drink," she said, transferring her mug from Claire to Lu's hands. "You'll need to replace all the water you lost…"

His lips curved slightly as he drank, his free hand on her back.

"Where's mine?" she asked, pulling at the hem of his new shirt.

Lu shook his head. "We're sharing this one," he said with a calm voice and steady stare.

Her heart fluttered, remembering the black shirt with the stretched collar.

"You've known Todd far longer than I have, and had plenty of opportunity."

145

"I've heard him ask you at least a dozen times," Nan offered.

"Me too," Claire chimed in.

Lu shrugged. *See?*

Lil rolled her eyes, shaking her head as she leaned into him a little.

"I can't wait for you to see Remi's…" He sighed.

*You know, you could have showed me both of them last night…*

*Yes, but the surprise.*

*Did Remi stop by the mountain while I was sleeping?*

*He did…*

"Come," Lu said, squeezing her hip as he drained the last of the tea. "We should get to work."

"Mmm," she agreed. "Uri threatened to take your timeslot if we're not making progress by the time he comes out from the kitchen… Said we had until the scones were done baking, I believe."

"Did he now…" Lu whispered, sensing the challenge. "Nan," he began. "Lil and I are taking a walk to the orchard and will likely be out for quite some time… Have Todd help Uri stack the wood and put the axe away. It will be a good excuse for you to get them out of your hair. Be sure to mention the axe if Uri gives you any trouble. He's particular about tools."

"You kids take your time, "Nan said, catching both their eyes to be sure the subtext that followed would be understood. "Just be mindful of the ditch… The

146

ground seems to have become disrupted over by that tree that's grown larger than the others…"

Lu wasn't caught off guard easily, but he did pause a moment before she heard him say, *We did leave that behind, didn't we…*

*It was pretty deep.*

*Well, I was motivated.*

"We can take a look while we're out there," Lil offered, cheeks pink with memory. "It might be something Lu and I can manage to fill in."

Lil glanced at Claire as her voice trailed off, her cousin's eyes wide as she likely put the pieces together. Of course, she'd known *something* had happened out there but Lil hadn't discussed the particulars with her.

"I appreciate it…" Nan said. "I don't want anyone twisting an ankle or breaking an arm should they fall in while harvesting apples out there."

"Don't overwork yourselves," Joan added. "Ask that one from the kitchen for help. We can send him through after he's done stacking wood."

*Should I grab shovels? For pretense? Lu asked.*

*No, Joan and Audrey won't be here when we get back, and it's not like they'd go out to inspect our work right away if they were. We just need to be quiet.*

*Challenge accepted.*

"We'll be back in a bit," Lil said, leaning down to give Nan a hug from behind bench. "You headed back in?" She asked Claire.

Her cousin nodded. "I'll give Duncan a hand out front after I try whatever Uri and Todd are making."

"I don't even want to know," Nan started. "I'm giving myself an hour away from their shenanigans, and that includes hearing about it… And if he moves my spices around…"

"Save me one," Lil chuckled, Nan's words trailing off as the distance grew between them.

"It's bigger than I remember, though, at the time, I hadn't cared in the slightest," Lu said from where he stood in the fissure. The uneven dirt walls came up to about his shoulder on one side, and well above his head the deepest point, roots brushing against him. "So, how will you fill it in?"

Lil took a breath, realizing her lesson had started. "I've moved ground before, but it would be too disruptive here, loud, and the trees would shift. It's like, a wide, sweeping undulation," she said, moving her hands to describe what she meant.

"When you say, *I've moved ground before*, you mean from this life, yes?"

She nodded, understanding he sought to prompt with his question. She hadn't been thinking of what she'd been capable throughout her existence, only since her most recent birth. "I've moved earth grain by grain, wove ribbons of soil like water, shifted mountains."

Lu placed a hand on the ground before him, hopping up and out, effortlessly.

"Feel it," he said, fingers reaching up at the base of her neck, into her hair as their mouths met in a kiss, parted.

"You're doing a poor job of trying not to distract me," she teased, taking a step back. Then, brushing an imaginary speck of dirt from his shirt and pretending to check for stains, she said, "Perhaps you'd better stay out of the ditch. I want to avoid washing this if I'm going to be wearing it later."

"It's cruelty to tempt me when I need to remove my hands," he said, eyes both burning and dark as he leaned against the nearest tree… the tall one.

Lil turned back to the rift in the earth, settling into her surroundings. The forest beyond, Nan's garden, the life therein, the surrounding fruit trees and the radiating warmth behind her; they became a song that hushed in the background as she focused on her connection to the earth, the stones, the soil.

In what seemed like only moments, granules of dirt shifted down from the side of the fissure where she stood, the side that rose higher than the other. Soil sifted gently down, and she found it felt somewhat similar to working with water.

*It should be moist,* she thought.

Lu's hand was warm on her back as he came to stand beside her, pulling water from the air to rain down over the fissure as Lil worked. It wasn't a torrent, but a fine mist, just enough to dampen the soil, to cling to the roots that had been left open to the air.

*The roots…* she thought, reaching to connect with the trees.

*It may help to connect with your body at first,* he said.

His hand slid up her back to rest behind her neck as she crouched down, placing a knee to the grass. She wove her fingers through the fresh, green blades, then pressed into the soil. She felt the trees and their roots, not as extensions of her body, but as something else, wholly of its own.

Lil released a sigh, finding relief in the connection, Lu's hands, and the cool mist just floating along her skin.

Working with inanimates, like minerals and water, required transferring an intention to shift, to pull, be elsewhere. But when working with life… With life, there existed an element of wanting to *be* more, of reaching, of growing, transforming, combined with a sense of permission, recognition.

Lil fed energy through the soil, pulsing with the mycelium. Tree roots lengthened, reaching across the remaining divide, knitting together, strengthening the closure as soil trickled in. The act was slightly draining, but not enough to feel empty. It felt good, something she'd enjoy relaxing after. Lil experienced a brief surge as she thought about the tea she'd had the night before…

*Open your eyes, Ilati.*

Lil hadn't realized she'd closed them.

Opening her eyes as she stood, Lil saw her work finished. Though the fissure no longer remained, the ground was somewhat uneven, with just a slight slope that, to any other, would appear natural. No grass grew from the freshly sifted dirt, but patches of small flowers sprouted, chamomile, fennel, and lavender in full bloom.

"Was it your intention to grow the herbs?" Lu asked, his voice a soft rumble.

"No," she whispered. "I was thinking of the tea from last night."

He nodded. "Do you still want to keep this shirt clean?"

In the time it took Lil to assess what dirt remained on her fingers, Lu had stripped the shirt over his head and scooped her up against him.

"Magnificent," he murmured.

Lil felt the mist follow, cool against her skin, as he walked them over to their tree, the big one, and leaned her back against the trunk.

"It's like birdsong in the darkness of morning, just before dawn," she whispered. Her arms around him, hands leaving streaks of mud over his shoulders. She brought her fingers to his cheek, then back around to his neck. "I know they'll sing, but before they start, it's almost like a hitch in breath, something hanging. I get that sensation before I do what I do, before I connect," she said, nodding toward the once-was ditch. "And then..." Her eyes moistened, and she sighed.

"They sing," he finished, his forehead coming to rest against hers briefly before bringing his lips to hers, softly, slamming a hand against the tree above her head, channeling the struggle of his restraint.

*The branches... impact,* she said. The tree was tall enough for the shaking leaves to have been visible from a distance...

He growled at the inconvenient accuracy of what she'd said, and turned them around until his back was against the bark, Lil leaning against his chest, and his groan morphed into a shared laugh.

"I do think Joan an Audrey would have enjoyed speculating," she said. "They're probably back inside, or gone home. Though Claire says they've been spending quite a bit of time here lately."

"No mystery as to why," he quipped, taking a few steps from the tree, lowering to a crouch to lay Lil down in a patch of grass at the perimeter of where the chamomile and fennel had spread. Lu reclined beside her, one leg between hers, leaning over her face with his.

She reached up, playing with the tendrils of his hair hanging forward. "First thing you grew," she asked.

"Apple trees, here," his low voice rumbled as a whisper. "You?"

"Same. With a seed from one of your apples, apparently. I was little, and wanted a tree over by the barn, so I pressed that seed in the soil with all my intention... Nan and I had a talk afterwards about drawing unwanted attention... it wasn't the first or last time we had that talk. I experimented at the Orn a bit."

"Did you try without seeds?"

Lil shook her head, her focus drifting to the leaves above them, the sky, then back to his eyes. "Not until up at the research station the other day, with a corpse I'd found in a lab, and that was an accident."

Lu's lips brushed against her forehead, then down her cheek as he nuzzled her hairline, then stilled, his grip tightening around her, low growl tapering off from deep in his chest.

"This is hardly an efficient use of training time," Remi said from somewhere outside Lil's field of vision. She twisted to see him approaching in tweed pants and a vest, his blonde hair down around his shoulders. "And I don't want to hear excuses about what you've been *growing*..." he added.

Lil released a huff of laughter. Remi seemed annoyed, but he wasn't really. She could see it on his face, even before the corners of his mouth turned up a little. The two of them were supposed to work together, though it didn't feel like she and Lu had been out there that long.

"No really, we worked," she laughed, pushing off the ground to stand beside Lu, leaning against him as he brushed off her back. Pointing over to where the ditch had been, she continued. "If you'd seen it earlier... We'd... Well, there'd been a cleft here, and I used the roots of the trees to assist in knitting it back together," she said, beaming at her accomplishment.

"A cleft?" Remi puzzled.

"When Lil learned who she is, we flew here for some privacy, and had an impassioned exchange," Lu stated with a glance up at the taller of the apple trees where his t-shirt still hung on a low branch. "There was some collateral damage."

Remi followed Lu's eyes up the tree, then over to the long slope in the ground where no grass grew, but patches of herbs blossomed.

"You cracked open the earth, didn't you..."

"Yes," Lu chuckled.

"Well, it wouldn't be the first time," Remi said, turning to Lil. "You filled it in?"

"Moved the dirt, worked with the tree roots, then unintentionally grew lavender, chamomile, and fennel," she said, waving a hand at the herbs.

"Excellent," he said, pondering something.

"Who is with Magnus?" Lu asked. "We can't all be here, Rem."

"You and Az are with Magnus, Uri is getting under Nan's skin, and I will be with Lil for a few hours, working on growth."

Lu narrowed his eyes. "You're not wearing your shirt, Rem."

Lil took a moment to reexamine Remi's attire. He clearly had on a white button-up under his vest, though she'd been expecting to see a t-shirt.

"I thought you left it in his room?" she said to Lu.

"I did."

"I have a shirt on," Remi said flatly.

"Yes, I can see that," Lu said. "But it's not the one Todd had made for you. He went through such trouble, Rem. The gesture…"

"*You* had him make the blasted thing," Remi huffed, almost letting Lu get a rise out of him. "I'm headed over to the school. I have a meeting with David, and-"

"If you're going to the school, I have the perfect thing." Lu reached into his back pocket, pulling out a rolled-up grey t-shirt. He unfurled the garment, holding it up in front of his own chest. There were no words on the shirt, just the detailed sketch of a greenhouse done in fine white lines.

"I left that in my room…"

"Yes, that's where I found it. And before you ask, all your pens and pencils are exactly where they belong."

"You're both fair game now that she's back," he said to Lu, wagging a finger between them as Lu casually rolled the t-shit back up. "Open season on the both of you."

A bubble of giddy anticipation began to grow within Lil. It had been several lifetimes since she'd last been subjected to her family's antics, and what a joy it was. Az had shifted the mountain once, just a hair, but it was enough to be disorienting, and had them all privately questioning if something was a little *off.* It wasn't until Remi mentioned it to Lil that Uri and Lu spoke up, and Az began to laugh. What a wonderful sound that had been.

Lu handed Remi the rolled-up greenhouse t-shirt as Lil pulled his *original* t-shirt down from the tree branch where he'd left it. She brought it to her nose, Lu's arm snaking around her, removing the garment from her hands.

"I'll be careful with it," he said, sliding the shirt back down over his chest. Lil placed her hand over his heart, over the stone that rested there. She tilted her head up as his came down for a soft, lingering kiss. "You two have fun," he said as the portal formed behind him. "Have Remi tell you what he did after the pen hiding caper. It was brilliant."

She heard Remi chuckle under his breath as Lu disappeared. She turned, looking at him expectantly.

"I carved the exterior of the mountain such that the entrance to your room appeared to be the anus of a colossal humanoid pulling their glutes apart."

Lil's eyes went wide as Remi smirked through the rest. "It took me a day to render it; a piece that large not needing extensive detail work. It took the four of us nearly three days to reshape back to a *natural* state."

"Worth it."

"Oh, totally," he said, opening a portal before them.

"We're headed to the school?" she asked.

He nodded.

"Mind taking a detour?"

He raised his eyebrows and fanned his hand out toward the portal, letting her take over.

Lil connected to the disruption in space until the vibrations resonated with her intention, her destination. And then they walked through.

# 10.

"This one," Remi said, holding the mug in both hands. He smoothed his fingers over the grey surface, pausing to press his thumb where hers had left a print in white glaze, feeling the tiny line and circle she'd etched there.

"Had you seen the Burney Relief before making this?"

Lil rolled her eyes at the mention of the Mesopotamian plaque. "Don't get me started," she said. "And no, I hadn't. I did, however, see the knocker every time I came in through the front door..."

Remi tilted his head with expected curiosity, set the mug down on the counter beside his t-shirt, and approached the entryway. The sunlight on his face was nothing compared to his smile when he opened the front door.

"Where did Magnus find this?" He asked, then sighed. "That man is full of surprises."

Remi closed the door and returned to the kitchen He ran a hand over Lil's hair, then rested it on her shoulder as he surveyed the space around them. "I could spend all afternoon here, and then some."

"We can," she brightened. "Why don't we?" Lil's mind swirled pleasantly with things they could do. She'd watch Remi putter around, answer questions as they came up, relax in the sunroom, paint, swim *then* paint...

Remi shook his head. "I have an engagement at the school I'd rather not miss. Their time here is so short," he sighed. "I'd planned to arrive a little early with you and get some work done at the cottage..."

"Let's stick with your plan, but, like I told Uri earlier, the house is here. You can come anytime, with or without me. Todd will end up living here eventually, I'm sure."

"Perhaps," Remi said ominously. "But changes are coming, and we know how unforgiving the ocean can be."

Lil's eyes followed his toward the wall of glass overlooking stones and water under a blue sky. Whether by erosion or tempest, the structure around them and the trinkets it housed would be washed away, would become sand, cosmic dust.

Lil stepped out into a darkness beside Remi, the small clearing surrounded by birch, and evergreens. A little stone cottage stood before them, metal roof and a deck off one side, fire pit with signs of recent use.

"I don't think I've been here," she said. But she knew where she was, at the house kept for him, or whoever held the title of *Recruiter.*

"No, you wouldn't have. You've stayed separated from the school since it was relocated here, until Magnus..." He approached the fire pit and had a sizeable flame built in no time. Lil sat down on one of the log benches, hands extended, feeling the fire's warmth.

"Do you stay here much?" She asked, glancing at several long sticks with charred tips leaning against another bench.

"I didn't at first, but I've been spending more time here the past few years," he said, then holding up the mug and shirt, he added, "I'm going to put these inside. I have some marshmallows if you'd like?"

"You roast marshmallows alone out here?"

"No…" he said, smiling softly.

"Two for me if you can spare it," she grinned. "I don't want you running out."

Taking the porch steps, Remi said, "She," then paused, tapping the railing. "Even if I were to run out of marshmallows here, the school has a supply in the pantry. The students will likely be having a fire themselves after dinner." Then he continued on into the cottage.

Lil pulled the crisp, brown shell of her marshmallow off of the soft, gooey interior still on the stick. Remi had just eaten his first, putting another above the flames as he spoke.

"I've seen your work at Nan's, and I don't mean the paintings… The anomaly in the orchard tree line, the flowers growing over what was once a fissure, apparently. You grew an apple tree from seed as a child, escapades at the Orn and, more recently, in the arctic. Have your abilities with growth been somewhat incidental thus far?"

Lil nodded, scraping her teeth along her thumb where a bit of marshmallow remained. "I have enhanced life recently, trying to practice. I grew dandelions from roots already there, enhanced some plants in my greenhouse. With the *incidental* occurrences, there's an effortlessness about it. I'm not really *trying*, but the intention is there, or a strong enough emotional outburst," she said, thinking back to the orchard. "When I put pressure on myself is when there's difficulty."

Remi lifted his stick, assessing for doneness. "There's something akin to muscle memory that you need to tap into, same as flying, the portals. You know all of this, of course, but for reassurance, it's worth being said."

Lil nodded, loading another marshmallow onto her stick. "Lu and I had gone over my history and were working when you arrived..."

"You should have started earlier. Uri told me Lu had been putting on a display of chopping wood most of the morning..." He couldn't hide the smile creeping up his face, nor could Lil. Pulling the toasted marshmallow from his stick, Remi examined the delicate char around the rim.

"I'm still putting my hands in the soil, or making contact of some kind to connect, when I intend to bring life to something. I tried with the roots in the orchard, but I wasn't able to connect my energy to theirs until I pressed my fingers into the dirt. I know... muscle memory," she sighed, inspecting her underdone marshmallow, then returning it to hover near the edge of a smoldering log. "It will come back, it always does... You'd think I'd have more patience, given what we are."

"But you're not as we once were, are you? One could argue that you've become something more. Living as we do," he paused, glancing toward the path to the school, then back to the fire, twisting the end of his stick into the flames so the last marshmallow's residue charred, rendering the tip no longer sticky. "Even I find myself effected by the limitations of the human timeline."

Lil thought of Thyra, of the few before her, of Estienne, of Remi's and Uri's children, and those Az had fathered, because there was a time once when he'd allowed it of himself. She thought of their descendants, the students just a short distance away. Her mortality had changed them all, bringing them closer to their creations than they'd ever had been.

Michael wouldn't have known the outcome of what he'd asked of her in the garden, only that it was what he'd been called to do.

"Practice," Remi said, interrupting her thoughts. "Practice small growth, but also reach out and feel your connection to life around you as often as you can, with or without interfering with it. Build strength in that skill."

Lil nodded, nibbling the last of the marshmallow from her fingers as the remains on the end of stick burned clean. She relaxed her eyes, focusing her vision on nothing in particular while she reached out to her surroundings. The air was crisp at her back where the heat from the fire didn't reach, the smell of fir trees and smoke prominent, other scents weaving through, the song of the forest in her lungs. She felt for the trees; they were there, but she couldn't get to them, couldn't make contact with her energy. She'd keep trying, but first…

Lil smiled to herself, a thought coming to her. Remi lifted a brow.

"I want to try something," she said, resting her stick on the bench and leaning a hand down to the dirt. She'd done it in the lab, and in the orchard… countless times before she'd been born.

Lil slid her fingertips into the soil and closed her eyes, acknowledging her connection to the trees she'd sought before making contact with the earth, but her focus wasn't on them any longer. She thought about the little glass jar of preserves Gunnar had taken from the kitchen when they'd visited the school.

Warmth spread through her, emotion and as a sensation running down her arms, blossoming beneath the soil, rearranging elements and infusing them with the spark of life. A smile began to spread across her face, knowing, and then she opened her eyes, watching as sprouts burst through the needles and moss. Little leaves formed, low to the ground, unfolding. Buds blossomed into tiny white flowers, four petals each stretching wide, reflecting the warm glow of the fire, hinting at what they would become. Lil felt something swelling within herself as the petals fell, their ripening remains brightening from red to orange and gold.

"Cloudberries," she grinned. "I thought about what I'd done the other times, and tried to recreate that. Remember when I would start by thinking of what I wanted to grow as if it were hatching from an egg?"

"I remember," Remi smiled, eyes sparkling with fulfillment as he sampled the fruit. "A rare treat to enjoy wild this time of year. We'll have to collect some to bring with us."


Lil vaguely remembered the hallway they walked down from her previous visit. She'd been rather overwhelmed while transitioning from the archives to the kitchen, then again upon meeting Remi, fleeing the tearoom…

Remi turned and paused in a doorway, small paper bag in one hand, extending his arm for Lil to join him. She pressed slightly to his side, his free hand coming to rest gently on her back as they looked into what she assumed was David's office.

Shelves lined the walls to her left and right, filled with books and the sort of priceless oddities she'd become accustomed to seeing in Magnus's home. The space felt old, but remarkably uncluttered with the exception of his desk, which had an *end of the day* look about it. A rather large stone carving of a lynx slept on the lefthand side, partially encircled by several piles of documents, each with a different manner of paperweight: a wooden pear, rock the size of her fist that she could have found digging out behind Nan's house, the shell of a moon snail, a nearly finished bowl of soup. The lynx statue, though, the style was too familiar to go unnoticed.

David sat there at his desk, engrossed in what he was typing, campfire blazing on the other side of the window behind him.

"David," Remi greeted.

"Remmond," he smiled. "And Lil, how unexpected, but welcome, of course."

"Nice to see you again, David," Lil said with a friendly wave, moving into the room with Remi, though neither of them sat down as David stood.

*How's plants class?*

Warmth spread with Lu's quiet words inside her.

"Lil and I have become familiar since her visit," Remi began. "And I think some of her unique skills would be useful here. I've asked her to help with the lichen project, and in getting our in-house tea production up and running."

*I grew cloudberries without a seed to start, but I still needed my hands in the dirt. We just got to David's office. How are Magnus and Az?*

"Yes, you two met here as I recall, or was it at a bar a few days prior," David smiled. "What a small world it is… Here you are, together again, and without Magnus?" A crease formed between his brows as he glanced from Remi, to Lil, then back. "I just thought, you and…"

*Magnus and Az are carrying on just fine in my absence.*

*Your absence?*

*Yes, something else came up and I was unable to remain in Iceland.*

As David searched for words, Lil came to the rapid realization that he thought she and Remi were *together...*

"Oh, we're not romantically involved," she blurted with more urgency than was perhaps necessary, her body humming with energy. Footsteps echoed from somewhere as she continued, "I'm..."

"Recently married," Lu said, his hand leading his arm in wrapping around her waist. Heat flooded her body with joy, and surprise.

*I found the prospect of dropping by irresistible.*

*Remi didn't know.*

*No. He's livid.*

"David, this is my brother, Lu. He'll be assisting me with my responsibilities here. The workload has increased considerably given the developments you and I discussed yesterday."

*You smell like birchwood fire and...* He brought her hand up to his mouth, kissing her knuckles. *Marshmallows...* the tip of his tongue darted out, briefly making contact with the side of her index finger.

"Of course. I'll need to bring it to the board's attention, but I understand completely and trust your discretion." He paused a moment, looking over the three of them. "Small world, indeed," he smiled. "You'll be heading out to the greenhouse then, Remmond?"

Remi smiled back, as if some secret were shared between them. "Yes, I'll make introductions and get everyone up to speed, though, I recall these two wanting to retire early…"

"David," Lil said. "I was hoping to have a word with Hamish while we're here, if that's alright?"

David's eyes flicked cautiously between Remi and Lu.

"They both know about the dreams, but please trust that the knowledge has not spread. Magnus told me you spoke to Hamish a little more about them, and I thought if I met with him, maybe he and I could uncover some details, maybe take the edge off the more troublesome visions."

"I see… I hope you can appreciate that, while the students are here, I am very much a guardian to them, and I take that aspect of my job seriously. I cannot have Hamish feeling ambushed. His first vision involving you occurred upon your arrival. I have additional concerns that meeting with you again may trigger further complications."

"I absolutely wouldn't want that," she said. "Only if he's comfortable, and we're not interrupting anything… And your concerns contributing to his distress are understandable, however…"

*How can I set him at ease?* She asked. *I could tell him… a little?*

Lu looked to Remi, a silent exchange occurring.

"Some of the things Hamish has seen, where he was unable to pinpoint the *when* of things…" Lil began. "He was not wrong in his descriptions, and it must have been so confusing for him. My life has been…. Long." She glanced from David to Lu, then she and Lu looked to Remi.

"Changes are coming," Remi sighed, then began to unbutton his vest as he said, "David, -"

"This'll take all evening at the rate you're going," Lu interrupted, pulling his t-shirt off in one smooth motion.

David, to his credit, only raised his eyebrows slightly at the sight of Lu's chest, perhaps having been educated amongst and then later teaching such a gifted set of children left the man not easily caught dumbfounded by the unexpected. What came next, though…

*Things are about to get interesting,* Lu said.

*About to?*

Feathered wings burst from Lu's back, neatly tucked behind him as not to cramp the room. David's mouth opened, though to his credit, just slightly.

"I could have done that myself," Remi ground out, rebuttoning his vest. "There was no need."

"The sun would have risen before you'd disrobed, Rem, what with the jacket, and the vest, and the shirt, all the buttons with that bag in your hands… You'd have missed your greenhouse rendezvous."

"*My* buttons," Remi scoffed. "This is the first time you've gone without a collared shirt in days."

"Oh, I've gone without a shirt, and then some, isn't that right," he purred, winking at Lil. "And whatever do you have in that little bag of yours. Are those berries?"

"They're not for you," Remi said, holding the bag a little closer to himself.

"They're the ones I grew!" Lil beamed, squeezing Lu's arm with excitement, and perhaps also jumping just a tiny bit. "He has to try *one*, Remi."

Lu growled as Remi held out three berries and placed them in Lil's hand.

"The first life she grew without seed, Rem, and you thought to keep them for yourself," Lu said before placing a berry in his mouth.

Closing his eyes, Lu leaned into Lil's hand as her fingers threaded through his hair. He sighed a low sound, and then the room became quiet, all eyes on the man whose office they stood in.

"We're immortal, David," Remi said calmly, almost a whisper. "I'm still the same, though, just a bit older than you may have thought."

David nodded, a reflexive movement that perhaps, on some level, served to lead his thoughts in acceptance.

"Berry?" Remi offered, approaching the desk with the paper bag extended.

David continued nodding, the action slowing as he reached a hand out, and took a single berry. The repetitive movement of his head stopped altogether as he put the fruit in his mouth.

"I have a knack for growing things," Lil said, calm and sweet. "And while these two are immortal in the true sense, as I once was, I ran into a bit of a snag quite

167

some time ago, rendering me *somewhat* mortal. It's a matter of reincarnation. I've lived many, *many* lives, David, and Hamish is seeing them in his dreams."

"The students here, yourself included," Lu said, "are unique in that you are all descended from beings like us."

"I'm concerned by your silence," Remi said softly, rounding the desk.

David turned in his chair, facing his friend of many years as he stood, back turned toward the others as Remi's arm came around him in a gesture that felt *very* familiar. "I'm feeling a little ambushed myself," David said with a nervous smile.

*Should we give them some space?* Lil asked.

*No,* Lu shook his head slightly. *He wants us to stay.*

"Should I call Raul?" Remi whispered.

"No," David replied with a brief shake of his head. "He'll be preparing dinner. I'm okay, really, it's just, I've not had a man sprout wings in my office before. And I know there'll be more," he sighed. "I know there will be other things we need to discuss."

"I can come by after dinner?"

"Yes, thank you. We can relax and discuss whatever else needs to be said."

Lu stretched his wings slightly, then said, "I'm putting my shirt back on, if anyone wants to get another look... No touching, Rem." He turned his back to David's desk, looked over his shoulder, then faced forward again as his wings vanished and the grey t-shirt slid back over his muscled form.

"Magnus knows," Lil offered, as David seemed to be settling a little more. "And a few family members back home."

"No one else...?" David asked Remi, with eyes that said more.

Remi shook his head. "I'll need to speak with her."

Lil squinted slightly, what else did she need to know?

"So, you see, David," Lu said. "The boy is quite connected. Some of our descendants have been known to have visions, predictive dreams, and those of our kind can initiate and become the focus of those phenomena. The things Hamish has seen have happened, or will likely come to pass, and it would be helpful for us, and for him, if we talk about it openly."

"He doesn't need to know everything," Lil added. "We don't want him to be more overwhelmed than he already is, but given his experience, he might be ready for more than we anticipate."

"He is a remarkable boy. They all are, all the children here," David sighed. "Hamish should be outside with some of the others, enjoying a fire," Rounding his desk with a hand on Remi's shoulder, he said, "I'll accompany you outside and approach the boy myself. If I sense any hesitation, you three can just continue on as planned with your evening. We can always try another time, especially with your visits becoming more frequent," he added.

*I asked Remi about Marshmallows,* Lu said, bringing her hand to his face, running her fingers over his mouth as they walked out into the night. *An offering could function as icebreaker with the boy.*

The light from behind them muted as the door closed, what illumination the windows provided proving no competition for the fire in cutting into the darkness. The greenhouse, though… The glass structure glowed with an ethereal quality, as if some bit of the moon had been whispered away from the sky and sealed within.

Ten children sat chatting and laughing around a blazing fire, no treats in sight.

*Marshmallows would probably be a welcome indulgence…*

"I'll just be a moment," David said, separating from them and singling out Hamish. The boy turned with a smile, and waved, sending a rush of hope through Lil. Lu felt it too, but Remi… Lil followed his focus to the greenhouse, catching some movement from deep within.

"The marshmallows, Rem." Lu said, pulling his attention.

"Cupboard beside the fridge. Leave the unopened bag."

Lu nodded and headed toward the cottage, disappearing with a crack once engulfed in darkness.

"The lynx on David's desk," Lil asked.

Remi sighed, placing an arm around her shoulders, face lingering in her hair before his mouth drifted to her ear.

"David and his husband, Raul, have been together for nearly twenty years," he whispered. "They met as students when they attended school here, then rekindled when Raul returned as faculty… While there may have been a moment between David and I, that time has long passed, and we are both better for it. We've shared much, our friendship strong, and our hearts captured elsewhere."

Hamish stood beside David, his smile huge.

"I'll leave you to it," Remi said, taking a step back, and walking toward the soft glow of the greenhouse. It looked very much like what had been drawn on that t-shirt Lu had taunted him with, but the rendering failed to capture the young woman with the auburn braid on the other side of the glass.

"I knew you'd come," Hamish beamed as he trotted over. "But where is the man with the beard. Oh, there he is," he declared, looking beyond Lil to where Lu approached, a half bag of marshmallows clutched in one hand.

"Hamish has assured me he doesn't need a chaperone," David started. "I hope you understand my position. I must stay at arm's length for this visit, though I'll interfere as little as possible.

Hamish shrugged, apparently not bothered much.

"And Remmond…" David said over Lil's shoulder, smiling warmly at discovering where his absent friend had gone. "He's in the greenhouse, of course. Shall we sit by the fire? The other students have started off toward the lake for an evening adventure, we should have some privacy."

Sure enough, little lights danced in the darkness through the forest, the children with their flashlights.

"I've brought some marshmallows," Lu said, holding up the bag as he settled down on Lil's left, Hamish to her right, David just beyond. "Lil got a head start, and says they're delicious."

*You tasted some yourself, as I recall.*

*Barely, there wasn't much left on your fingers.*

There may have been a hint of excitement in Hamish's eyes, but it was laced with indecision as he looked to David.

"You're in charge of what goes into your body, Hamish, but I recall seeing a bag similar to the one Lu is holding not too long ago. I saw it passed around the campfire from my office window, pausing several times in your lap. You should consider how many you had, and how your body will feel if you continue."

"I had four," Hamish sighed. "And I'd feel totally gross if I had another one, even though they taste delicious, especially when they're gooey."

"That they do," David said, reaching for the bag. "And if I limit myself to one, I don't think my appetite for dinner will suffer."

Lil smiled. Turning her focus to Hamish, she said, "Remmond and I are good friends, and we had a couple marshmallows each before heading over to visit. I hope you don't mind, but David told me a little about the dreams you've been having, how overwhelming they can be. He mentioned you've seen me in them."

Hamish glanced away to where Lu sat, then his eyes flicked back to hers as he smirked. "I've seen *him* too."

*I told you...*

"Pleased to meet you, Hamish," Lu said, extending his hand toward the boy. "You can call me Lu."

"You know my cousin, too," Hamish said as they shook hands.

"Indeed, and he speaks of you fondly. Perhaps I can assist in facilitating a visit sometime soon."

"I'd like that," Hamish said. "So, you wanted to talk about my dreams?"

"I've seen things happen to you, Lil. I've seen good things, or, *normal* things. I saw you flying one time! A couple times, really, and him too," he said, nodding toward Lu, "And Master Remmond one time, and these other two guys. You guys have so much *extra*. I think those flying ones are my favorites, I feel like I'm flying too, wings and everything."

"And sometimes scary stuff?" She asked.

He nodded.

"I've had some big-time scary dreams of real things," she offered. "I've had a lot of real-life scary things happen to me, too. My mom and dad died when I was little. Sometimes I dream about that."

"Were you... were you little more than once?"

Lil nodded. "I've been little more times than I can count on my fingers, toes, and your fingers and toes, and Lu's, and David's... And I think there are more fingers and toes in the greenhouse, so let's add those too."

"What about the kids at the lake?" Hamish asked with a bright enthusiasm Lil was thankful for.

She nodded. "Hamish, I've lived and died hundreds of times, I've flown with feathers and *everything*, and had the *best* fun ever, but the scary stuff is a part of it too. Have you ever dreamed of me fighting?"

He nodded.

"And maybe dreams where I might be dying?"

He looked as though he might cry, almost, as he nodded again. "I think those were the older ones though. The one I see now that feels the most real, is one where I see you being carried, and I can see a dragon, and I think that's who is carrying you. And you look so tired…"

*Whatever could have made you so tired, I wonder…*

Lu leaned forward, addressing the boy gently. "We're pretty sure that I'm the dragon you saw, Hamish, which I'm sure might sound a little outlandish… But you'll recall the wings you saw…

Hamish nodded.

"We have all *kinds* of extra," Lu smiled. "Including dragon stuff."

Hamish glanced down to Lu's arms, a puzzled look on his face as he tilted his head. "Do you ever wear a watch?" he asked.

"No," Lu smiled. "I've never had much use for one, what with all the traveling we do. I'm mindful of where I am, where I'm going, what time of year it is, things like that."

"Speaking of time," David started, giving Hamish glance. "We've got a few more minutes, but I'm cutting it close with dinner."

"You can go," Hamish said. "I'll be ok."

David didn't speak, just raised his eyebrows.

Hamish sighed, "Okay, a couple minutes."

"We should get going too," Lil smiled. "Don't worry about the dragon stuff, alright? Were there other dreams that seemed from now?"

"Well, there was one in the woods, and you shot your bow, but it feels like that passed. You turned out ok but the two guys didn't make it. Oh, and I saw wolves."

"Happened, and I'm fine," she smiled. "Anything else?"

"One where you're sleeping and there's a man on the stairs and another close behind, and they shoot you with something sharp, then there are so many men, then they're in a pile…"

"That happened too," she said. "And it was scary, like the time in the woods, but I'm here and I'm fine, Hamish. Though, if you have others, please tell David right away. Sometimes you'll see things before they happen, and it might be helpful for us, but try not to get overwhelmed. Gunnar told me sometimes you stack stones and talk about your dreams, and I think that's good. I drink tea, and swim, and I have some poetry that helps me."

"The stones help, and I like being in the kitchen," he smiled, holding his fingers out toward the fire.

"How's your hand?" Lil asked.

"My hand?"

"When we first met, you'd just cut yourself in the kitchen."

"Ohhh." He held up his palm and grinned, no stray marks to be seen. "That healed up by the time I got outside."

*He heals fast, even for them,* Lil said. *He'd apparently sliced his hand deep enough to stitch just before we met.. He came to tell David, then went right out to class.*

*Indeed. There does seem to be something more about him; I can't quite put a finger on it, though. Gunnar's cousin… On that side… That makes him Uri's.*

"You two are talking," Hamish smiled, his golden hair and amber eyes reflecting the warmth of the fire, reminding Lil of the cloudberries she'd grown.

"Another one of our *extras*," Lu said with a wink. *Incredibly perceptive.*

*They all are. Can you imagine Magnus at this age?* She bubbled with laughter as Lu conceded, Hamish looking on at their silence in wonder.

"Lil," David said, standing with his confiscated marshmallows. "I know it was your plan to do some work here after our chat, but I intend to stay in this evening, and I've asked Remmond to come over to discuss new developments. I anticipate Marissa might come along, she's the woman you would have been collaborating with in the greenhouse. I just need something familiar tonight, I hope you understand. Perhaps you can settle in over at Remmond's cottage."

"Of course. We'll reschedule," Lil smiled softly, then to Hamish she said, "I feel like we should hug, what do you think?"

"I think so too," he grinned, arms out.

Lil bent down for a squeeze, inhaling the scent from the campfire that wrapped around him, a smell like burning wood, and hope.

# 11.

"The stones were floating around us," Lil recounted dreamily.

She and Claire had Nan's living room to themselves while Todd was in the kitchen, foraging for snacks. It was well past midnight, and they were sitting on either end of the couch, feet under a shared blanket. Claire wore the soft, grey sweatpants Lil had given her, an olive-green Henley style shirt, her hair in a ponytail. She also had on those malachite earrings she loved, and her bracelet, now with two beads: green matching her earrings, and the obsidian from Lu.

Lil wore the same soft pants as Claire, black racerback tank top in case her wings came out to play. Uri hadn't informed her what he planned on covering during their session. He'd been training with Gunnar out back for hours, and Lil's turn would be next. She'd been cozied up with Claire and Todd beside a pleasant fire, taking part in a favorite pastime: watching nature documentaries with the sound off and narrating voices for the animals. Nan, upstairs, somehow managed to sleep through their laughter, though the entertainment had transitioned to Lil's storytelling.

"Can we rewind the conversation to the part where Lu was a *Dragon*?" Claire asked, wide eyed.

"He changed back when we got to shore…" Lil said, sitting up straighter. "Please tell me that was clear. You didn't think that he was still, I mean, if I had been in a similar form, it would have worked, but-"

"You've been a dragon?"

"I've been a lot of things, Claire."

"Dragons?" Todd called from down the hall. "You guys said you'd wait!"

Lil and Claire laughed as Todd walked in with a giant bowl of popcorn and a scowl on his face. He wore sweatpants and a sweatshirt in matching heather grey, slightly tattered at the cuffs. The hoodie was unzipped, revealing a dark grey shirt with the words *Illyrian Training Camp* on the chest.

Lil pulled the blanket back, and Todd tucked in between them.

"One bowl?" Claire asked skeptically, raising an eyebrow.

"It's to share," Todd remarked. "And I don't appreciate you talking about dragons while I was in there monitoring the popcorn… and seasoning it."

Lil sighed, almost blushing as she explained. "It started as an entirely different conversation, Todd, which was less about dragons and more about things I *think* you'd prefer not to hear the details of…"

His expression was blank for a moment before understanding flashed in his eyes, and he grinned. "Like about why the lights went out and we had to wrap our phones in tin foil the other night?

Lil nodded.

"Yeah, I don't need to know anything about that," he chuckled warmly, funneling a handful of popcorn into his mouth. "But I love knowing you're glowing out there," he added, releasing the bowl to offer his hand for a high-five.

"I was just telling Claire about swimming in the ocean with Lu the other day; he transformed himself into what you might call a dragon. The body moves differently in water with that form; it feels... nice."

"You didn't change with him though?" He asked.

Lil shook her head slowly, expression a little somber. "It takes a while to have control over things, and morphing my body into an entirely different form, however familiar it may be, takes practice, and it isn't a priority right now. I'm not always around long enough to have the experience... It's been hundreds of years, at least."

Claire and Todd's expressions began to sink, the mood transitioning.

"I love you both," Lil said. "It's okay to feel whatever you're feeling, and I can't tell you my deaths have been pleasant, or right, but *please*, don't make this your burden. I live with the weight of the injustice, but I don't carry it, and neither should you. Easier said than put in to practice, I know... and I've had a bit longer than you guys to work at it," she smiled weakly.

Heaviness hung in the air with an understanding that Lil's long life had been, for quite some time, broken by a series of deaths.

"What does it feel like," Claire whispered.

Lil knew the question had nothing to do with shape shifting. She wasn't asking about wings, or scales. Before Lil could begin to form an answer, she heard Todd's voice.

"I've gone under the waves more than once," he began. Lil sensed he hadn't spoken to interrupt, but to take the edge off; give her some time. "I was afraid when it happened, afraid I might not make it up, but nothing has come close to what I felt that night when those guys came for you. When I got cut, my blood was draining out, but I felt me draining out with it." Todd took a moment to compose himself before looking at Lil, glassy eyed. "I don't know how you've done it so many times."

"It's different. When I die, I know I'll come back," she said, as if to reassure him of something.

He shook his head.

"But it wasn't peaceful for you, ever," Claire added, voice fragile. "You've never passed in your sleep. You're not even *meant* to die, are you...?"

Indeed, she was not. It went against the nature of her soul. And with a human form that wasn't susceptible to illness, it was always violence that took her. No, Lil had never passed in her sleep.

"It's a lot like that draining feeling you described, but it doesn't stop," she said.

She found the human experience of passing was surprisingly similar to that of her own, though she couldn't claim to know exactly. She'd both read accounts and had them told to her firsthand. Those who relayed their stories were alive at the time of the telling and had, of course, not been dead at any point, only dying.

Death, once completed, could not be undone. Those were the stories she'd heard from Lu.

"First, I feel like I'm fading into myself and also emptying. Then, I feel separate from my body, rising."

Claire sucked in a breath, "Like the dream I had..."

Lil nodded. Claire had told her once that she'd had a dream of floating into the ceiling and looking outside. Claire rarely remembered her dreams, so she seemed to hang on to the memory.

"Yes, though you weren't in any danger. Dreams allow the living freedom to explore the universe inwardly without a tether to waking life, though in some instances, lucidity is maintained and a body's attachment to the soul loosens a bit," she smiled. "Some have described it as an *out of body experience*, which is not dissimilar to what I encounter, only... dreamers return."

One of Todd's hands gripped the bowl, while the other rested over his mouth, and Claire stared intently at Lil from the other side of the couch.

"And then..." Claire whispered.

"And then, it's disorienting." She could almost hear Lu's agonal roar through the past, his voice pleading with her to stay, the presence of the others... How it felt to slip away, set adrift before an unrelenting undertow pulled her in a violent rush toward a place of dark dormancy...

"Alright, but what's it like to be a *dragon*?"

"Todd!" Claire scolded, kicking rapidly against his thigh.

"Ow, Claire!" He scowled, then laughed as he lifted the bowl. "If you'd knocked this over, then Lil would have had to pick up all the popcorn with her *magic powers*," he joked, "and we can't have her exhausting herself before training."

"He's only trying to lighten the mood," Lil said, unable to keep herself from smiling as she leaned forward and mussed his hair. "And I think it worked." She grabbed a handful of popcorn and looked toward the hall as Uri and Gunnar appeared in the doorway. Uri had his feet and chest bare, wearing only loose black sweatpants that allowed for a wide range of motion. Gunnar wore black sweatpants as well, with the addition of a plain grey t-shirt and a barely visible sheen of sweat over his skin. Uri had a seemingly ever-present gleam of mischief in his eyes, a subtle smile on both their faces.

"You're up next, kid," Gunnar winked.


Claire gripped a chunky, grey knit blanket around her as she walked toward the orchard where Lil and Uri moved in the darkness. Gunnar kept pace with long strides beside her, his expression smitten and amused, another rolled up blanket under one arm. Todd had practically flown out of the house behind them, already passing them on his way to the trees.

"I thought you guys were going to wait," he said excitedly.

"Just warming up," Lil smiled, stretching out her limbs beside Uri at the edge of the apple trees.

"Are you guys sparring hand to hand? Blindfolded?" He asked excitedly as he neared.

"This isn't Kickboxer, Todd," Claire sighed, too tired and too familiar to filter sarcasm with him as they came to a stop beside Lil and Uri.

"They used *resin* and *glass* on their gloves in Kickboxer," Todd said, tone serious as he corrected her. "*Bloodsport* is the one where he had to fall back on his blindfolded training because his opponent through salt in his eyes."

"Are you really fighting?" Claire asked, turning to Lil with her nose a little scrunched up. "It didn't occur to me that you'd need help with that. I mean, I've seen you… that guy by the barn, heck, Brian the other night… If someone is close enough to hit you, wouldn't you just freeze him?"

Lil tilted her head to Uri, who answered, "What we're doing is about more than an exchange of blows, it's about waking her senses, detecting attempts delivered in stealth."

"And though we *can* freeze someone," Lil began with a smile, leading Uri with her words.

"It's no substitute for pummeling them," Uri grinned. "There's something to be said for using the hands in all aspects of life; with dough, with clay, the earth, in combat. We typically take precautions with Lil… There are risks not worth taking, though she's more than capable," he winked. "Her brilliance is a treasure to witness."

Uri crouched and pulled something from a bag he'd left at the base of the nearest tree. Passing Lil the long strip of fabric he'd dug out, Uri turned back to Todd and said, "Nice shirt, by the way."

"Thanks, it felt like the right time."

Lil watched Uri's lingering somewhere in his thoughts. He took a breath, shook his head, and said, "The Suriel, am I right?"

Todd's face changed, becoming more serious, as if Uri had seen inside him. "*Yes*," he said with one hand coming to rest on his heart as he let out a sigh.

Lil approached the nearest apple tree as Todd and Uri talked, her smile unrestrained. That she didn't know what they were discussing wasn't as relevant to her as seeing the relationship that had formed; the coming together of different facets of her life, ones she so cherished. She wondered, of course, about the little gem that had affected them so, but her curiosity was secondary to her delight for their bond, and her eagerness to get started...

Without making contact with the bark or soil, Lil reached for the nearest tree, attempting to connect to the life essence she felt there.

"Alright, spectators," Uri said, transitioning into training mode. "Take a few steps back, settle in, and no interrupting, no matter what you see." They didn't hesitate to follow his instructions, Gunnar setting down the large blanket for them to lounge on.

Uri turned his amber eyes to Lil, one hand coming to her cheek, sliding down to rest on her shoulder, the other hand taking the strip of fabric he'd handed her. "When my gaze met yours that night," he began, "I saw the depths of an ocean around the dark universe waiting. The joy I felt when those lights shattered nearly brought fire to my skin, knowing you were in there, bursting, ready to come home..." He sighed, flashing her a smile, holding up the cloth between his two hands. "We've done this before," he said, his voice gentle, disarming. "I am going to blindfold you. You can remove it, but it won't help if you do that. I need you to trust me, and trust the exercise. Remember, it's *meant* to disorient you.

184

Her eyes darted to Gunnar, feeling a wave of nostalgia. He'd been with her when broken glass rained down on them in the bakery. He'd sat with her, watching the Chihuly sway in the museum, had been the one blindfolding her on their journey to the school. Lil saw as much as felt his smile until her eyes closed and a swath of fabric secured the darkness.

She became aware of Uri's heat as he stood before her, the scent of fire, ginger, fresh dough and mayhem... until it was gone.

She'd barely detected any movement, only a whisper of air over her skin before registering his absence.

Lil became breath, waiting potential, as she listened to the sounds of the surrounding night. If she could find her center and lift a lake, open a portal while haunted by-

A flick at the tip of her right ear jolted Lil from the memory, followed by a tug at the end of her braid, then Uri's forearm at the back of her hand when she deflected his next attempt.

Lil leaned back as fingers grazed her throat. She continued to tilt as she grabbed his arm, and he swept her legs out from under her. His free hand gripped her side, his arm around her back swinging her up, lifting her until she felt weightless for an instant, his grip detaching and Claire gasping as Lil soared higher.

Lil tucked her legs until she'd repositioned, pointing them down. Her arms went out as her trajectory peaked, gracefully flourishing as she touched earth again.

"*She's awake*," Uri said, and though Lil couldn't see him, she heard the smile beaming through his words. Lil brightened, then she heard air brake with a high-pitched vibration to the left of her ear followed by the unmistakable sound of metal sinking into wood just ten paces behind. A knife.

They'd done this before, many times. The first throw was a courtesy to let her know the game had changed, he wouldn't miss again.

"Oh god," Claire gasped.

Lil stood in darkness, hearing Uri grumble, shift, then Todd whispering, "Tamp that shit down, Claire, the distraction could get her hurt. They know what they're doing."

Lil let the words drift away as she refocused on her breathing, until she was wholly aware of everything, yet pulled by nothing.

Sensing the release of another blade, Lil bent her body to avoid impact. Another, and her body was twisting, left palm touching down for support before she sprang back up, unscathed, right hand shooting out, fingers wrapping around the knife she knew would be in front of her shoulder. She released, and the dagger was airborne.

"Lil! Caire screamed, her cries becoming muffled, as though she were struggling for air. "Lil! She tried again."

"Just relax," Todd soothed. "This is part of her training."

A grunt followed, the sound of a large body hitting the ground.

"Gunnar!" Claire shrieked. "This is not part of the training! He's out of control!"

Lil's hand reached up for the mask, then a blade rang past her ear, blood trickling from her cheek.

"It stays on," Uri whispered beside her.

Three more blades rushed rapidly toward her, too many to grab at once.

She slowed her breath, drowned out Claire's screams, then *everything* slowed, projectiles continuing but as if they traveled through syrup. The knives drifted until Lil caught them, not with her hands, but with her mind. They hovered, suspended around her as she pulled them down, one by one, fiercely flinging them with unwavering confidence in her precision.

Through some heightened awareness she continued this way: catch and release, anticipating what was coming, twisting as Uri changed his position, blades coming from the front, from behind, from above. Lil continued knowing where to move, where to throw, until there was stillness again, until she couldn't sense Uri or anything else coming at her. Claire and Todd seemed to be holding their breath, the night song continuing at a murmur...

"Take it off," Uri whispered, his voice too low for her to get a read on what he felt. "Take it off and open your eyes."

Lil reached up with both hands and pulled the blindfold down, adjusting quickly to see Gunnar, Todd, and Claire sitting on their blanket like they were enjoying a midnight picnic, not a hair out of place on any of them.

Lil's eyes darted to Uri, the grin on his face, the fire in his eyes, the *knife in his chest*.

"You got me!" he laughed with pride, pulling out the blade.

In what seemed like one quick movement, Uri dropped the steel into his bag, extinguished his arms, charged at Lil, and spun her around. By some centrifugal phenomenon her heart felt lighter, as if it were flying outward, releasing bubbles of joy on its way up.

"Impressive, kid," Gunnar said, with a soft smile and strong emotion. They were all beside them when Uri put her down, Todd with his hand raised and Claire looking relieved. Lil high-fived Todd as Gunnar pulled her in for a hug. "I expected nothing less," he added, "though I was surprised you didn't use ground disturbance to your advantage, or send a team of taloned warriors after him.

"She's done it before," Uri laughed. "Though not in this life… First and *last* time I trained with you in a jungle. It was brutal, and you were fucking fantastic. Now, pull that blindfold back on," he said. Lil couldn't help smile as he turned to shoo the others away toward the blanket, calling out, "We're not finished here."

Uri glanced back at her, raising his eyebrows with expectation until Lil pulled the blindfold back down, tightened it, and waited.

A strong wind blew, lifting her hair. Heat rose from the ground like fire, spiraling around her as an ice-cold chill pushed against her back. The fluctuating temperatures blasting her were a distraction, but one Lil suppressed when the first strike came near, perhaps when it was still a thought not yet born to action, because it was nothing less than graceful as her body moved in response to his. There could have been music playing, and perhaps there was, what with the way the night continued to sing as she and Uri danced.

Lil found herself spinning, then felt two fingers pressing gently at the center of her forehead, stopping her altogether. Uri pushed, and she followed, falling backward into his arms. She was rolling in darkness, in the smell of damp grass and earth at the floor of the orchard, arms still around her.

Thunder cracked and they were tumbling like they'd fallen off a cliff. Her wings begged to be released, tingling beneath her back, but she resisted, feeling her body lurch against Uri's chest as their speed reduced. They were gliding, and then there was impact. She smelled wood burning, shouts in the distance.

"Listen," he said, his words low, textured against her ear. "Observe."

He went to the ground, her back against his, and then he was gone.

"I don't know where we are," she breathed, heart racing. She needed to glean clues to her surroundings, information to feed Lu, but that wasn't right… He'd felt her soul return after death every time, locating her before rebirth.

Uri surrounded her again, his voice in her ear. "It's not so we can find you… He will *always* find you. If you've survived long enough to listen, they don't plan on killing you. Observe. Keep calm. Keep *them* calm… Learn what you can about the opposition until we come for you. We'll spend more time with this lesson later. I'm hungry."

Thunder cracked and they were rolling again, upright against a hard surface. They were alone outdoors. Daylight peaked at the edges of her blindfold, and people spoke casually beyond whatever walls surrounded her. She heard a conversation in French become audible then drift away, a couple speaking English lingered, then they too were gone, there was… Dutch. Many people speaking Dutch, but it was particular… Belgian. The smell of bread hit her suddenly, and she knew.

"Ghent. We're in Ghent, somewhere near Himschoot. I can't *believe* you brought us here in daylight, Uri," she said, delivering an affectionate whack to his shoulder.

"Wait here, I'm going to grab a bag of croissants to leave in the woman's kitchen so she finds them in the morning..." He said, his mischievous laugh growing distant as he left her. Blindfolded.

"What's left of them," she teased, knowing he could still hear. Uri could eat his way through a bakery in a matter of hours without breaking a sweat. She didn't know how he was going to resist consuming whatever he walked out of Himschoot with... Another mystery was where he kept the money to pay for this bounty with just those sweatpants on. She didn't recall any pockets, or him wearing shoes for that matter. Greater still was the question of why she still wore the blindfold when he'd left her alone, against a wall in an alley, while he was off procuring pastries.

*Leave it on.*

Lil startled as Lu's voice moved through her, his instructions halting her hands before they reached the fabric over her eyes. Lil hadn't heard him arrive; no crack of thunder preceded his words, only the sensation of his nearness rising through her as he drew closer.

His presence pressed on her, though his body had yet to make contact. It was a weight that molded around every curve, filling her with the scent of smoldering embers.

Lil's blood hummed, charged and reaching for him, skin flushed. His breath moved over her neck, her ear.

"Open your mouth."

Lil's lips parted, an act of trust and anticipation. Something light brushed against them, her tongue barely grazing the tip of his finger, then a dense cloud of whipped cream began to dissolve like a delicate cloud. Something akin to a moan escaped her, subtle, riding her breath on its way out, sweet cream, spices, and his lips melting into her.

*I do adore your sounds.*

# 12.

"Brian texted me this morning…" Claire trailed off, fingers worrying the bottom button of her green sweater.

Lil sat beside her cousin on a bench overlooking the orchard and lavender field, air crisp, sun brilliant as it passed through the trees. She had returned from Ghent alone, emerging from the orchard wearing naught but Lu's *Original* t-shirt just before yoga.

Claire had been… Well, she'd not been not pleased.

When Uri came back on his own, and the portal closed behind him, Claire had immediately become agitated. She'd been convinced Uri had taken things too far, and Lil had been the victim of a training accident. Lu had given strict instructions that he not be interrupted, so Remi and Az had been brought in to provide reassurance.

Lil raised her eyebrows. "You've been texting with Brian for a few days... What's different?"

"He wants me to meet him for coffee." Claire scrunched up her nose and waited for what she thought would be a firm objection. "But not at Nan's."

Understandable. The location came with a bit of baggage for Brian.

Lil took a deep breath in and paused to think. Brian wasn't Lil's favorite person. He'd overstepped with her, often. Things had become a little rough that last day they saw each other but, other than that, he'd been respectful, his ineptitude with boundaries aside. Claire's relationship with Brian had only lived for few months, but it was an important experience for the two of them, and the closing deserved some thought, maybe more than Claire had given.

"I'm not opposed to the idea," Lil started, "but I think you need to consider what you want, what you need, potential outcomes, and if it's worth it. What do you want?"

"I'm *not* trying to get back together with Brian, but I feel like things weren't left in the right way. I'd like to feel comfortable seeing him professionally, and socially. I mean, I'm busy as hell right now, but at some point, if things ever calm down and I'm out with friends, I'd like for it not to be uncomfortable if he's there. We've been texting, and I think we're at a place where we can see each other, and I think we should."

"I'm going with you," Lil said, Claire's eyes going wide. "I don't think it's a bad idea for you two to find healthy closure to your romantic relationship, and a healthy start to whatever comes next, but I don't think it's a good idea for you to go alone."

Claire squeezed Lil's hand and sighed. "Yes. Exactly that."

Phone in hand, she began sending a message to Brian.

"He's out on the water this morning, but should be back by now."

A few moments later Claire looked down at her phone again.

"He needs to wrap some things up before meeting us. He can be at a coffee shop near him, Yaal's, in about an hour and a half. It's right by the water," she scowled. "It's so close to him, he could just scoot over there on foot in five minutes. Why make us wait?"

Lil tilted her chin down and raised her eyebrows. "Really, Claire? Because work stuff. You know better than I do how he is about work, and you're the same way," she smiled.

Claire relinquished a shrug. "True. And work is so relentless right now."

"But you love it."

"Are you kidding? *Of course* I love it... This whole thing with the lichen has just taken over. It can be a challenge to cultivate. It's not just one organism but two, well, three actually, or at least we think it is. Growth is extremely slow... unless *you're* helping it along... There are some challenges for what Magnus has in mind... but I'm on it."

"Need my magic touch?" Lil asked, wiggling her fingers

"If only. Can you imagine if I could get lichen to grow like kelp? Hmmm... you *did* help Dr. Zhang, though, and you're helping them grow it up at Gunnar's old school. Doesn't it breach some ethical interference guidelines you guys keep?"

"Yeah, but I think things are a little flexible right now..." Lil trailed off, considering how much Claire knew. "The blonde guy at the mammoth, and that your friend saw... that was one of us."

Claire's jaw loosened, her mouth parting.

"I mean, one of my kind," Lil clarified. "It was... we think it was the one who's responsible for rendering me mortal. It's a long story, to say the very least, but he reached out to Lu, apparently, to get my attention." Lil let out a sigh. "You know how with gardening things can get overgrown, and sometimes need to get cut back? There's something like that going on here, on a larger scale... with people." Lil wasn't sure how much to say; but it was Claire, and they had time, so she said everything... from the garden to the flood, from Lu's first meeting with Nan, to the smell in the barn, and the stones on the shore in Iceland.

"That's... that's heavy," Claire whispered. Lil saw the tears building before her cousin brought a sleeve to her eyes. "And beautiful, like a song..."

"Yes," Lil breathed. "Exactly that."

They were silent a moment before Claire asked, "So, will you meet with him? Michael?"

Lil nodded. "We just want to look at a few things first. Lu, Az, and Remi went out to do some investigating after they finished up with Magnus earlier."

"Was this before or after you disappeared for a few hours?"

"I didn't *disappear*, Claire. I knew exactly where I was, and if you need details: Lu met me in a Ghent alleyway. I left the blindfold on and, well, my clothes couldn't be salvaged afterwards because-"

"Further details not needed, thank you," Claire laughed, cheeks pink and eyes watering. "So, the others are investigating what Michael has been doing?"

"Yeah, and I'll probably meet with him tonight or tomorrow," Lil sighed. "But until then, you and I get to hang out. That means tea, tarts, and hitting some waves with Todd... I've missed you guys. It's only been a few days, but they've been *busy*."

Claire checked her phone and chewed her lip a moment.

"Text?" Lil asked.

"Oh, yeah."

"Brian?"

"No... I need to stretch my legs," she said, standing up and taking a few steps. She glanced at Lil's back and flapped her hands as though she were imitating a fledgling bird. "How's progress coming along?" she grinned, flexing her eyebrows. "It must feel amazing. How is it to have muscles and, I mean, whole functioning body parts that come and go from you like that?"

"I was disappointed at first, but progress has been really good. It's hard having something attached to your body that you can't control." She shook her head. "I felt like a toddler. Having memories of flying made it even more frustrating because I *knew* I could totally own the sky, then as soon as I spread my wings I got tossed about. I can laugh at it now, but I was *very* frustrated at first..." Lil paused, a look of excitement spreading over her face as she began to walk with Claire. "Do you want to see them?"

"Yes! Wait... can we? Its daytime and we're outside."

Lil looked around, waving off Claire's concern. There was no one else in that section of the garden and very few people in the shop, but taking a walk would make things safer. There'd been a time before, when she could have walked with her feathers out, taken to the sky midday, but much had changed since then.

"Come on," she said. "Let's go to the orchard. You're not missing out on the wings."

Claire released an excited squeal, clapped her hands, and linked arms with Lil. They strolled toward the trees, and Claire pulled out her phone again, typed, and put it away.

"Brian?" Lil asked.

"No, just checking something. So, Uri didn't have a shirt when I saw him in the air..."

"I've been wearing open back clothes," Lil explained, gesturing to the shirt she'd changed into after returning from Ghent, Lu's *original* tee tucked safely away. "The open back helps so I don't, you know, rip through anything. There was a time when people were a lot more easy-breezy about nudity, but that was a *long* time ago..." She paused when they were a few apple trees deep, sliding her arm away from Claire with a wink.

A shimmer began to spread beneath the surface of Lil's skin, a building spark until her body released, unfolded, expanded, and she adjusted her posture to accommodate the weight. Joy blossomed between them, Claire's eyes sparkling and smile widening, like a child watching ladybugs dance in the air.

"Oh Lil, they're so amazing. I've seen Uri's, and that was a pleasant shock, but this is *you*," she marveled. Her hands hovered at her side as she moved in so close

Lil could feel breath on her feathers. "There's gold in parts... How do you do that?"

"They're a part of me and just appear as they should be, I suppose. The first time they manifested in this life, it was Lu who drew them out. I didn't even know what was happening, it was like muscle memory or instinct."

Claire hit Lil with level eyes and total seriousness. "Can I touch them? Only if it's okay with you, obviously. Your body, your choice."

"Of *course!*"

Awestruck, Claire reached out slowly, almost hesitant.

"Just go for it," Lil laughed. "And try to remember that they're just a part of my body. Imagine yourself caressing my arm or my foot with the same *delicate awe...*"

"Hey, you go and sprout a third foot and I'll caress and marvel at that thing just as much. Until then, it's gonna be these massive wings."

"Marvel away," Lil said, shaking her head with a smile that wouldn't fade. "But let's set a ten-minute limit this time. I want to visit a bit in the shop before we head out... Todd's going to be so grumpy if he misses this... I can call him while you pet my feathers," she laughed, holding out her hand for the phone.

Claire hesitated, looking around...

Lil's smile weakened a little, her eyes questioning.

*Claire is either sexting Gunnar or something is wrong. She's being weird.*

*You're still at Nan's?*

*In the orchard showing off my wings.*

*Is Uri with you?*

*No, he's in the shop with Nan, Todd, and Duncan. I was going to call Todd to come out here but-*

Lil's head snapped to the side as the ambient sounds around her silenced unnaturally. Claire's uneasiness filled the air like a bad smell. Instead of drawing closer to Lil, she took several steps away...

*But what?* Lu demanded, concern in his voice.

Two humanoid forms rolled out in front her in a blur of movement, one swiftly coming to a crouch, the other a little less graceful but with just as much enthusiasm. As a third figure appeared, Lil barely had a moment to register the guns aimed at her, before steady streams of water pelted her face and body.

"I'm sorry," Claire shouted as Todd, Uri, and Remi assaulted her not with squirt guns, but Candy-colored pump rifles, each with a water chamber the size of a fire extinguisher. Once she'd been thoroughly drenched, which occurred in a matter of moments, the team lowered their weapons.

"Todd," she sputtered, half laughing. "I can't believe you guys. You too, Remi?"

But they weren't done… Todd reached into a fanny pack and pulled out three baggies, each the size of his hand, in hues that rivalled the brilliance of his gun, and threw them up in the air just over her head.

Instead of reacting, Lil watched, transfixed by what was enfolding. When the projectiles reached their apex, Lil heard something of a chuckle escape Remi as he ruptured the bags from a distance, sending bursts of bright lemon, magenta, and cerulean powder raining down on her. Then Uri threw another bag, this one showering her in glitter.

Roaring of thunder exploded in front of her, Lu striding toward her, eyes blazing, wings flared out to shield her as he assessed the threat.

Lil's arms went around him, his eyes locking with hers. He scanned her body, his expression transitioning from deadly to relived, puzzled, and then deeply amused as he beheld the brilliant color covering her face and torso, most concentrated at the top of her head, shoulders, and wings.

"I'm fine," she said. "Just decorated."

His eyes wandered from hers, back down her body, tracing a finger through the pigment on her chest, pulling at the hem of her shirt as he explored the valley between her breasts.

"You hadn't any gold?" He rumbled to whoever listened.

The birds began to chatter again, and while she heard Uri and Remi's laughter, Lil knew Todd and Claire would likely remain terrified a bit longer, what with Lu storming in battle-ready. Wherever he'd come from had been raining, or he'd been in a river. His shirt was plastered to his skin and dripping, hair slick, beads of water nestled in his beard. Soaking, he'd rushed in before the dust settled, leaving a fine layer of the jewel-toned sediment over his body and wings.

"You're wet," she said.

"Indeed," he grinned darkly. "Az and I were meeting with a contact in Borneo."

"Todd!" Remi shouted.

Without hesitation, several more bags went up. Lu could have stopped them all, but instead he turned, colors bursting above him, and raised his eyebrows at Remi.

"You orchestrated this?"

Remi flashed his teeth, proud.

"Todd," Lu said, turning to address the young man. "You have no idea what you've gotten yourself into."

"Locked in for life," Uri chimed in. "I told him there's no turning back once he set foot in the orchard. He's the one who came through with the powder on short notice."

Todd always knew someone.

"Duncan went to that Holi thing in March," Todd explained. "He's got *tons* of these baggies at his place. The glitter wasn't me though…"

Claire cringed…

"You too!?" Lil gasped.

"I got it at the craft store…" Claire smile-cringed.

*I'm flabbergasted.*

"I thought maybe you just got roped into getting me out here," Lil laughed.

Claire shook her head.

"Well, I can't go back to Nan's looking like some exotic hummingbird," Lil smiled.

"Oh, I think we'd be well received," Lu smiled, her grip tightening on his arm as he leaned in close to her mouth. "Joan and Audrey seemed to enjoy watching me sweat in the yard,

I can't imagine they'd mind listening to the two of us rinsing off in the outdoor shower."

She inhaled quickly, then looked over his shoulder to see her cousin's mouth open with no words.

*Or perhaps we clean up in the orchard,* he said, taking a few steps back. He winked, then burst into flames, wings spread wide like a phoenix.

Remi nodded and disappeared through a portal while Uri gathered Todd and Claire toward him. "Alright kids," he called out. "You two won't want to be here when the flames die down, trust me. Eyes over here, Sunshine."

"But we have plans," Claire protested.

"I won't be late," Lil said, mesmerized as Lu tucked his wings in, fire receding from his hands as he reached for her. "I just need to run back to the mountain really quick… to change."

*

Not a spot of stray color remained on Lil as she and Claire walked into Yaal's café. She felt her cousin's strength, but heard the tired sigh as she spotted Brian. He stood at a sunlit table by the window, holding an empty mug. JD put a reassuring arm over his shoulder and leaned into his ear, likely with words of confidence.

As Lil and Claire approached, JD stepped back to give them room. Lil found herself watching closely as Brian put his hand on Claire's arm. With difficulty, Lil resisted the urge to slow his movements to a stop, as a reminder. The last time her cousin had interacted with him, Brian had not been respectful. If she saw Claire tense, even once, she was going to pull the plug and get them out of there, leave Brian frozen with JD thinking he'd had a stroke.

JD moved next to Lil, his body fluid and casual, his eyes warm and excited.

"What? No thermos?" He teased.

Lil turned, smile coaxed, his playfulness taking the edge off.

"I should have brought it. Ordering tea at another shop... it feels like I'm cheating on Nan."

"Please," JD scoffed. "Their matcha is sweetened and they stir it in with a spoon. They *do* have a small but exceptional variety of coffees. That's their niche. Let's skip it, though, and get you some tea." He raised an eyebrow but Lil hesitated, she just wasn't there yet.

"First off, they're teabags," he continued, "and second, I'd like to, finally, be allowed to get a drink for you. I could run a cup under the faucet and serve you tap water, if that seems the least offensive option."

"If they have chamomile and mint bags, you could get one of each in the same cup," Claire offered.

Lil rolled her eyes. "Chamo-mint. Two bags, one mug, hot."

"Yay!" Claire cheered.

"For here or to go?" Brian asked cautiously.

"Well, we're going to be here, right?" Claire responded, looking at Lil, who nodded.

"Great," Brian smiled. "We can still go for a walk and bring the mugs back after. There are no bug mugs though," he added with a smile, nudging her in the shoulder. He was trying.

Claire smiled back.

"What will it be then?" JD asked.

"Jasmine," Claire answered.

Brian extended his empty mug. "Another coffee." Then he stood and said, "I'll just go up with you. You're gonna need four hands to carry it all back."

Lil and Claire sat down at the table, Lil looking over to see Brian and JD at the wooden condiment bar. She imagined JD took his coffee black or had some elaborate and precise routine about what he put in. Must have been the latter because there he was, pouring in bits of this and that, stirring away.

Brian arrived at the table and put Claire's mug down, but remained standing.

"Five minutes," he said, placing his hand on hers. "Give me five, maybe ten minutes. Let's go take a walk. Sally is cool if we take the mugs for a bit and bring them back; I come here all the time."

Claire gave Lil a look, a look that said she wanted to go but needed Lil to cut the last thread holding her back.

Lil nodded. Claire was a grown woman and didn't need permission, but it was a delicate moment, and they had a trust between them. She needed time with Brian to calm the leftover turbulence, and Lil knew better than anyone how the ocean air could be soothing.

As Claire and Brain left, JD sat down across from Lil. The sunshine spilled through the window in a way that was warm, but not forcing either one of them to squint. It was pleasant.

Lil looked down at her cup.

"I haven't sipped from a boxed teabag in a *very* long time." She took a sip and, fighting the instinctive grimace, smiled, saying, "No really, it's not terrible..."

They both laughed.

"I wasn't brave enough to try the matcha," he confessed. "I went with the Guatemalan beans."

JD breathed in from atop the mug before taking his first sip. Eyeing Lil, her cup, and then looking back to her face, he said, "You'd better drink it hot if you're going to drink it at all. I can't imagine it will get any better cold."

He glanced at his watch then to the counter. "Want to split a cookie?"

Lil shook her head, unsure. "Do they have anything with puff pastry?"

"I saw dark chocolate croissants."

"Get two."

"You got it," he smiled, and headed for the counter.

Lil knew the pastry would be nothing like Nan's, and to Uri's there could be no comparison, but they'd help the tea go down. She drank about half and paused. Heat was the only discernible positive, though the tea did feel soothing, almost numbing her throat on its way down.

JD stood chatting with the woman at the register. Sally, she supposed...

Glancing out the window, Lil drank down the rest of her substandard chamomint. Pushing the empty cup aside, she slid the back of her hand over her hair, over her shoulder, and down her other arm. Her hair was warm from the sun coming through the glass. Inside her body, heat spread from the tea. She imagined a time when she's sprawled on a warm stone in the mountains, the cool air around her, sunlight on her skin.

She rested her head on her arm, her hair sprawled out, eyes closed. She felt like a cat, basking: so warm, so cozy.

A broad hand rested on her back. She delayed, but eventually opened her eyes as the hand slid away. She saw JD unbuttoning his cuffs to her left, rolling up his sleeves. In the process, he revealed a rather expensive looking watch on his left wrist, some type of diving style. It had a military look to it, but expensive, not that she had an eye for that sort of thing, but Lil had seen the type of watches Magnus wore. This was of a similar caliber. On his right wrist, she noticed, as her eyelids drooped a bit, he had a tattoo. It was scaled and wove up his muscular forearm, disappearing to a place she couldn't see. There was a clawed foot there, perhaps.

Thinking was making her tired, so Lil closed her eyes again. She felt the hair bushed away from her neck, and a warm hand resting there. It was gentle, then it was gone. Then she felt it again, low on her arm, sliding down. She opened one eye about halfway again. JD had two fingers on her wrist. He was looking at his watch. The light was bright, but also heavy.

She closed her eye again as he took his phone from his pocket with his left hand, his right... it must have been his right resettling on her neck.

The clicking from his phone echoed, and then the world moved.

# 13.

Lil lifted what she could manage of her eyelids, but the sun made them so heavy. She was against JD's chest; he was holding her.

"Your dragon arms," she whispered with great effort, and no help from her tongue.

"The better to hold you with," he smiled.

*You want to wake me from my sun nap. I wish I could smell you in my sleep. I bet I could, but I can't reach my hand.*

*What? Where are you?*

Lil didn't respond, soothed by Lu's voice and distracted by the cool air as she was carried out of the café. She remembered the mountains again, basking on the stone. She just needed to settle back into the heat.

*WHERE ARE YOU?*

*Dragon arms. The tea was so bad, but the table was a warm nap, and now it's cold out here. I'm moving. Carrying. No, carried... I never got my croissant.*

The black vehicles were like a blur, stopping suddenly in front of them. The back passenger door to the middle car opened.

Her heart picked up pace a little. The vehicle wasn't right. She drove a truck.

*There's a car. It's not mine.*

*Lil, WAKE UP! Don't get in the car! We're coming.*

205

Lil opened her eyes wider as things became darker. JD's body shifted considerably, another set of hands joining his around her. She found herself in the back of an SUV, windows tinted.

The vehicle shook violently as a thunderous crash sounded around them.

"Two in the street at our six," a voice said from the front.

Another loud crash.

"Vehicle three compromised."

"Expendable. Leverage in V-One."

There had been three cars, they'd taken her into the middle one.

Lil was eased down until she laid across the back seat, her head on JD's lap and her legs somewhere else, as though they'd drifted off to sea and sunk to the bottom with her slipping consciousness.

She woke to a pinching at her arm, it felt tight. A soft toothpick moved in her mouth, then it was gone. She heard men's voices, and then there was Lu in her head, the sound like heaven.

*Are you belted in?*

*I, I don't think so.*

She managed to open her eyes a bit before they fell closed again.

*He's holding me. My arms and legs are heavy.*

*I need to intercept the car, but you could get hurt if you're not belted properly. We're going to follow in the air and make a plan.*

He roared in her mind, frustrated, raw, and powerful. Like him. Like her.

She listened.

Lil was lying down in the back seat sprawled across two men. She didn't know who held her legs, but her head rested on JD's lap. He was stroking her hair away from her forehead with one hand, holding his earpiece in the other. Tossing the device into the passenger's seat, he looked up to the driver's eyes in the rearview.

"Your audio still good?"

"Yes, sir."

His hand returned to its work in her hair as a man at her feet took his hands from her briefly.

"She's hot," he said nervously.

"Keep driving," JD said, reassuring the driver, his voice unfaltering.

"She's shaking, *vibrating*," the man at her feet said.

"It's getting dark, fast, sir." That was the driver.

"Put your headlights on."

*Your body is working hard to clear whatever they gave you. You'll need to eat and rest when we get you out of there. You've managed to work up an impressive storm.*

*I'm working up a sweat, too.*

She could feel Lu smile.

*Indeed. Your humor and desire are a good sign. How is the driver?*

*Driver is managing. My thoughts are more coherent, but my mouth isn't cooperating when I try to speak. Tongue is thick, heavy.*

Lil felt the hands on her leg moving up the inside of her thigh.

Startled, she released a sloppy vocalization and grabbed onto JD, fisting his shirt in her hands while sluggishly kicking at the other guy. The stranger's hand stopped suddenly, squeezing Lil's leg as JD clutched the bastard's throat.

"Was curious... vibrating..." he managed.

"Open the door and get out, Stephen."

The man's eyebrows rose, but he reached for the handle.

*What was that? Are you ok?*

*The guy holding my legs got handsy.* Lu growled, the sound immensely soothing. *JD instructed him to throw himself from the vehicle for it. And he did.*

*Interesting. JD you said?*

*Yes, I went with Claire to meet Brian. They're all friends. I drank something.*

*I'm right with you, working on the best way to get you out.*

A long pause followed.

*Remi has the discarded man. We will leave him secured with Gunnar for the time being.*

JD leaned over, pulling the door closed.

"There was no excuse for that," he said. "Tom," he continued, attention up front, "make sure someone swings back for Stephen."

"Yes, sir."

A loud *THUD* sounded from the roof of the car, then another, and several more, like stones rained down on them. The vehicle swerved, then righted as the banging continued.

"Hail, sir."

"Keep driving," JD responded casually. "The plan is solid. They won't jeopardize her safety by attacking at this speed."

He put a hand on her wrist, two fingers on her pulse.

"Charlie won't take off in this..." The driver said with concern.

JD sighed, bringing his mouth close to Lil's ear.

"Lil, you're affecting the safety of a treasure I've waited quite a long time to hold. Can you guess what that treasure is?"

Her eyes rolled as she struggled to keep them open.

He cupped her cheek. "You. *You* are my most precious treasure: the girl who evaded my uncle's efforts at sea, causing a storm that should have taken you down with it. You were lost to us for two decades."

JD released a sigh as he continued, still stroking her hair. "I was sent in as liaison to the Orn about a year ago after we found you again. It was an effort to keep a clear head upon finally meeting you at the bar. I made that tea when I left, with the instructions written on your napkin... I imagined it was your mouth I tasted as I drank," he whispered close to her ear. "I make it often."

That he would take the liberty of fantasizing such a thing was repulsive, but he'd said something else... his uncle... the ocean.

JD attempted to look into her eyes.

"The severity of this storm is impacting the driver's ability to keep you safe, and that is unacceptable. I need you to slow your racing heart. Calm yourself and the storm as best you can, or I'll have to help you with more medicine. I don't want you like that, but I can't allow you to injure yourself."

*He will medicate me further if I don't rein things in. Someone mentioned taking off and not being able to fly in this. He said I evaded his uncle twenty years ago at sea, and that I'm his treasure, and he's been waiting for me. He's... being affectionate.*

Lu growled. *He's a relation of Malcom's, which is rather concerning.*

Another pause.

*We're either going to throw some trees down ahead of the car so they'll slow to a stop, or I can just levitate the vehicle, decrease speed in the air, disable it, and set you down.*

Lil had trained to stay calm, to stay focused, to listen...

*I can stick it out a little longer; it could be useful. He clearly doesn't want to hurt me.*

*Your body is extremely vulnerable,* Lu said, *but your mind is clear. This is your choice, but it makes me very uncomfortable. I'd like to get you out of there now, and crush them,* he snarled. *Rip them open with my hands and teeth.*

*The threat will continue after the men in this car perish. If he reveals something useful, maybe we can end this in a bigger, more long-term way.*

*I can interrogate him when he's DEAD,* Lu snarled.

*Just give me a few minutes.*

Lu's growl was strong. *Do NOT let him medicate you again.*

*It won't come to that.*

*I'll be right here with you.*

With another sigh, Lil burrowed her head into JD a little more, repositioning.

"They came," she murmured, her tongue still heavy as her limbs.

"Your guardians," said a male from the front passenger seat. It was her first time hearing the voice; he sounded about the same age as JD. "There have been accounts of them coming to your aid, and here I am, seeing it for myself. It's a wonder they're so persistent in keeping you for themselves given the history."

"She's in no state for analysis or academics, Jonah," JD warned. He moved his hand behind her neck, massaging the base of her head. Whatever threat JD held was not heeded, as the man up front continued with increasing enthusiasm.

"Don't give me that nonsense. She's perfectly capable of listening, and plenty interested. We infiltrated a fanatical group a few generations back, The Guards of Eden. They're absolutely insane, but their network is surprisingly extensive, and they have records going back thousands of years. They associate you with some creature sent by the devil to disrupt *God's plan*," he snorted. "Their manifesto is… colorful, but ancient people seeing humans with a longer lifespan, zero susceptibility to illness, and flying no less… it lends itself to stories. The descriptions of you though, they line up. There are beautiful depictions of your likeness, of the stone necklace you wear, but none hold in comparison from what I can see, though I wasn't supposed to see you just yet, was I," he asked rhetorically, releasing a short laugh before continuing in a more serious tone. "Magnus has a business relationship with our uncle that could complicate things, but it won't be a problem once you get settled with us. We went a little rogue in moving forward with your retrieval. I have a feeling it's going to take more than finesse to smooth things over with our uncle. JD, of course, is the finesse, not me; I like the lab and the library. If only we could have persuaded Daniel…"

"The interpreter of dreams," JD scoffed under his breath. "How aptly named our brother was."

"His middle name could have been Ajax, or perhaps Achilles," Jonah said, craning his neck to look toward her. He appeared slender with ash blond hair, wire rimmed glasses. "And there you are, holding the arrow. Would he be Menelaus or Paris?"

"Our brother does not embody the whole of the Trojan war, Jonah," JD groaned. "How much coffee have you had...?"

*He has a brother in the car who's oversharing, and another somewhere else.*

*Lovely. Can I dismember them yet?*

"My allotment of coffee should be as limitless as my potential, JD, and she should know what's going on. There's no greater input than what we can get straight from the source. I've waited long enough to speak with her, haven't I? My family," he continued, speaking directly to Lil without concern for reprimand, "has postulated that you are a species which branched off from humans, but have *fertility issues*, to be blunt. There are accounts recorded in Genesis of male angels pairing with human females. We suspect your kind are those that the humans of the time labeled *angels*. Whatever the backstory, the fact that the ancients recorded interspecies pairing is intriguing. My family has postulated that the men of your species can breed with human women, but perhaps not with their own females, resulting in weakened genetics in their offspring, as far as your species' superior abilities. There are accounts, granted they are biblical, of people living hundreds of years. Were they of your kind? Progeny of your kind? Mated to and sharing something with those of your kind? And what of the females of your species and their reproductive tendencies? It's been said in stories throughout the ages that blood is the fluid that gives life, *eternal* life. There is more than enough fiction out there on the subject, but we wonder if there isn't a bit of truth grounding it. There's a great deal we don't understand, but are excited to get to work on."

Lil managed a sharp inhale.

"*Tact,* Jonah," JD grumbled, giving considerable leeway to the man up front compared to the one whose hands had moved too far up her leg.

"We are not going to drain you of your fluids or keep you restrained in a lab..." Jonah continued. "We took a cheek swab and a couple vials upon getting you in the vehicle. Beyond that, maybe you can help us to come up with a plan for what methods of investigation might be most useful. I don't want you to think we're recruiting you as a test subject. We want you to be a part of this, *JD especially,* though I don't think Daniel will entertain the idea, and neither will Uncle. There's no greater specimen than Daniel, honestly, not of our species anyway. No offense JD, though you make a fine runner up. Remember, you were on retrieval duty, brother, so while you may pet the cargo now, once he sets his eyes on her in waking life, that'll be the end of it..."

Lil didn't hear hail anymore, but the light outside the windows remained dim. How she was able to stay calm during such an unsettling confession was beyond her. She'd been abducted by a man who Claire had wanted to set her up with. Of course, her cousin would've had no idea his agenda was to hand her off to his brother, who would mate with, impregnate, and use her power to enhance his company's prowess while her body fluid extended his life. Because it seemed like that's where Jonah thought things were headed. Lil couldn't fault Claire for not suspecting.

JD looked down at her. Running a knuckle over her cheek, he said, "I know you're still drowsy, but it's for your safety and mine until we can get to a secure location, then you'll have time to get to know us in a more relaxed environment. It'll be well stocked with the herbs you like for tea. No bags," he smiled.

"Where?" She asked with a whisper.

"With me. That's all you need to know."

Her head rested on the lap of a dangerous man. But still a man.

"And let's not forget Daniel," Jonah said.

*I've been promised to his brother, apparently. They're hoping I'll breed with him and make them immortal. They took my blood and a cheek swab while I was unconscious. Bringing me to a secure location, but won't say where. Get me out of here before I blow up this car.*

She felt a sudden lurch of the vehicle as it left the ground.

"Sir?" The driver questioned.

"Wait it out. Alert Charlie, put V-one on standby."

Lil felt the wheels slow to a stop beneath her. The jostle of being set back down on the ground was a comfort, knowing she was closer to getting out of there.

JD glanced up to the man who'd been driving.

"Charlie up to speed?"

"Yes, sir. En route, backup with sound."

"V-one?"

"Coming back around, sir."

"Stay in the car please, Jonah," JD said before sliding out from under her head and exiting the vehicle. Jonah, to her surprise, stayed put, but the driver got out and stood beside the door.   Lil thought for a moment that JD might be leaving her in there as well, but he reached back in and put his hands on her. He was gentle, but firm enough to pull her out.

"Come on, beautiful," he said, helping her to her feet and leaning much of her weight against himself. "It will keep us both safe, they won't risk you."

Lil looked up and saw that they were in a field, surrounded by forest on all sides but where the grass met a road.

Lu stood not six meters away, flanked by Remi, Uri, and Az. Her heart nearly sang out loud at the sight of them.

*I don't want you to fall, Ilati, but I cannot tolerate his insolence any longer.*

*You could always freeze him, then rip his arm off to extract me.*

*The idea alone warms my heart.*

Lil turned an eye toward JD and noticed the corner of his lips hinting at a smile. How could he possibly find joy in his certain death?

A commotion of doors slamming followed by shouting pulled Lil's attention. The noise came from a vehicle at the road, a black SUV.

"Get your hands *off* me, Brian!!!!"

"Claire. *Claire…*"

213

Lil's cousin came around the vehicle, stomped on his foot then struck him in the head with her elbow as he folded over, taking a few steps back. Two men exited the vehicle, maintaining close proximity as she berated him.

"I am *not* getting back in that truck, and I am *not* going with you. I don't know what is going on, but you are not to hold me like that! Don't even come *near* me," she seethed.

"It's either me or one of them. Wouldn't you rather I hold you?"

"*No one* is holding me. Lil!" Claire screamed, meeting her cousin's eyes with both panic and relief.

The situation had been delicate to begin with, but concern for her cousin's safety was too much. There would be no more listening to see what she could learn at this point. Only a monster would have involved Claire.

*Get her out of here,* Lil said, the ground trembling beneath her words.

She had more energy than she'd thought, but not enough control, not yet. After visually confirming her cousin hadn't been hurt, Lil glared up at JD. If Lu didn't end him immediately, she was going to do it herself. She didn't yet possess enough power to coerce the earth into opening up and swallowing him whole, but she could clamp her hands around his throat. It would be immensely satisfying; she just needed to raise her arms up first...

JD rubbed Lil's shoulder, pulling her in closer.

"She'll be fine," he whispered, as if to comfort her, then looked up with confidence and said, "Lil is coming with me. Claire is here to assure cooperation. To be clear, I don't want to hurt Claire, she's a lovely young woman, but as a means to an end, I'll use what I must."

"Brian!" Claire shouted with pink cheeks wet with tears. "He's psychotic! How could you be a part of this? Do you see what he's done to her? She can't even stand on her own!"

# A Story in Song

Brian had really outdone himself as far as poor choices went. That he was gingerly touching the injured side of his face and working his jaw before he spoke gave Lil a small sliver of satisfaction.

"His company has the resources to make big changes, globally, Claire," Brian said slowly, as if educating a child. *"That's* where she needs to be, and you know it. Besides, they have chemistry. And don't tell me some nonsense about the volcano guy," he added, pointing at Lu. "JD comes from a strong family; she'll be safe, and they'll foster her potential. She could right the wrongs of humanity, Claire. The earth is *dying.* I don't know what Lil is, or exactly why she's here, but I know it's not to sit around Nan's, painting pictures!"

Lu raised his eyebrows at Lil, asking without the need for words between them, not even in their minds. One would expect such a decision to take more time, as it should in most cases, but for her there was no more pause than a heartbeat. A line had been crossed.

*He's all done. They all are.*

Brian made a pained, strangled noise, anguishing briefly before collapsing on the ground.

Uri was by Claire's side instantly, quicker than the two men from the car in grabbing her. With a crack of thunder, they were gone.

And there was no more leverage.

The two other men who'd come with Claire fell to the ground, as did the driver of the vehicle Lil had been in.

JD stood strong, unflinching and straight-faced as they collapsed before him.

*The boys are getting rather antsy,* Lu started, *and there's only so much of this I can tolerate, Ilati, but I thought you might like to sink your teeth in first.*

Beyond the rolling thunder overhead and harsh wind picking up once more, the sound of blades could be heard, slicing through the air, a loud crack as lightning struck a few meters away.

*Missed...* she sighed.

*You're just tired. You've trained extensively with Uri, and were worked rather hard afterwards as I recall.*

*Quite hard, yes.*

*Fortunate for both of us the recipe for your invigoration is similar to what works best in easing you to sleep... Do you need help waking, Ilati?*

If Lil's cheeks hadn't already been pink... she almost forgot where she was for a moment, but then JD's hand was on her wrist, two fingers on her pulse. Lil had been feeling her mind clear since back in the car. When she'd remained steady as the ground rumbled, Lil had known her muscle strength was returning as well. She felt power running through her body like the blood pumping through her veins, and it was strong.

JD must have made a similar observation.

Lil licked her lips; they were dry, as was her tongue.

"You shouldn't have brought her here." She whispered.

JD looked down at her and sighed. "We tried. I sent two of ours to speak with you at Nan's, but I accept the heat for that fault. One got jumpy, and mistook Claire for you. But then I sent them to *talk* to you in the woods, *calmly*, and you made it clear that a conversational approach was no good. There were more, sent to subdue and retrieve only, but with that failure I had to step in and do it myself. I didn't want you to associate me with the acquisition because I want us to have a foundation of trust as we work together moving forward. I shouldn't have *needed* to bring Claire today, but you've continued to be uncooperative."

Lu's growl filled the entire field, rustling leaves and penetrating her entire body, lighting Lil from the inside out with molten warmth that leaked from her center to her extremities.

JD's face twisted into one of anger and frustration, apparently having met the limit of his tolerance as well. With what care he could manage, he leaned Lil against the vehicle. He then turned to face Lu, tore his shirt open, stripped it off, and threw it to the ground. The black and red dragon tattoo coiled up his arm and over his chest, rippling as he flexed his muscles, openly challenging an immortal.

Hamish hadn't seen her with Lu in the water after all…

"The Drake family mascot," Lu said, as if making a casual observation. "Wearing this animal, it makes you feel powerful, yes? Tell me," Lu rumbled, "Do you wear the dragon to strike fear? Should I be afraid of the picture you've had drawn on your skin?"

Jonah stormed out of the vehicle and slammed the door, shouting, "You keep selfishly trying to retrieve her, but it's pointless! Your kind cannot breed with her; you need to pair with humans. You have no *need* of her!"

The audacity. There they stood, after chemically restraining her, and this fool throwing an entitled tantrum…

"Jonah," JD warned, but whether by coffee or too much time spent contained in the library, Jonah, to his detriment, was not quiet.

"Tell me, young Drake," Lu began, addressing JD and ignoring the outburst. "Has Uncle Malcom sanctioned this escapade of yours?"

"Our uncle has always had a Machiavellian philosophy about getting things done," JD replied vaguely, but from what Lil had heard in the car, it didn't sound like Malcom had known.

"There is no future for you together," Jonah began again. "We will never stop until we've brought her into a family of dragons, where she-" His mouth closed and, in spite of his best efforts, he was unable to open it again.

Reflecting on the original betrayal that had caused her vulnerability left Lil fuming. The human beside her should have been *thanking* them for the diatoms that provided him with breathable air, for everything around them, for planting

217

the seeds that gave him *life*. His very existence traced back to her work in the garden. He knew nothing of it though, nor should he.

"Young Drake, you are profoundly misinformed, and there is no purpose in my enlightening you. I'm fairly certain your offenses outweigh your usefulness at this point." And with that, Jonah went up in flames, though it seemed a surprise to Lu, who turned toward his companions with a brow raised in question. Lil followed his line of sight, her eyes stopping at Uri. He'd returned without Claire, and wore a mischievous smile on his face.

Saving Jonah for a living interrogation was no longer an option, then.

Lu sighed. "I said *fairly* certain, Uri".

Uri shrugged, smile unmoving.

Lil raised her head, her body humming with a low vibration, a subtle glow hovering over her skin.

JD reached into the pocket of his trousers and pulled out a pre filled syringe with a cone tip instead of a needle. A nasal syringe. The palm of his other hand came over her mouth, fingers moving to block one of her nostrils, though they stopped short, his body frozen in place.

And the eyes of a raging ocean storm locked with his.

Lil slid out from under his hand, leaving it suspended in the air where her face had been.

His eyes flared, unable to speak.

She took the syringe from his hand, released the spray to the ground, and dropped it.

"I don't need potions to keep you still," she said, then turned her back to him and walked away.

*Do you wish to head back to Nan's with Az, Uri or Remi?* Lu asked as she approached.

"I don't want to be separate from you," she said out loud to his heated eyes. Her arms went around his waist as his came up her back to her shoulders, fingers on her neck. His scent of deep earth and sweet, spiced warmth cascaded into her body, eliciting a sigh.

*His repulsive hands have been in your hair. We're bathing immediately after I shred him.*

Lu's lips were soft, his mouth strong and warm.

The arms he wrapped around her were the same ones that had thrust her against that tree in the orchard, the ones she'd seen coal and water drip down, that had held his body above hers, the hands that had smeared shimmering paint as they gripped her...

Lil's lips, still joined with his, stretched a little farther as a smile formed.

*Did I mention I found a stone vessel filled with gold powder at the mountain? I was poking around and there was this little jar, so familiar, and when I lifted the lid...*

Lu growled into her mouth with a heat only an immortal could survive, and Lil savored every moment of the fever that surrounded her. Him. Through sound and smell and taste, their bodies merged, a reminder that nothing, not even death, could keep them apart.

Their reverie was muted by the beating of metal through sky, their eyes flicking up to find two helicopters appear low over the trees.

Through the open sides of the flying machines Lil had expected to see guns. Instead, she saw massive, flat squares and circles mounted with men standing behind them, wielding whatever those things were. They looked like solar panels and satellite dishes.

"If you impair the driver alone, the vehicle could crash some distance away and cause unnecessary casualties," Lu advised.

Uri stayed on the ground as Remi and Az nodded and flew out, helicopters angling their broadsides towards the incoming threat.

About four meters from his target, Remi banked left, then sailed up only to be violently propelled backward a great distance by some invisible force. He recovered as he fell, landing on his feet with eyes wide.

When Az was hit, he wasn't catapulted. Instead, his body froze and flickered, as if fragments of him were fading in and out. Eventually, he fell to the ground in what looked like a state of unconsciousness.

Lil stopped breathing as she watched his body take the impact.

Az groaned, pushed up on one arm, then his knees, stood and shook his head.

Uri hovered above Lil and Lu, plotting his course as both helicopters turned, waiting for him, one on each side. He angled out to the left, the respective chopper adjusting its position, then he cut low to the right, swept up, and with a loud crack, he vanished.

The two machines spread out.

With another boom, Uri ripped back into sight, reappearing in flight below the helicopter off to the left. His arms swung out, a great flame extending from each hand like swords on fire. Arcing his weapons upward, he sliced through the chopper with martial grace.

The detached rotor from the severed machine continued to spin, its trajectory less than ideal for Lil. Lu tucked her into his body, taking her to the ground beneath him, narrowly escaping the path of the blades. She looked up from underneath him, Az and Remi's concerned faces turned toward her.

They scowled to the sky where Uri hovered still.

"Sorry," he shouted with a grimace. "You ok?"

His distraction with Lil's condition provided the other helicopter with an opportunity to attack. When Uri swung back around it was already on him, blasting him down to the earth. It appeared they were holding him there, aiming one of those unusual weapons at him, causing him to flicker slightly like Az had.

Lil looked to where JD had been left a statue. Her sudden transition to the ground unfortunately allowed him to regain control of himself. She watched from beneath Lu as JD removed an earpiece from the fallen driver and retrieved a messenger bag from where Jonah had been seated. After slinging the strap across his bare chest, he secured the earpiece and began giving instructions, signaling with his hands.

Lu grunted, his body tightening above hers. Lil twisted to catch a glimpse of the helicopter's refocused efforts, weapons in the air now trained on Lu.

*Whatever they're using, its destabilizing my form. The others are all afflicted as well. We're going to rematerialize offsite and return. It will just be a moment.*

*I'll have this all cleaned up by the time you get back,* she managed with a smile.

*Your humor is refreshing, but this weapon of theirs does sting a little.*

And with that, he was gone.

The searing pain was manageable, but it was some other unsettling sensation that rendered Lil immobile. There was a humming, as if every atom in her vibrated together at the wrong tune. She wanted to escape herself, but was trapped in a body that was too busy coping to cooperate.

JD approached. The signals he gave to the chopper must have been to stop the assault because suddenly her body no longer felt like it was on fire, her disorientation clearing, albeit slowly.

He looked down at Lil and grinned. "Military *love* The Drakes."

He crouched next to her and stroked her hair. "One is using infrasonic, low frequency high intensity sound. The other is using something akin to microwave and electromagnetic technology. We weren't sure what would be effective, hell, we didn't even know if we could blow these guys up with explosives," he chuckled. "I stressed nonlethal though. The last thing I wanted was for our girl to become a casualty again."

She tried to lift herself onto her side, the hand stroking her hair sliding onto her cheek.

"I have to apologize, but I was given strict instructions to sedate you before getting you in the air or near water."

His palm continued to slide over her mouth as he brought another nasal syringe towards her face. She ungracefully swatted at it, managing to send the thing flying into the grass.

"I *really* wish you hadn't done that."

He gathered her weakened arms in his hand and pushed them down to the ground, putting one knee on top to hold them there.

He swung his bag to the front, explaining, "The darts and the spray are more short term. I would have liked to just work with the spray, giving non-invasive doses as needed, but we no longer have time for this foolishness."

He pulled out a case, opening it as he continued.

"This sub-dermal implant was designed specifically with you in mind, though we have adapted it for other applications. The medication in there is fantastically potent, so a small amount goes a long way, allowing us to fit it in this tiny little guy." He held up the syringe housing the implant he intended to place. "There's a release mechanism in there that can be accessed remotely." He tapped the remote sitting in the case next to the syringe-like devise. "This allows us to dial it in for someone with a special metabolism, like you," he winked. "We want to keep the right amount flowing without going overboard."

Lil tried to remain calm under his weight as he talked her through what he was doing. She reached out with what senses she could, smelling the soil. She inhaled deep, stretching her fingers, digging the tips into the earth. She felt life around her, waiting. The roots of the nearby trees were strong, and responsive to her pull. She'd recovered enough that she could probably put up a good fight but this, this would be better. Though tempted to lift the corner of her lips into a subtle smile, she kept her hope to herself.

"The needle has a bore large enough to place the implant so, it's got a bit of a kick. Nothing you can't handle." He gave her hair another stroke then firmly gripped the back of her arm. The pinch was like a skewer threading through her flesh.

Lil felt a little dizzy, probably from the shock of having had it done. She was able to keep her eyes open, but couldn't control what they were doing. Maybe not shock then.

"You'll feel it settling in right away, that's normal. The fluid surrounding the implant is a loading dose to get you started," he said, fingers down at her wrist, monitoring her pulse. "And not a moment too soon, you were really heating up again."

His expression of confidence changed then, transforming into one of panic.

Lil's energy was rapidly waning, as was her consciousness, but with what little she had, she continued to feed the roots. They grew longer, thicker, coiling relentlessly around his legs.

The pressure on her arms released as JD rolled off, the heat from the second helicopter crash exploding over her like a warm blanket. The rotor blade didn't come for her this time, but with a crack of thunder, Uri was by her side. He hovered over her, lifting her eyelids to assess her pupillary response to a flash of fire over one of his fingers. He checked her pulse, sniffed at her skin. Then another series of loud cracks vibrated the earth and air around her.

Lu crouched over her, Remi and Az at his side, their attention outward, surveying the area.

"She doesn't smell right," Uri reported, barely moving out of the way as Lu took over. His knees were planted on either side of her legs, his hands gripping the ground beside her head, his nose pulling in the air hovering over her skin.

*Where is it?* He said, his frustrated words echoing through her mind.

Lu moved down her torso, then back up, traveling over her arms. His eyes narrowed, targeting the already healed injection site. He let his nose, then his tongue run along the skin covering the unwelcome invasion. Lil clenched her fists and arched her back as his teeth sank in deep enough to remove the implant and a bit of flesh with it. He expelled the offending material into his hand, returning his mouth to her arm as he passed the capsule to Uri. Lu continued to suck out blood and the chemical that had leached into the area, though unable to draw back what had already circulated. He held his tongue in place for a moment or two over the gash he'd created, assisting her already accelerated healing.

Lil felt the thick, fluid fog that had overtaken her beginning to thin, the somnolence clearing enough to feel the heat at her arm, and the body cocooning her. As she'd called the roots before, she wielded her heavy limbs, using all her strength to intertwine her legs with his, sliding her fingers up the back of his neck and into his hair until cool air passed over her once injured arm, and his mouth seamlessly connected with hers.

A moan escaped under her breath with a sigh, thankful for Lu's weight grounding her, for the languid kiss pulling her into consciousness.

*Your sounds…* he whispered, and with his words she heard what wasn't said, his emotion, the fear of her loss, her vulnerability, and with it his own. *I'd like to hear more of them, but there's something to be taken care of first, and it unfortunately requires that we detangle…*

She smiled against his mouth, unwrapping her legs from his and letting them fall to the ground. Like leaded extensions of herself, they hung down as he lifted her up and secured her in Remi's arms.

Lu turned then, and looked down at the man Lil had restrained with roots to the ground, the man whose purpose had become no more than the nutrients his decomposition would provide the earth.

"You put something inside her body," Lu growled. "Hear me now, *Drake*... Death will be no respite."

His roar was deafening. His wings flared out, not with feathers but with dark, leathery skin and talons. His form grew to an incredible size, changing in shape, until a massive beast of scales, wings, claws, and fangs stood before her, a creature she knew like the depths of the ocean.

His head dipping down close to JD's, Lu's voice boomed, vibrating from his body and the air itself.

"You're not a dragon."

Lu raised his front foot, what would have been a hand in his human form. The back of his most prominent talon passed over the trembling man's cheek, twisting so the tip just barely punctured his soft skin. Lu dragged the claw down slowly, skipping JD's neck and passing it down his chest, blood chasing his movement.

Still held firm by the roots of an old maple tree, JD watched in horror as Lu's face descended toward him, mouth widening into a ferocious grin. Teeth sandwiched his bare torso, creating an unpleasant pressure that quickly became unbearable, until he was separated, his pain likely receding with the blood and other fluids leaking from the two halves.

Lu released JD's remains in time to see the life leave his eyes.

"There will come the briefest sense of peace as you slip away from your broken body," he growled. "While you feel yourself lingering in the unknown, waiting for something, on the verge of forgetting this world... know that I remember, and it's me that you are waiting for.

There would be no calm light and sense of peace to greet him as he passed from his torn vessel. There would be no rest for the wicked in death, Lu had made that vow to himself when they first came for her, and the promise was no burden.

Lil rested her eyes a moment as Remi placed her back in Lu's arms, his form having returned to what it once was, though he retained some of the red splatter from his earlier work.

Her eyes opened briefly, a gentle smile blossoming while her eyelids fell again. She inhaled deep, and sighed.

*You mentioned bath,* she said.

*I did.*

# 14.

Lil's reflection hovered on the surface of Lu's eyes, steam rising from the surrounding water as he cradled her neck, fingers working through her hair.

Nan's old claw foot tub in the upstairs bathroom wasn't as accommodating as the pools of their mountain, Iceland's hot springs, a lake, or the ocean... So, Lu sat on the tile floor, his bare arms submerged with her.

They'd all arrived not fifteen minutes prior with the exception of Uri, who'd had about a ten-minute head start to smooth things over. Everyone from Nan's had raced out to greet them when they thundered through the air and between the trees, Remi and Az flanking Lu, Lil still in his arms, him without a stitch of clothing on, all of them battle worn. It almost reminded her of the first time she'd arrived with Lu in the orchard.

How dramatically things had progressed since then.

Lil's gaze had found Gunnar first, his countenance of silent fury and his wide stride keeping pace with Claire, who'd been running, eyes frantic, chunky grey blanket sliding from her arms. Nan had said she wouldn't fall victim to the chunky blanket knitting craze, but a few years back when Birdie Peterson brought over a basket of mist colored yarn the diameter of a garden hose, she'd caved.

"I'll kill him," Claire's shaky voice rang out as she collided with Lil and Lu, wet cheek sliding against skin. "Oh, thank god you're ok. I'll kill him. I'll kill them both, I don't know how, but I will. Those *bastards*."

Through the chaos of smells, Lil had inhaled the grapefruit and Rosemary lingering in Claire's hair, the scent of lavender and cookies on the blanket.

*I should get down and give her a big hug,* Lil had said, still securely held in Lu's arms. *She really needs it, look at her.*

*No.*

"I'm so sorry," Claire said into the space between Lil's shoulder and Lu's chest.

"No, *I'm* so sorry," Lil countered. "I'm sorry you were dragged into this. I never meant for that."

"It's my fault, Lil. If I hadn't brought Brian into things… I still have a key to his place. I'll kill him. There's a bacterium I was working on before the lichen took over, or I could just throw him down the gosh darn stairs."

"You won't get the chance," Lil said, soft and serious.

Claire backed away, and with a half knowing whisper she asked, "You let him go?"

It was one thing to wish a person dead… but the truth of someone whose arms you once welcomed around you, dying, however hurtful their betrayal, is far different than a thought exercise. Whether convenient or tragic, though, facts were what they were, and Claire wouldn't want to be denied the knowledge either way. Besides, she couldn't exactly hide from it. Men had died.

Lil looked into her cousin's eyes, and shook her head.

Claire's expression stilled, and Gunnar slid an arm around her, securing the grey blanket in place. With his other hand, he reached out and touched Lil's face, nodded to Lu, then brought his attention back to Lil. His smile was soft, but heavy with emotion.

"Kid."

"Gunnar," she smiled, placing her hand on his as it slid away to make room for Nan, who'd started her own inspection.

"I thought they weren't going to attack again," Nan huffed. "Come, let's get you all inside. Uri hosed himself off; he's upstairs drawing a bath for you. Todd's at the shop clearing out the last of the patrons, but still, you'd better put away your feathers, boys."

Lil found some lightness in the idea that Az, Remi and Lu were eons Nan's senior, but somehow, she still saw them as *boys*, and they tucked their wings away at her request without question.

"I can walk, really," Lil offered half-heartedly as they all charged toward house.

Lu's chest vibrated against her with an almost inaudible growl.

Lil understood his position, knew she could protest, could assert her independence, show just how quick she was bouncing back to full strength, but why? If she was honest with herself, she still felt a little slow. Besides, the closeness calmed something in both of them, and she sensed the whole of the group felt a little more at ease with her enveloped in his protection, given what they'd just been through. There was another kind of strength, perhaps, in allowing oneself to be carried. The bath though…

"Nan, I can just rinse off in the shower out here, really. The cold is no bother. I don't need to-"

"Oh, I expect the rest of them to rinse off *thoroughly* before tracking all that dirt and blood into the house, but Lil, you're taking a bath. You need heat, you need calm, and I don't know what you have planned for after this, though I'm certain it's not a nap, but you could also use a cup of chamomile with lavender, and I need a glass of port."

And so, Lil agreed to go inside, showering briefly to rinse off the bulk before soaking in the heat Lu sustained.

"I can't hide in the bath all day," she sighed, feeling her head move slowly from side to side in Lu's hands.

A strong glow pulsed around him, and a fire in his eyes just beyond her reflection.

*No, but you can take a few moments.*

*The water might not get cold, but time still passes,* she whispered back through their minds.

His hands her were a comfort but, like Lu, she lamented the tub's inability to accommodate both of them. The shower was adequate for two to step in, though, and had kept Lil from steeping in blood and soil. It was a test of both their abilities not to crack the tiles while they were in there.

Lu lowered his hands, still cradling her head, allowing the warm water to cover her face. She closed her eyes, sinking into the feeling of being surrounded by dark warmth. Relaxing her mind, Lil opened to the river of thoughts she'd been diverting.

She saw the blood and soil, the frightened look on Claire's face. Lil felt the sun falling on her like a blanket in the coffee shop, roots waiting just beyond the earth at her fingertips. Her limp body being carried, the fear in Lu's voice. The waves. Wings. Her necklace, his. His *hands*. She felt Lu's tongue licking the gold off her skin, beads crashing to the floor, the arrow going through her chest, ice water running over bare feet, blood seeping from her body into snow.

*Claire had wanted to meet with Brian,* Lil began. *She wanted to meet him for closure, and told him I'd be coming for support. I thought he'd invited JD for balance… JD and Brian got our drinks at the counter while I sat with Claire, then Brian and Claire took their drinks outside.*

The water around her became hot briefly, but Lu kept slowly moving her head beneath the surface while supporting her; slow and gentle and listening.

*I let him bring me a drink. Why did I do that?*

*You felt comfortable, and you weren't wrong to let yourself trust a few of the creatures you'd bonded with… And as questionable as Brian had always been, it was reasonable in that moment to have felt safe. As you cannot flourish in an existence confined to the mountain, you must allow yourself this vulnerability.*

No breath moved from her mouth, but she released something of a sigh.

Lil looked up through the water, admiring how the rippling movement changed Lu's features, the soft glow over his skin, all around him, shadow and light undulating. The center of each eye a black hole, pulling her always.

Lil raised her head just above the water line, maintaining eye contact as she broke the surface. She was more than half tempted to drag his body into tub with her, but the resulting displacement might leak through the floor before they were able to persuade the liquid into a nearby drain.

She glanced beyond him to the teacup resting beside unlit candles, to the sink, then she looked over to the separate shower, a recent convenience. Nan's arthritis had been bothering her a few years back and she wasn't quiet about the challenges of climbing over the edge of the tub. Lil *mistakenly* made mention of the ailment to Magnus, who wouldn't take no for an answer when offering to have the upstairs bathroom renovated.

The water rippled as a muffled laugh moved through her, swaying further as she sat up, leaning into Lu's mouth for a kiss. He smiled against her, waiting for Lil to share what had brought a bit of light to her thoughts.

"I was thinking about Nan and Magnus, their banter. You should have seen them during the shower-installation-negotiation drama."

His eyebrows arched; lip curled up. *Continue.*

"He threatened to have grab bars put in, claiming she was acting so foolish he questioned if she suffered from *mental decline*. Come, look."

She brought the memory clear into her mind, slowing down to let one of the exchanges play out until a rumble broke through Lu in low laughter.

"She has brought me so much joy," Lil sighed. "Especially inadvertent joy as a result of her carrying on with Todd or Magnus. This morning, I caught myself wondering if I'd be like Nan when I'm elderly: strong and warm, spry and wise. I lost myself for a moment. We were in the kitchen. She had her apron on and, when Magnus called, she wiped her hand and answered the phone, but there was still flour in the creases of her skin. I ate a maple scone and watched her smile so genuinely she almost sparkled. I forgot myself, imagining my body wearing the weather of my years."

Water trickled along her skin, forming drips. His hands moved over her, slow enough not to pull her attention from her thoughts. He soothed, and listened.

"Then I heard Uri's voice, and my reality slipped, blending..."

*It will be like this for a time; having those moments come and go.*

She nodded. *I remember.*

His hands slid down her back, dipping down low before rising back up and releasing a hot flow of water over her shoulders as she leaned into him.

"Magnus was going to Malcom's," she breathed. "He's there now."

"We've not vetted the location for security, but that we're unexpected will be in our favor. A relatively small gathering at his home isn't where he wants to have an altercation. And your abductor claimed he was not working on Malcom's orders. There is a very high likelihood the old man is still optimistic about civil discourse, and desires to get past the unsanctioned incident from earlier today."

Magnus could give them the location; they'd travel directly.

"We need to go," she said softly, with conviction and rising urgency. "Now."

The unlit candles flared to life with Lu's unspoken response, flames licking upward from the wax pillars on a small table beside her, and clustered around the sink. He hauled her out of the tub, holding her in his arms as water sluiced downward, never reaching the floor. Instead, the liquid rose up, hovering around them.

"Remi and Az went to the mountain for fresh clothing. Rem returned and is contacting Magnus as we speak to ascertain an exact location. Az stayed behind to gather something for us to wear." He moved his arms, sliding her body down against his until her feet rested on a towel.

The suspended orbs of water twinkled, floating around their bodies, reflecting the fires still burning throughout the room.

His teeth grazed her ear while she sent silent thanks for the way his scent clung to him after a shower.

"Do you have a preference?" he asked. "For what clothing Az should return with?"

His teeth ran across her jaw, returning to compress the flesh of her lobe.

"Something with an open back."

*

Lil stepped down from the stairs, releasing the bottom of her dress that had been gathered in hand. Black silk flowed over her from neckline to ankle, at which point something interesting happened with the color. The dark hem hung over several silk and silk chiffon layers in varying blue, green and grey shades, like the night sky laid atop the ocean, waves illuminated by some unknown source. A handful of tiny little beads scattered across the expanse like stars. Atop it all, Lil wore her hair braided pinned and, her long neck a pedestal.

Lu, in one of his black suits, stood just behind her, his heat at her exposed back, the two of them pausing a moment before moving toward the sitting room. In that instant before the others looked up and took notice, Lil observed at her family. She saw Nan with half a glass of maroon liquid at her lips. Remi stood beside her, the phone passing between them, presumably with Magnus on the other end. They really shouldn't have been taking too much of the old man's time while he was at Malcom's. Would Magnus's behavior raise suspicion? Perhaps not. Magnus wasn't his only guest, and they were both men perpetually on-call in some capacity.

Claire and Gunnar sat together on the couch, their faces relaxed. The chunky grey blanket wrapped around her remained open on the side where Gunnar sat, his leg touching hers. Az sat by the fire with Uri couched beside him, both in suits of some sort. They were looking at Claire and Gunnar, something akin to paternal pride brightening their faces.

They were blended together, her kind and theirs, her lives, her family. She leaned back into Lu, his arm banding around her, hand snaking up to the side of her neck. Her fondest memories were from a time when there was a fearless sense of community amongst them and their creation.

*There is indeed a sense of home here.*

Gunnar looked up; meeting her eyes with an expression so sweet she could almost hear the song in his heart.

*I feel his love for you, unconditional as Uri, Az or Remi's.*

*Or yours,* she teased.

*That is an animal so different it deserves another name, one there is no word for.*

Claire followed Gunnar's line of sight, her face brightening as she saw her cousin.

"Lil, you're so beautiful. I nearly forgot…" Her face seemed to fall slightly. "I nearly forgot what happened." Gunnar reached for her hand as she continued; her words reflecting the light returning to her face. "When all this is over, I'm getting in that mountain closet of yours. I don't care if I need an oxygen tank or a spacesuit; I know Magnus can get me whatever I need. I want in," she laughed. "I don't want you to think it's just the dress, though," she added. "I mean, it looks like you're wearing the sky on a moonless night, but it's you that's beautiful."

"Do I need to pick my nose?" Lil quipped. "I'll totally do it if you need me to."

Nan rolled her eyes. "If you're going to start that, you'd better have a plan, because I'll not have you *wiping* it on the furniture, as I'm sure Todd does. If there were ever a hidden camera in the shop, heaven help me, I'd probably be shut down."

"He's not *that* bad, Nan…" Lil laughed, coming to Todd's defense. "And Claire, we can *totally* play dress-up when things calm down a bit."

Lil eyed the empty chair by the hearth thinking it would be nice to have a seat for a bit with Lu beneath her, his body molding to hers… The fire roared, wood snapping and the base, flames flashing white as the light seeping from her skin.

*Your train of thought is a bit of a distraction,* his whispered. *A delicious distraction we unfortunately don't have time for.*

Lil flushed, leaning into him further.

*The entertainment isn't over it seems,* he smiled against her cheek, her neck.

*What's that now?*

*Wait for it…*

Todd came through the front door with his bat and a walkie talkie, wearing a beige knit beanie hat, and dark grey long sleeves under a light grey t-shirt that said *Backdoor Man* under a stick drawing of a surfer going through a wave tunnel. His expression was worried and alert, ready, until he saw Lil and his face relaxed.

"You cleared the place out quicker than I expected," Nan said, though it was more of an accusation than an observation. "I have insurance, but if the place burns to the ground because you didn't shut things down properly, Todd, I will not be pleased."

"No need to completely close up shop. It's just Joan and Audrey playing cribbage, and Suit Guy. They can hold it down."

"Hold it down?"

"Yeah, I locked the front, flipped the sign, and gave Joan a walkie talkie so she can communicate with me." He leaned the bat against the corner of the wall and clipped the walkie talkie to his belt loop. "I told her to call if they were leaving, needed a refill they couldn't handle, or if Suit Guy needed anything. They all know the deal and they're cool with it."

Nan was poised to make an argument. Between her predisposition for getting into it with Todd and the recent military assisted abduction attempt on her adopted child, Nan was a little on edge and less inclined to see reason. Before she could speak, though, Todd calmed his voice with the perceptive maturity Lil knew he was capable of, but that was perhaps a surprise to Nan.

"They're regulars, Nan, and we're having a family emergency. I belong here, and they'll be ok. If anything, they feel proud to have been entrusted to protect the shop. I called in Duncan and a couple guys. They're on their way over to help out, and Joan's gonna let them in. If you need me to, I'll head back down when things are more settled here, but, like I said, family emergency. I should be here."

Nan sighed and approached him. Todd leaned back ever so slightly, as if weighing the odds of being struck, by her words or her hand. Nan's eyes though, began to tell a different story. She'd melted, and what water remained had collected there.

"You've grown up overnight," she said, pressing her palms to his cheeks and pulling him in, her arms wrapping around his waist. "I'm not entirely sure I'm ready for it."

She pulled back just enough to read his shirt and, with a sigh, patted his chest.

"Selective maturity, but I don't think I'd alter that a bit," she smiled.

He released a breath and grinned. "You still got some greys left Nan. I wouldn't be doing my job if I stopped making an effort at changing them over."

With the residue of Nan's affection still lighting his face, Todd, scanned the room, fixing his attention on Lil and Lu. "Someone needs to tell me what the hell is going on. Lil went out with Claire to meet that jackass for coffee. It couldn't have been an hour later when I saw Uri flirting across the counter with Audrey, then his eyes went wide and he flew outta there, excuse me, *ran* out so fast I'm not sure I even saw a blur." Turning back to Nan, he said, "You apologized to Audrey and said there was a family emergency, then told me to call in Gunnar and *mind the shop* while you went back to the house. Gunnar blew through not too long after, but I heard nothing. When you finally called," he took a deep breath and sighed. "When you finally called asking me to close up, I heard Claire crying in the background, screaming that they still had Lil. Forty-five minutes ago, you told me Lil made it back, but asked me to wait until everyone left before I come up to the house. It's been crickets since then, Nan. I've been in the dark."

Lil could feel him, his concern, what he'd waited through while maintaining at the shop with the regulars carrying on. She gave Lu's hand a squeeze and walked over, Todd's arms going wide and wrapping around her, his head to her shoulder.

"It was crickets," he whispered. "She said you were fine but I was worried. I knew you'd been taken, and something happened to Claire. I nearly died last time; I thought you would too."

"We met Brian and JD at a coffee shop. Brian and Claire went for a walk. JD put something in my drink and carried me out while the girl at the counter was in the back doing who knows what. I was in a car, and things got creepy. Lu and the guys followed in the air. Things got stormy. Lu lifted the car and put it down in a clearing. There was a showdown. Claire was brought out of another vehicle, used as leverage…"

Lil took a breath and glanced around. She was trying to keep things brief, light, clinical. Emotions were raw for everyone in the room; for those who'd been with her in the field and those who'd waited at home, not knowing. Todd deserved to hear, and those who were still recovering deserved to process what happened without reliving their trauma. A concise rundown would be good for all of them, without sinking into the details. It was during this sliver of time while Lil pondered how to move forward with the conversation, that Claire spoke.

"Brian and I were by the water when he got a text from JD that Lil had fainted." Claire looked off to the side, likely seeing what she remembered as she replayed it. "He said JD had a car on the way and would take her to be seen, that we should follow. We raced to the shop and saw her limp in his arms through the

239

window, then Brian was pushing me into an SUV as JD came out. You looked so peaceful, Lil, but I knew something wasn't right. You *never* get sick. It was like an electric shock of warning ran through me, but then the car lurched forward, and I heard the impact of their arrival," she said, waving toward Uri and Az. "When they took off in the sky. I didn't know if the storm was from them, or from you, but Brian tried to comfort me, saying that JD would take care of you, but then Brian started in on how it was selfish of you to keep your gifts from the world…"

Lil felt a low tremor in her core and up through her feet as a growl emerged from Lu, so low she doubted anyone human would register it as sound.

"Uri brought Claire back to Nan's safely," Lil said, picking up where her cousin left off. "We determined Brian was no longer compatible with life, so he didn't make it. JD brought military via helicopters," she sighed, shaking her head.

"And then you gave 'em hell?" Todd asked, raising his eyebrows at her.

"Hell is Lu's department," she winked, turning to meet heated eyes. "And he is thorough in anything he sets himself to."

"Anything worth doing, as it were," he rumbled.

Lil moved back to Lu, sliding her palm over his outstretched hand as she approached. He pulled her in, sending a flicker through the room as the fire roared and their soft glow pulsed gently to life.

"Were there any survivors?" Todd asked.

"No," Lu rumbled, his hand smoothing over Lil's back, gently pressing her further into his body.

"There's that one I picked up off the street," Remi said, looking to Gunnar.

Gunnar nodded, "Secure in the barn, he's not going anywhere."

*The one whose hands were on you in the vehicle?*

Lil nodded, seeing Az smoothly exit the room not a moment later.

*He's taking care of it,* Lu said, fingers trickling over Lil's neck.

She couldn't help the feeling of peace as she stood there, or the sigh that escaped her. She couldn't help noticing how Lu relaxed as she melted against him. His breath pulled at her as he inhaled, and Lil wondered if she was the only one who heard his body respond.

*You smell like rain, apple blossoms, and a northern forest at night,* he rumbled. *I'd like to sink into you and wrap the rest of you around every part of me like vapor. I'd like to do a great many things that must wait, unfortunately, until after we meet this man.*

"It was made clear that Malcom had called off the operation," Lu said, addressing the room. "But Lil's abductor was uncooperative in following that order. We had plans to meet with Malcom in a week's time, but we're altering our course to depart immediately for his chateau in France. He's hosting a gathering. Magnus is there presently, and plans to receive us. Malcom is, as far as we know, unaware the attempted abduction transpired, and that we intend to visit. Malcom previously professed his desire for civil discourse, and we believe it is still his intention to do so."

I don't like this," Nan worried. "It's too soon."

Lil suspected she didn't like Magnus's involvement, either.

"We'll bring Magnus back with us," Lu said.

Claire managed a smile. "He'll love making an exit like that with you, can you imagine? Though it will be quickly followed by feeling a little scrambled, speaking from experience."

"Don't you beat yourself up, Claire," Uri said, leaning toward her. "It can be tough on first timers, but you'll get acclimated soon enough. Some even start to like the ride." He gave an exaggerated waggle of his eyebrows.

Claire froze, Gunnar gave a hint at a scowl, and Uri laughed, leaning in further and reaching a paw-like hand over Claire to muss Gunnar's hair.

"Calm yourselves, I'll take you both, of course. Hallstatt; I can jet you guys over there tonight for breakfast their time. We can scoot back after, or you can stay at a place I have, then maybe we put some beach time in."

"I think it's best if we stick to our positions for the time being, Uri," Remi advised.

"Yes, but *after.*"

Az returned with the same fluidity he'd left with, settling in near Uri by the fire, as if he'd never gone.

"Are you staying, Uri, while they go to Malcom's?" Gunnar asked.

"Yeah, I'll be on shop detail, and it's a good thing too. Nan still has some kinks to work out with that ma'moul recipe.

"There most certainly aren't any *kinks*... I'm familiarizing myself with the dough."

"Nan," Lil interrupted, or attempted to, anyway.

"And you've got *this* mold, and *that* mold, and the mold you carved from the blasted tree you liked to sit under before the war took it. You've got cookie molds like my cousin Vivienne had shoes, and let me tell you-"

"The molds have done nothing to you, woman, don't blame your learning curve on the them."

Nan took a breath as if she were going to start back up, but Lil managed to edge in before she could get a word out.

"Nan, we need to go."

With no distractions left, Nan's face shifted, raw with something that had touched them all.

"Keep safe," she pleaded, closing the few feet between them. Looked up at Lu, Nan placed a hand on his cheek. "This face," she said with a smile, then pulling her hand away she hugged them both at once. "She's tough. You know more than I what a beautiful force she is, but please, *please* keep her safe."

"I'll keep her safe," he promised, to Nan and to himself.

"And…" Nan whispered.

"And him too."

# 15.

The branches above appeared like black lace against the night sky, the forest silent but for the movement of air from their arrival. Lil had a sense of deja vu that, while not terribly uncommon for one who'd walked the earth so long, elicited a pause. Lu found her eyes then, remaining silent as he waited for some acknowledgement; to what, she wasn't sure.

"Uri notified Magnus of our arrival," Lu began. "He'll meet us imminently at..." He paused, then nodded. "He'll be waiting at the front entrance of the estate."

Smooth steps took them over soft ground, the trees seeming to part for them. Not a twig snagged, not a leaf clung.

Upon emerging into a field, Lil took in the sky first. Unobstructed by limbs, the darkness above revealed itself, bespeckled with stars. The display wasn't as extensive as what the mountain provided, but it was still a beautiful sight.

The fragrant earth hummed with abundance, and there was something about the shape of the landscape... A place changes over time, like any form. Life ages the human body: hair lengthens or is cut short, hips widen, skin loses elasticity.

The trees before her were fuller, a few more here and a few less there, but the face was the same. Turning toward the country road, her breath caught. The house was different, but the stone wall and the unpaved drive were where they had been hundreds of years before.

Lil felt warmth at her side as Lu moved in close, the others processing their own revelations.

*Remi suspected when Magnus gave the location,* Lu said. *And what with the journals…*

Lil sighed. She had lived many lives in many houses, and with many people, though only a few brought her a sense of family, belonging. This place was not one of them, save for her brother, Estienne. There'd been no tragedy then, that much could be said. She'd been able to find joy, pure, simple joy at that, but there was nothing compelling about the life she'd lived there, other than that it was hers, she supposed. There would always be a bit of wonder and mystery to an outsider looking in, and that's what Malcom had found. He had stumbled upon a chapter of her life, followed the details like a map, searching for bits of treasure left behind. She couldn't find him wholly responsible for his interest, though, as she and Lu had called to him from his own history. He wouldn't have known how to read the journal as a map otherwise.

"It would be rude to arrive without a gift," she whispered, her voice like silk through the air.

"Your presence is the gift," Remi offered, an attempt to keep them moving, but Lu stood observant and amused, eyes on her.

She knelt down and slid the fingers of her left hand down into the cold earth, warming it.

"I don't need the seeds or spores," she whispered.

"You are the seed," Remi said with soft veneration, seeing what she meant to do, but perhaps not yet why.

Lil began to channel something like a message, sending it through herself into the soil. She delivered instructions for what the atoms at her fingertips should do, persuading them, infusing the breath of life that they could continue on their own under her guidance. Lil's right hand joined her left, massaging the earth, leaving trails of green shoots sprouting rapidly upward. She held her hands firm as the shoots strengthened, as large, flat leaves began to fan out, increasing in number and height. Thick stems grew forth, producing pink and purple flowers hanging like bells down the powerful stalks.

"He will delight in the gesture," Lu mused.

Lil handed the harvested flowers to Az, and extended her hands toward Remi, not wanting to get her dress too damp as he rinsed away the mud.

Lu scooped Lil up into his arms, releasing a flutter of giggles from her along the way, holding her horizontally with her belly down as if she were a child he assisted in pretending to fly.

"Not an errant drip, Remi, we have an event," he said, with all sorts of seriousness that made Lil's laugh more robust before she was able to slow and catch her breath.

Remi rolled his eyes before a trickle of water formed in the air, collecting above her hands. The dirt beneath her fingernails was effortlessly called out into the flow, which gathered into suspended spheres, instead of splashing to the ground.

*You could have done this, easily,* she said, though it was not a complaint.

*Yes, but I'm holding you. It's best my focus remains on my hands instead of yours, for now. It's a very important job... one slip and-*

Lil let out a yip and a cracking laugh as she suddenly dropped several centimeters, Lu's hands still firmly curled around her. Her body made sharp changes in direction as he moved her to the left, right, back, all while water splashed over her wrists, mist spattering her face, and Remi groaning under his breath.

"Are you having trouble controlling your stream, Rem?" Lu asked, mocking with the grave seriousness someone would offer a loved one with an emerging illness. "She has bathed extensively, I saw to it before we left, do you remember, darling?" he moved his fingers in a wave as he continued to move her about.

Even Az had his lips curled. He tended toward a quiet disposition but wasn't immune to emotion, far from it. Az felt *everything* with the same profound strength he was capable of upon release.

"Yes," Lil smirked. "I recall."

"So, you see, Rem," Lu continued. "We only need her hands to get wet, not so much with all this spray all over her arms and face."

"I think they're clean now," Lil said, her laughter settling. The spheres of water began to coalesce, then faded into steam as Lu heated them, probably thinking it best before Remi retaliated. They didn't have time for a bout of foolishness turning into a mud pit.

Light leaked from the house's openings like breath escaping into frigid air, making visible the unseen. Set into a grey stone archway, the front doors were tall, worn, and open. Two large pots of lavender sat on either side, as it had been when she'd grown up there. Lil may have written about or sketched them once while drawing one of the children or cats sitting in the doorway... The house she approached was not the same structure she'd lived in, the original home had not survived in-tact, but the lavender was there. Perhaps he'd expected her to come, but more likely this was something Malcom did for himself, a secret indulgence that connected him to her past, like the land, and the journals.

Magnus appeared, illuminated in silhouette, framed by the stone doorway and holding a ceramic cup. She'd expected to see him sooner; perhaps casually leaning against the stone wall, politely cursing their tardiness as they started down the driveway. Instead, he emerged when they'd nearly reached the steps.

"He took a call as I excused myself," Magnus began. "He received a text, rather, then stepped outside stating he would just be a moment. There were two other gentlemen at the table with us, a younger son and a nephew. He is a man who rarely takes calls during these things, but then again, so am I, and I've been corresponding with you."

Magnus paused for a deep breath, really taking them in. His eyes caught on the flowers still in Az's hands, and a hint of mischievous delight washed over his face, infusing Lil with a renewed sense of joy.

"If only we had a jar of strawberry jam," he said, before turning back inside for them to follow.

As the lavender had flanked the doorway outside, they found silent security standing vigil within. Lil caught them nodding to Magnus but her eyes were soon busy, darting about the room. A modest chandelier hung from the high ceiling, and the floor had a black and white mosaic design moving outward from the center. She could have sworn it was similar to the one in the old house; the tiles appearing cracked in the same place... Two of the servants' children had been trying to help carry a stone sculpture through and dropped it. Lil had kept the children's involvement with the damage a secret, of course.

The left wall in the entryway was exposed stone and mortar, but refined and finished looking. On the wall to the right hung the portrait of a grey cat with copper eyes; his fur giving the appearance he'd been playing in ashes. He had a distinctive scoop missing from his left ear. Lil remembered when he'd returned to the yard with the injury, bloody and triumphant. The feline in the painting was posed on the mosaic tiles of the original entryway. Lil knew because she'd once sketched him thusly, her drawing having obviously inspired the painting she was staring at.

Pulling her eyes away, she looked straight ahead down a corridor with an intersecting hallway running left to right. On the other side there were trees instead of plaster and stone.

"Is that an atrium?" she asked.

The old house certainly didn't have one of those.

"Yes, but we'd better skip that for now and head towards where I last saw Malcom. News of your arrival will spread quickly, and one does want to maintain height with the upper hand."

"*Cendres?*" Remi whispered.

Lil turned to see him gazing at the painting, his eyes lost to memory. The feral cat had taken an immediate liking to Remi upon their meeting, the two becoming nearly inseparable during his visits. She'd seen it as a sign that her brother's friend had good character, as the only people Cendres tolerated until that point were her and Estienne. When Lil had awoken to who she really was and it became clear they wouldn't return to the house, Remi considered going back for the animal, but ultimately did not. Like many things they left behind, the choices made had to be accepted and left as well, though not necessarily forgotten.

Magnus led them to the left through a study or lounge with deep blue and green hues lined with aged wood and books. A well-dressed man sat on a couch, distracted by his phone, and two women stood by a long window, talking. One wore a long, flowing red gown, the other a short dress of black lace with long sleeves. Both were adorned with gems at their ears, necks, and arms, eyes turned toward Lil, brows arched.

Lil hoped Magus was taking them on the most direct path rather than threading them along a parade route of some kind. She followed with Lu at her side, Rem and Az behind, traveling through two more rooms before entering a hall that seemed to run the length of the house.

Magnus had described the event as a small gathering of fifty to seventy-five people, but with the late hour, numbers had dwindled a bit. Still, quite a few bodies moved around, dressed in luxury. Lil would have blended in had she been mortal, but given the unknown status of her group, late arrival, and that ethereal quality most couldn't quite put their finger on, she and her companions turned heads.

Magnus paused by an open doorway, calling her with his eyes to peer in.

The room had tall, rectangular windows that, upon further examination, were in fact doors. Through the glass and the darkness, she saw a terrace where a few people milled about, the beginning of a garden beyond. Within the room, a warm glow was cast from both artificial light and fire. There were several occupied seating areas to the left, comprised of couches and overstuffed chairs where a male member of the catering staff was removing a dish from an end table. Two men stood by one of the doors leading outside, and off to the right, three men sat at a small table.

Lil felt a rush of recognition pass through her, and Lu's arm snake further around, sliding over the silk barrier.

Malcom. He sat there, turned to the side, speaking with the two others. His hair was silver and cut short; his face smooth and build strong. He wore a white shirt, his suit dark grey, jacket folded over the back of his chair and, from what she could see of his face, he'd aged well. She'd seen pictures of him, of course, before, but never come this close while *knowing*... He hadn't been on the water when they came for her, and she was unsure if he'd been there in Siberia. But he'd been at the auction a year ago, one she'd attended with Magnus, where she'd bought the ring she'd pretended was a wedding band.

One of the men sitting with him had short blonde hair and pale skin, the same frame as Malcom but muted somehow; his son perhaps? He looked to be in his late forties with a face that held a strong resemblance. The other man was built like Gunnar, with dark hair and fair complexion, though there was something bronzed about it. He looked roughly the same age as the blonde, but had features that brought to mind a man she'd seen killed earlier in the day.

*Daniel. Jonah spoke of having another brother,* she whispered, Lu's arm and fingers flexing over her torso. *He made a point of reminding JD that I was not theirs, but meant for the other brother who would be none too pleased at the attachment JD had formed...*

Lil felt Lu's body curl around her further, vibrations from a long, slow growl moving through her as they continued to observe what was happening in the room.

Malcom's two companions appeared relaxed but leaned in just a little as he spoke. It occurred to her as she watched, that Malcom looked the sort of man who would have a cigar in his hand. Though Malcom wouldn't, she supposed, as it would decrease his longevity. And he certainly wouldn't be the type to hold one for the sake of posturing, so no cigar was to be seen, not in his hand nor anyone else's there. She wondered about his allowing for the intake of alcohol, noting the drink in front of him. To taste slowly, perhaps, while remaining in control. She watched as his posture changed, seeing that he maintained his position but no longer paid attention to the man speaking to him. She sensed he was about to turn.

Lu followed Lil's lead, and moved out of view, the others as well, before Malcom caught sight of them. *Not quite yet*, she thought.

A young woman in a black uniform approached from down the hall. She held a tray that seemed too large for the single glass it supported. She had blonde hair neatly twirled into a low bun, and quite the eye-catching silver pendant. The piece was long and sleek with a curved bottom that almost seemed separate from the top three quarters. The whole pendant was about fourteen centimeters in length and two centimeters wide; rather large to be worn by someone in service wearing a uniform, but there was minimalism in its design. The earrings she wore were interesting as well; long thin cylinders of silver. It added a modern elegance, she supposed, something the class of clientele would find appropriate.

The blonde woman's eyes went wide upon seeing Lil, flicking up and down quickly, pausing at Lil's chest, darting to Lu, then behind them and back but not meeting Lil's gaze. She'd almost thought there was a flair of recognition when the young woman registered her presence, but it was far more likely that she was caught by something else. Lil might not have her wings out, or skin glowing bright, but something wafted from her like the smell of a storm coming, something humming in the air that creatures could sense but not identify...

"Pardon me," Magnus began, intercepting the young woman with his authentic charm. "Malcom Drake asked that these be brought over to where he's seated. We had them brought for him especially." He carefully gathered the foxglove as it was passed to him, and offered it to the woman.

"Of course," she nodded politely, allowing Magnus to rest the flowers on her tray. "I'm with catering; I'll just have someone from the house help me find a vase." She turned to retreat but Lil placed a hand gently on her arm.

"That won't be necessary. Just bring them as they are, if you please. He'd prefer it that way."

To her credit, the woman didn't bat an eye at the request; though Lil did sense impromptu floral arrangements were hardly the strangest demand that could have come the server's way in crowds like these.

"Of course," she smiled politely. "I'm bringing a drink to one of the gentlemen at his table now."

Lu stood with Lil just inside the doorway. Magnus, beside them, watched discretely as the server approached Malcom. She placed the drink down in front of the fair-haired man, then gathered the length of flowers in her right, tucked the tray under her left arm, and laid the foxglove down on the table. Malcom became still as she explained, perhaps using the moment to gather himself. The woman from catering stood waiting, but instead of responding to her, he slowly turned his head toward the doorway. Piercing blue eyes connected with Lil's, blue, but with striking gold lining his pupil, bursting out like sun into a clear sky. His face went through a series of subtle expressive changes: surprise, relief, interest.

The woman with the tray maintained polite awkwardness.

Without request, Lil and Lu moved forward toward the table, not waiting for words. It's what they came for.

Magnus followed the prompt and moved along with them, Remi and Az fanning out, with Az staying closer to the doorway. Lil felt calm, powerful, and ready. She had arrived, and with Lu not in front or behind, but beside her. She knew from her fingers to her core that she could pause the beating hearts of everyone in the room and, while it was hardly her primary concern, the dress she wore felt amazing.

A fire burned deadly calm within Lu as they crossed the room, heating Lil's skin with his proximity, warming her blood from the inside.

*Should I make a comment about being inside you?*

A flush rose to her cheeks, but she didn't reply.

His palm scorched as he placed it against her back. *Say the word and I will raze this structure to the ground along with its inhabitants in a torrent of fire while seated inside you.*

Malcom stood as she neared, almost close enough to reach out and touch, enough for a woodsy scent to reach her.

"Daniel, Karl, if you'll excuse me."

He said it as though he were pardoning himself for leaving, but made no move to do so. The fair-haired man cocked his head a bit from his seat as the unexpected realization set in, that it was he and the other gentlemen that Malcom expected to depart. The dark-haired man rose, looking directly at her. His eyes were the same striking blue as Malcom's, gold all around the center almost shimmering, though with Daniel it pooled a bit on the right side, a wedge of sky obstructed altogether by sun. The asymmetry was not something she would identify as a flaw.

He looked at her with curiosity and something almost intimate, as if he knew her. The feeling was one sided, though, and he would be disappointed if his expectations aligned with those voiced by his brothers.

The blonde remained seated, swirling his drink as he looked up at her, evaluating for himself the value of the insult he'd been subjected to. First, his gaze met hers, face relaxing as though taking in a pleasant smell. Then, his expression took a predatory shift. Lil saw the spark of delight in finding something worth pursuing, savoring. He took a sip from his drink, eyes roaming downward, then there was another change. It occurred at just about the bust line, where her stone rested. He coughed and stood immediately, face frozen by blood run cold.

"Of course," he managed to say. "We'll just head out back for a bit of fresh air."

"Fresh air and nothing more," Malcom said flatly, with subtext she was thankful for. His son and nephew were aware of her identity, operations run to *acquire* her, the unplanned nature of her visit. It was plausible they would be motivated to take some type of action had they not been directed otherwise.

"Nothing more," The blonde repeated, then both the men nodded to her, eyed Lu, and made their way through one of the large glass doors. That same woodsy scent floated toward her as they passed by, noticeable, but not cologne. Lil couldn't help but wonder if it was something familial, or if they'd been somewhere together beforehand.

Another uniformed woman came in as they left. She had dark hair in a short braid, the same style of earrings and necklace as the server who'd handled the flowers. *They're part of the uniform*, Lil thought. It made sense given the atmosphere. As the staff member passed into the hall, Lil looked around the room and through distant doorways, seeing another woman with the same jewelry, and a man… he didn't have the necklace or earrings, nothing on his fingers, but his silver belt buckle was clearly custom made. It was long in a similar way to the necklace on the women, but horizontal, and with bilateral rounded ends that seemed almost separate from the main piece, hinting there might be a hidden, functional aspect to the adornment. Lil almost smirked imagining the server coming to a client's rescue by pulling a wine key from the intricately crafted piece.

"Would you like a drink?" Malcom asked. He spoke slow and strong, his voice textured with age.

In her periphery, Lil saw the blonde server who'd been standing mute suddenly brought to life, looking back and forth between Malcom and his new guests, eyes downcast when they fell on Lil.

"No, thank you. I had a very strong cup of tea not too long ago."

Lu, Remi, and Az went deadly still where they stood. Magnus continued on, though, tending to what Lil suspected was black tea with cognac. He made a face as he sipped; it had cooled.

Malcom turned to the woman with the tray she still clutched in front of her chest. "I won't be having anything either, if you could go see to the other guests, please. Thank you, Miss."

He brought his attention back to Lil, though she supposed he'd never really lost focus on her.

"Lily, dear, this is Malcom Drake," Magnus began with casual formality. "Malcom, this is Lil."

"Thank you, Magnus," Malcom replied, eyes never leaving her. "I was made aware, just before your arrival, of the tea you drank earlier today... and the events that followed. I'm relieved to see you well, and that you appear to have an interest in exchanging words." His voice was smooth and cautious, as one might be when approaching a feral animal. She appreciated that it required him, on some level, to acknowledge her position of power, but still, there was something off-putting.

"Perhaps if we took a seat," Magnus suggested, raising his brows, not waiting as he moved toward an empty chair by Malcom.

*Az and Remi will stay where they are, though I wouldn't mind having one outside.*

Lil nodded, and Az crossed the room, exiting through the glass doors a moment later. She sat down facing Magnus and Malcom. Lu pulled a seat so close to her, their thighs touched, his arm around her back, fingers running gently over her shoulder.

"You're as sublime as I remember," Malcom sighed, then, with the voice of a leader, he said, "I had explicitly called for the operation to be terminated. Had there been survivors, they would have been swiftly and severely disciplined. I'd thought adherence to orders would have been engrained... foolish boys. I've only seen images of the aftermath, though Daniel..." His fingers explored the flowers on the table, a pleasant smile on his face. "I was unable to obtain the remains of the two men I first sent to speak with you, but I was able to view the second grouping." A knowing smile teased at his mouth, a chuckle escaping. "I had the vehicle transported in cold storage as it was, so decomposition wouldn't set in. Tell me, which ones were yours?"

He was asking which bodies she was responsible for.

Lu's distaste rumbled like low rolling thunder.

Lil reached her hand to his neck, fingers delicately pulling along his hairline. She squeezed and his eyes rolled back, lids easing down slightly, sinking into her touch.

Malcom was too blinded by her to see Lu as he was; larger than his body, than the room. He could not be contained, only remaining in what form suited him.

"I rather dislike being hunted, Malcom, whether for kill or capture," she said, as a matter of fact. "I've come to ask, as politely as I am able to manage with one who has tried to ensnare me like *a creature*... I'm requesting that you and your people discontinue your efforts. I have enough to worry about with those who solely seek to end my life, and it was by your people's hand I lost it the last time. We're here with you now to find a peaceful end to your pursuit."

Magnus watched the exchange with focused curiosity, only occasionally glancing down at his drink as if making a tough decision.

Lu extended his hand forward, motioning with his fingers.

Magnus pulled his brows together in question.

258

"The cup, old friend."

Magnus slid his cup toward Lu, who passed it back with steam wafting upward.

Malcom appeared quite excited by the feat, his eyes still drifting back to Lil as he asked, "Do they die as well? It's not something we've found ourselves concerned with, having focused on you, as the female."

The way he spoke, like Jonah had in the car, like Brian of his whales, as though they were subjects in *his* study… the audacity. Magnus blew on his tea, Lu's hand blazing with heat on her back. She wondered if Malcom was a man who could be reasoned with, or if he was like Jonah and Brian in that capacity as well.

"I don't know what you are," Malcom continued. "I think your kind have been here since the beginning. I think people thought you to be angels, and perhaps the foundations of many myths have you to thank for their origin. I'm not a monster," he sighed. "I am, however, human, I'm powerful, as far as my species is capable, and I'm interested."

"Interested enough to ambush a child at sea and kill her parents, to stalk me in the woods, shoot at my family."

Thunder rolled in earnest outside, but no rain fell. Lil was escalating, but in control.

*No complaints, Ilati. Do you think he needs to take a pause?*

Lil reached out and into Malcom until his tongue was like stone, his arms granite, and her skin luminous.

*I do love the way you glow when you're worked up, Lu said,* his skimming over the skirt of her dress and- *Pockets? I approve.* She felt his heat on her thigh as he slid between the folds of silk and rested there.

She released Malcom, who took in a generous breath, and exhaled.

"I don't take pleasure in tormenting you," he professed with a hint of sweat on his brow. "Nor do I enjoy losing men. I was forceful and unrelenting, and in a sense, I was not successful, but here you are."

"I am," she said. "Though I'm not clear on what it is you're after aside from just that. When I was immobilized earlier, Jonah had... He mentioned body fluid, a desire for lengthening mortal life, of breeding, and your nephew, Daniel..."

"It must have all sounded very coarse at the time, but I admit, I had hoped your blood might reveal something. It is my belief that myth takes inspiration from life. Ambrosia, the fountain of youth, holy communion, vampirism; it is my hope that these elements have some truth to them. Documentation of the Nephilim was canonized, for goodness' sake."

"Those children are mortal but with longevity greater than humans, though that lifespan returns to one somewhat typical as generations pass. There have been many children seeded by my kind, but always born from the womb of yours. It's possible that I could, and it was once asked of me..." She trailed off.

"Tell me, Malcom," Lu asked. "What do you know of the self-professed *Guardians* of Eden? We know them as the *Condemned*, but people don't always see themselves for what they are."

"Self-professed indeed... Yes, we infiltrated their organization some time ago and came to acquire a great deal of material, copies of course. The Guardians have been following you from the beginning, it seems, or so they claim, and they don't appear to be as interested in your entourage. They think it their righteous duty to put a stop to your wickedness, Lil, believing that you are a demon who can become a serpent, who steals children and corrupts men." His analytical eyes searched hers, perhaps for a reaction, for truth. "The crux of their beliefs is that you, my dear, were Adam's first wife, and responsible for human kind's banishment from Eden."

Lil took a moment to hold his gaze while dimming the lights in the room. She plucked one foxglove bell from its stem, floating it low over the table toward Malcom. He rested his hand beneath it, watching as the flower gracefully settle down against his palm. Then Lil grabbed ahold of his wrist, startling him from his enchantment. She pressed her palm against his with unforgiving strength, again calling his eyes to hers. She channeled a flicker of power that, to him, would have felt like a deluge. The life between their hands transformed, thick roots descending as a green sprout spiraled through her fingers. He tried to pull back, but she was unabating, maintaining her hold on his hand and his eyes.

"I am the breath of life, Malcom," she said with the power of oceans, yet smooth as glass, her voice calm and terrifying. "I am the index finger of god."

"Forgive me, I…"

"Did the material you found also say that I was not a participant in a marriage to the organism I created, as I was paired from my creation with another, the first of our kind and the blueprint for love as you understand it? Did these documents you discovered explain that it was my recommendation the human be made with an equal, or that it was *I* who fashioned him from blood and earth?"

Magnus casually grasped his mug and brought it down from where it hovered several centimeters over the table, reaching for Malcom's glass and doing the same. Lu, Remi standing by, and Az still outside; they didn't bat an eye. Malcom's face went lax, however, eyes drifting from Lil's to the rising foxglove bells before him.

"The advice was ignored and I was not asked, only *told* to breed with the creature until it expired. Only then would I have been allowed to return to my purpose of creating and seeding new worlds with life. When I refused this blow, I was then further insulted by having my immortality muted. My *entourage*, as you call them, are those who refused to participate in the injustice."

Lil couldn't imagine what her existence would have been like without them; not just Lu, but Az, Uri and Remi. What would life be like for Lu without the others? He would be alone during the moments when her body fell, when he waited for her soul to be reborn.

Flowers drifted gently down as Lil released a calming breath, Lu's hand on her neck, her shoulder, his thumb pressing in.

*I'm so saturated in thankfulness for you, it both lifts and weighs my heart down,* she sighed. *What would it have been like without Uri, Az, and Remi?*

*We have enough past to let go of, without reliving moments that never were. Leave that diversion to the humans who seem to enjoy it so. Stay here, with me, in the place of what is, and things yet to come.*

*Sound advice,* she cooed, leaning into his hand. *What are your thoughts on this encounter so far?*

*Aside from your magnificence, and astounding self-control...*

*He's terrified,* she said.

*As he should be, though he is clearly enamored. I suppose I shouldn't burn anything to the ground just yet.*

*Your proposal was persuasive...*

Malcom looked to Lu as if seeing him for the first time, his eyes open to what had been lurking before him...

"He is the one you were paired with, in the beginning?" Malcom asked.

Lil felt Lu flex a little for his own amusement, casting an unaffected gaze back at their host who took a sharp breath in. He would have, in that brief moment, felt the universe closing in on him, pressing with its vastness.

"Malcom," Magnus began. "Forgive me for not introducing the others, this is Lu. By the doorway is Remi, and Az has gone outside. You'll know their names now, should the need to address them arise."

"*Lucifer?*" Malcom tentatively asked, questioning the obvious.

Lu left one hand on Lil, and with the other he gave a flourish, silently confirming his identity.

"By name... or reputation?"

He was asking if Lu was the keeper of the damned.

"I prefer not to talk shop in mixed company."

Mixed being their kind and Malcom's. Human. Though, they made exceptions.

263

Magnus was content to witness the mystery unfold, he'd once said. Drawn to secrets, to puzzles, to his treasures. The man was a vault, and he delighted in keeping what was his. Lil shared Lu's hope that Malcom had similar values, that he would be satisfied with the power of knowing, of being a part of the most elite inner circle in present existence.

Malcom looked to Magnus, who seemed to be enjoying himself immensely, then back to Lil. She imagined he'd trained himself well not to reveal with his face what he was feeling, but he couldn't hide his reverence.

"You really are an angel," he breathed.

"That word comes with baggage," Magnus advised, "and is a term they don't use for themselves; perhaps they prefer that we don't either."

"It is our hope that you can understand…" Lil said. "We cannot get involved here. Whatever interest you had in using me for science, or for some personal experiment, for weaponization; we cannot get involved that way."

"You say you cannot get involved here, but you *are* here, walking amongst us with the power of a star running through your veins… the definition of limitless. I'm having a hard time, it's just… your disinterest in collaborating, it's confounding.

Magnus looked down at his mug, and then smiled up at Lil with what she imagined the love of a father or a grandfather should be, how Nan often looked at her, how she felt when they held each other. It was warm, and honest.

Magnus turned to their host, and said, "You cannot capture the sun, Malcom, only what it gives."

Malcom appeared contemplative. He had, no doubt, a multitude of plans for her collaboration, and flexibility can be a challenge for some. Could he adapt, or would Lu have his ashes?

"You are asking me to retire my enterprise in exchange for your story. And if I want to be a part of the story?"

"You're already a part of the story."

"Indeed, but I'm not ready for the story to end."

"Reputation," Lu said, just the one word as he stared at Malcom.

"Reputation?"

"My name," Lu said, pausing to let his voice resonate, for the connection to be made and the discomfort to linger. "The man who disobeyed your orders, Malcom, he and I have only just met, but have a very long time to become familiar, because this is not where it ends for your kind. Your bodies rot upon expiration, but the soul passes… though it must go through me first." He'd had one of Lil's hands in his and brought it his face, rubbing his chin over her palm, then resting it in his lap while he stroked her arm. Lu tilted his head toward Malcom, raised an eyebrow, and with his dark charm added, "Not everyone makes it."

It was a good thing Malcom hadn't been eating or drinking, as he surely would have aspirated. It was, perhaps, only by a lifetime spent testing his limits that his body remembered to breathe.

*Subtle,* she teased.

"It's not a warning I give lightly or often… perhaps ever."

Lil gave a little shake of her head in agreement. They'd not even detailed that bit for Nan or Magnus. "Anyone you would have told didn't need to know."

"You have our story," Lu said. "And you have a choice."

Malcom's upper arms expanded, pressing against the fabric of his shirt as he flexed his biceps and hands. Eternity was a chain he couldn't break, couldn't negotiate. Lil felt the struggle wafting off of him, could almost taste the bitterness on her tongue, his conflict necessary for transformation to occur. Malcom was a means to an end man, and he'd just learned there was a different end. With the loss of his old endeavors, as elaborate as they were and as determined as he had been, a new door had opened, and he was not blind to opportunity.

The pith on Lil's tongue faded as the subtle scent of chocolate took over, and the bitterness sweetened. There was a sense of the man there too, something woody, but he wasn't close enough for Lil to get a read on it.

Their host took a breath, looked to Magnus, smiled and gave a subtle shake of his head. He took a long pull from the remaining amber liquid in his glass, and nodded. "You make a compelling argument."

"Not much room for negotiation given that last bit, is there?" Magnus commented.

"It's a position I don't often find myself in."

"Nor I, and I don't envy you."

Malcom looked at Magnus, then to Lu, and Lil. He drank the rest of what his cup held, and announced, "I agree to your terms."

He'd want more, they usually did, but this was a start; a good start. Malcom would need to restructure things on his end. Lil was hopeful that his other employees, his family, weren't like JD, and Jonah. She hoped they followed orders, but would be ready if they didn't.

"You'll have to forgive me," Malcom continued. "I've not yet thanked you for your assistance up north. The actions of my nephews today are all the more offensive given how indebted I am."

"What of the second helicopter?" Lu asked rather directly, wasting no time in getting to the point. She knew he and the others had gone to investigate Michael's work earlier that morning, but was not yet informed of the outcome...

Malcom took a moment, took a breath. "I've discussed what transpired with Magnus, as much as I can account for. There was an *unexplained* explosion, that part you're familiar with... The station was a complete loss, and for that we are thankful. Magnus can fill you in on what you acquired, but of the helicopter... It landed, the crew departed, and they made an unknown amount of contact before all but one of them were intercepted and quarantined. They have since died. It is not contained."

"It wasn't meant to be," Lu said, and though it wasn't news to Lil or Magnus, the statement struck Malcom, shifting in his relaxed façade.

*Our investigation revealed things are as we suspected, widespread and irreversible...*

"The earth has a way of maintaining balance," Lu continued, "but from time to time it needs a little help. We've not served her well in this capacity, as a result of the *creative differences* Lil touched on earlier."

"You've not met with him yet?" Magnus whispered, voice heavy and directed toward Lil.

She gave a subtle shake of her head, Malcom observing the exchange, eyes sharp.

"We'd planned on making contact this afternoon," Lu said, "But the day took an unexpected turn…" The undercurrents of undissolved fury didn't go unnoticed by Malcom who stilled, wary of stirring Lu further. Magnus's brows rose a bit as the growing flames in the fireplace whirled, sending out sparks.

Lil crept her fingers up into Lu's dark hair, spreading them out and grasping firm at the roots, massaging with every pull, pressing the heel of her palm into his neck.

*You don't play fair,* he growled, eyes closing.

*Shall I stop then?*

*No.*

She felt his hand sliding against the silk of her dress, back into the pocket he'd discovered earlier.

*Don't you dare burn a hole in this dress.*

Then his skin was against hers, fingertips resting on her thigh, a soft glow blushing with the flush of her cheeks.

*You started it…*

Magnus cleared his throat. "Though I would not have known you otherwise, would not have been born for that matter, I believe what Michael did in the garden was reprehensible, and please forgive me, Lily dear, for using his name. It appears, Malcom, that a former colleague of our friends here has initiated another cleansing of the earth, as it were." He paused a moment to give Malcom a chance to ask questions, but their host only nodded for Magnus to continue.. "The trouble we've been managing with the arctic, the Southeast Asian outbreak, and who knows what else... Several airports in the latter region are closed to all flights," Magnus continued, turning to Lu and Lil. "I'm not sure what your investigation turned up after you left Iceland this morning, but hospitals in the regions affected most are overwhelmed; running out of beds, out of *oxygen*, medical workers are dying, mass graves... The United States, Canada and the UK have restricted incoming flights, and are working out quarantine protocols. Germany and France will have something in place imminently, from what I hear."

"It will afford some time," Lu said. "A drop in a very large bucket, old friend."

"Is there anything..." Magnus trailed off, the question obvious, perhaps the answer as well.

"Is there anything you can do?" Lu asked, giving a smooth, slight shake of the head. "If by some strange miracle the human race came together to eradicate these waves of pestilence, Michael would likely just accelerate the melting of polar ice. We've not yet determined if the recent spike in volcanic activity is a result of influence, but it's likely. A change is coming, and it's coming fast, that the few who survive might adapt and later thrive. Be thankful for every breath, be thankful for tonight, and enjoy yourselves. We'll speak with Michael afterwards, but before we do, Magnus... We may have made assurances that you'd be returning home with us. The choice is yours, but I know which option I'd prefer. She was quite worried when we left."

There was no need to explain who *she* was.

"Yes, justifiably so. I wouldn't want to upset her further."

To their credit, neither Malcom nor Magnus complained about the impending apocalyptic outcome. They didn't protest or attempt negotiations. They didn't question further why such a thing would be necessary. Their concern was only for what could be done moving forward. Magnus would likely do fairly well; his family history having protected him from illness thus far, and he certainly had resources. Malcom, Lil had a feeling he would survive what was coming, but Nan… Claire, Gunnar, *Todd*... An electric pull formed around her heart at the thought of their vulnerability.

*Let's speak to Michael before we let our minds wander too far,* Lu said.

"If I might humbly ask another favor," Malcom began.

"Humility, Malcom?" Magnus quipped. "Never too old to try new things I suppose. Perhaps I'll try coconut water."

Lil didn't think she'd ever eat or drink anything from Malcom's table, but the banter between the two men felt familiar; comfortable.

"Correspondence. I've rather enjoyed the journey, and I know it's a favor I don't deserve, but I'd like to continue on, for whatever is left of what we have here. Seeking you out was as thrilling as it was frustrating. Finding you in present day was exhilarating, then there was finding you in *time*. The pursuit of your past was compelling, and still is. What you've described, the proverbial storm coming, looks to challenge the already short lives we have here, and I'd like to maintain contact for what's left of the ride, so to speak. I have questions, and they may seem trivial, but so many things in life are, and yet they have such an impact.

Your name was Lil in Siberia, I've seen it so elsewhere, but it was Manon in this place. Why?"

"Stubborn woman," Lu huffed under his breath.

"Apparently the woman who birthed me couldn't be swayed. Truthfully, the name never felt my own, nor did the woman's affection. My brother, though, that love was true. He understood me, encouraged my independence and my antics, and I adored his indulgence…"

She noticed Malcom's eyes drifting down to the flowers, a mischievous smirk flirting at the corners of his mouth. He'd read about her antics.

"You gave a copy of the journal to Magnus…" She started. "Are you in possession of the others? I know I wrote more than one, and I know better than most how things can change their form with the passage of time." Decomposition, decay, the house that once stood, the brother who'd once lived, a dress she'd once worn, parents… "I thought you might have something else."

"Would you like them returned to you?" He offered. It was an honest question, and she believed he would do so if she asked it of him, but those bits of paper meant more to him now than they did to her. They had become her past, and his discovery.

"No, but I would like to borrow copies. I can pass them on to Magnus when I'm done," she smiled.

Malcom nodded. "I have copies here. The originals are in another location, at my primary residence. The copies I'll send home with you tonight, if you'd like, but first, I would enjoy taking you to a special room, one I think you'll connect with."

If he'd somehow gone back in time and had Cendres stuffed…

# 16.

Lil turned a corner, and the hallway opened on one side. She'd caught a glimpse upon first entering the house, through a corridor segmented by pillars, had seen the abundant greenery on the other side. As they neared their destination Lil heard the trickling of water, smelled mint and citrus.

A narrow flower bed thick with herbs lined the wall as they entered the atrium. Moss grew between the stones underfoot as they passed through, giving way to mosaic tilework. Lil had the feeling she'd left the chateau and entered the lush courtyard garden of a Moroccan riad. Had Malcom found her former life there as well?

Light from the arches and latticed railing wrapping around the second floor lit the tops of the trees that grazed them, branches full, heavy with ripe oranges. Large ceramic pots of herbs had been thoughtfully placed, filled with rosemary, basil, mint, thyme, and lemon balm. A woman sat on the edge of a small wading pool, her legs dangling in, shoes set beside her where a man positioned his legs the other way, remaining dry. Her feet swirled, the movement eliciting a lovely sound, but trickling water continued elsewhere, calling to Lil.

She found water bubbling from the mouth of a sculpted fish, the centerpiece of the fountain from her previous life there, the original, intact and nestled in the heart of the home as if the new structure had been built around it.

Lil approached, smoothing her palm over its cool, wet curves. A question hung there, answered when she stood tall, leaned in, and dipped her fingers into the cavern of the fish's mouth. It was empty. Hundreds of years ago she'd hidden a pearl… and written about it in her journal.

Slowly she turned her head and looked over her shoulder where Lu stood close, an easy, nostalgic smile lighting the depths of his beautiful face. Beyond him stood Malcom, flanked by Remi and Magnus, curiosity sparkling in his eyes. She felt Az there with them off to the side, somewhere through the greenery. Malcom had been watching her, as they all had, though she suspected only he and Magnus knew what she'd sought in the fish's mouth.

*The pearl,* Lu whispered, having read the journal by the fire in Iceland. Had Remi recognized the fountain from his visits?

*It's not here, though…*

Her attention flashed back to Malcom who casually brought his arms in front of him, and slowly removed a cufflink from his shirt. He rolled up his sleeve to reveal a watch on his left wrist that could have been out of Magnus's collection, though no doubt it had some custom element that would render one unable to find a duplicate. Malcom transferred the cufflink to his right hand, removing the one on that side as well, transferring the set into his pocket. This was a performance, she realized.

Surely he wasn't trying to flaunt his forearms... He was in great shape, something that wouldn't have escaped Nan's observation were she to have been present and not too repulsed by the memory of his attack on her home.

Malcom began rolling up his right sleeve slowly as he had the left, revealing a thin leather bracelet and the tip of a scaled tattoo like what she'd seen on JD. As his wrist tilted, Lil saw a flash of light reflecting off something white there on the cord... a pearl.

A quick rush of breath entered her, heat flaring against her body as Lu moved in close. He'd seen it too. Lil's eyes flicked up from the pearl to see Malcom staring right at her, delighted.

"You found it," she whispered.

"Yes, I did. And what a marvelous trail of breadcrumbs you left... What a treasure I found."

Malcom reached up and pulled an orange from a branch above him. He peeled the fruit's skin off in a coil and brought it to his nose.

"I love this smell."

Setting the peel down on the ledge of the nearest ceramic pot, he separated the orange in two and extended his hand, offering half. Fresh fruit was usually safe, and it had just been plucked from its tree... Lil put her palm out, holding the fruit there for Lu. It wasn't until he sampled a segment and nodded that she tasted one herself.

Magnus appeared deep in conversation with Remi, eating an orange of his own. Az remained unseen.

# A Story in Song

*Do you think Magnus will gut him for that pearl, or just fantasize about it,* Lu asked.

*He has my artwork everywhere he sleeps; Magnus doesn't need pearls from my past. Besides, I don't think the gut would be his style... How* would *he end someone?*

*They do have weapons training at the school... He seems like a fencing or bo staff man, if he were to use a tool in hand.*

*Sniper. He's so patient. I bet he'd watch a man drink a cup of coffee and read the paper through his scope, politely waiting until the target finished before taking his shot.*

Lil found herself able to inhale a truer sense of Malcom as she stood beside him, what remained beneath the scent of orange. He smelled like whiskey, leather, and Grampa Pat's sweater.

"How did you find this place?" She asked.

"The same way I found you."

*And how was that exactly? Was it through the Condemned again, or coincidence? They'd met briefly at the auction a year prior, Magnus later sharing he'd been captivated with Lil's painting.*

Malcom had the same look in his eyes that Magnus got when he had a tidbit dangling there. The old man delighted in having the upper hand when it came to information, secrets, depth.

"We were fairly certain you'd used the Condemned to find her in Siberia," Lu said. "But we'd structured her childhood for avoiding detection. Your attack on her at sea was the first time she's come near to death at such a young age in quite some time."

Malcom nearly grimaced at the word attack.

"Chance," he began. "I was meeting a friend to do some sailing, and discovered a little girl sitting on the dock, enjoying a book while her parents loaded supplies aboard their vessel. She appeared to be reading music, and I noticed her bare feet kicking the water in time with what she must have been hearing as she read. The height of the dock should have left the water out of reach," he said, meeting her eyes, "but it rose up to meet you. I wondered if you'd even noticed, but didn't dare interrupt, especially once I saw the stone pendant resting above your lap at the end of a long necklace. The story of that stone, of a woman who swam with dragons, has been told in my family for centuries."

Lil's hand went to her chest, smoothing over the carved images like braille, as Malcom continued.

"I wasn't ready when I saw you. I thought I'd lost my chance, but then I dreamed of you, as I had before Siberia. I saw where you'd be clear enough to instruct others. After the failed attempt to retrieve you at sea, the dreams changed. I saw you in the past, the long past, I saw you here at the chateau, the way it once was. I learned as much as I could about the area, put feelers out at auctions and estate sales, private collections. Eventually I acquired the journals, which led me to the land here, and then the dreams changed again. I saw you swimming in the present, in the ocean. I watched you create works of art over the years, and then a business associate showed me a painting... and I saw the artist buying a ring."

"*You* dreamed of her?" Lu asked.

"Daniel as well, though not of the present until a week or so ago. It really ramped up around the time we attempted contact."

They'd known the Condemned to have some among them with visions of her, and then there was Hamish...

One of the catering staff approached, the dark-haired woman who Lil had seen earlier. Her job description likely included either fading into the background or appearing fully present, personality adapting to the needs of those she worked for, ever accommodating. Their server had become the latter, at the moment.

Lil looked beyond her, seeing through the greenery and the courtyard's open arches to where several other members of the catering staff milled about in the surrounding hall, dissolving into the shadows. None of the others had trays, though, and there were very few guests in the area aside from her companions and the couple at the wading pool conversing with a male server.

"I brought your drink, sir," the woman smiled brightly as she approached Malcom. "And a strong tea for the lady."

A strong tea... Lil's senses stood at attention like the hair on her arms. Lu felt bigger beside her, his arm tensing around her waist.

"I didn't order another drink, and when asked, the lady declined as well." Malcom spoke with kindness, but was firm in letting the woman know there'd been an error. "A harmless mistake," he added as a dismissal.

Strong tea; those had been Lil's exact words.

"Oh, Deirdre must have misheard," the woman offered. "It's no trouble to take them back, but surely you don't want to waste good whiskey."

To the server Malcom would have appeared, in that long moment, to be deciding whether he was irritated or amused. While Magnus wore his thoughts openly, Malcom was more trained in wearing a mask, but Lil could see they were both working at the same thing... working out a puzzle. They all were, though her kind could boast a faster pace.

*Does catering staff usually persist so?*

*No.*

Lu pressed against her. Malcom stood at arms-length, Remi about ten paces to Lil's left with Magnus, and while Az remained silent, she felt him there in the darkness, stirring within his stillness.

A throwing knife appeared suddenly, hovering beside her head. Lil's inhuman reflexes stopped it before she knew it was coming, before her adrenaline had a chance to spike.

Time, like the knife, seemed to hang as she observed the blade. Then the tray, tea, and whiskey crashed to the tile floor, releasing the moment back to full speed.

Remi rushed toward them, Lu's growl taking form as Lil plucked the suspended knife from the air and followed Lu's stare to the immobilized server. Loose strands of dark hair framed the woman's face, necklace missing its bottom segment, fingers clutching one of her earrings. The blade Lil held in her hand had been hanging from the server's neck.

All the female catering staff had been wearing them.

Remi and Lu took formation around her, assessing.

"Go," Remi shouted.

Malcom stood on the other side of her protectors, between their bodies and the wading pool, not a fiber of fear woven into his composition as he took stock of their surroundings.

Chaos building around her, Lil began to connect to her intention, The Mountain strong in her mind. Trickling water continued just behind her, the scent of oranges and mint still flooding the air, Lu's heat still radiating through the silk of her dress as the air started to shimmer and she looked over Remi's shoulders. Everything in that moment seemed so crisp as she watched Magnus go down.

"*Go,*" Lu shouted, echoing Remi in her ears and in her mind.

But she would not.

Shock spread like electric ice through Lil's chest, raw anguish flooding in as the portal faded, and her eyes flicked to the blonde server, frozen in place with arms raised above her head. The woman's fingers remained as they had been when she'd released the knife embedded in Magnus.

Lil broke through the perimeter of bodies. If their hold had been in earnest, they could have contained her a little longer. They valued her life, but also what it meant to be living, they valued trust, and autonomy. With no time for discussion in the moment, they would adapt, but never restrain her.

Lil's wings burst from her back as she raced past the pool. The male server spun toward her, pulling a knife from his belt buckle, but Malcom was on him before the blade launched, tackling him to the ground.

The woman at the wading pool screamed, her ankle wobbling, limbs splashing as she recoiled from the scene. The man she was with snaked one strong arm under her two, pulling her out and carrying her from the courtyard. He put his cellphone to his ear and gave a series of hand gestures that Lil assumed meant something to whoever he was communicating with further down the hall.

Magnus nodded at Lil reassuringly as she neared. Though still conscious, his breath sounded wet. Remi knelt beside him, hands already at work.

Lil flared her wings to shield him as she turned toward the blonde server, holding her motionless. Lil placed her left hand around the woman's throat, slowly adding pressure. Lil could have pressed the blade from the dark-haired woman into this one's chest. She could have stopped her heart from a distance. She could have changed the acidity in her blood until it burned, paralyzed her diaphragm without laying a finger on her flesh… But Lil remembered voices she'd heard once in a dream, echoes from waking life long ago. Lu had been carving a stone cup for her to drink from; he'd been asked why he chose to do things with his hands that could easily be done with his mind.

*Because it feels good*, he'd said.

Because it feels good.

There was no thunder, no flash of lightning, no rain beating against the glass overhead, and the tremors underfoot were minimal, because Lil was in control. With calm breaths so slow they were almost undetectable, she dropped the blade from her right hand, and put her palms together, blinding light escaping from between them. Lil brought a radiant hand to each of the woman's ears, dread transforming her subject's countenance while the rest of her remained frozen. A fine vibration transferred through Lil and into the wicked specimen, a creature who'd forfeited a miracle for ugliness, willfully risking the end of her life to strike a deathblow to an innocent man, to *Magnus*. The woman's eyes began to lose focus, overcome with the gift Lil bestowed upon her.

"*Stay*," Lil commanded. "Stay long enough to feel something beautiful come from this body before you leave it."

Green coils squeezed out with the light from under Lil's palms, still pressed against the woman's ears. Blood trickled down the tendrils sprouting from the offending creature's mouth and nose. Vines grew, leaves unfurled, and white moonflowers bloomed along the body as Lil brought it to the ground.

"You did terrible things," Lil whispered over the mound of blossoms, "but you were not a waste."

Lil turned to Magnus, Remi still crouching over his body, singing a song with no words.

Magnus's eyes still shone with love for her as he held on. Love remained even with a blade meant for her between his ribs, even after seeing her dispatch a woman's soul, making the corpse food for a new garden.

Lu's arms came around her, warm and strong. She took in a shaky breath and let it out as he placed a hand on her back. A rush of calm released as her wings retreated, and he pulled her further into his chest. Gentle trickling from the fountain continued, but it was Lu's scent that soothed as Lil inhaled deep; fertile water, damp earth, embers and myrrh. She let five fingers trail up his shoulder while her head rested on the other, his body a cocoon.

*Az has three; the first one and two from the hall. Malcom has the other.*

She glanced back to Malcom, who had a male server on the ground, unconscious and locked in a rear naked chokehold.

"Getting old doesn't mean getting soft," he grunted.

Releasing the deadweight of the server to the ground, Malcom stood swiftly with the nimble movements of a much younger man. Putting a cellphone to his ear, he said, "Code black, code grey. Catering staff, all of them. Two females and one male still inside and unaccounted for, possibly more. No quarter given. *No quarter*. Set up a perimeter, separate and hold any unknown guests. No, they're with me and they're enhanced, assist but do not challenge. Wings." He paused, looked at Lil, and added, "She's free to go without interference."

His people wouldn't have been able to contain her, not now, but the gesture was well received.

Lu rubbed her back as he nodded to Malcom, "Remi will assist with the perimeter."

A loud crack like a sudden blast of thunder sounded through the courtyard, then Uri appeared, alert, assessing, ready. He made wide strides toward her, his hand going to her cheek while Lu's remained around her torso.

"Magnus," she said. "Remi healed him; he'll be ok."

Uri nodded, but continued looking her over, judging her condition for himself before stepping toward Remi and Magnus. The old man stood, a little shaky on his feet, but from nerves not injury.

"You didn't bring a spare shirt, did you?" Magnus asked.

"She'll find out either way," Uri smiled, something between a grin and a grimace, as he put his arm around the old man. "I'm glad you're patched up," he added as the space before them began to shimmer, "because traveling this way can feel a little like eating too many Danishes. And before you say anything, *I know*... it's nearly impossible, but I've almost managed it."

The two stepped forward and dissolved.

Remi had a distant look about him as he stepped toward the fountain, wet his hand and perhaps his mind with a memory before briefly glancing at Malcom.

"Apologies for the ceiling," he said, and shot up toward the night sky.

Glass blasted out of his way, gracefully circling upward and outward in a contained spiral. Lil marveled a moment at the beauty of it, the shattered remains sparkling like dancing stars, like a galaxy from a distance.

"He was close with your brother," Malcom said cautiously after having clearly noticed Remi's moment of depth by the fountain. Malcom had read her journals, all of them, and though she'd been discrete, she had made observations.

Lil nodded, thoughts of loss from the distant past fleeting as she looked back to the mound of moonflowers.

"I should have showed restraint until we'd interrogated her..."

"We have others," Lu said, eyes darting to the woman who'd thrown the first blade, down at the unconscious man Malcom had rendered thusly, then over to the immobilized women on the ground with Az standing by. Lil hadn't noticed him emerge from the shadows, but such was his way.

Several men and a few women began lining the hall around the courtyard. Malcom held up his hand and gave a short burst of gestures, signals to them, then approached the dark-haired server, still frozen with broken glass and a tray at her feet.

"I wouldn't mind assisting with the interrogation," he said to Lil. Then to Lu, he asked, "You plan to take them offsite?"

*Not Nan's,* Lil said. Her family had been through enough.

*Patagonia?*

*Let's just take them outside as a start,* she said. *Malcom's people need to get the house cleaned up, make sure guests are safe...*

"If you're unsure, I have locations," Malcom nearly chuckled. "Or, perhaps if Magnus would be so kind as to host?"

"Iceland," Lu nodded. "I'll have Uri inquire, but we may be able to accomplish what's needed just outside if adequate privacy can be provided. Will disposal be a problem, or do you need assistance with the remains?"

"We have methods, but," he turned to the moonflowers, the curve beneath them having become indistinguishable from a pile of earth. "You work quite a bit faster, and with far greater grace than we are able. I do have a holding room here, perhaps we can provide temporary storage, and when things have calmed down a bit..."

Az grabbed the male server and a female with long, honey colored hair banded in a ponytail. Between his wide arms and their stiff bodies, he easily scooped them and carried them up into the night sky. The remaining Condemned remained lifeless on the floor with the exception of the dark-haired woman who'd thrown the first blade.

*Three retained should be enough,* Lu shrugged, but barely.

*I'll take Malcom but I refuse to carry him.*

*No wings then.*

The space in front of them began to ripple, losing definition.

Lu allowed the server use of her feet, compelling her forward. Lil felt his other hand on the exposed skin of her back, then under the silk as he followed the curve of her body, resting on her hip.

Lil passed through, Lu on one side and Malcom on the other under her firm grip. She remembered how it felt before she'd awoken, remembered Claire's reaction to the method of travel, and didn't want to risk Malcom becoming compromised by disorientation.

As the rush and silence came upon her, Lil focused on Lu's hand, ever warm against her skin until they arrived in the back garden of Malcom's estate. The sound of crickets was joined by movement of Remi's wings overhead, and the muffled thump of the female's body hitting the soft ground as Lu released her with what care she deserved.

Malcom took a few steps. Bending slightly at the knees, he paused a moment to take a deep breath, and let it out with a powerful vocalization.

Excitement bright in his wide eyes, he said, "One hell of a ride." He grinned, like he'd just jumped through a waterfall and come out the other side invigorated. She wondered if Magnus had arrived at Nan's with similar verve. Malcom, of course, benefitted from having not been recently stabbed.

Lil recognized the familiar silhouette within the changes time had brought to the back garden. With all that was going on, a piece of her that wanted to wander, to explore how the flora had evolved in her absence. She let go for a moment, imagining herself running through the moonlight, into the trees, Cendres close behind.

She turned at the rising heat against her back, Lu's arms coming around her. She slid her hands under his shirt, explored the hard curves hidden while his hands swept up her back, her skin humming where they made contact, radiating.

"I miss the bonfires and dancing," she whispered. "The heartbeat of the drums pounding on…" Knowing he was behind her in the darkness, chasing her as she darted through the forest.

His hands heated, steam and light hovering around them…

"That was before your time here," he said.

"Long before."

"Your glow in the distance was like a single star behind a cloud in the mist of the woodlands, fueling the frenzy you lit by those fires…Your skin was painted… your tresses free," he growled, hands sliding up to remove the pins from her hair, nimble fingers unbinding braids until a cascade of curls hung down, still damp from her bath.

*I don't think I can wait to have you in the water again.*

*The brook isn't far.*

They were both overtaken; by the memory, by the moment, by their gravity. On the cusp of turning to run, Lil took a deep breath, bringing the night into herself. She smiled and closed her eyes, taking the smoldering, earthy spice of Lu's scent into her lungs. There was something else there though, something the shifting air brought to her, something woody and familiar. Her arms loosened, hands sliding down Lu's body as she looked beyond him. Why hadn't she noticed it before?

*What is it?* He asked.

She stalked around to the immobilized female server and scrunched her nose. Turning to Malcom, Lil was only half joking as she asked, "Do you two share a hope chest?"

Malcom arched an eyebrow and cocked his head, oblivious to the nature of her question but swelling with curiosity.

*Their clothes have this smell, like a sweater Nan wears. It was Grampa Pat's, and you know how she keeps that chest with some of his things and the blanket.*

*I'm familiar with the garment.*

Lu approached Malcom, who stilled himself as any man with sense would have done when approached by a beast too close to run from. Any understanding the old man may have felt they had between them took a back seat to instinct, and so he stood without moving a muscle as Lu drew near, breathing in from around the man's head.

Knowledge passed through them, not with words, not with their voices or in their minds, but a simultaneous awakening.

*It's not their clothing,* she whispered.

Lil remembered Lu in her bed at the ocean house, bringing her hand to his face, remarking on the scent from the cone she'd found atop a cairn on the shore. *Cedar.* She'd had such a strong association with Grampa Pat's sweater that she'd nearly forgotten…

*Michael.*

Lu twisted and brought his nose to the woman's neck, inhaling deep and growling low, sending a ripple of disturbance through the ground under their feet. Michael's scent wasn't just in the fibers they wore.

*It's seeping from their skin.*

Lu brought his attention back to Malcom, staring into him with an intensity that should have robbed the man of his consciousness. "How do you know this woman?"

Malcom shook his head, "My people hired her company at our usual caterer's recommendation when they encountered an emergency and needed to cancel. I've not worked with her company prior to this."

Lu turned on the woman. "Tell me what I want to know," he commanded, allowing her the temporary ability to speak.

"I saw her here in this garden, with her hand in the fish. I had the first vision over a week ago. When they became clearer and I saw Mr. Drake's face, we did what was necessary to be here to protect humanity from another day of her evil intentions, as is our purpose as Guardians. Our numbers are unfathomable, and-"

Her voice was cut off, because her words were no longer necessary... and because Lu's attention had been pulled somewhere else, rendering him into that state of predatory stillness.

Lil felt it, felt something *other*. In her periphery she saw Remi and Az staring directly at her. Shared knowledge passed through them, awareness that something was happening, and it was not to do with the Condemned...

A current ran over her like cool air, charged, then she felt the ocean of that moment pull back before the wave struck.

Like meteors fallen from the sky, two pairs of feet pounded into the earth. Both beings were built well; muscular, each with a set of enormous feathered wings. Gabriel stood to the left; dark eyes, dark skin, dark curls cut close to his head. He wore loose pants, though there was no shirt to hide the strength of his form. Cassiel had landed to his right, chestnut hair in loose waves banded back, the same loose pants and absent shirt.

A wall of earth and stone rose from the ground, encircling Cass. In the fractured instant before Lu moved, his roar echoing through the surrounding trees. Lil's heart sent frigid threads into her blood, like snow pumping out from her chest, spreading through her body.

The winged visitors hadn't made their presence known to her since the flood; hadn't cared to, or dared to, more likely. Az moved in close, his arm coming around, tucking Lil into his body. Remi dropped low but stayed circling overhead.

By the time the icy tingle hit Lil's fingers, Lu had taken Gabriel to the ground in a blue of feathers and fire. The reverberation through the earth traveled so far, Lil saw birds taking to the sky in the distance. Light poured from Lu's eyes and mouth as his palms pressed into Gabriel's shoulders. He fought hard. Lu had his opponent's body pinned, but there was more than strength of muscle at work. Light and power continued to pulse from Lu's hands, and as it did, Lu rotated his fingers toward the center of Gabe's chest. The flesh seemed to part beneath Lu's fingers, opening to receive them, and Gabriel began to flicker, becoming corporeally unstable. Lu lifted him slightly, then slammed him back down, retracting his fingers, cocking one arm back and striking Gabriel in the jaw. Blood sprayed from crunched bone and split skin, healing almost as rapidly as it was broken. Gabe's head bounced off the ground, lolling as it repaired.

Lu leapt off the recovering body of his adversary and stood waiting for some explanation as to the purpose of the intrusion.

"If you won't let him speak to her," Gabriel grunted, "let *us*."

With a thunderous crack, Uri emerged from thin air, making long strides until he stood beside Lu. His arms outstretched with blazing beams of flame extending from either hand like swords of fire. Though their bodies formed a wall in front of her, Lil still caught sight of Gabriel rolling onto his side, pushing up on his knees, trying to see through to her.

"If we worked as one," Gabriel began, "we could command a great purge, one that could prune back, if not eliminate, this human plague that chases her through each life. We could refresh the garden and prevent her from being *hunted*." His voice was strong, but strained, tired.

"So, she should agree to work with you?" Uri asked with disgust, "And what, have her human family *slaughtered* again? We are aware of what Michael has started, and we'll meet on our terms."

They'd planned to meet within hours, but the point remained that the others were out of line in their approach.

Gabriel got to his feet, his body seeming heavy. "Something has to change; this can't go on as it is now. The garden is not well," he said, his voice nearly breaking as he tried again to see through to Lil. "It's painful to watch…"

"Painful… what could you possibly know of it?" Lu asked, with a flat, low voice more terrifying than if he'd shouted. "You have been *absent*."

"It was *you* who left," Gabriel seethed. "We've always been here, and we witness *everything*."

"Witnessing…" Lu growled. "With obedient hands folded in your lap."

The small dome of rock and soil continued to undulate where Cassiel stood encapsulated. Dirt and stone flew outward at various points, presumably from his efforts to break free, but Az was strong and calm as the mountain, making repairs, prepared to stand as long as needed. Lil leaned against him, glancing to the other side of his body where the Condemned huddled together, released from their immobility during the tussle.

Malcom leaned in, his posture remarkably steady given the series of disruptions the evening had presented.

"You said it was your own kind that did this to you, that made you mortal?" he asked.

Lil nodded.

"And these two pricks…?"

She nodded again. "They were a part of it. They sided with Michael in the garden, unable to see around orders given. They sang a song that only our voices can carry, muting my immortality and rendering me vulnerable."

Lu was still, releasing a low, almost subsonic growl. Uri, though, he had only just arrived.

"Were you watching when her family sacrificed her to gods that don't exist?" Uri shouted, his words burning as he released them. "She was a *child*, Gabriel. Do you remember when they still burned witches? We barely got her out when... I can't..." he sighed. "There have been too many moments."

"Every time," Gabriel started, "*Every* time she dies our hearts ache with loss only to be filled with hope again when she is reborn. We watch, forbidden to interfere on our own, and not whole enough to move on as we are called."

Lu spoke then, low, and with a chilling fire in his voice. "It seems the rules of engagement don't apply to your *leader*, or were you not watching when he came down to get his hands dirty in the mud with us?"

Lil watched the transformation of emotion as Gabriel began to regain control of himself at those words, saw the questions blossoming behind his eyes.

"Explain."

The rock surrounding Cassiel fell away, his arms thrashing and punching with fury and triumph, as if it were he who had broken free and not Az who had released him. The manic ferocity calmed quickly as Cass assessed his surroundings, seeing Gabriel and Lu had somehow come to an agreeable state of nonviolence while he'd been waging battle within the stone capsule.

Regaining his bearings, Cass approached Gabriel with caution, and then he saw Lil. Their eyes met with a spark of ice in her chest. Cassiel's face softened as he closed his eyes briefly and scented the air, appearing almost on the edge of peace.

Remi touched down in front of her, blocking the view as he touched her cheek.

"I'm ok," she said. He might have been able to sense it, but the words still meant something. "I'm a little nervous about Uri not being with Nan, and with these two here... with what happened last time." Before the flood, when her family had been killed to *motivate* her. "I know they're probably okay, but his moment…" she let out a ragged breath. "It's a lot."

"And why it means so much for us to be with you now. Uri will return soon, he just needed to be here."

"As much as I'm nervous, I'm glad he's with us."

*I can always feel you, but if you were closer, our bodies would be touching.*

Lil heated, a pleasant distraction from the current situation, or was their current situation the distraction, and it was Lu bringing her back to the constant? He called her to him, but also to the forefront of what was happening, giving her permission she didn't need, but was thankful for. Lu, those surrounding her, they acted as an unrelenting barrier. They did so to protect, and to provide her with the choice to engage when she was ready, on her terms.

Remi shifted back to surveying the area as Lil looked to where Lu stood. Uri's flames were away, but his wings remained ready. Lu's feathers were again hidden and his shirt gone, leaving the smooth skin and defined muscles of his back in full view. His head swiveled slowly as he glanced over his shoulder, catching her eyes.

*It's your choice,* he continued. *You could return to Nan's if you wanted, or to the mountain with Az… But I'd like you here…*

*And touching,* she clarified playfully.

*We all have our strengths.*

*And you have them all,* she laughed. It was true. Her kind shared the ability to control substances, wielding and reorganizing atoms, calling and manipulating energy, feeding life. They tended to have more of a knack in some areas over others, a reflection of personality perhaps. But Lu far surpassed them all in almost everything, brute strength included. There was something about what Lil could do though; creation without a seed... She was like the stem cell for all life, a trait unique to her.

*I was made to balance something magnificent,* he said with a heated whisper, *and great strength was needed for your counterpart it seems.*

He turned to face forward, continuing his conversation with Uri and the two others...

*Ok, I'm coming.*

*All the strength indeed,* he purred.

Remi nodded to himself in her periphery and approached the cluster of servers, calling forward the woman who'd brought Lil the unrequested tea; the woman who'd tried to stab her.

*Remi is bringing Malcom and the Condemned who smells of cedar, that we might rub Cass and Gabriel's noses in it, as it were.*

Lil huffed another laugh, *I'll bring Malcom.*

Az slid his arm gently away as Lil placed a hand on Malcom's back. "Walk with me; they just want to examine you."

Lil felt his instant apprehension, not likely a familiar feeling for him. "Nothing invasive," she said, reassuring as much as she could. "You just have a scent we're intrigued by. I'll be with you, okay?"

"In for a penny..."

Az hung back while she walked with Malcom on her left. Remi broke off to her right, moving with the Condemned toward Uri. She could feel Gabe and Cassiel's eyes on her, their bodies humming in reaction to her approach. She met their gazes as she fit against Lu's body, his waiting arm wrapping around her. Gabriel was as Cass had been; centuries unspoken, his stare sharp and then softening, searching. He opened his mouth as if to say something, but stopped when Lu's head ticked to the side in her periphery, a warning.

Gabriel refocused on Remi and the woman with him.

"This creature is one of the Condemned, as you call them?" He said, then shifted to face Malcom. "And this other one... from the family that has hunted her for use as an asset?"

"Yes," Lu offered.

"And killed her in the process..." Gabriel added, looking at Malcom with disdain. Then to Lu he said, "You should have never interfered with that shipwreck."

"Never interfere," Cass agreed, shaking his head.

"You oppose interference, and yet, here are these two specimens, reeking of your master."

The suggestion that Michael was their master was offensive on its own, but to imply he'd been in such close contact with humans, to have left his scent on them, was a blow that had to sting.

"Michael's involvement is undeniable, and warrants a conversation. You suspect he's working with these creatures?"

"You remember Frejya?" Lu asked.

Gabriel released a breath. "Remember? If I had selective memory, she'd be among the last forgotten."

"She was breathtaking," Cass whispered, his eyes flitting to Lil's before returning to Lu's stare, the growl having not gone unnoticed. "I've only known one other to be so beautiful, and so bloody lethal. Had a serenity about her," he added, looking to Gabriel. "Remember her playing with those ice cats?"

They certainly had been watching. Lil heard that the others had come around, testing the waters during Freyja's time. Something passed between Lu and Remi then. Had he known how close the two had been to his daughter?

"I always said she took after her auntie," Remi sighed, nostalgia weighing his smile as Lil caught his shimmering eyes.

She turned then, to the two who had betrayed her. Lu grinned in her periphery, his fingers reaching up to her hair where it floated off her shoulders. When her eyes met Gabriel's, his went wide, they would grow wider, though, as he learned what she and Lu had discovered.

"And other than by her appearance," she began, her voice steady and strong, "How did you know it was Remi's seed that had grown into Freyja?"

"She aged slowly," he answered, more breath than voice. "She had greatness about her."

"All their offspring did; she could have fallen from any of us."

"When the wind lifted her hair back, you could smell snow and evergreens, even in the dead of summer amongst the flowers…" Gabriel's eyes went wide as his words trailed off.

Cassiel's jaw loosened as the word, "No," escaped him with very little conviction.

Their reactions hung for a moment, until Lu stepped forward, his voice low, steady, deep. "Because you could smell *him*," he said, head ticking toward Remi. "She shared the scent of her father, as did, her children, and theirs. That greatness-"

The twin jabs in Lil's neck were almost enough to distract from the warm fullness in her abdomen, radiating up into her chest. She felt hot, and full, but there was also a sense of depletion. She'd felt this before…

Eyes slipping down, Lil saw a hand still around the knife tilted up inside her, cutting sharp to one side. She saw the bloodied ends of a silver earing in the server's other hand; the server who smelled like Grampa Pat's sweater, eyes blazing with the glory of her accomplishment.

Lil slumped, Lu's arms easing her down onto the grass. The ground was damp with what continued pouring out of her, and with what leaked from the severed head beside her, the woman who'd impaled her, eyes still wide.

# 17.

She was emptying.

Lil poured like water from a pitcher, the liquid within her vessel finite and depleting.

One of Lu's arms remained around her, his free hand pressed against her wound, Remi's Left hand on Lu's, his right on her head, light leaking from where they made contact.

"Tell me again about what you've witnessed. Tell me of the pain, Gabriel," Uri fumed, fire burning around his arms and in his eyes. His voice sounded like it had traveled through deep water, muffled and distorted. Lu's rumbled, but his attention stayed with her, not in the circle of bickering and helplessness that surrounded them.

Lil felt the weight of her body sinking into the ground, sinking beyond the arms embracing her. While a solid part of her remained heavy, another part released from it, bringing a sense of weightlessness from discarding the tether.

*Wait...* Lu implored, his words as saturated as his eyes, his tears hot on her cool skin.

*There is a dish of caramels in our room,* she replied. Lil had meant to mention the caramels after making the discovery, but then Lu had experienced their flavor second hand, and a series of distractions ensued.

She felt him smile against her.

*And your mouth tasted of elderflower and rosemary after you found them,* he purred. *Gunnar sent the confections with Uri. I'd have left them in the garden, but they'd not have lasted until you woke.*

She felt his breath on her body, heard the sigh through her mind before he began...

*The first time you felt the fire between us,* he asked, his question coming as a sorrowful whisper.

Lil felt the bittersweet of blossoms unfolding and petals fallen as she answered. *From the first time I dreamed of your voice, I didn't want to wake. From the first time I smelled you about the barn, I didn't want to leave. From the first time I felt more than the ocean's fingers through my hair, I didn't want to return to land... But when water ran black with coal down your arms, I tasted salt from across the room, and I felt the heat between us stronger than the flames lighting your face...*

She felt the same heat again, all around her. *The first time you smiled to yourself, alone,* she asked.

*When I put on your apron.*

Lil felt the tangled joy and sadness of the memory coming through. *I was so flustered packing, I nearly came back down undressed...*

*We would've been extremely delayed in our departure had you chosen that course of action, though I can't say I would have been disappointed.*

While Lil could feel the vibrations and the heat beneath his words spreading through her, she no longer felt his breath on her skin, or the moisture from his eyes.

*Stay a little longer,* he pleaded. *You'll return in the blink of an eye. We'll fall toward the stars and feel the sea over our skin together again, but don't leave yet...*

She ached. He could hold her soul, but not indefinitely, not long enough to repair what had been done.

*When I'm born again,* she whispered, *bring me to Claire. She and Gunnar...* Lil's eyes had long since closed, but the depth of exhaustion was just beginning to reach her mind. Thunder from Lu's chest moved through her like some effervescence, lifting that disconnected part of her with it, further, upwards. Her eyes were closed where she lay on the ground, but she had detached from her corporeal form with another kind of sight, watching instead from where she floated.

Lu used what power he had to hold her hovering soul as long as he could, as he'd done in the past, but she always moved on.

They'd formed a circle around her remains. Malcom, quite possibly for the first time in his life, looked stricken. Az appeared terrifying as Lu; Uri distraught, Remi contemplative. The other two, those who'd once betrayed her, who claimed they'd ached with her loss, beheld for the first time the wrenching agony of her passing, and their discomfort was apparent.

The bodies of the condemned were lifeless just beyond, further still the soft glow from the chateau built where an old home of hers had once been whispered memories of a pearl well-hidden, and a cat…

The rumbling thunder below her intensified, drawing Lil's attention back downward.

"She's… she's not healing," Cassiel said. Eyes frantic, he looked to Lu, then to Remi. "How much time does she have?"

"Moments," Remi whispered. "It's by her divine nature and our hands that she's remained this long."

Cassiel, fraught with concern, shuffled his restless wings as he turned to Gabe, and said, "I'm going to Michael; this can't continue."

"We don't have time for inquiry, Cass," Gabriel snapped, though it wasn't Cassiel he looked toward, it was Lu.

"She's still here," Lu said with guttural urgency, twisting to looking over his shoulder toward the stillness, toward Az, toward eyes darker than his own. "It's not too late."

The atmosphere shifted around her, a pause between breaths. Then an engulfing sound like the voice of a mountain came forth, evoking the total silence of anything other than itself.

Az was singing.

Lil felt the magnetism of her remains pull her downward as the monolithic sound continued. Then his voice was no longer alone. Lu's joined him, the haunting harmony passing through her, all of her, everywhere she was.

The scene suddenly went dark, not for lack of light, but because Lil's eyes had been closed. She felt the weight of her body around her soul, felt the limits of the impaired, mortal form.

Sound washed over her from all directions as the others joined, overtaking her with their collective voices merging together. Though powerful, the song's crescendo came not as a torrent, but something rather gentle. As if carried on a smooth, vernal breeze, an unseen veil fell over her like mist along the forest floor catching dawn's light. The veil settled not on, but within her as the song found its purpose; the key moving a lock into place, and opening.

Stillness subsided as their song faded.

Lil's soul took a breath, her body took in air, and her eyes opened.

The night sky was as it had been; stars hanging like distant secrets above. The infinite existed as a backdrop to the faces looking down with fatigued expressions, faces marked by despair and hope.

Cass's mouth parted, his hand on Gabriel's shoulder as the latter leaned in. Then Uri exhaled for all of them, scrubbing his hands over his face, over his shaved head, cheeks streaked with tears. Az stood still, but for the nod he gave her. Remi knelt at her feet, countenance not unlike what he wore when they first met at the school, when Etienne first brought him home, when she held Frejya.

They'd sung for her, all of them. Az, Lu, Remi, Uri, Cass and Gabriel. They'd done more than heal her body, they had returned her immortality to its rightful state.

Another three sets of feet hit the ground guided by three sets of wings: Sab, Raz, and Raphael. Their faces, the forest, the heavens beyond; they were all in the periphery... eclipsed by Lu.

His eyes shimmered with water and burned with the fire encircling that infinite blackness within. He looked at her with the depth of time passed, with spans so vast they couldn't be measured in years. Agony lingered there, but so was there an exploding plume of awe. Like ink in water, tendrils of hope bloomed, overtaking the desolate absence with darkness; a darkness where worlds are made, where dreams are born.

Lil felt it within her as well, that jet stone becoming liquid, moving outward from her heart as radiance. The resulting glow lit his face, and the display of red streaking his skin. One of his hands, slick with what had been her mortal blood, slid down her cheek to the back of her neck. His other hand still rested where the blade had torn through her dress. He glanced down only for a moment to where his tentative fingers stroked newly formed skin, unblemished and luminescent. Then, he met her eyes again, and his tears fell to meet hers like stars turned to water.

A hand went to Lu's shoulder, then another, a web of those who'd waited, conducting whisps of crackling light over their skin. Their foreheads came together above hers, a nest, a cocoon, welcoming her home.

She felt the impact of another hand, not on her body, but through the connection made. Malcom, then Cass, Gabriel, Sab, Raz, and Raphael.

"I'd like very much to dissolve the grass below," Lu breathed, the air around him thick with the scent of storms, earth, and combustion. "Fall into another sky, and have you to myself."

"Don't you Remi," Uri scolded.

Lil's cheeks reached to meet her wet eyes, fluctuating between tears and laughter, her emotions spreading through the others like long awaited rain.

"Later," she sighed, her eyes locking with Lu's. "We have an abundance of later."

The cluster of them took a collective a breath. Sab, Raz, and Raphiel illuminated as to suspected condition behind scent shared by Malcom and the Condemned who'd nearly sent Lil into another cycle. Lil kept her distance from them, The Others. Gabe and Cass had sung for her, but her return to immortality didn't erase the past, and reconciliation would take time.

Lil's hand went to the bloody hole in her dress where the knife had been, her neck where the poison had entered from the Condemned's earring.

"Nan," she said, eyes flicking from Lu to Uri. "I need to make sure they're alright."

"Not like that, you're not," Uri shot back. "I'll go."

"She's seen me worse."

"She's seen you worse *today*," he said, using her point to make his. "Then Magnus arrived after surviving his own brush with death. Give the woman's heart a rest." Drawing closer, his voice softened as he tipped his head to rest against hers. "I'll check on them, and we'll wait together for your arrival. Maybe you and Lu can do that thing he likes, where he just burns the clothes off."

"We'll be close behind," she whispered, smile forming to match the grin Uri wore as he pulled away, and disappeared.

Lu's eyes settled on The Others. Not Cass and Garbriel had used their voices, but the three latecomers, who'd not acted.

"We came when the song called us," Sab said, answering Lu's glare.

"And what of Michael?" Remi asked.

Sab looked to Cass and Gabriel who shook their heads.

"There are a few places we can look," Raphael said, "We've not seen him in some time."

While Remi joined The Others, trust being what it was, Az followed Malcom inside. The man had offered assistance with clothing that Lil could get to her family sooner, and they'd offered one of their own to assist in clearing the chateau of any unwanted company.

While the Condemned were no longer a threat to Lil, they were still a plague, and could threaten her family. And while she could have gone to the mountain to change, there was something about the gesture, and the moment to pause it provided them with.

"Thousands of years," she sighed as Lu sat before her on a low garden wall, about the height of his hips.

"The blink of an eye," he finished, inviting her to sit by his side. "You'll want to keep the dress?"

She nodded. "It marks too big a moment to incinerate." She selected a small stone from the ground, smoothing her thumb over the surface as she sat, leaning into Lu as his arm came around her. "There'll be plenty of opportunity for fire. We can burn off whatever Malcom turns up with."

His eyes lit, then became distant. "All is well at Nan's," he said, relaying Uri's report. "Magnus suffers only from an abundance of attention." He stopped abruptly, listening again. "Remi… they've trying to locate Michael…"

Though it had only been minutes, they could travel fast, and knew where to look.

"He'd have felt the song."

"There's no doubt, but they cannot find him."

Lil placed the object in her hand down on the wall, the scent of cedar flooding her mind with the memory of a young boy stacking stones in a garden.

"I know where he is."

# 18.

The thunder of their arrival faded, giving way to the sound of light rain in the darkness. Small, intermittent drops created a chorus of gentle taps announcing the location of every leaf in the front garden. The sound of the forest beyond blended together as one.

The Arboretum had not been built, but grown, stone by stone. Even with the large structure of the school and its outbuildings, all those tucked in and sleeping safely inside, Lil still felt the unmistakable sensation of being deep in the woods.

*He's here.*

Lil put out her hand, tracing down Lu's arm until their fingers wove together. She'd felt Michael upon first breaking through the air, but as they rounded the corner of the new library, Lil breathed in the subtle scent of crushed limestone and cedar warmed by the sun. Something else far fainter lingered there...

Tangled with the scent of Michael, and the rain, she smelled lichen tea.

Her breath caught then, at the sight she beheld.

# A Story in Song

Two figures sat on a rock wall in the garden. To some they might have appeared as just a man and a child side by side, but they were so much more than that. The bright-eyed boy was the one who'd cut his hand, who'd dreamed of her: Hamish. And he, the one who sat next to the boy, had a golden sheen over his skin, catching what ambient light lingered in the darkness. His long hair, like his skin, reflected what the stars offered. He was not a man; he was Michael.

They each held mugs, steaming and fragrant. Hamish was gently concentrating on the stone he'd been setting atop a cairn built between them. Michael watched the boy patiently with contentment and knowing; aware of her arrival, but not yet ready to turn.

When the stone had been balanced, two sets of honey-colored eyes looked directly at her.

Pleasant surprise brightened Hamish's face as she approached. "You made it," he smiled. "I've had this dream before, but I wasn't sure it would happen," he added, eye's flitting to the small tear in her dress.

Lil hadn't changed. After realizing where they needed to go, there was a heightened sense of urgency, and she thought it appropriate he see for himself what had happened. In hindsight, perhaps she should have, thinking the boy might be sensitive, but time had passed and there she was, wearing the evidence of her attack and her triumph.

Beside Hamish, Michael smiled as well, though it was faint, burdened.

Lil had waited for that moment on the wall as much as she'd avoided it. The urge she felt to erupt upon arrival had been diffused at seeing the boy there with Michael, at the peace between them as they stacked stones together, drinking tea.

There would be no explosion with the boy present, but Hamish would soon depart, and more than words would be spoken in his absence.

Lil unlaced her fingers from Lu's and sat beside the child.

"I dreamed of this," Hamish smiled. "It was the first one where I knew you were going to be okay." Taking another sip from his mug, he glanced up to Lu where he stood beside her. "Hey, Lu."

Lu smiled, nodded.

Hamish looked over Lil's shoulder toward the tree line. "Master Remmond," he smiled as Remi emerged from the path to his cottage. "He was in the dream too, and those other guys with wings. Are they here too? Did you guys *fly* here?" His face became quite serious then, as he asked, "If I got permission from master David... could you fly me?"

"A conversation for another time," Lu said, soft and low, a hint of a smile at the boy's refreshing brightness. He brushed a hand over Lil's neck and shoulder, then leaned against a tree beside the wall. He had the strength not to growl, but Lil felt the undercurrent of power looming. There was no caged beast within him, but one that sat patiently, relishing the absence of bars.

Remi strolled over, crouched before Hamish, and looked into his mug. "I'm glad to see you're drinking the tea," he said, "but it's rather late, wouldn't you say? What time is your first commitment tomorrow morning?"

"Sunrise," the boy sighed.

"Perhaps you should say goodnight and head in. Come," he said, standing to his full height. I'll walk with you."

Hamish slid off the rock wall and put his arms around Michael, *hugging* him. When he pulled back, Michael handed him an empty mug.

"If you don't mind returning this to the kitchen," he smiled. "Thank you for the tea, Hamish. I'll share another cup with you in a day or two, but you should continue drinking it in my absence."

The boy nodded, and turned to Remi. "Are there more?" he asked, looking around the darkened grounds.

"Yes," Remi answered, placing his hand on the boy's shoulder. He gave Michael a brief, contemptuous look before returning his gaze to Hamish, and escorting him toward the school. "Some colleagues travelled with me. I've known them for so long they're rather like brothers. You'll meet them soon enough, but not tonight."

Their footsteps and quiet conversation were silenced as the door closed behind them, giving way once again to the gentle rain pattering throughout the garden and the forest beyond... Until another sound joined the night chorus.

Lu's growl was deep, but the undulations were more than a rumble, they were intentional in their pattern.

Lil turned her head, lingering a moment on Lu, breathtaking and foreboding as his song. Then, another voice rang out like harmonizing thunder from somewhere in the woods; Az. Lil took in a breath, feeling the vibrations around her, surrounding Michael...

He gritted his teeth, golden light seeping from him in waves as Uri's voice joined. Both he and Az remained unseen, their song washing over her like a beautiful storm and holding Michael, painfully, in place.

"I'm not one of your dead," Michael ground out.

"No, they only have one mortal span with which to inflict their sins upon others," Lu roared as the others sang on. "You've spread your suffering over lifetimes, Michael; *her* lifetimes."

"I sought her out," Michael huffed, wisps of gold light flaking from him like tiny falling leaves, the soft edges of his form, rematerializing as they dissipated.

"That she should work alongside her tormenter?" Lu countered with disgust.

Lil breathed deep, not for the oxygen, but for the stability it brought her, for the rhythm of it. She breathed, feeling the music move through her, around her, from her, and she parted her mouth.

Rich as earth, light as air, and deeper than the darkest heavens, Lil sang of *herself*. She had a great sense of opening as she released music such that the rain, the leaves, and what filled the space between seemed to be singing with her, no particle left unmoved.

She closed her eyes, and with the ache of a thousand years doubled over again and again, she wove sound and light into her target. These threads were embedded with her fury, love, and loss, condensed, undiluted, and they did not slice clean as they entered Michael, but branched out like tenacious roots, clenching and clawing with abandon as they carved.

Lil continued to sing as all other sound fell away, until it was only her voice moving through the night. She sang until catharsis soothed, truth saturated, and the comforting scent of deep earth and embers, cardamom, and myrrh, enveloped her again.

When Lil's voice finally faded to breath, her eyes opened.

The garden was calm. Sparse drops of rain fell slow in the darkness, sparkling and illuminated by the light that still emanated from her. The surrounding forest had returned to its slow, almost undetectable respiration. The heavens remained as they were.

If Michael's soul had been mortal, the garden would have been painted red. Instead, he sat on the stone wall, dull and hunched in contrast to the cairn which still stood balanced by his side.

Her words were soft but clear as ice as she addressed him. "I wanted to tear you apart."

"You succeeded," he sighed. His eyes had always been like a lion's, golden and unwavering… but there with her on the wall, she saw something else as he looked at her, more than rain on his cheek. Lil sensed his ache to make whole not what she'd torn apart, but what he had.

"Your soul is as it has always been…" he paused wistfully, "*Radiant*… and now, once again immortal. I felt the song as they brought you back."

"Did you feel the knife go in as well? And the poison?" She asked, her words delicate and powerful.

"I'm sorry."

Two words, like the ocean in a drop of water. Lil had never known him to apologize. It wasn't in his nature.

"We were meeting with Malcom Drake when the Condemned struck," she said. And with a voice that carried the weight of lifetimes, the weight of the garden, she whispered, "They reeked of you, Michael."

Lu's growl moved low beneath the sound of the rain pattering gently on the grass, the stone, her skin. But his presence went unacknowledged by Michael, whose focus remained on Lil, and on something far more distant.

"Gabriel and I came often, watching as you did what none of us had before: living amongst the creatures in the garden. They still knew then what you were, as much as any of them could. We watched as they cherished you…" he sighed. "And we watched as they turned."

The moist air was cool against her back, Lu's hand warm, his scent enveloping her…

*I'm here with you,* he whispered. *The others are near; I've asked them to give us a moment.*

"What a tragedy it was," Michael continued, "for the thread of creation passed to them to be used for weaving a tapestry of lies, assigning you responsibility for the death of their children."

"We tried to explain the truth of illness," Lu rumbled from beside her.

"But the story of your defiance in Eden had been retold too many times," Michael went on. "Easier to blame you, than to punish a microorganism… Those that struck the first blow against you," he paused, closing his eyes a moment. "I hadn't intended for that when you were rendered mortal, but we aren't meant to know, only to carry out what we are called to do. And I was so called to intervene."

Lil felt a pulse of heat and pressure from Lu's hand. They'd known the story thus far, until Michael's last words… Michael, who had a reputation for staunch opposition to anything but minimal interference.

"I came often to speak with the Condemned, as you call them. *Stubborn,*" he added, shaking his head. "I came with no disguise, and still, they would not relinquish their quest to end your life. There was a woman among them, Ninella. She was *infuriating.*"

Michael closed his eyes again, taking a breath as the edge of frustration passed, and then Lil saw something else wisp forward. His expression calmed, and there was a hint of serenity. Serenity… and some distant amusement had found him, his lips turning up slightly at the corners. "I can still smell her hair. She had a blend of oils she used. They were pleasant, but the natural smell of her hair still managed to come through… Far more intoxicating. Never, aside from some of my more entertaining disagreements with you, had I found myself so exasperated. She was by no means immune to fury, either, as many of the pots in her dwelling didn't survive my visits. And they were not always empty when they met their end. I found myself, more than once, picking grain from the cracks in the floor… *Me.*"

Imagining it was enough to bring Lil's lips ticking upward.

"Neither one of us was able to see reason, nor could we seem to resist one another. We had a son, who she raised among them. He lived long, but even with my blood in his veins, he was mortal, and died as the result of tragedy, though not before fathering several children of his own. Ninella couldn't be swayed to reason after his loss, devoting herself to the Condemned entirely until she too met the fate of all mortals."

They'd thought Michael ignorant of such attachments of the heart, but he'd known the love of a woman, the death of a child, the passing of a family. And he'd left his legacy to grow without his guidance in navigating their divine traits.

"You gave them *sight*, Michael. They used that gift to hunt me *mercilessly*."

He nodded slowly, his heart so heavy she could feel the weight of it in her own chest. "It's been said that we don't make mistakes," he said with resignation.

"Those who say it are mistaken," she suggested with a soft smile, encouraging him to continue.

"I'd sought to stop the Condemned from their assault, only to arm them with their greatest weapon… I thought the flood would take them," he whispered to the trees, to the memory of what he'd done.

"You thought the water would hide what you'd done, no matter the cost," Lil said sharply.

"Not to hide," he ground out. "And it's not that I didn't care… The sacrifice of your family was worth it to manage the problem I'd caused, was worth saving you. I had intervened too much. My own offspring, my lineage, *twisted*, becoming the wicked instruments of the monster I had meant to defeat. I thought the flood would take them all, but it wasn't enough."

Lu's fingers gently traced over Lil's back, threads of warmth trickling through her.

"What of Malcom, and Hamish?" She asked. "They are not Condemned, but they are undoubtedly yours, Michael."

"Malcom descends from my time with Ninella. His ancestors broke away to seek greatness apart from the cause, so much so that any knowledge of the Condemned had been completely lost by the time you and your *dragon* intervened with that shipwreck."

Lu rumbled at the word *dragon*.

"I met Hamish's mother by chance, a breath of fresh air. Perhaps I sensed what it was of our kind that sparkled in her..." he trailed off.

Gunnar hadn't mentioned how the boy's parents had died... It was Hamish's mother that had been Gunnar's relation, and it was Uri that the cousins had in common. The coincidence would have been too great for Michael to have met the boy's mother by chance. He must have followed his line from the Condemned to Hamish's father, then sensed his spark in the boy. Was his legacy the reason behind the urgency of his plans for the earth?

"You must have sensed yourself in Hamish. Did you know his father before he passed?"

Had connecting with the youngest generation of his line prompted some need in him to take part, to nurture as the rest of them had? To provide a better world for the boy to live in?

Michael paused. His eyes flicked to Lu's for an instant before returning to her. For a being not caught off guard often, he seemed almost puzzled... His expression suggested that it wasn't so much an internal struggle that perplexed him, but the foundation of the question itself; that she had even asked it, that she needed to. He'd assumed she knew something, but what?

Lu's fingers slowed their movement over her skin.

Michael's face was free of confusion, eyes clear. "I am the boy's father, Lilitu. Hamish is my son."

The tapping of light rain on leaves and stone continued; small drops taking their time to fall. Lil heard the landscape like a drawing made with sound, but between her and Michael, there was stillness.

"How," Lu breathed beside her. "The boy is less than half human, what with the addition of Uri's lineage flowing through him. How has no one noticed? How have *we* not noticed?"

"I've concealed him effectively thus far; though only so much can be done… as you well know."

"His mother," Lil asked, "was she… *aware?*"

"Elin… She had a small café. Loved to cook. I was visiting a northern forest and there she was, with two of her friends, sourcing food for her creations. She was a beautiful soul, so strong, but without *angst*. Elin hadn't been corrupted by the indoctrination that had ensnared Ninella. So strong…" he mused. "So strong, and so fragile." Then he closed his eyes and took a slow breath, savoring a memory. "I can almost smell her still, like citrus and summer… No, she never knew what I was. She knew I was different, knew I couldn't stay, but she thought me human."

"He'll need to be told," Lu said, his voice solemn. "You can hide him here for a time, but his peers will wither around him. His cousin is of two lines and will age slowly, but even he will grow grey while Hamish remains a young man. *That,* you cannot conceal."

"He shouldn't need to be hidden," Lil said, meeting Michael's eyes. Az stalked out of the darkness in her periphery, barely visible along the tree line. She turned, though, at the sound of a door opening in the distance. Remi walked out like a storm barely kept offshore, a wall of mist thickening rapidly behind him, spreading out to shroud the school entirely.

Lil hoped the sleeping students hadn't seen the spectacle that had played out in their garden. She felt a brief twinge of remorse for having not thought of shielding the children sooner, risking their exposure her song.

*Remi saw to their continued slumber while we sang,* Lu whispered as he leaned in, mouth tracing the hairline along her neck as he inhaled.

Uri came from the forest then, making no adjustment to what burned within him. Eyes lit with fire, his steady steps threatened, but did not disturb the earth.

"They know," Lu said casually.

"Clearly," Michael drawled.

Lil leaned further into Lu as he dipped his head back down, inhaling again.

*I love the way your fragrance lingers here with such strength...* She felt his tongue make contact as he moved his lips to her neck. *Like the earth rising to meet the rain, almond and apple, flesh exposed at my mouth...* The sound he made was like a low purr, laden with satisfaction. *Deep earth, smoldering... My scent remains on you still.*

Immortality did not affect some things, as blood still rushed to her cheeks at hearing his words.

"The boy is vulnerable," Michael interrupted, paying little attention to Lu's disapproving growl, or to Remi and Uri as they arrived. Instead, he turned back to Lil. "Hamish is not so different from how you once were; not fully human, not fully immortal. Certainly, you're aware of the benefit your concealment provided."

319

Lu maintained his body flush against Lil's as Remi approached and laid a hand on her cheek, his eyes like open sky reflected on a mountain lake. He took a few steps back to hold a wide stance, and *stared* at Michael. Uri appeared before Lil in Remi's place, resting his forehead against hers, releasing a long breath; a moment of vulnerability. She breathed in the love he exhaled. His amber eyes flicked up to hers, flames still burning but seemingly more contained; not dampened, but controlled. He moved threateningly toward Michael before pausing, and, like Remi, taking position a few meters from them, standing watch.

Az had ceased his advance somewhere between the forest and the stone wall, nodding to her, brushing his hand over his heart as he settled in.

"Things are changing," Lu said, low and ominous as he turned his head toward Michael. "Are they not?" None she knew, human or otherwise, would want to be on the receiving end of Lu's eyes when he looked like that.

"Pestilence?" Remi asked.

Michael nodded. "Among other things. I've put the wheels in motion. It cannot be undone."

Uri swore under his breath.

"The changes were undoubtedly overdue and would have happened in their own time," Michael began. "Though a controlled burn is favored, is it not? I attempted contact with you, Lilitu, but I could not wait. To protect... to protect what is dear, I moved forward... The garden will have transitioned considerably by the time Hamish has grown out of his childhood," he continued, then his eyes widened as thunder cracked around them. Five sets of feet carried five large bodies over the ground, and as they began coming through the trees, their eyes sifted through the landscape, before settling on Lil. A range of emotion worked over their faces, expressions of frustration, shock, and longing.

"A son," Gabriel's angered voice rumbled as he approached with the others close behind. *"Here*, Michael? And not the first child, as the fruit of your lineage has been *hunting* her since you took it upon yourself to interfere… While the rest of us were prohibited, and blind to your transgression, you were breeding with humans and seeding the greatest threat to her mortal existence, a state *you* inflicted upon her."

"They know as well," Lu stated, the belated nature of the disclosure clearly intentional.

Michael's jaw clenched before his expression flattened, his voice laced with dry tolerance. "That *we* inflicted, Gabriel, and yes, you have demonstrated yourself to be an enlightened historian. The *primal pair* and I were just reminiscing," he added, gesturing toward Lil and Lu. "The conversation was thorough in its coverage of my offspring, and we've since moved forward to discuss current events." He surveyed the five new arrivals, those who'd stayed with him after he'd betrayed Lil in the garden, those who'd had asked no questions, who had been silent before they sang. "Does anyone wish to share with the group what developments have been made with regards to this planet's landscape and human population?"

Share with the group.

Gabe and Cassiel were fuming, but held their tongues. Instead, they used their energy to damp down their frustration, assess their surroundings. Their eyes flitted around, seeing the school, the gathering at the wall, perhaps realizing the potential for serenity in the space.

# A Story in Song

It was Gabriel whose eyes rested on Lil first, his shoulders relaxing. Perhaps something had started to heal between them since he'd arrived with Cass at Malcom's. It may have been the emotion she sensed when they'd seen her, that they'd risked wrath to make contact, Gabriel's willingness to learn the truth of Michael's actions on earth alongside them, or his presence with Cass at her last brush with death. Whatever the reason, Lil didn't find herself inflamed or disgusted by him any longer, though there were still wounds.

"We were not fully aware until just recently…" Raz began, his thick black hair bound in a braid, white linen pants contrasting against the warm brown of his skin.

"We've been working in a support capacity," Sab added, white hair hanging down around his shoulders. He wore linen pants like Raz, though Sab's were the same dull brown as his eyes. *We*, he and Raz had said. Never *I*. Never personal responsibility, only following orders. It turned her stomach, threatening to derail her mood and thoughts.

*I could do without their voices tonight,* Lil whispered. Cass and Gabriel had been with her when the Condemned struck, had used their voices to sing her home, but the other three…

Lil had risen and laid a torrent into Michael. Though she was strong, immortal once again, there was a weight that threatened to reform within her, and it seemed to require she breath steadily to reduce its size. She believed herself to be arriving at an emotional limit.

Lu's growl prohibited any further commentary from Sab.

"I died for the last time tonight," Lil began, her skin luminous, her demeanor calm and foreboding as she addressed The Others. "I have had an eventful day, this evening even more so… My tolerance has run *extremely* thin, and there is no information you could produce to make the sound of your voices worthwhile in this moment."

She was not blind to the twinkle in Michael's eye. He ground his teeth in frustration when she asserted herself defiantly *to him,* but when witnessing her might wielded elsewhere… Lil always sensed she'd brought him something akin to fraternal pride, and it had been a long time since he'd had the opportunity to indulge thusly.

Lu purred, the vibration and heat he emitted both relaxing and invigorating her.

"Do what you do best, and remain silent" he rumbled, meeting the eyes of the three who'd arrived latest at Malcom's. Cass and Gabriel had raised questions in the first garden, Lil recalled, something having at least stirred in them before they'd carried through with their given orders.

"It was at your instruction," Raphael began, providing his attempt at justification to Michael with caution. Auburn hair curled around his ears, chestnut eyes not grasping his infraction.

"You were complicit," Michael said abruptly, eyes meeting those of Sab, Raz, and Raphael. "We will discuss potential modifications to protocol later, but at present you are a hindrance to our progress here. You're to take a walk; by the ocean, in the desert, it matters not so long as you don't remain here. I'll find and brief the three of you when we've finished."

After the three departed without a word of protest, Lu wasted no time in addressing Michael.

"We have ideas based on what we've seen," Lu began. "What does the timeline look like from your angle?"

"Weeks, maybe months," Michael said frankly. "Geographical changes have been underway for some time, drastically expedited by the creatures themselves. They just needed a nudge here and there to synchronize the transforming landscape with the waves of microorganisms unleashed." He paused a moment, tilted his head. "Ten to fourteen days and the global population will have reduced by fifty percent. An additional reduction of fifty percent by twenty to twenty-four days, at which point geological changes should start to ramp up, and we can begin to work logistically with survivors."

"The destruction will be enough to ensure peace for those who remain?" Remi asked.

Intervention of this kind was a very delicate business. Too little, and any impact made would be soon forgotten. Too much chaos drawn out would promote anguish and suffering too long-lasting, creating a landscape riddled with marauders and cruelty. The intervention was meant to bring peace, and for that the devastation would need to be rapid in execution.

Michael sighed. "Your collective collaboration would make for a more compassionate timeline."

Lil closed her eyes, recalling the ocean on her skin. The sensation of undulating water, of smooth, wet stones under her body on Iceland's shore was so strong, for a moment she felt she'd returned from a dream rather than exploring a memory.

*I asked you then, as I have every time you awoke.*

He'd asked, if given the choice, would she consider. For centuries Lil refused contact, but this time had been different; this time Michael didn't wait for a response. He hadn't used targeted brutality to force her hand. He'd just moved forward without her.

She felt an ache in her heart for the suffering her absence would cause, and perhaps an ache of another kind.

*We decide the extent of our involvement, but Ilati...* His words were heavy, saturated with the blood and tears of the past, with hope.

*We cannot remain absent for this,* she sighed, turning her head up as she leaned back into the warmth of his body, inhaling comfort.

*No.*

Lil opened her eyes, finding herself where she'd been before they'd closed: in a garden again, in Lu's arms, looking through unshed tears at Michael. He'd had experienced more than sons; he'd known mortal love. He'd picked rice from between floorboards, stacked stones with a boy.

The water coating her vision hovered a moment before falling, stretching his golden glow out into a halo. His eyes pulsed like soft stars in that moment, sharing something as they regarded her.

She blinked, and Lu's thumb was at her cheek, wiping what had fallen.

"You mentioned working with survivors," Lil whispered.

Michael swallowed, recovering from something, and nodded. "As you stated, we shouldn't have to hide, nor should our offspring. There was a time when we walked among them, when you *lived* among them openly. I tasted it briefly in the beginning, and with Ninella," he added briskly. "This will be the dawn of a new age, as it were, a time for adaptation or failure to survive. We will be present without dampening what we are, as will our children. Hamish will have a chance the others of my unfortunate lineage were never given: to be nurtured, to steward the earth." While it wasn't in their nature, Lil felt something akin to regret in Michael's voice as it trailed off, regret and the faint spark of possibility.

*Imagine flying over the lavender fields in daylight*, Lu said, his words carrying the promise of sun on her feathers.

*Will the fields survive this?* The plot of land seemed inland and high to stand a chance…

*Yes, but it will be a short walk to the shore afterwards.*

Lu nodded to Remi, who then joined Uri in conversation with Cass and Gabriel. The four spoke low, and without detectible animosity. Az remained at a distance.

"Our involvement does not mean a return to the way things were," Lil began. "But we will come together for this."

Michael nodded, and it truly seemed he was hearing her.

"I have a family here," she continued. "A human family. After everything that's happened today, with what's to come, I need to spend some time with them… Before we get started."

Michael nodded again, then looked to Lu for input, browse raised.

Lu's palm heated Lil's back, the green of his eyes bright against the brown, slipping into a deep black. His hand slid up her spine, curved around her neck, and stopped at her jaw. As his thumb softly grazed her mouth, Lil tasted the salt lingering there, what had been her tears, before his lips molded to hers.

*We will depart shortly*, He said. *A concise conversation is all that's needed for now. Then another breath before we get to work.*

*Nan must be a wreck...*

*Uri will give assurances when he arrives ahead of us*, Lu purred, pulling his mouth from hers to flash a subtle smile weighted in delightful suggestion. *We won't be going there directly.*

"Come," he said. "Let's wrap up for tonight."

Lu ticked his head to the side as he and Lil turned, an invitation for Michael to walk with the two of them, to join them in speaking with the others. But Michael didn't move.

"Lilitu, a moment, if I could."

Lu stopped, then slowly rotated his head toward Michael. The depth of his eyes held an entirely different promise than what they offered under Lil's gaze.

Lil knew the choice was hers, and she felt Lu's ease the moment she made her decision. He kissed her once more, inhaled intensely around her mouth as his lifted into a soft smile, then he moved steadily on toward the others, alone.

Lil noticed for the first time that Michael had a small pouch resting at his side. He picked it up, reaching inside as she drew near. He removed a small round thing, placed it in his mouth, and chewed. A cookie?

Michael's eyes sparkled, his skin shimmering gold where the light caught. "It's not in our nature to be separated thusly," he began. "We are meant to be ten, not six."

The statement hung for a moment, Lil processing the implication.

"The more time I spent here, the more…" He paused thoughtfully. "I can never fully understand *your* experience: growing from birth within a family of creatures, or the experience of those who left with you, who stayed with you throughout the cycles… But with what time I have spent among them, developing *connections* and such…" His words trailed off as his gaze drifted to the stones stacked on the rock wall, then to a row of windows on the top floor of the school. "I might grasp now more than I once could, the hesitation to leave this place. But we are not *leaving*, Lilitu, we do not abandon the first child to go birth a second. Can you remember, still? We were *everywhere*, then…" He took another small, round cookie from the bag and placed it in his mouth, the action followed by crunching sounds and the release of a sweet, spicy fragrance mingling with the subtle scent of cedar that lingered around him.

"Are those gingersnaps?" She asked with a raise of her brow and almost, *almost*, the hint of a smile.

Michael nodded, his face soft as it had ever been. "Hamish. He saw that our meeting tonight would not be a dream, and baked them to bring along," he sighed. "They're quite good, and warm more than my palette."

He offered the bag without ceremony, and she reached inside without hesitation, equally relaxed in disposition as she took a bite. A breath of satisfaction left her, the spices in her mouth contrasting nicely with the crisp air and cool ground under her feet. The soft grass felt fresh and wet, and the clouds like a blanket, slipped from the heavens, exposing what had long been waiting.

"You've been living short spans, perpetually," Michael stated gently. They'd stopped walking, and she sensed him looking at her, though she kept her eyes on the stars. "Five years here, several hundred there; these small bursts have denied a core impulse of your being. You have created a magnificent garden on Earth, Lilitu, lived within, have become a *part* of it…"

There was a truth she hadn't been ready to drink from, a deluge that threatened. Lu's warmth was at her back, his arms around her again, his breath at her neck. He would support her, but he wouldn't protest verity.

"…You have a purpose beyond this atmosphere," Michael concluded with a whisper.

And she breathed, "I know."

# 19.

"That's enough for tonight," Lu breathed, guiding Lil back a step, away from Michael, the wall, the weight of what had been said.

Then the grass shimmered beneath her, and the two of them were falling.

Ground gave way to sky, to the roaring storm clouds that enveloped them, flickering and sparkling with brilliance.

Lil breathed in air she wasn't sure she needed anymore as Lu pulled away to look at her.

They beheld each other as they plummeted, lingering in the love of that moment, the long-awaited glory of it, until his wings shot out. The surrounding clouds moved as if his feathers had pushed them, parting in half before dissolving into wisps of mist, then dissipating altogether.

The darkness beyond waited, open and black as the center of Lu's eyes, though with flecks of stars and less impending intensity. If one were to somehow manage to set those eyes on a scale against the infinite above, she knew the balance would tip down ever so slightly on the side of the two dark rounds pulling her in.

# A Story in Song

*Never again will you wait to fall toward the stars, Ilati... never again.*

And she would never again be born, or die. The cycle had ended, and along with that thought were a thousand others threatening to spill over. Lil let herself have the long moment, the pause before another breath taken. There would be an after, and there would be a reckoning, but not yet. First, she would have the stars, she would have Lu, and then she would take the next breath.

Lu angled his wings, cutting upward through the air, slowing their descent. The water beneath appeared tranquil as glass, though it was the ocean. The resulting reflection was so vast, it allowed the night sky to encompass them as a sphere, interrupted only by the almost imperceptible horizon. Lil lifted the skirt of her dress, dipping a toe to into the surface, disrupting the stillness with concentric rings moving outward.

They could swim, but perhaps that was a moment for after.

Lil looked from the water to Lu's eyes as they hovered. She inhaled deep, then pushed off from his chest with both hands, her own wings flaring. She remained at Lu's height, several meters away while he stared hungrily, eyes blazing. She knew that predatory look, the ferocity of it sending a welcome flare of warmth accelerating through her.

Lil lifted the skirt of her dress again, dipping a foot and playfully sending a splash of droplets toward Lu. The water turned to steam before making contact with his skin.

He sprang forward with incredible speed, but Lil reacted just as fast. She leaned backward, wings slicing through the air like a living fan as Lu dove over her. He turned, eyes locking with hers, feet skidding across the ocean surface, wrinkling the night's reflection as he slowed.

Lil raised her brows, goading him.

Lu flapped his wings, sending slow, powerful gusts toward her, the air dense with vapor as it reacted to his heat. Though a soft fog materialized, Lil could still see Lu's form clearly, and it was changing... Before her eyes, Lu had increased in size by double, almost three times. The chain of the necklace he wore tightened around his neck.

What had remained of his clothing were shredded.

Feathers fell around him, dissolving in the air and water. As his wings continued to beat, they became dark, leathery in appearance. The wings of a dragon. As his smile formed, the pronounced lengthening of his canines became visible, sending a delightful shiver down her spine.

He charged again, but this time she surrendered, absorbing her wings as they collided. The growl from his chest moved through and around her, intoxicating as his scent, though nearly dwarfed by the thunderous sound of the rippling space behind her.

She'd expertly manifested the portal just prior to his strike, the momentum from the impact taking them through.

Her feet met dry sand, and then her back, gliding gently across the shifting desert ground. Ocean had been replaced by dunes, but the night sky remained. Lu brought them to a stop, digging the taloned tips of his wings into the earth just above her head, creating a cocoon above them.

He rested his giant palm over her torso, his fingers curling around the neckline of her dress, the heat of each digit skimming against her skin. Lil kept her eyes on his, on the unfathomable darkness he welcomed her into. Slowly, she reached for his other hand and guided him to the zipper at her side.

"Were your hands a bit smaller," she whispered, "you might find this simple task more manageable…"

His chest rumbled and his head lowered, mouth at her neck. His body shifted until the chain around his neck was loose once more, his size as it had been when they fell.

The zipper slid downward, and then the dress, until there was nothing between them but their story written in stone, two cylinders resting over her heart.

His lips brushed her ear, followed by his teeth pinching at her lobe, his smile against her skin.

"I could smell it…" he whispered with a low growl. "Your memory drifted across the water like the scent of ripened fruit in an orchard…"

Only one of his hands made its way back up her body, moving slowly over the rise and fall of her curves.

Lil reached down, grasping his forearm, feeling the rhythm of his muscles beneath her palm, and then she brought both her arms around him. Lu gently cradled her neck in one hand, his thumb stroking down to her clavicle and up to her jaw; while the other hand traveled up to her hip, and gripped firm.

Stretching her arms over his back, Lil felt her way up to his neck, felt the landscape of him. He raised her hips as her fingers entwined with his hair, both of them responding to the divine need that was a foundation of their being.

## A Story in Song

Her skin had maintained a soft glow since they'd fallen, but as she glanced down to where their bodies met, Lil saw orange and carnelian flames flickering over Lu, wrapping around both of them. His fire could turn bones to ash, but her flesh wouldn't burn, not anymore. Instead, she reveled in the heat, what they made together.

An indescribable hum was building between them; the dunes singing around them harmonize with it.

Lu's hands dug into the sand on either side of her head. Golden grains mounded up to his wrists, and then sank down into a void rapidly filling with fresh water. Lil felt the cool liquid flooding beneath her, seeping into the sand and trickling in tiny rivulets along the contours of her body. The fizzling hiss of steam bubbled up around them until Lu allowed his flames to recede, though his skin maintained the same glow she radiated.

He took her hands from behind his neck, guided them over their heads, and pressed them into the sand beneath the shallow water. His expression was both content and feral as he hovered over her, his movements slow and strong, his gaze intensifying as he studied her face. Lil could just make out the moving sparks of energy orbiting them in her periphery, but Lu's proximity, the space that was and was not between them, wouldn't permit her awareness to wander.

Their parted lips joined, creating another explosive connection.

A building force began spreading outward, like an entire universe forming rapidly within a budding flower, waiting to burst with bloom, fragrance, with sweet reward and the promise of new life.

*Show me,* she whispered.

Through his eyes, Lil saw her body glowing like a moon among the rippling reflection of stars. Shallow water came up just below her ears, becoming much deeper further beyond her reach. She followed the drifting tendrils of her hair to see water lilies… their flowers blossoming, leaves unfurling across the surface… grasses, reeds shooting up. Young trees grew strong along the banks, dangling vines with green fruit that became yellow, then darkened. Dates. An oasis.

She let go.

While most of Lil's body clung to Lu, the rest of her released like a burst of fireflies, twinkling into sentient starlight as she diffused through the air. Lu erupted like a roaring thundercloud, the ground vibrating violently beneath the parts of them still connected in solid form.

Frenzied euphoria calmed like waves after a storm, lulling to serenity, as the sparkling mist returned to settle around them, rejoining their bodies.

Lu brought his nose to her hairline, breathing her in. His beard grazed her face, his breath caressing over her. His scent was so intoxicating that her eyes rolled and closed for a moment, focusing without sight on the water meeting her skin, his pulsing body inside her, his tongue along her clavicle.

She opened her eyes again, holding Lu's stare as she guided him onto his back.

"Mmmm," he groaned as she ground against him, sand molding to his form, around her knees.

Lu tilted his head back, his hair drifting, water undulating against him. He let his arms go loose, partially submerged at his side as Lil leaned forward. She sank down until her nipples pressed against his skin, her hips still working against his.

When their rhythm had worked again to that ledge, wet fingers gripped Lil's thighs, Lu meeting her thrusts, until another explosion of heat and release flooded them both.

Lil stretched out over him, then slid down to rest on her side, her head on his shoulder.

"Are you hungry?" He asked, his fingers stroking along her torso. They made the most pleasant sound as they dipped slowly through the water.

Lil smiled, certain a blush had found her cheeks. She didn't feel the need to eat for sustenance as she once did.

"Not for food, then," Lu said with a self-satisfied smile that she found utterly endearing.

Propped up on his elbow, he lowered his face toward hers, and Lil brought her tongue peeking out just enough to slide over his lower lip. His sigh was like a song, calling her muscles to loosen, her mouth to open a bit wider. Her fingers skimmed along his thigh, trickling water over his skin as she moved upward.

Another drawn out breath escaped Lu as he eased back from Lil's lips. This time, the sigh was weighted slightly, leaden with the memory of time's passage, and of their obligations.

"I think we've a few more moments of peace before our return," he said, repositioning their bodies so he sat at the edge of the watery drop off with Lil between his legs facing outward. "And more than a few moments afterward."

"Mmmm," she responded, leaning her head back into his hands. They would have time, time unencumbered by the threat of death inevitable. "I'd like to return to Ghent. I had some pastry there recently, an experience that was nothing less than *rhapsodic*."

"And was it the pastry or the presentation that left this lasting impression?"

"It would be unfair to compare the two, but they did enhance one another."

"What shall we do after Ghent?"

"We?"

His fingers stopped moving and Lil smiled, Lu chuckling softly as he started working through her hair again.

"I want to swim," she said. "I want to swim together as we once did and... when's the last time you went sledding?" She asked, as the thought popped into her mind. "Claire asked if you'd ever had, and I realized how long it must have been."

"When was this?"

"The other day on the phone," she smiled, recalling the conversation. Tilting her head back further, Lil added, "She said she thought it unlikely you had."

Lu's brows both lifted and pinch together. "Of course I have," he stated, as though Claire were there to hear him refute her assumption. "I'm immortal, and I know how to have a good time."

"Todd said almost the same thing exactly," she laughed.

"Bright young man... So, we have Ghent, swimming, and a family sledding trip. I have a few ideas of my own..."

Lil leaned back as Lu combed his fingers through her hair, listening to the low tones of his voice move through stories and ideas kept waiting, sharing her thoughts as her hands massaged his calves.

When they emerged from the water, Lil rinsed the sand from her dress, though some of the blood remained. Lu dried the garment, steam still rising as she slipped it on. Lil could have provided this service of herself, but it was the gesture… whether combing her hair, making her tea, or drying her dress, it was about the gesture rather than who was capable of what task.

"I don't know whether I want to preserve or burn it," Lu said flatly, his fingers delicately smoothing over the torn silk.

"You're not burning it. This garment will live out its days in a drawer or on a hanger at the mountain," she sighed. "We should probably get going. We'll need to rinse off, get dressed before we head to Nan's."

"What do you plan on wearing?"

She eyed him. The question was off, and his expression too casual not to be mischievous. "I don't know… Why…"

"I believe there was mention of gold."

She inhaled slow and deep. "I can't wear gold to Nan's…"

"There won't be any left."

# 20.

Mist softened sunlight welcomed Lil and Lu as they passed through the orchard and put the fields behind them. It was as though the fog had waited with Lil's family for her return, parting with their collective sigh and lingering concern.

The pair were met by loved ones not running toward them, but standing with uneasy stillness in the garden by the house, faces haunted and hopeful. Lil felt warmth spread through her, the sensation of tiny bubbles rising and bursting within at the sight of them.

Uri stood tall to the left beside Todd, Claire and Gunnar, followed by Magnus and Nan, Remi and Az a little off to the right side. Uri's Grey T-shirt had faded red letters that said: *Self Starter.* Todd's was grey as well, but with black letters that read: *Post Mortem.* A play on his brush with death, apparently.

She wondered if he'd had one made for her and Magnus as well.

*He does get those shirts made remarkably fast,* Lu commented.

*He says he knows a guy.*

A Story in Song

Claire had on her Malachite earrings and sage green cardigan, two beads on a bracelet visible just past the cuff. Gunner stood beside her in jeans and a black thermal. Nan's loose-legged, grey knit pants grazed the ground, and the wide neck of her lilac sweater reached across her shoulders. Magnus had his arm around her. His grey trousers and white shirt were covered by Nan's pinafore… the one with the blueberry stains.

Nan made contact first, pulling Lil in close before stepping back with shaking breath to inspect her abdomen.

"I changed out of the dress," Lil said softly. Instead, she wore faded jeans, flats, and that fitted black shirt with the long sleeves and low back. "There's no mark left behind," she added, lifting the hem briefly to reveal unblemished skin.

Nan exhaled with relief as she pulled Lil back in again for a long, firm hug. Milestones of Lil's human life had been marked by the feeling of Nan's arms around her; moments of joy, fear, and contentment.

"I think my heart could use a bit of a rest after this," Nan sighed, the words ringing true in Lil's chest as well.

Magnus put his arms around both of them. "I'm glad you made it home, Lily dear." Then he gave Lu a healthy pat on the back.

Nan's hand stretched out, cupped Lu's cheek, then slid down to his shoulder where she gave him a little squeeze. "Thank you," she said, "for every part you played in their return."

Because it was more than Lil who'd survived and come home to her.

# A Story in Song

Lil barely had time to process embracing Todd and Claire before Nan started waving her hands around, ushering everyone inside with promises of opportunity for conversation *after* their bellies were full, or at least not empty.

Spoons clanged against ceramic as food was scooped from bowls and platters onto the plates set atop a crowded wooden table. The plan had been to meet at Nan's for breakfast, but Lil and Lu were delayed in in their arrival, resulting in a gathering that felt a little more like a late brunch.

The kitchen was too small to contain them all, and with Nan's preference that their plates remain on a table rather than their laps, the seldom used dining room had been prepared with a modest feast for the ten of them.

Lil had lingered in the kitchen a while the others shuffled through to start eating. Gunnar paused, his large frame leaning silently against the doorway to the dining room. He extended his arm, seamlessly pulling her in toward himself, resting his cheek atop her head.

"It was a long wait kid." His voice was low, carrying something ragged as it traveled through his chest and into her ear. "I thought you might not come back the same as you were…" He inhaled, released his breath. "Wondered if I might meet you as a child again."

It had been close…

"Did Lu share with you the nature of his unique relationship with the dead?" She asked.

Lil's hair moved under Gunnar's chin as he nodded.

"I left my body," she sighed. "I know you were filled in, with as much as someone looking on could report, but Lu and I were able to speak to each other briefly as I separated… while I was passing, and he held on. I asked that he bring me to you and Claire upon my rebirth." Closing her eyes, she whispered, "I've never asked for such a thing before."

*Had you slipped through my grasp, I would have done it,* Lu said from the other room. *Never again, Ilati,* his voice soothed. *Come, sit at the table with our family.*

Lil pulled back from Gunnar enough to see him wipe below his eyes. She did the same.

"The memories of my youth will have to be enough for you now," she said, letting out another deep breath, and patting him on the chest. "I'm all done dying."

The modest dining room housed a long table set for ten, spread with food enough for all without feeling crammed. No one had been positioned alone at the ends, but sat five to a side.

Lil settled in opposite Lu on one end with Claire, Gunnar, Todd, and Uri on her side. Lu next to Nan, followed by Magnus, Remi and Az on the other, all of them tucking in. A door at Lil and Lu's end led to the kitchen, at the other a door to the hall. Windows lined the length of one side, letting in the natural light. While Lil sat with her back to the scenic view of the garden and the trees beyond, she was graced with Lu's face across from her, the remains of their morning glistening in the sun.

Nan narrowed her eyes at Lu. Absent malice but heavy with curiosity, she cleared her mouth with a sip of tea and asked, "Now, what have you gotten yourselves into?" Her fingers fell loose as her hand casually gestured to his beard and neck. "Is that powder? There are gold smudges all over your skin but none on your clothes. Don't tell me you're using those glitter soaps."

Uri made a choking sound from down the table, and Remi turned his head to look away, the upturned corner of his mouth still visible.

Gold filled the creases of Lu's hands, smeared across his neck, a slash marked the crown of his head. The epicenter, though, was his mouth: a metallic gleam unevenly coating his lips and beard. What flesh his clothes didn't cover displayed a shimmering accent, telling the story of where he'd been.

"A painting project at another location," Lu answered, casually selecting a warm vanilla scone from its basket. "These-smell delightful."

He kept his expression relaxed, but Lil saw what lived under the mask he wore. He was wickedly pleased, both sated and greedy.

"What were you doing, drinking it?" Claire laughed. Uri let out another choking sound, unsuccessful in disguising his chortle as Lil's cousin continued to point out the obvious. "It's all over both of you."

Gold remained on Lil's skin as well, in defiance of Lu's efforts, though none remained at its point of origin. The swirling details had once been intricately applied from her shoulders down. What streaked along Lil's neck, over her lips, cheeks and through her hair... that was all his doing.

"I can get you each a damp washcloth," Nan offered, moving to rise from the table.

"It stays where it is," Lu said, looking to Lil over the rim of his cup. His eyes burned with a fire that hadn't died down since his tongue first laid a path through her golden landscape, a fire that hadn't died down since they'd first drawn breath.

Nan's brows shot up, then she paused with a critical eye, assessing. She had the look of a seasoned woman who'd raised children several times over. She glanced between Lil and Lu, then further down the table, to Uri, no doubt.

With words that were spoken deliberately slow and well-articulated, Nan said, "Let me preface by saying it warms my heart to know the two of you are able to enjoy each other's company, especially given all that you've been through, however…"

Lil felt Claire go still beside her, and she was willing to bet Todd had stopped chewing, avoiding any sudden movements that might attract Nan's focus. They knew what was coming next, what to prepare for when Nan slowed and intensified her speech like that…

Someone was going to be scolded.

"Yesterday," Nan began, catching Lil's eyes, "if you'll allow me to refresh your memory, dear, you were drugged and abducted. You came home looking appropriately disheveled, but you cleaned up *well*," she added with an honest smile after a pause and nod of recognition. "And do you remember how Todd reacted when he came through the door? How he felt after having been left in the dark?"

He'd been left to manage the shop, to shoulder responsibility while being beside himself with worry, and rightfully so.

Lil nodded, hearing Todd shift in his chair down the table.

"Mmm," Nan went on with a tilt of her head. "And then you went off to confront the man who'd been responsible for the invasion and attempts at capture. Claire had quite the experience. They early killed Todd. And Magnus," she added with a slow shake of her head. "When I heard thunder out back, and it was Magnus…" Nan closed her eyes a moment. Magnus took her hand in his, and she sighed, "We knew you'd been attacked again, and again we waited. I'm an older woman, at least by mortal standards. Magnus and I, we know what it's like to lose people, people who weren't reborn that we might be given the promise of holding them again. I sat with him by the fire wondering what would become of your body if you died. I pondered on whether the skin you wore would dissolve into the ether with you on the way to your next life, or if you'd leave your flesh behind like the rest of us. I grieved that I might not see your face again, or have the comfort of ashes to throw into the ocean. We waited for *hours* until Uri showed up and gave us the short version, that you'd died, but they'd restored your immortality. He said there'd be nothing more that could harm you, that we should all get some sleep and you'd be along for breakfast." Nan paused for a steadying breath, then turned to Lu and said, "After the day and night we endured, I'm fairly certain that whatever this was,' she gestured again to the evidence he wore, "could have waited until you'd at least checked in."

A sinking ache gnawed at Lil's heart, though it was surrounded by a fullness, saturated with love. Nan had been holding those words in all night, for days, since raiders had come to her home willing to kill for what they sought. Perhaps she'd held on to some fear longer still, since Lil had been brought to her doorstep as a sleeping girl in Lu's arms. Perhaps Nan had always held a little bit of breath, wondering when she'd need to use the number kept by the phone.

"Nan," Lil pleaded with a whisper, the distance between them suddenly seeming too great. Lil stood and rounded the end of the table as Lu moved his chair back enough for her to seamlessly slide onto his lap. She leaned over into Nan's arms, tears falling on Nan's shoulder.

Lil felt Lu's hand around her waist, then warm on her thigh, one of Nan's hands resting behind her neck, another rubbing her back. The old woman was soft, and had the familiar scent of lavender and things baked with love. Lil let out a ragged breath as she noticed Nan twisting slightly to look out the window.

"Don't worry, I won't make it rain," Lil sighed with a shaky laugh.

"I raised you, dear," Nan said, pulling her face back to capture Lil's eyes with hers. "You can't blame me for looking."

"You did raise me, Nan," Lil said, giving the woman's hands a gentle squeeze for emphasis. "You *raised* me. The scope of my existence is not a rug to sweep your importance under. It was your arms that carried me to bed when I fell asleep before a movie ended, your stories I grew up listening to, your eyes *glaring* at me when my finger went into the batter too many times. Your unconditional love. You are part of me; the me that is here, now, and the me that will continue on. I love you, Nan, and I know there are rooms upstairs, but I really needed some time away with Lu, to just relax, stretch… to connect."

Lil leaned back into Lu's lap, and he eased her head against his chest.

"You were with me," he began, addressing Nan with thoughtfulness and clarity. "You were with me while I grieved. I entrusted you with her care when she was last a child. And though she has recovered from mortality, we still sit at your table, because of our love for you." He ran his cheek over the top of Lil's head, inhaling her scent, his eyes drifting toward the window. "The day has been long, and the compounded lifetimes have been longer, Nan. We took the time we needed, and it was time best spent at a distance from others."

"It's my fear talking," Nan sighed and reached for Magnus's hand. "I love the two of you, and you've gone and grown wings."

"Won't be able to keep me away," Uri said with mouth half full, grinning at Nan as he chewed. "I worry you won't manage on your own now that that you've felt my fire in the kitchen."

"Fire," Nan mumbled, rolling her eyes. "You're a pain in my ass is what you are. If your palette wasn't superb and your hands magic, I'd have thrown you out."

"You'd have tried."

"She's all talk," Todd said.

Nan glared at him.

"Mostly talk," he amended.

"I know what she is, and I know her heart is going to melt when she tastes the pie I made," Uri announced, getting up from the table. "I told you what I would bake when I first arrived," he said from the kitchen.

He returned with the round dish in his hands, and looked at Lil.

"Lu planted the orchard before you were born," Uri said. "Your childhood, this whole life, you ate his apples not knowing the weight they carried. You grew a tree of your own with the seeds. I told you I'd bake you something with the fruit from both trees because the story sings to my heart. Now let the music fill you as you eat. Come."

A pulse of light flushed over Lil's skin, settling into a soft glow as the overhead chandelier briefly flared on. She locked onto Uri's amber eyes with tears welling in her own. Lu's hand trailed down her leg as she stood, pausing as Uri held up a finger.

"You can thank me by eating," he said, pointing at the pie. "Pass your plate down. You too big guy."

Lil and Lu passed their plates, their story filling them as they ate. The food quieted everyone's mouths for a time, but as conversation flowed again, Lil put a hand on Claire's shoulder.

"Let's go make some chai," she said.

Claire's face flashed with concern, Nan asking the same wordless question.

"I think we're all going to need a cup," Lil said, heading into the kitchen.

Claire and Nan followed, then the three women set to making a drink they'd consumed together for some twenty years, a drink for soothing storms, both inside and out.

"No, the *bigger* one," Nan said to Claire, who sat crouching in front of a large cabinet. "I'd rather the obscene size than risk the pot bubbling over onto the stove, and the- Yes, that one."

After they'd sourced and added the ingredients together, Claire calmed her nerves with an old wooden spoon, stirring what simmered. Through the scent of spices that filled the kitchen, she caught Lil's eyes, and asked, "Will we still see you?"

"I'll have... *obligations*, so you won't see me as often. But you'll see me. Like how you split your time between the Orn and Nan's... Though I don't think I'll be able to keep my hours at the shop."

Nan huffed an amused breath as she ladled out the tea into mugs. "Times change," she said. "Todd has really grown into something of a young man. With him taking charge, Duncan and the other kids, we'll be just fine. Remember, I ran the shop long before you two started taking on hours."

The three of them carried in cups until everyone was seated with their hands around a warm mug, in a collective moment of spices and silence.

*Ready?* Lu asked.

Lil nodded, took another sip, a breath, then started in on disclosing the forthcoming challenges

it was then that the nature of forthcoming challenges was disclosed. Nan was right in sensing changes coming, but Lil knew, however wise the old woman was, Nan hadn't suspected the devastation being discussed. She hadn't suspected billions would be taken by illness and a changing landscape, or that, with Lil's help, the Ten could make those changes in a matter of days. Nan had wisdom, and foresight, but her eyes grew wide as every other mortal's at the table, becoming somber as the revelation sank in.

"I might need you to go over this again," Nan started in a remarkably calm voice. "The word *after* was clearly mentioned at some point in reference to a time following this apocalypse of yours. Forgive me if I'm incorrect, but it also sounds very much like everyone on this earth will perish in a week's time. *Everyone*, do I have that right?"

"No, not all… but most." Lil answered.

"What do we do now?" Claire asked.

"Live," Magnus answered; his voice and eyes soft as he looked across the table.

"You have always known you would die," Lu said. "You've known that you, and all those around you would pass, and yet there was no frantic scramble, no panic. You lived. You lived for joy, for the bittersweet, and the journey between them. You have lived to feed the thing that drives your kind to wonder, to love. Continue to do that."

"There must be *something* to be done," Nan said. Her defiance was strong but her confidence in her claim faltered even as she spoke the words. "That tea Claire had been working on…"

Claire shook her head. "The tea won't save people from earthquakes or floods. It will only protect against the one pathogen, and there's not enough for the world to drink."

"We're implementing these measures because of their potential for devastation," Lil said. "Our intention is for not all, but most, to lose their lives."

"Believe me when I say there is nothing you can do that will affect the global outcome, and you should not attempt such an intervention," Lu said. "There are ways to ready yourselves for the coming storm. Magnus, we have things to discuss with you, related to the Orn."

Magnus nodded. "I expected that might be the case."

"Good, there's not much time, but we'll make use of what we have when I return. I have an errand to run with the three down the end. Don't get excited, Todd, I mean Uri."

A silent exchange took place between Uri and Lu, Todd looking back and forth between them like a dog watching a tennis match.

Lu shrugged; Uri grinned.

"Ok, you're coming," Lu said, then he, Remi, As, Uri, and Todd all stood together, pushing in their chairs, Todd displaying an entertaining combination of emotions.

"We shouldn't be more than two hours, and I expect you all to be well rested and prepared to have some fun when we return," Lu said, winking at Lil.

"Fun?" Claire asked. Her expression was appropriately distorted at the prospect, given the impending devastation, everything they'd learned.

"Joy and the bittersweet," Lu said. "To honor what moments you have, that others might not."

Claire nodded in understanding, though still appeared unsettled. Lu's arms were already around Lil.

*Whatever are you up to?* Lil asked.

*Rest up*, he teased, sliding a hand behind her head as he leaned in for a kiss.

*I don't require sleep anymore...*

*And thankful I am for that or we'd have arrived even later,* he purred, bringing his thumb up to her lip and slowly grazing over a golden smudge he'd left there. *It would have taken you hours to recover.*

And when she'd woken refreshed, it would have been another struggle altogether to leave without further delay.

*

The five who remained at the house cleared the table, letting routine and togetherness work their earthly magic. It was perhaps an hour or so later that

Nan and Magnus had gone out to the garden for some fresh air; the younger three wishing to give them some space. Claire leaned against Gunnar at one end of the living room couch, her feet tucked under Lil's thigh at the other end.

"Do you still keep in touch with your families, the ones from before… from other lives?" Claire asked.

"No."

There were some she thought about more often than others. Over the last one or two thousand years, the idea of immortal beings, of wings and such, they weren't as accepted and her perpetual youth may have been troublesome for her families and their ancestors.

"I maintained contact with some, but only for a short time. There were many I would have liked to revisit in their older age, once I'd been reborn again and awakened to who I am… But it takes so much time… Reentry into their lives would have complicated things, perhaps been selfish. I still looked the same, and had danger following me. The Condemned will follow me still, I suppose, though they will find their mission to end my life a more challenging endeavor," Lil smiled, then pinched her brows and said, "I wonder how my change will affect their visions…"

Gunnar rumbled with consideration. "You said not all would be taken, but what of the Condemned?"

"Not all, but most," she said, her words hanging. "We'll make ourselves known to the survivors, be part of the recovery.

"Do you still sleep?" Claire asked.

There was a time when Lil and Claire sat together on the couch, albeit without Gunnar. Claire would tuck her feet under Lil's leg just so, and the two would talk about their dreams. Claire would sip her tea, enraptured by stories of where Lil had been while her body slept, of the ocean, of flying, and of the man whose face she couldn't see.

"Not the way I did before. The practice is refreshing, but I don't *need* it the way your body does. I don't yawn. My eyelids don't become so heavy that I cannot lift them, and I won't become ill if I deny myself. I can dream, and it's been a while, but as I recall, the challenge is in relinquishing control rather than struggling to gain it."

Lil paused, her mouth stretching into a broad smile at the interrupting words only she could hear; Lu's voice detailing what he'd planned.

Leaning back against her side of the couch, Lil reached for her mug, fighting the grin she wore to take a sip.

Then she said, "rest up."

*

Nan's breath formed a cloud in the cold mountain air, her cheeks pink as the gloves she wore. The lavender band on her ski goggles matched her snow pants… and Magnus's.

"I'm too old for this shit," She huffed.

"Nan!" Claire shouted, shocked at hearing the woman curse, then laughed, "Didn't you say you wouldn't let your age define you?"

353

The reflective coating on Nan's goggles prevented any of them from seeing through, but Lil knew the woman had rolled her eyes.

Nan, Claire, Todd, Gunnar, and Magnus all dressed head to toe in brightly colored ski gear, and stood on a snowy mountain top aside Uri, Az, Remi, Lil, and Lu. It was a special kind of miracle that magenta ski pants had been found in Gunnar's size, or Uri's for that matter, but Lil didn't ask questions, and allowed herself the joy it brought her. Uri matched Gunnar in pants and boots, but where Gunnar had a black jacket and gloves, Uri remained shirtless, as did Remi and Az. Lu's chest was bare as well, save for the stone suspended from around his neck. Their story, his promise. Lil had hers tucked under a black shirt, the one she'd worn in Iceland.

And brighter than anything Todd wore, was his unyielding smile at the spectacle they all made, and the triumph of having contributed to it.

"You know what they say: you only live once," he said to Nan.

She turned to Lu with pursed lips and cocked her head, as if asking him to confirm Todd's accuracy.

Lu nodded. "Just the once."

Claire and Gunnar got on one sled; his massive body positioned behind hers. Todd had his own sled, Nan and Magnus on a large inflated tub, reclining side by side, each with handles to grab hold of. Az stood behind Gunnar, Uri behind Todd, and Remi had one hand on each of the older mortals.

All at once, as though a silent countdown had ended, those with wings began to run.

They pushed the sleds as fast as was deemed safe, until their wings spread out, taking them into the air, hovering above those on land. The idea was a precaution given the age of some riders, and the potential for injury. Should one fall, their respective flier could have them scooped up before they hit the snow.

Lil sat on her sled as Lu ran behind, then gracefully crashed against her body as they jettisoned down the mountain at an exhilarating speed. She didn't need a flier, and he hadn't been on a sled in lifetimes.

Lil could feel the bright excitement of the others dancing with her own; it was as loud as their screams of delight ringing out over the snow.

Those without wings were flown back to the top for round after round of sledding until Todd fell on his back without energy enough to finish a snow angel.

Uri stood over him with a thermos. "Hot chocolate for when you find the strength to sit up," he said. "Groan all you like, but I'm not wasting the good stuff if you're just going to spill it. This has cinnamon, two sticks, and almond extract…"

Lu brought his mouth close to Lil's ear, his skin and breath radiating heat through the cold air. "One more. Me and you, let's go."

He ran behind her and jumped on as they accelerated. With the wind whipping around them, Lil turned in his arms, her eyes meeting his before she closed them, then brought their lips together. She heard his wings flair, felt as they caught the air, and her body lifted. She heard the surrounding sound of thunder as they passed into where, she did not know.

# A Story in Song

The atmosphere felt drastically different from what Lil had experienced during her mortal lifetimes. Her body adapted immediately upon entry to the extreme temperature and high levels of sulfur, carbon dioxide, and nitrogen that would have been incompatible with her human form. With open eyes, she took in the dark, rocky landscape, moons, and dusk barely lit by some star that was not the sun she'd known since the garden.

"I met with Gabriel earlier, while the others were procuring goggles and gloves," Lu began. "I allowed him to bring me here. Traces of oxygen and water… they've made slow progress."

Something had been missing. The new world had been waiting for her, for them; waiting for life.

Lu nodded.

"When you're ready, she'll be here."

Like the strengthening of rivers swelling inside her, Lil felt a fullness building within, echoed by the tears beginning to form in her eyes, like the clouds rapidly manifesting in the sky.

Water fell.

Her fingers raked his hair as his mouth met hers, and Lil felt his smile, coaxing.

Water fell, and fire burned. Flames burst around them, making wet ash of their clothing.

Water fell, and water rose. An ocean formed around them in what may have been moments or days, but the star had not yet risen from dusk's mirror.

*Time*, she said, her body floating beneath the surface, Lu hovering just below.

# A Story in Song

*Only hours for earth,* he said. *But we should return soon.*

*Soon, but not yet...* she said.

Lil twisted in the water to face him, then dove down into the darkness, her luminance the only light in an ocean of black. She turned again from the depths, her eyes on his as he watched her transform. She had been aching to do so for so long...

Lil swelled to an immense size, her dark scales like blue stone in shadow though somehow radiant.

Lu's eyes seemed almost as wide as hers, his body floating in water before her as the moment hung around them. He rested his hand on the expanse of her forehead. There were no words.

And then he was gone, but only from her sight. Lil felt him in the darkness below, looming as he often did, becoming larger, until a dragon without wings undulated unseen beneath her. She felt the black of his eyes watching; felt him seeing her from the abyss, where he waited to unleash himself.

Anticipation swelled, and then erupted the moment he did, his massive form shooting toward her with the force of a thousand years doubled over again and again. His smooth scales glided over hers, and she over him, their graceful bodies spiraling around one another as they swam.

# Epilogue

The rumbling of their passage quieted, though it took a few moments more for the birds and insects to resume their summer chatter over the sound of distant waves. Through the orchard, Lil breathed in the scent of lavender fields, beehives, salted air of the ocean just beyond. She breathed in the scent of fertile earth, smoldering sandalwood, embers, and rain.

Apples hung from the trees, not yet ripe. Lil cradled one in her hand, feeling the fruit swell until stem separated from tree. The crisp, sweet, tang of its flesh released a refreshing liquid in her mouth as she bit down. She could almost taste him… deep and earthy.

*It has been said that smell influences taste… should I stand farther away?*

Lil opened her eyes to meet Lu's.

*Don't you dare.*

He came in closer, took a bite.

She could have become lost watching him, but footsteps had joined the insects and bird song.

A man walked slowly out through the garden to meet them. His silver hair had been turning white for some time, but his broad shoulders still filled out the black t-shirt he'd stretched snugly over them. Nan would have had something to say about that...

Without hesitation, his arms wrapped around her, Lil's head finding a familiar resting place at his chest as he nodded to Lu.

"Kid."

The word was like another layer of him blanketed over her, a safe place for the pinch in her heart. She breathed in and sighed against him. The last mortal keeper of her childhood memories smelled like caramelized sugar, rosemary, and grapefruit.

"See, I told you they were coming," a child's voice shouted from somewhere inside the house. This was followed by a young girl of about seven years dashing out, screen door slamming and blonde hair trailing behind her. A long, thin string of silver encircled her neck, two small stone spheres strung on it: one black, one green.

Gunnar took a step back so she could give Lil's waist a hug.

"Hi Auntie Lil," she said, smiling bright.

Lil bent, bringing herself eye to eye with the girl, "Hey, Flora, ready for school? I thought we could visit one more time before we head over tomorrow."

"I've *been* ready," she laughed. Then, with a more serious expression, she lowered her voice and said, "Grampa Guns is hesitant…"

Lil raised her brow at Gunnar, then glanced back to see the girl's attention had already flitted elsewhere. Scanning the garden and beyond with a critical eye, Flora searched.

"Unka Lu!" The girl called out, triumphant and running off toward the distant shadow he stepped out from. Lu had a way of disappearing into things, and Flora delighted in finding him.

Gunnar adjusted his arm over Lil's shoulders, the two of them walking toward the apple tree Lil had planted between the shop and the old barn. The tree was about a century old, but the bench close by was new. Gunnar and his grandson, Flora's father Jacob, had built it together in the new barn, a space they used for woodworking and all manner of things. There always seemed to be a project. Over the past year Lu and Gunnar spent some time alone on a few big things, repairing and renovating the old barn being one of them.

Lil sat with Gunnar on the bench by the house where she'd grown up, where he'd raised a family, where loved ones had passed. They sat in relative silence, save for the sounds of the garden in summer, for Flora and Lu's voices in the distance, the waves, and that of waxed paper unfolding.

Lil leaned into Gunnar's shoulder, his arm resting across her back as the caramel melted over her tongue, soft, sticking to her teeth.

"Lu met her once when he lived here with Nan, before I was born. She had been a child," Lil said.

Gunnar nodded, and some time went by before he spoke. "I don't know how he survived your deaths with his sanity intact, but I'm thankful for it…"

Claire's passing had been hard for all of them, as it had been with Nan, Magnus, and Todd. The impact ran deep through Gunnar and Lil, and woke an old ache for the others. Lu was reminded of Lil's former affliction with mortality. Remi, Uri, and Az suffered the same memories, but with the addition of those they'd loved and lost, those who were never reborn.

Remi and Uri were not strangers to mourning, having felt the death of more than one companion. Decades, sometimes hundreds of years passed before they'd consider opening their hearts to another. Az, though… He had not explored romantic love again, not after the first time.

That which made Gunnar a descendant, of both Az *and* Uri, gave him vitality and slower aging. He had years left before his heart would grow tired enough to stop beating, but wouldn't feel another passing like Claire's in that time.

"Are *you* ready for school?" she asked.

"I was ready to teach once, then I met *you*. Time has passed since carrying a girl out of the garden on my back… more than a lifetime."

The crinkle of wax paper sounded again preceding Gunnar's placement of a caramel into his mouth. As she leaned in closer, Lil's head rested just below his shoulder, the scent of ginger and memories on his breath as he exhaled over her.

"You ok kid?" He asked. The arm slung around her flexed, his hand giving her a gentle squeeze. "I'm not the only one she left behind."

Claire had asked once, if Lil ever kept in touch with her families from lives passed, and Lil had answered honestly that she did not. Times had been different then.

No headstone marked Claire's organic remains, no indicator for one to find comfort in closeness to the husk she'd left behind. Lil knew well it wasn't the body that rested, in fact, what remained of Claire's body was very much active, what with the decomposers having done their work, and new life sprouting forth, as it was meant to.

Lil didn't visit bodies, but the memories shared. She made chai. She visited the hives and lavender. Sometimes Lil wore Claire's green cardigan, though a few buttons had been replaced over the years. She surfed at night, kept a keychain that made her laugh. She wore the apron with blueberry stains and, *on occasion*, buttered her scones.

Someday she'd sharpen knives on wet stone, and eat caramels.

"I wear the sweater a lot," she whispered.

His head moved slightly, a subtle nod against her hair.

"I wrap in the grey blanket..." he said. "Sometimes when I'm drinking that chai of yours with that blanket around me, I can feel the echo of her feet tucking under my thigh."

"Her feet were always cold," Lil smiled, and sighed. "The sweater still carries a bit of her smell."

Lil kept Claire's sweater in a box, like Nan did with Grampa Pat's things, only Lil used stone, not cedar, and she lined it with fresh sprigs of rosemary.

"Her scent fades," he said. "But the rosemary helps."

It did.

The small paper bag rustled again, and a covered caramel appeared before her. She unwrapped it, and welcomed the smooth texture, slowly flattening as it melted on her tongue: apples and some subtle smoky essence he'd managed to capture. Lil was nearly submerged in the flavor when she heard a deep voice singing low, a song passing through air, through the ground and into her heart.

*"Ladybird, ladybird, protect these leaves, eat all the aphids, then dance in the breeze."*

Gripping Gunnar's hand, Lil turned, a sweet ache filling her chest.

Like a blood mist rising in the garden, Ladybugs lifted from stems, leaves, and petals all around Flora. They came together to form a swirling red stream that, to the little girl's delight, spiraled around her.

The young girl turned toward Lil and Gunnar where they sat on the bench, excitement radiating from her, an invitation to come closer. They stood and approached slowly, then the first dragonfly landed on Flora's hand.

A delightful gasp escaped her.

"What's that one?" The girl asked.

"Blue Dasher," Lil said, crouching down beside her.

"And what's the red one?"

"Cardinal Meadowhawk," Lil smiled, tears prickling at her eyes. "Do you know who taught me how to name the dragonflies?"

"Nana Claire."

Lil nodded.

"She liked insects, I think. We have some cups in the house with things pressed in them, like bees and dragonflies. Grampa Guns said she made them."

The red ribbon of ladybugs exploded as the ground moved beneath everyone's feet. The actions seemed simultaneous, but no, the earth had shaken first, and continued in the insects' absence. The tremor tried to blossom into something more, then it too faded away.

Lu lifted a curious brow, and Flora took Gunnar's hand. The vibration seemed to start up again with a bit of a rumble in the air, as if the space around them were trying to speak. As the sound and movement faded once again, Lil saw Gunnar's face had a knowing look about it, mouth quirked up at one side. He was amused.

Flora released a giggle, but Gunnar's head ticked to the side with a lovingly stern expression, putting stop to it.

"You smiled first, Grampa Guns."

It was true. He did. Then he made a sound in his chest or the back of his throat, a stifled laugh.

"I was quiet about it," he said, backing up as the resounding rumble erupted in earnest before them. "Come on; let's give the boy some space."

The sound of the storm created neither rain nor clouds, but a shimmering portal some ten meters away from where they stood. Thunder roared until a man stumbled into the garden as though the ether had spat him out. Broad shouldered, he stood tall as he recovered. Work boots, brown pants and a white t-shirt stretched over his muscled form, fabric smudged with dirt. His golden hair appeared close cut, but long enough to lay flat on his head. His eyes flashed with triumph before his attention landed on Lil and those with her, staring back at him. It was then that his expression held a flicker of some bashful innocence. And though a youthfulness carried through, and Gunner would perhaps continue to refer to him as a boy indefinitely, Hamish had been a grown man for some time.

*He's improved,* Lu said. *Remi and Michael have been working with him, but Hamish was barely opening and closing portals around the school grounds last I saw.*

*And the students watch him practice?*

*Indeed.*

Lil nodded. It would be good for the children to see an elder persisting when there was struggle, especially their headmaster.

"I knew you'd be here," Hamish smiled as he walked toward them, his brows shooting up in an expression of asking.

Lil wasted no time in putting her arms out, letting him come in for a hug. She made an attempt at encircling his bicep with her hands, then looked into his eyes. They were like crackled honey.

"Are you building cairns with boulders now?" She teased. I can't even get my fingers around… They touched last time, I'm sure of it."

Lil smiled as his cheeks flushed.

"How's Willow?" she asked.

His face maintained its hue, brightening, perhaps. "Oh, Will's lovely. She wanted to come, but I've only been successful in transporting a few times…"

*He's afraid of Remi,* Lu chuckled.

*Stop. Remi has known him since he was a boy. He loves Hamish, and Marissa did too.*

*Rem's still her father.*

"We'd planned on seeing her tomorrow," Lil said, then, turning to Lu, she added, "I still want to pop over for a visit later today though."

"She's expecting you," Hamish said.

"Of course she is," Lil smiled. "And I don't suppose she baked anything in anticipation of the visit…"

"There's a tart cooling."

"Apple?"

He nodded.

"That woman is divine…"

"She is indeed," Lu added. "By more than half."

Lil caught Flora whispering to Gunnar.

Crouched beside her, he asked, "Do you not want to go?"

"I *do* want to go; but I want to stay out here a little longer…"

Flora put her hands out slightly at her sides, stretched her fingers, and gave them a little flap.

Warmth spread through Lil at the sight, then feathers spread out as she called her wings.

"Please take me flying, Auntie Lil. It's been so long, I have so much fun, and if I could take myself I would, but…" She used her eyes and hands, gesturing to call attention to her lack of necessary parts.

Lil picked the girl up, Flora's legs swinging over each of Lil's hips and locking behind her back.

"I don't know…" Lil said with an exaggerated glance toward Lu. "If I take you, he might chase us, and then I'd have to go *fast*…"

Lil turned her back to him, knowing Flora could see over her shoulder, could still peek between her neck and wing.

"What's he doing?" Lil whispered.

"He looks very serious. I think he moved, but it's hard to tell… I think he saw me," she said, quickly turning her head away.

Lil took a few cautious steps for the sake of performance.

"Look again, what's he doing now?"

Flora tilted her head slowly.

"He's smiling."

"Can you see teeth?"

"No… Yes!"

Lil dug in her heels and took off in a sprint through the garden. Flora's legs squeezed tight, her laughter like flower petals in the wind behind them.

"His wings are out!" she shrieked, fists holding tight, cheeks pushed high. "He's running!"

"Should we go left or right, Flora?"

"I don't know!"

"Left or right!?"

"Up!"

Lil's wings flared, wind flowing strong beneath them, lifting.

And in the light of the morning sun, they took to the sky.

# Acknowledgements

This duology is like a set of twins, written and born at the same time, and so my acknowledgements are much the same, though I did leave a couple out of the acknowledgements. Mike, I have you in my phone as "Freight Train," and you were one of the first people to read my work years ago. You shared your thoughts, you shared Andrea's marmalade, and you took me seriously enough for me to keep going. That momentum turned into this, and every other book I'll write. Massive thank you to Kerry and Melissa. You are two of my original champions. You read my chapters when they were chunks of thoughts. You imagined the taste of Gunnar's caramels and laughed at Todd's shirts before anyone else. You sent me The Rock. You sent me a Story in Stone gift basket (Shout out to Our Green House.) Kerry, you made me one of Lil's mugs! You both encouraged me to keep writing, and took this journey seriously when I was unsure. You've been gracious with your time, gave me tough love when I needed it, and I am beyond grateful to have you both in my life. So much more than a book club. Becka, Colleen, and Caroline too; you came in after these stories were born, but have been there for my triumphs and my tantrums, cover design and (insert vomit emoji) formatting. You've read, supported, and promoted my work. I am grateful.

Thank you to my parents for reading my first draft... steamy bits and all. As a daughter, feeling your enthusiasm and pride was everything. Love you guys.

Thank you to my spouse. I love you. You pull my leg, you cut my grapefruits, and you do all the little things. You've read my books, been a second set of eyes, and now we can chat about my friends from work! (Characters.)

Thank you to my daughters for enriching my life and keeping things beautiful, interesting, and sometimes a little bit gross. I love you.

# About the Author

Kristen Cornwall is a writer, an artist, and a great many other things. She likes maple in her tea when she wants it sweet, enjoys the seasons in New England, croissants, and listening to birds (though it's a little love/hate when days are longest and they are awake before she really wants to get started.) She likes being in the woods and by the ocean, and reads often. She occasionally makes crepes.